SOMEDAY WE'LL
FIND IT

SOMEDAY WE'LL FIND IT

JENNIFER WILSON

HARPER TEEN
An Imprint of HarperCollinsPublishers

HarperTeen is an imprint of HarperCollins Publishers.

Someday We'll Find It
Copyright © 2022 by Jennifer Wilson

Library of Congress Control Number: 2021943587
ISBN 978-0-06-304465-4

Typography by Corina Lupp
22 23 24 25 26   PC/LSCH   10 9 8 7 6 5 4 3 2 1
❖
First Edition

For my mom, who would've never left if it was up to her.
And for Carly and Cassidy, who I could never leave.

OX OX OX

SOMEDAY WE'LL FIND IT

One

River and me started going out one night when I got drunk, passed out, and woke up to him all over me. I never really knew he had it on for me before that, but I got a pretty good idea from the way he was going at it.

After that, we were a couple.

It's good to be River's girlfriend. His truck runs most of the time, so he can pick me up at my cousin Patsy's and take us out to his granny's old house, where we've all been hanging out all summer. None of my boyfriends has ever been as crazy for me as River is.

Which is why, in all the time that we've been going out, I've hardly asked River for anything. So when I want him to take me into town today, he puts up a little fight.

"Why you have to go and make a cake for Patsy?" River leans back against his old truck that's half white and half rust and gives me that raised eyebrow and smile combination that just about melts my heart. It's a slow smile, more on one corner of his mouth than the other, and every time I see it, I'm right back to when we first started hanging out at Granny's, with River lording it over everybody, turning away enough people at the door that you felt real special when he let you in.

River's not big—a little scrawny, if anything—but he has this way of moving—standing, even—that makes me notice parts of his body I wouldn't normally look at. He puts his arms around me, and the July heat pushes us closer together, heavy on our skin. There's not even a tiny breeze blowing through the soybean fields to cool us off.

"Because she's my cousin." I kiss River's neck. "Because it's her birthday." I play with the ends of his sandy hair where it flips up from under his baseball cap, but he's nowhere near saying yes. Yet.

"I have the afternoon off. Don't you care about that?" He turns that look on me, all big sad eyes, then pulls me close and gives me kisses that start out soft but real quick show me what *he* cares about. Before I know it, my mind is tossing eggs, sugar, and butter right out the window, telling me Patsy won't notice if I don't make her a red velvet cake like she had at Bridget and Lonnie's wedding three years ago.

I push away from River, catching my breath and my good sense as I step back on Granny's gravel driveway. I shake my head. "No fair."

River reaches for me again, and I duck up under his arm and jump in the truck.

"Besides, you told Lisa you'd go back this afternoon."

River works for his mom, painting houses, and they are always either on-again or off-again, depending on how much River has screwed around on the job and pissed her off.

"Shit. She won't care," he says, but he gets in on the driver's side.

"You promised me," I remind him, as I scoot over on the bench seat. "You said you'd keep working as long as she wanted you. Without any fighting."

River leans in so close he's almost on top of me, picks up a long blond piece of my hair and plays with it. He brushes my forehead, my nose, my lips with it, all while giving me that white-hot smile, so bright against his summer tan. "And I've gone almost every day, haven't I? I deserve a reward." He looks at me with those clear eyes, like blue jeans that have been washed until they fit just right, and then he's kissing me again.

It kills me that I can't do this for him, stay out at Granny's, kiss and everything all afternoon long. But then I picture Patsy's face when there's no cake for her birthday, no present from me. It takes everything I have, but I pull my head back.

"Cake," I say, barely able to talk. "Please."

River sighs. "Fine." He pulls out of the driveway and down the lane from Granny's so fast it's like the cops are chasing us, attacking every turn like he's taking a bite out of it and wolfing it down. I knock against his tan arm, tacky with sweat from the humidity that's all around us like another person in the old truck.

Patsy's dad, Uncle Leo, told us a long story about dew points making it hot and sticky here in Illinois all summer, but me and

Patsy just nodded our heads till he was done, because knowing why something is doesn't change how bad it feels.

I don't think River's pissed about leaving Granny's, but I don't say nothing more, just scoot right up next to him, fitting up under his arm like we were made out of the same piece of wood, carved apart, and just now fitted back together again.

I still can hardly believe it's me and River here in this truck. That for a whole year he picked being lonely, and waiting for me, over any of the million girls who were throwing themselves at him, right up until me and Chris broke up. But he swears it's true.

We pass fields of corn, then beans, then corn again. Fine, chocolate-colored dust coughs in the windows and settles on every damn thing, getting between my back teeth and making me sneeze. I trace River's cracked, bitten fingernails, his hand almost the same size as mine, then I slip my finger under the light-blue hair tie on his wrist and pull it away from his skin, rubbing the red dent it leaves behind. Something about touching the little hairs on his arm feels all intimate, close, like I'm touching somewhere I shouldn't, even now after we been together all these weeks.

"Maybe someday you'll make a cake for me," River chokes out, wheezing as the truck jumps a big chuckhole, raising a new cloud of dust. "If you care enough." He plants a kiss in my hair, gets a flyaway blond piece stuck in his mouth, and pulls it sharply out of my head as he jerks away. I push on the spot until it's not stinging anymore and straighten my tube top.

"You want red velvet, too?"

"Hell no. None of that fancy shit. Chocolate with chocolate frost— Fuck!" River fishtails the truck as it slams into a chuckhole and stops. I'm tossed practically on River's lap, and the truck is caught in the bear trap of a giant hole.

River opens the door, and we both just about slide out, the truck is tilted so far over. We head up to the front, and River squats down and puts his shoulder under the bumper. He goes all red as he pushes up with his legs, rocking the truck back, but it stays completely stuck.

I crowd in next to River and put my palms on the bumper to help. It's hot and dusty and slick from where River already tried to push. My shoulder mashes up against him, and for just a second it's enough, but River's feet slide out from under him, and he lets go of the truck to catch himself.

"Pretty stuck, huh?" I ask him.

"The fuck do you think?" He slams the hood with a fist, and I take a step back while he stomps off, spitting in the dirt.

River might cool off all by himself, but more likely, he needs a little help. I tiptoe over to where he stands, hands on his hips, staring into the corn like he's trying to force a tow truck to come out from between the rows. I sneak up under his arm and go all soft, put my head on his shoulder, and make the baby voice he likes.

"What're we gonna do, River?" I open my eyes wide and pull up closer to him near the driver's side door. The motor ticks as it cools, and the hot metal of the cab burns my bare shoulders, but I just wait him out.

Heat pours out of River, and I'm sticking to his neck. A drop of sweat slides down his nose and lands on my cheek as I run my hands up his sweaty back and hope my touch can cool him down some. He closes his eyes and takes one, two, three loud breaths through his nose. When he opens his eyes again, good River is back, and he looks at me through cool, clear, blue-jean eyes.

He pushes off the truck with one hand, while the other arm snakes around my neck. We start walking.

"You're fucking magic, you know that?" he asks me. "Anybody else, I would've punched out the windshield or broke my toe kicking the truck, trying to get it free. You just look at me all sideways and next thing I know, I'm leaving my truck in the middle of the road and trying to hitch a ride home."

"Sorry my phone doesn't keep a charge. We could've waited here," I tell him. "Patsy's supposed to get a new one for her birthday, so I'll probably get her old one."

River just nods and pulls out his chewing tobacco from the back pocket of his cutoffs. He settles a new pinch in his lower lip and keeps walking like there's a hundred-dollar bill at the end of the road if we get there soon enough. He doesn't say nothing about how if I hadn't needed to make Patsy's cake, we wouldn't be out here in the first place, so I just try to keep up with him.

River's fine with his tennis shoes, but my flip-flops aren't doing so good on this gravel road, catching on chunks of rock as we go past row after row of soybeans. "Might as well be barefoot," I say, catching myself on River's arm.

The sun pours down on us, and I left my goddamn hair tie

back in the truck. I grab at River's arm and pull the blue one off his wrist.

"Oh no you don't," he says, grabbing it back from me. The sun sparks off his smile as he snaps it back in place. "You're the one who made me promise to never take it off."

River picks up even more speed, and I walk faster, trying to catch up. "You sure I said that?"

"I still can't believe you don't remember."

"I was drunk."

"You were. Drunk as hell and hot as fuck," he says. "Any guy who didn't keep that promise is a damn idiot."

I got nothing to say to that, so we just walk on without talking. At first, it seems quiet out here on the road, but after a while I hear birds chirp from every direction, and a far-off airplane hum. I lean my head back to find the plane way, way up in the sky, its jet trail the only white in the hazy blue. I can't believe it's been almost six years since my plane ride with Mama to New York City.

I slow down even more, watching the jet trail, and like it was yesterday, I remember the smooth plastic airplane tray folded down in front of me, the rumble of the jets under my seat as we cruised over the clouds. My nose tingled from the ginger ale bubbles when I took a sip, and the seat belt buckle kept me fastened in tight.

I half expect to turn my head and see Mama leaning against the airplane window, her white satin sleep mask and earplugs blocking me out so she could catch some beauty rest before her interview for the Japan job. A hundred other people on the plane and all I remember is feeling completely alone.

I'm jolted back to the road as my flip-flop catches on a rock and shreds itself in half, landing in the middle of the road. "Dammit!" I hop all over on the good foot, just barely catching myself before I fall flat on my butt. I shake my head to clear away Mama and the plane ride.

Just thinking about her makes shitty things happen.

"What?" River asks, a few feet in front of me.

"Screw it." I hop out of the other flip-flop, scoop them both up and toss them into the ditch before I can start to cry.

"Aww, Bliss. Now what?" River asks, heading back my way.

I take two steps, little tiny ones to try and miss the biggest rocks. The white gravel pressed into the tar is hot as hell and sharp as shark's teeth, and I blink away a few tears. I'm never making it to Patsy's cake. I never should've even tried. There's nowhere to step that doesn't hurt, and there's no way I can make it to town like this.

"My flip-flop." I look at the tall grass on the side of the road, try to guess how many jagged steps to get there. I get up on my tippy-toes and inch over, every step a billion agonies. The grass between the road and the corn looked soft and cool, but it's not a whole hell of a lot better than the road.

River looks down at my bare feet and turns his back on me. "Hop on."

"You sure?" The air is thick and hot, and we might as well be swimming in it.

River holds his hands behind him, and I jump up, piggy-back. We make it maybe five steps before River's sweaty hands start to slip on my sweaty legs. "Jump me up," I say, and he bumps me higher.

"Shit," he says as I slip away from him again, landing on the sharp rocks of the road.

I tie my heavy hair into a knot to keep it off my neck, not near as good as a hair tie, but I'll take anything right now. "The road is too sharp," I tell him. "I can't go any farther."

River looks off over my shoulder, scanning the road back to where we left the truck, and says, "Empty as fuck. Nobody's coming."

I look ahead towards the blacktop off in the distance. "You go ahead. Get a ride, then get Long Tom or somebody to come get me."

"Really?"

"Uh-huh. No sense both of us sitting around."

River puts his arms around me, our skin clammy where it touches. "You sure?"

I nod. "Either one of us gets a ride, we'll text Long Tom."

River nods back. "Fucking Patsy," he says. "I hope she likes her cake." Then he kisses me and walks off.

Two

I watch River until he's just a speck on the road, then I look around me. There's a clump of bushes about a half field away that looks like it has grass growing around it, and I decide right then and there that I'm going to go sit in that shade.

I have to tiptoe through the grass clumps on the side of the road. I can practically see the water in the air, and I can't hardly stand it when I brush up against myself. My skirt is droopy, and I can only take two or three steps before I have to pull my tube top up again. It twists around, too, so I've got a lot of things to fuss with as I make my way to the little patch of shadow.

The bushes are like a million miles away. It's hard to tell when everything looks the same: corn on one side, beans on the other, as far as I can see. I stop for a minute and finger-comb my tangles up in a braid, wishing I'd made River give me that hair tie. It is mine, after all. I shake my head and fix the tube top again. I'm giving this to Patsy for keeps if I ever get off this road and back home. Even if she doesn't give me back my good shorts. We're just cousins, but ever since Mama left me with Aunt Trish and Uncle Leo, we've been a lot more like sisters. Sometimes even sisters that occasionally like each other.

There's a car coming towards me from the direction of Granny's. I squint my eyes through the thick summer haze until I can make out that it's a red truck, raising a mane of dust all around it.

The truck bounces closer every second, and I shade my eyes to see better, coughing on the dust.

It comes to a stop right in front of me, tires crackling and popping on the bits of gravel. It's a big, big truck, twice as big as River's, with four doors and a superlong bed, and somehow, it's still shiny, even after coming down in the middle of all this dust. The windows are tinted, and all I can see is a reflection of hot, sticky me with a braid that has mostly come undone.

The window glides down and a blast of cold air washes over me. I'm so happy to feel it I don't even look at the driver.

"That your truck?"

I snap my eyes wide open at the question. It's a guy, probably my own age. He looks at me with a half smile on his face and rests an elbow on the window he just put down. He looks vaguely Asian and completely amused.

Something about his face is comfortable, like I know him from somewhere, but he is for sure not from around here. I know all four hundred kids at my high school, five hundred if you count the ones who just graduated, and he is not one of them.

But he looks reassuring anyway. Maybe it's because the heat doesn't even touch him. His dark brown eyes are soft, a little turned down at the corners, and one of his heavy eyebrows goes up while the other goes down. He's half smiling, like he sees something funny.

"Over there? Your truck?" he repeats. He jerks his thumb back down the road.

I smooth my hair, forgetting it's half in a braid, and find my voice. "There was a chuckhole." I pull out the rest of the braid and gather up the hair on top of my head.

He nods.

"We couldn't get it out. We were heading into town to see if . . . what?"

His white teeth flash at me in a grin that lights his whole face. Why is that so funny? He points at the ground.

"How far were you going to get without any shoes? Lots of sharp rocks on this road." He face-palms his forehead and gets immediately serious. "Oh my gosh, you must be miserable. Here."

I jump as he swings his door open and hops out. He's taller than River, but not by much. His plaid work shirt is as shiny as his truck, and his jeans are dirty but new. He waves me in.

"Climb in. If you want, that is. It's a whole lot cooler than out here." He squints up at the sun, then bows as if he's a butler and puts his palm out with a swish.

Definitely not from around here.

Still, he does not have to ask me twice. He could be a

world-famous serial killer and there's no way I would not get in that cold truck. He's not stocky like the farm guys I know, doesn't have the shoulders and arms that come from working in the fields year after year. But his skin is a sunburned soft brown, and he seems like he knows his way around the truck. Who *is* this guy?

Who cares, as long as he has air conditioning. Lots of air conditioning. I turn both the vents towards me, close my eyes, and eat that shit up. I don't cool down all at once, but some of the stickiness leaves my neck and arms. The only thing that would make this better is . . .

"Water?" he asks. He stands at the door, pointing at a water bottle on the dash.

Spooky.

"There's no ice, but it's cold." He looks up at me, and I am positive I've never met him but sure I should know him from somewhere. I swipe the bottle and try not to chug it or spill it down my chin. What I'd like to do is pour it right over my head.

"Whoa, there. Not too fast." He laughs.

Everything I do is such a joke to this guy. His eyes are all crinkled up again and he sways a little bit back into the door. I pull the bottle away and wipe my chin. I should be pissed, but his grin just makes me feel like he knows what it's like to be dying of thirst somehow.

"Sorry," I say.

He waves away my apology. "So, what do you want?" he says. Again, with the laughs, and again I have that feeling that

I should know him. Maybe he's two years ahead of me? Nope. I knew all the seniors when I was a sophomore. And he doesn't look that old.

"What do I want?" For a second, I forget what we are talking about. What do I want? Maybe I have heatstroke, because a picture of Mama and me pops into my head real quick. We're on pink rafts in our very own swimming pool, maybe in California, and we're laughing at some inside joke.

"Do you want me to call a tow? Or maybe give you a ride?" he asks, slow like he thinks I don't understand him.

"A ride. Sure." The picture of Mama breaks into a million pieces and disappears as I take another swig of the best water in the universe.

He raises both eyebrows at me, and he smiles even bigger. His smile is sort of squarish, and you can see each tooth, instead of one straight line.

"Just scooch on over. Move that stuff out of the way."

So I do, and soon we are both on the bench seat of the truck. It's so big, with a back seat and high roof, but it seems real small all of a sudden. I fuss with my tube top one more time when he's not looking, set the papers—some kind of music book and some receipts—between us, and smoosh my back against the passenger door. It's not a brand-new truck, but it's a hell of a lot nicer than River's old piece of shit.

He puts on his seat belt and grabs the gearshift.

"Where to?"

"Anywhere but here," I say, thinking about swimming pools and snowy mountains and places far, far away.

"Anywhere?" He looks at the dashboard, then back at me. "I guess I could get us as far as . . . Indiana before I need gas. Or would Iowa be better?"

He sounds half serious, and I half believe he'd do it. "Can you take me back to town? I have to make a cake," I add, for no reason at all.

He makes a big fake sigh, and says, "I suppose we'll save Iowa for another day." He goes forward a few feet, then stops all of a sudden.

"Oh man. What am I, an idiot?" He turns in the driver's seat and rakes a hand through his choppy black hair. It's real black, not like Patsy wants to dye hers, and there's lots of it. It looks like it would be soft.

I raise my eyebrows back at him.

"I'm Blake. Blake Wu." He takes his hand off the gearshift and puts it out to me.

I look at his long brown fingers stupidly. I have honestly never shaken hands with someone my own age. I feel like an idiot, but I go ahead and stick my own hand out and put it in his. Surprisingly, he does have a few calluses, but his hand is warm, and firm, and I relax just a little bit shaking it.

"And you are—?" Okay, sue me. Nobody ever taught me this shit.

"I'm Bliss," I say, and my whole face is hot. He's still shaking

my hand, and the air conditioning isn't working very well anymore. "Bliss Walker."

"Pleased to meet you, Bliss." He looks at me with a soft
smile. "Bliss Walker."

He leaves my hand alone in the middle of the truck and
shifts into drive. "All right, Bliss Walker, let's get you where you
need to go."

Fields of sharp-leafed corn go by out my window, then darker,
lower soybeans, then corn again, and then we're back in town.
We don't pass River on the way, so I guess he made it just fine.

Blake has this concentration about him as he slows down
for the turns to Patsy's house, like he's driving a china cup that
might shatter if he makes a mistake. He eases to a stop in the
driveway, so slow the only way I know that we've stopped is
Blake jumps out of the truck.

I reach over to open the door at the same time as Blake pulls
it open from the outside, and I almost fall out. I didn't know
actual real people open doors for each other outside of old-time
movies. I feel like a total idiot for not knowing what he was
trying to do.

"I'll walk you up." He nods at the front steps.

"I'm good," I tell him. I can't tell if I'm breathing the air or
drinking it, it's so thick. I take another gulp when I realize how
close we are standing, how dark his eyes are, how the corners
of his mouth turn up just a little bit. We stand there between
Blake's shiny red truck and the tiny front porch like there's a

string stretched between us that we can't quite cut.

"Thanks—" I say, but he says "Don't—" at the same time, and we both stop talking, then pause, laugh, then both try again at the same time. I nod at him to go first.

He grins. "Don't try walking to town barefoot again."

"I'll think about it," I say. "Thanks for the ride." Out of nowhere, my arms reach out and give him a hug, like that's how I thank every strange person who shows up out of nowhere on a country road. He goes to hug me back, but he doesn't start until I'm almost done, and our arms get all tangled up together.

I quick pull away from him, my head spinning, and just about run over to the porch steps. "Thanks again."

"Let me know if you decide to go to Iowa," he says, then adds, "Bake a good cake," and drives off.

It's not cool inside the house, and it gets way hotter once I start cooking, but I fly around the kitchen making Patsy's cake. I drink, like, a gallon of water, and once my phone charges I text Long Tom to see if River made it to town, and River answers.

River: We're stocking up. Beer and shit for Granny's.
Me: Truck ok?
River: No problem.

River doesn't even ask how I got back here, and I sure don't tell him—he'd probably be able to tell I hugged Blake just from the way I text his name.

Like always, I wash up Patsy's dirty dishes from breakfast and lunch, adding them to the baking shit. Just as the timer goes off, the front door slams open.

"Don't come in here," I yell at Patsy. I pull the cake pans out and set them on the counter to cool as fast as I can.

"What's going on?" Patsy asks from the front room, all sing-song. I know she can smell the cake, but I still want it to be a surprise.

I stop cold once I walk in the living room. "Holy shit, you did it."

Patsy shrugs, then shakes her shoulder-length, inky hair that was plain light brown when she left earlier. "Happy birthday to me! You like it?"

I nod at her. "Black, huh?"

"'Raven Black.' Box dye for the win. The world has enough blond and beautiful people. Some of us have to work with what we have."

"Ha, ha." I push her with my shoulder. "Well, it looks good. Real good."

Patsy wants to go to beauty school to do hair and nails and shit, but it's super expensive. And besides, Aunt Trish keeps telling us how she had a bad experience back when she was in "the business" where she lost her salon, and now she won't let Patsy even think about it. But Patsy thinks about it more than just about anything, watching tutorials online and practicing on herself and me any time she gets a chance, no matter what Aunt Trish says.

"And Mom can't say a thing, now that I'm eighteen," Patsy says, gathering her hair into a ponytail.

"Better hope she doesn't."

Patsy grins at me and goes off to take a quick shower. I really should've told her about meeting Blake, and River's truck, but then she might think it's a big deal, when really it wasn't. I hurry into the kitchen to get the cake frosted before Patsy's done.

Three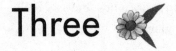

Most people love birthdays, but Patsy takes it to a whole other level. She's been crossing off the days on her calendar, she's had her outfit planned for weeks, and she picked out tonight's menu down to the exact brand of cucumber buttermilk dressing she wants.

Aunt Trish just shakes her head when she sees Patsy's hair, but she keeps her mouth shut. While me and Aunt Trish fix dinner, Patsy comes in and out of the kitchen, reminding us of all her birthday wishes, pointing at the zillion and six pictures of phones and cases she's had stuck up on the refrigerator for over a month now.

"I'm sorry it's just a small celebration tonight," Aunt Trish tells Patsy. Patsy and me look at each other and try not to smile. We're gonna celebrate the shit out of her birthday on Saturday, with more beer and more people than we've seen in a while out at Granny's.

"That's okay," Patsy says. "Later on, I'm going to go buy a

lottery ticket. Since I can, now that I'm *le-gal*." Patsy sings the last word as she leans against the counter and watches me chop the carrots into the salad.

"Waste of money, if you ask me," Aunt Trish says, wrinkling her nose. "No one ever wins those things."

Aunt Trish bends down to get the Parmesan chicken out of the oven, and she almost drops it when Patsy says, "Which day should I get my nose pierced?"

The oven door slams. "You know how we feel about that. The hair is one thing, but . . ."

"You said when I was eighteen, I could decide for myself," Patsy says. "I'm a real live adult now. Might even get a tattoo."

"Well if you're such an *adult*, you can just move on out and support yourself. Tattoos and all. I could practically buy a new car with what I'd save on groceries," Aunt Trish says. "And once you're moved out, I can finally have my sewing room." She looks dead serious as she says it, then walks out of the room.

I stare after her as it hits me: if Patsy moves out of her room, Aunt Trish expects it to be empty. But I live in that room, too. If Patsy goes, do I have to go? Patsy looks at me with big eyes, and she must be thinking about living on her own and supporting herself, too, because all the birthday joy has completely left her face.

"She wouldn't," Patsy says.

"I hope not," I tell her. I especially hope not, because the only reason I am here is because Aunt Trish and Uncle Leo allowed Mama to dump me here five years ago. Almost six. And

I have worked my ass off so they hardly notice they have a whole extra person to take care of all this time, helping out around the house and not making a fuss over anything if I can help it. It would sure suck if they plan to kick me out next month when I turn eighteen.

Patsy shrugs, and her face clears. "It'll never happen." She checks her phone. "God, this old piece of shit sucks. I can't wait for my new one. Do you think they remembered to get me a case, too?"

"How could they forget?" I wave my hand at the pictures stuck up all over.

Patsy stares at a pink case covered with fake diamonds, then sighs. "I wish it was Saturday already. River didn't forget, did he?"

"He didn't forget." I lay out the last of the silverware on the table and try to keep from looking at the microwave, where I hid the cake. The frosting didn't come out too good, but the crumbs I tasted were perfect, so I think Patsy will like it. She better: it's my whole birthday present for her.

Uncle Leo comes in the front door and calls out, "Is there a birthday girl in the house?" He stops for a second when he sees Patsy's hair, and says, "Who's this?" but then he opens his arms wide, and Patsy gives him a big hug.

Pretty soon, we're all chowing down on Parmesan chicken, salad, and cheesy mashed potatoes. "Isn't this what we had last year for your birthday?" Uncle Leo asks.

"And the year before, and the year before that," I tell him.

We all smile at Patsy's food choice, then Aunt Trish asks for the salt and pepper, so I get up and bring them to the table.

"Thank goodness she finally gave up the chicken nuggets." Aunt Trish shakes salt onto her whole entire plate.

"I thought she was going to turn into a nugget," Uncle Leo says, and laughs.

"Nuggets?" I ask.

"Before your time," Patsy says, her mouth full of salad. "I ate them for about ten years running. God, I loved those things."

I try to picture it, where I was when they were eating chicken nuggets every year, but all the hotel rooms blur into one hotel room, and all the towns are mixed up into a pile of towns. All that time, Patsy and Aunt Trish and Uncle Leo had been having birthdays together without me.

Aunt Trish pats my hand as I reach for a drink of water. "You would've had nuggets, too, if you'd been here. Patsy sure did love them." It's nice of Aunt Trish to pretend it doesn't matter that I wasn't here all those years they were busy being a family, but it doesn't change anything.

Everyone's plates are empty, so I hurry to put them in the sink like any other night. As soon as the table is clear, I pull out the cake and light the candles. In their glow, the cake doesn't look so lopsided, and the crumbs in the frosting don't look like freckles on pale skin.

I carry the cake to Patsy, and she smiles so big as we sing "Happy Birthday." They look so happy there in the glow of the candles, Aunt Trish on one side of her and Uncle Leo on the other, full up with love for their birthday girl. Patsy's blue eyes dance along with the candle flames, and it's not hard to guess what she wishes for before she blows them out. The smoke from eighteen candles makes a screen between us, and I wonder what I'll wish for when it's my turn.

Patsy cuts the cake, and the minute she sees it, she says, "Red velvet? You remembered!" And her smile washes away every fight we've ever had and leaves only Patsy: secrets in the dark, braiding my hair, trying new makeup ideas on me, always there no matter what, even if I grabbed the last Diet Coke or took too long in the bathroom. Patsy passes around the plates. "Oh my god, it's even better than I imagined," she says, with her mouth full.

"You've really outdone yourself, Bliss," says Uncle Leo, another bite of cake on his fork, ready to eat. My face heats up. I like to help out in the kitchen, and it turns out I'm not terrible at it, but I don't like anyone making a big deal about it.

Patsy goes to take another bite of cake, but she stops with the fork halfway to her mouth when Aunt Trish nods and says to me, "You have a real talent, honey." She makes a happy noise and takes another bite.

For one whole second, it feels like I'm important, included, and then I see Patsy's face. She looks at the red velvet cake—my whole present to her—like she wants to pick it up and smash it into someone's face, probably mine.

"Well, it's for *Patsy's* birthday," I say, trying to get them to refocus their attention.

Uncle Leo, clueless as usual, says, "People don't make things anymore. It's all just consumerism and who has the newest gadgets. It's so nice to see someone who values a gift from the heart." He smiles at me real big around his last bite as Patsy pushes her plate away.

Aunt Trish says, "Aren't you going to finish? Bliss worked so hard." Patsy's mood is as black as her hair as she picks up her fork and starts shoveling bites of cake in, hate-eating it until it's almost gone. Uncle Leo says again how good it is, but I don't dare take my eyes off of Patsy, who is about to bust, she's so riled up.

All these years, and Patsy thinks there's only a certain amount of good things in the world, and if I'm getting some of them, that means there's less for her. I take their plates and my half-finished cake to the sink, and when I come back to the table, Patsy is twisting her head around, probably looking for the big stack of presents that should be here somewhere. Or envelopes full of gift cards or money.

But there's only the counter heaped with dishes, and the table that just has water glasses and balled-up napkins on it.

Aunt Trish clears her throat, her cheeks all pink and a goofy grin spread across her face. Her and Uncle Leo stand up next to Patsy's chair, and Uncle Leo even bounces on his toes a couple times, which is not normal for him unless there's baseball involved. Or fishing.

Patsy's face changes from pissed-off to confused to excited, the longer they stand there saying nothing. I start to think they bought her a brand-new car, or maybe a trip to Paris or

Hollywood or something. Or maybe they finally changed their minds about beauty school.

There's a little wobble in Patsy's voice as she says, "What's up, guys?"

Uncle Leo puts his arm around Aunt Trish, and they look at each other like they just invented the wheel. "Ever since we found out we were pregnant," Uncle Leo starts.

"Almost nineteen years ago," Aunt Trish adds. They smile at each other again, and it's kind of cute the way they're looking at each other, all nervous and happy.

"Every week, after work on Friday, I would go to the bank," Uncle Leo says.

"Every week," Aunt Trish echoes.

"Whether we were broke or flush. Every week I put the same amount in a bank account for our baby. For you," Uncle Leo says, and I swear he's got tears in his eyes.

Aunt Trish pulls out a little notebook with flowers on the front, opens it up and pages through it until she finds what she's looking for, then she puts it right up in Patsy's face. "Every week he went, and we kept track of it, how it grew, how it started with practically nothing, and here it is, all grown up!"

"Just like you," Uncle Leo finishes. "Happy eighteenth birthday, sweetie."

Patsy takes the book from Aunt Trish and flips through the pages. "What is this? Is this money?" she asks, her voice all quiet.

"For school," Aunt Trish says.

"Or trade school, or nursing school," Uncle Leo adds.

"Or dental hygienist—Stacey Wilkins's daughter makes real good money as a—"

Patsy's face is a disco ball, her smile sending speckles of light to every corner of the room. "OH MY GOD, beauty school!" she breathes, then she grabs me and hugs me and dances me all around the room with her. "Beauty school! Oh my god, thank you, thank you, th—"

"Oh, honey, no," Aunt Trish's voice cuts through the dancing. She puts her hand on Patsy's arm.

"This is for real school," Uncle Leo says. "Not beauty school."

Patsy goes all still, and her eyes jump from one of them to the other and back again. "What the fuck?" she says, an arrow from her mouth straight to Aunt Trish's chest.

Aunt Trish flinches, but then she says, "Sweetie, we couldn't allow you to waste . . . we've worked so hard to—"

"Beauty school is the only school I'm going to," Patsy tells them. She squeezes the book in her hands as she walks back and forth. "Ever."

"B-but—" Uncle Leo sputters.

Aunt Trish narrows her eyes. "We will not *allow* you to—"

"You act like this is a gift." Patsy's like a bear that was woken up in the middle of its winter sleep, roaring and growling all over the little kitchen. "But it's just you wanting to control my life."

Patsy looks around the room like she's searching for something to hurt, or break, or burn into a thousand pieces, and her eyes land on me where I'm standing over in the corner all small, trying not to be here at all.

"So, I guess you made one of these books for Bliss, too? Added her in every Friday? Watched her numbers grow? Or don't you think she's going to *real school*?"

Aunt Trish's face is shredded, and Uncle Leo holds his stomach like Patsy punched him, and neither one of them answers her, they just stare at her with big round eyes. Patsy shoves the book at me. "There. You take it."

I push it away. "Patsy, it's not for—"

"If I can't use it for beauty school, I don't want it." She throws the book down at my feet. "And you might as well have it, since nobody's decided *your* future down to the last dime."

Nobody's been planning for my future at all, I guess. I stare down at the crumpled book, its flowers all mashed up, but there is no way in hell I'm touching it.

"Honey," Aunt Trish says, and reaches for Patsy, but Patsy pushes past her.

"Happy fucking birthday," Patsy says over her shoulder, stomping off.

Four

Uncle Leo isn't bouncing anymore, and Aunt Trish looks down at the book and up at me all horrified and says, "Bliss, honey, we just . . ."

Patsy slams out the front door, her arms full of all her beauty cases. I duck my head and chase after her. By the time I get outside, Patsy is in her car and backing out.

"Wait," I call, but she peels out down the street before I get to the end of the driveway. I stand there, left behind for the second time today. At least I'm wearing shoes now. *Let me know if you decide to go to Iowa*, Blake had said. I don't need to go to Iowa, but I do need to find Patsy.

I put Blake out of my mind and text River to please come get me. When I look up from my phone, I see all of Patsy's makeup and hair stuff in the garbage bin where she tossed them.

I pull the beauty cases out one by one while I wait.

River drives me all around town, and we finally see Patsy's

car at the little park by the fairgrounds. We walk out to where Patsy is sitting on top of a picnic table, watching a Little League game across the park and drinking from a pint bottle.

I set her cases down on the table with a thump. "You forgot these."

Patsy gives them a major side-eye, then lifts the vodka to her lips, drinking like she's in a contest to see how quick she can empty the bottle, not caring if anyone sees.

"Emergency pint?" I ask.

There's a small pop as Patsy pulls the bottle from her mouth, nods, then offers it to me. We keep it stashed in an empty box of cookies in the back seat of Patsy's car, but this is the first time we've needed it.

I take it, then hand Patsy the bright pink plastic case with all her nail shit. "Here," I say, then take a gulp at the vodka.

"I don't need it," she says. She shakes her head, and her newly black hair falls over her cheeks. "Ever again."

"Bullshit," I tell her. I put the case in her lap.

Patsy lays her hands on it, like it's a newborn baby somebody just passed to her. She runs her fingers over the latches like a new mother counting fingers and toes, then pops it open. Tears run down her cheeks again, till her face is shiny with them.

"Plumb Purple," she says in a little squeaky voice as she touches the bottles. They clink together heavily as she says their names. "French Kiss—my first polish, and Bitchy Red—my last one, I guess."

"You aren't done, Patsy," I say.

River sits next to me on the picnic table, half listening to us. Across the park a little kid runs around the bases while parents cheer like crazy.

"They had all that money," Patsy says, the open vodka bottle resting on her chin. "They saved it all up, and they won't let me use it." She remembers the vodka and tosses back a few swallows, then holds the almost-empty bottle out to me, a little wobbly.

I take it and hand it to River, who finishes it off, wipes his lips with the back of his hand, then says, "So fuck 'em. Save up like you've been doing and go anyways."

I grab Bitchy Red and shake it, the marble inside the polish *tick-tick-tick*ing as it mixes it up. "Come on."

Patsy shakes her head.

"You know you want to."

She turns away, wiping at her cheeks. I grab River's hand and hold it out to her. "Here. Do River's nails."

River pulls his hand back, laughing. "The fuck she will," he says, but I hold on tight and keep his knobby-knuckled hand in front of Patsy, who can't keep herself from looking at River's fingernails, and then back at the red polish.

"River needs some Bitchy Red . . . don't you?" I say, and look at him all helpless and sad. "For Patsy's birthday present?"

"Jesus Christ," he says, but he doesn't move his hand.

"Do it fast, before he changes his mind," I tell her, and Patsy's hand stops hovering over the polish and squeezes it tight. She opens it up real quick and grabs River's hand before he can get away, making the first red mark on his pinky fingernail and filling up the other nails in neat swipes of the brush.

"Oh, Christ. You'll take this shit off before we go to Granny's, right? I can't have no one seeing it." River looks like he's going to pee his pants watching his nails go from normal to bright red, but he lets Patsy keep painting away.

Patsy nods, and her dark black hair falls across her face as she concentrates. Patsy and me used to look a lot alike, back when I first lived here. But we didn't change in the same ways as we got older. I'm taller and she's got more meat on her bones. Our eyes are still the same basic blue, but hers have more ice in them than mine do. And she's way better than me at fixing herself up with makeup.

"Look at that," she says, tilting her head this way and that to look at her paint job. "Drunk as fuck, and I'm better than a salon." She quick does River's other hand, and he looks so damn cute with his hands all flat so they can dry, the red polish setting off the light-blue hair tie on his wrist.

"Now me," I say, and stick my feet on Patsy's lap. The vodka is hitting me some, so I close my eyes and lean up against River while Patsy starts in on my toes. The smell of the polish floats over to me and calls up Mama so clear I can almost hear her, like she's here in the park with us. I remember the last time we got our nails done together.

It was right after our New York trip, when Mama brought us here to Lakeville for our first visit in seven years.

"You and me, Bliss. Matching paws and claws, to celebrate my new job in Japan."

I was so goddamn excited to have fancy nails for the trip, pestering Mama with all our plans about what kind of house we'd have in Japan, and if the food would be weird, and what we'd do on such a long plane ride.

We were sitting at the drying table after Mama paid, hands under one orange lamp and feet under another, and I asked her for like the hundredth time if we'd have to use chopsticks to eat all our meals.

"Stop," Mama said.

"But I should practice, don't you think?"

Mama looked up at me across the dryers and gave me a little closed-mouth smile. She took a deep breath. "I guess now is as good a time as any to give you the news. You won't have to worry about chopsticks because *you* get to stay *right here* in Lakeville while I head off to Japan. Isn't that wonderful? You get to stay with Trish and Leo and Patsy." Her face opened up in a grin so big it was like a scary jack-o'-lantern.

"What?" I tried to make it not true by shaking my head over and over at Mama. "No. No, no, no."

"Yes! I never in a million years thought it would work out like this, baby, but just think of all the fun you and Patsy can have. It'd be too hard, with me gone day and night, and you not knowing one word of Japanese or ever tasting one bite of sushi before. You just wouldn't like it, baby girl."

The orange lights of the dryers got all blurry from the tears that came out of nowhere. I reached up to wipe my eyes, and Mama said, "Ahh-ahh! Don't ruin your nails!"

"I'll be good, Mama. You know I can." My voice wasn't much more than a whisper, almost lost in the fans of the drying lamps.

"Oh, baby. You have been so good, Mama's barely had to lift a finger all these years. But you'll like this. You and Patsy will be like sisters. And just think: I'm the face of the company! The face of SMOOCH! It's what we've been working for all this time, you and me. You'll see. It'll be so great."

"But you said we would live in Japan." My nose was running, and the tears poured out of my eyes. I had to turn my head to wipe my nose on my shirt, and even that didn't slow it down none.

"Settle down now. I can probably come back next summer."

"Mama—" I snuffled and tried so hard, but my nose and eyes wouldn't dry up. "Mama, I won't ask to model, I'll be so—"

"Okay, I'm busted. I can see I have to tell you the truth. I've never lied to you before, and I guess I shouldn't've started now." Mama looked over at me, her face misty through my tears, blond hair floating around her in a shimmery haze.

"Truth is, they said you can't come. That I need to go alone. Erika—you remember my agent—says we should wait until SMOOCH can't live without me. Then I can have some bargaining power. But I just can't bring you with. Lord, how I wish I could. I'm gonna miss my Bliss girl."

"The whole year?"

"At least until summer."

"They don't want me. Patsy doesn't want me."

"It was Trish's idea you stay here." Mama looked away from me, then down at her toes. "Time's up!"

My lights were still on, but Mama said we were done, so we were done. I bent to put my sandals on and when I looked up, Mama had gone out the door and was standing on the sidewalk. She was a stranger, a stranger who was already far away.

"Mama!" I burst out the door and grabbed her around the waist from behind. She was still here. She was still real. She was still Mama.

"Bliss, whatever the—?" Mama used her elbows to pry my arms away. "Now look what you've done. You've smudged your nails. All that time, just wasted."

"Um, hello, Bliss?" River says, shaking my shoulder. "Get this shit off of me, Deke and them are headed to Granny's, and I want to get there before they do." I look around the park, at Patsy putting the polish back in its case, shake my head to clear Mama right away, and pull Patsy to her car so I can drive us out to Granny's since I'm way more sober than her.

Patsy doesn't cheer all the way up, but at least she's not crying the whole time we're out at Granny's. She goes around asking everyone who comes in what their plans are for the future, but most people don't have a fucking clue.

"I'm gonna go on that bachelor show, what's it called?" Long Tom says, out on the front porch having a smoke. "Have six or seven girls fight over me."

Deanna punches him on the arm and says, "Good luck," and he laughs with her.

"College, probably," says Cracker. "Only way I can get my old man to pay for me to leave home."

"Is he telling you what to study? Or what not to study?" Patsy says, crowding up in his face as he sits on the front steps. "Because you should get to pick for yourself. Everybody should."

Cracker looks at her like she's selling ice in the winter. "Fuck if I know. I guess if he's got a good idea, I might just check it out."

River says, "Do what you want, Patsy. I mean it. I turn eighteen, I'm getting that Class A license and my own rig, and I'm out of here so fast, the only thing I'll bring along is Bliss here. See the world." River takes his hand off my leg to tap his can of chew and pinch a dip into his lower lip. As the tobacco smell sifts into my hair, I look out from the porch and wonder if he'll let me be the one to pick where we go. Maybe the ocean? Cold and deep, stretching out so far you can't see where it ends way off in Japan.

Or the mountains. Up so high there's snow all the time and the air is so clear you can see all the stuff you left behind.

Anything but miles and miles of hot, dusty cornstalks with their arms reaching out across the sharp rows, or squatty soybean fields with dry weeds standing like forgotten memories. Anything but the hot, sticky, butt crack of the country.

River adds, "Then Granny'll for sure give me this place at last, since she had to move in with my mom, so we have a place to crash when we're not on the road." He pulls me close up under his arm. "Just me and you, baby."

I picture the whole farmhouse all to ourselves, wide-open kitchen and three entire bedrooms I could fix up and live in any way I please, without Patsy or Aunt Trish having a say. I'd paint everything white. Bright white walls and white cabinets, all cool and clean next to the wood floors. I'd fix up the garden out back, so there's flowers in every room, and tomatoes on the windowsill getting just the right amount of ripe. I don't need a book full of money. Or anyone to save it up for me. All I need is River, who wants me right next to him, whatever he's got planned.

Patsy finally gives up and sits down on the glider with a beer. People have came and went all night, a few at a time, and it's starting to get dark. Deke's girlfriend, Nevaeh, brings all these cookies her and her sister made, practicing for the fair. We stuff ourselves on caramel-chocolate crunch bars and tof-fee crumbles and mostly sit around listening to scream-metal music and talking about all the crazy shit that's gone down this summer out here.

"I'm surprised you let me back in, River," says Cracker, from the porch chair he's sharing with his girlfriend of the week. "After me and Deke tried to have that campfire in the kitchen."

River leans back in his favorite lawn chair and puts his feet up on the porch railing. "Shit, Cracker. You'll notice that was over a month ago, and I just let you in for the first time today." He spits in his Mountain Dew can. "You wouldn't be here now if Deke hadn't took away your lighter." He pulls me onto his lap and balances us both in the chair. The last light of the long evening makes the sky all purple, and it's getting hard to see faces clearly. If it weren't for the music, I could sit out here forever and ever.

Long Tom laughs and scratches at his raggedy brown beard. "Lucky you aren't Shane and Billy—they won't never see the light of day here after River caught them pissing in the bathtub."

"Who even does that? Eeewww!" says Deanna, cuddled up with Long Tom.

Deke and Neveah go inside to turn up the music, and Patsy smirks over at me from where she sits on the glider, still about half-drunk from the vodka. She knows I hate the scream metal, and she knows that River loves it.

Way down the lane a big-ass shiny black SUV turns in, makes its way up, and parks in the drive.

"The fuck is that?" asks River. He dumps me off his lap, takes his feet off the railing, and sits up tall like one of them birds that puffs itself up all big when another bird wants its food.

Long Tom runs his hand through his beard and squints out at the SUV. He tosses back the rest of his drink and sits up as the doors open and guys pour out of the car. "Oh, yeah. I saw Nathan Cranston and them clowns at the store today. They're all back from college and looking to party. That good with you?"

Nathan Cranston. My stomach turns over, and I try to keep

it still by pouring a beer down my throat. I move back against the house at the same time Patsy moves forward and leans out over the railing. Nathan's family lives catty-corner across the street from Patsy, and she's had a thing for him ever since she was, like, ten years old.

My memories of Nathan are . . . less good, and if I never see him again, it'll be way too soon.

"I dunno, Tommy. Looks like they already got started," River says, his eyes narrowed at the six guys who almost fall out of the SUV. They stagger past the headlights and up to the house like they own the place.

"C'mon. They're good people," Cracker says, but he sets his beer down and goes to stand at the top of the steps by River. "When they're not all fucked up."

River is scary good at knowing who will behave and who won't, and I can tell he's not having it.

I force myself to look at them.

"River, my friend," says Nathan. His smug smile has not changed one bit in the years since I've seen him, like everything in the world belongs to him.

"Nathan." River stands tall on the top step and looks down at where Nathan and them sway in the heat. In the dark, their faces are all shadowy, and their eyes catch the last of the light. Nathan lurches away from his buddies, towards where me and Patsy stand on the porch.

"Hey, Nate," Patsy says, not *too* pathetic. She waves down at him.

He smiles at her, a loose, liquid smile. "Patsy." He swivels his head around until he lands on me. "And Bliss." His smile gets bigger. "Nice night for a party."

I just about crawl out of my skin hearing him say my name, all hungry and grabby. I shiver and lean back even more against the house.

"It *was* a nice night," River says.

I have never been so glad for River as when he comes over and puts his arm around me. I hang on to him as he pulls me over to the top of the steps with him.

"Long Tom said we could join you." Nathan takes the first step to the porch.

Just then, one of his friends hauls off and pukes in the bushes, making the other girls squeal and run inside.

"Yeah, maybe some other night," River says. "Earlier in the party."

"Oh, come on, River," Patsy whines. "It's my birthday." She smiles at Nathan again. I want to block her from him, keep her safe, keep his smile from lighting up her face.

Nathan looks from River to me, over to the bushes, and back to River. "It's a free country. We're all friends here," he begins.

"All of this"—River waves an arm around at the house, the yard, and the fields—"is mine, Nathan. And tonight, we are not friends." River's eyes do not match his easy smile one bit.

Nathan just stands there, hands out, like he's still asking for something. His eyes keep sliding off me and back to River, but he finally fumbles his keys out of his pocket. "Guess I was wrong about this party. Happy birthday, though." He smiles with every one of his teeth, then jerks his chin at one of the other guys and points at the puker. "Load him up."

Watching Nathan stalk back to the car, I half want to puke in the bushes myself.

"Thanks a lot, River. Ruin my birthday the rest of the way," Patsy says, and slams back into the house.

River kisses me real good, calming down the stomach Nathan riled up. "They'd have fucked with the house for sure," he says, and pulls me back inside.

Five

River wants us to stay the night, but Patsy's still pissed at him for not letting Nathan in. So just before midnight, Patsy puts out her last cigarette and pulls away from Granny's. She's got the windows all open as we blast down the highway, and my hair whips across my face, getting in my mouth no matter how many times I brush it away. I put my window up and enjoy the break.

Patsy puts my window back down without even looking at me. The dank night air rushes in and fucks with my hair again.

"She's gonna smell the smokes on you no matter what," I call, swatting hair away from my face.

Patsy just drives.

Whatever.

"We're almost out of gas," Patsy says, looking at me with her eyebrows up.

"So?"

"So, it's your turn."

42

Shit. "I . . . can't." I hold out my empty hands to her. "I'm flat broke." I've been trying to save up for a car of my own, but every time I get more than a few dollars, Patsy needs it for gas money or River needs it for beer. I spent everything I had this week on ingredients for red velvet cake, but I can't hold that over Patsy's head, especially not since the whole thing with the birthday money.

Patsy stomps on the brakes at the stop sign. "Of course you are." She lurches forward. "You're flat broke, Nathan can't come into my party, and I'm never going to beauty school, even though I'm some kind of rich. Some goddamn birthday." There's nothing for me to say, so I just close my eyes and ride the rest of my buzz all the way home.

Patsy and me say hi real quick and stumble past Aunt Trish and Uncle Leo, who I can guarantee was passed out in the recliner not two minutes ago. Aunt Trish's eyes are all puffy, but I don't look at her any longer than I have to. We need to move fast unless we want to talk about Patsy's birthday, which I sure as hell do not.

Patsy somehow doesn't get caught for smelling like an ashtray, and she books it to her bedroom, which looks like a tornado went through it. There is no way in hell I'm tripping over everything to get to my side of the room, so I turn on the overhead.

"Off," she barks from where she's already in her bed, clothes scattered in her wake. I ignore her command for my own safety. She's got her face to the wall and the yellow comforter up to her ears, even though it's about a million and six degrees in here. The ruffled trim pushes up her blacker-than-black hair so it's standing up almost straight, and the pissed-off is rolling off of her in waves.

"What are you mad at me for?" I ask, catching my foot on one of her shirts. I reach the first pile of her crap on the floor and toss it over onto her bed. The second pile follows it. Next is her outfit from tonight. I about gag on the smoke smell before I throw it on top of her, too.

A hand comes out, gives me the finger, and shoves everything back on the floor at the foot of her bed. "You could have made him," she says.

"Made who?" I say.

"River. He had no right to kick Nathan and them out," she finally spits over at me.

I haven't seen Nathan in years, but it took all night for my stomach to settle back down after he left. "It's River's granny's house. He has all the rights," I say, as I stub my toe on her tennis shoe and toss it at the bed.

It lands by her feet, and she kicks at the covers to knock it off. "He didn't have to be such a dick about it. To Nathan, or to you." Patsy pulls the covers over her shoulder and turns away.

"When was he a dick to me?"

Patsy's voice is muffled. "When isn't he? Why do you stay with him? I mean, sure, he's hot, and Granny's is a great party place, but he's a real asshole."

The floor is almost clear now and I make it to my trundle

without stepping on anything else. "River's my boyfriend."

"He treats you like he owns you. And you just take it."

"I take it?" There's shit on Patsy's desk, too, and I bump my head on the bulletin board as I reach for it. The board sways like it's going to fall. It's covered with postcards from Mama—lots at first, not many the past few years—and a faded picture of me in seventh grade dressed up for Culture Days in a bathrobe kimono, holding chopsticks and a sign that I thought said *love* in Japanese. I grit my teeth and steady it with my hand, then grab Patsy's pink bra and the zebra-print cami off the desk chair and send them flying.

The cami lands on Patsy's head and she pulls the comforter tighter. "The way he talks to you? God. And the worst part is, you could have any guy in the world. And you go and pick River."

"But River waited for me, Patsy. For, like, a year. Over all the girls he coulda had." I dump my clothes in the hamper. "I could never leave him. He loves me."

She rolls over and looks at me, her eyes glittering from the ceiling light. "River loves you. Priceless." She throws off the comforter, knocking the cami onto the floor. She stomps over to the light, slaps it off, and stomps back to her bed. The mattress springs squeak under her weight, and she scrabbles around to cover herself all up again.

I start to remind her about the red velvet cake, and the park, but I shut my mouth and click on my reading light.

"Fuck you," Patsy says. She reaches over and pulls the plug of my light right out of the wall.

I sigh. "Happy fucking birthday," I tell her. In the darkness, I sit on the edge of the trundle and bounce on the flimsy mattress. There's not even a box spring, just a metal frame. It's supposed to fold up under Patsy's bed and only be brought out for company, but it's been unfolded, for me, for almost six years now.

I stretch out on my matching yellow comforter—bought back when we were trying to act like twins, when Mama first left me here. Patsy and me swore we were gonna go everywhere together and do everything together and be sisters instead of just cousins.

My stomach lurches as I remember Nathan's hot eyes out at Granny's tonight. Nathan is one reason Patsy and me went back to being cousins, instead of sisters like we planned, all because of him picking me over Patsy a long, long time ago.

I close my eyes to push Nathan far away in my memories, where I usually keep him. My head spins a little from all the beers, just like it was spinning after the hug with Blake earlier today.

I still don't know what came over me. Probably the heat. Either way, it's a good thing I'll never see him again.

Thunder rolls into my dreams, filling the air and shaking me awake. The room is greenish dark, sticky, and still, as if it's waiting for the world to end.

Then the thunder cracks, splitting my ears and my hungover head wide open. *Oh no. No, no, no.* I have to get down to the basement before the storm gets any worse. I pull the comforter around me and hurry down the empty hall. The sharp, warm smell of coffee tries its best to make the house feel homey and safe from storms.

But it's not good enough.

I hurry down the stairs and go straight to the beanbag that sits farthest from the high-up basement windows, safest from lightning strikes and tornado-force winds. Back when I first got left here by Mama, Patsy would come and sit with me when there was a storm, both of us with afghans over our heads, looking out at each other through the openings like we were fish caught in rainbow-colored nets. Patsy would tell dumb jokes or sing loud enough to drown out the thunder, and sometimes it nearly worked. Sometimes I'd feel almost safe.

If the power stayed on, Aunt Trish would let us watch a movie through the afghans, and when the power went out, there was a whole shelf of flashlights right behind the beanbag, and Patsy would hold hers up under her afghan-covered chin and make funny faces until I laughed.

Nowadays, Patsy barely even notices that there's a storm, never mind that I might be down here waiting it out. I don't come down here every time, and I almost never put the afghan over my head. Not unless it's a real tornado warning.

The thunder can't make up its mind whether it's a rolling storm that builds up louder and louder, or a bunch of cracks that sound like they are tearing up every tree between here and Granny's place.

When will this shit be over? I need it to be over. Now.

"Bliss?" Aunt Trish calls down the stairs after a thundercrack that I'm pretty sure was in the backyard. She calls again. "Are you down there?"

Before I can answer, a giant wave of thunder rolls over the house. I let out a squeak. Why did I have to drink so many beers last night, is what I want to know. My head is bad off enough without the thunder. What will we do if a tornado peels off the roof of the house like a pop-top?

"Want some company?" Aunt Trish stands over me, holding out a Diet Coke. I take the can, and Aunt Trish gestures to her green smoothie. "I can make you one of these, if you want?" She sits on the sofa next to the beanbag.

There's another flash, and a crack of thunder. Jesus Christ, where is the afghan?

"No, thanks," I say when I can finally answer. She knows I don't like breakfast. "Is there a tornado watch?" I take a long fizzy drink of my Diet Coke.

"No sirens. Just a storm. Should blow over soon."

"How soon?"

"It's already calming down. Hear?"

The rolling is a little quieter, and so is my head, thanks to the Diet Coke.

Lightning flashes, and I close my eyes while Aunt Trish counts, "One thousand one, one thousand two . . ." all the way up to five before the thunder cracks, so we know the storm is five miles away.

Aunt Trish's voice sounds like Mama's voice with my eyes closed, and I remember a long time ago when I didn't used to be scared of storms. Mama would sit us on the bed of whatever hotel or motel we were in on the modeling circuit, pull the blankets over our heads, and every time the thunder roared, she would scream and grab on to me. I remember laughing, thinking she was fooling, until the time when the storm *was* a tornado warning, with screaming winds and pounding rain. We had to hide in the hotel's dark, creepy storm cellar with the other guests, and Mama held on to me so tight that when it was all over I had eight little round bruises on the outside of my arms and two on the inside from her grip.

Every time, though, Mama would count, "One thousand one, one thousand two . . ." with every lightning flash until it was safe to get out of bed again.

After Mama went off to Japan and I stayed here, I started to get afraid of storms, even though everybody told me there was nothing to worry about. Even though I count to see how far away the lightning is. Even though nothing bad has ever happened. I wonder what Mama does. Maybe that's why she's still in Japan: maybe there's no tornadoes there.

The storm passes and Aunt Trish says she needs some help in the storage room. My hangover is still there at the base of my head, and I wish I could go back to bed, but I feel so bad about Patsy's birthday, I get up and follow her in.

"There's a tag sale at church next weekend, and I want to clear out some of Mother and Daddy's junk. It's for a good cause, and I have an idea that we could use this room for something," she says, her pudgy arms just barely hanging on to a giant box.

49

There's nubby carpet on the floor, and the walls have this brown paneling on them. It's kind of dark, but without all the shelves, this *could* be an actual room for something.

I turn in a circle, seeing it with new eyes. There's enough space for a bed over in the corner, and even though there's no closet, it'd be enough for someone who just wanted a space of their own.

But there's a shit ton of boxes down here, and Aunt Trish will never part with this stuff, so there's no point in even wondering how it would look with a bed, and a dresser, and maybe a desk or a mirror.

"'Love,' 'leave,' 'let someone have,'" Aunt Trish says, dragging in two laundry baskets and a giant black trash bag.

"Seems like an okay system. What is this stuff?" I ask, as we haul two big boxes from the shelves to the middle of the room. I'm only limping a little bit from walking barefoot yesterday.

"Most of it was Mother and Daddy's." She rips tape off one box while I pick at another, trying to open it. "But this . . . oh, look here." Aunt Trish's voice sounds like when she sees a puppy, or a baby, or one of those stupid commercials where some old guy finally gets a visit from his kids. "It's your baby things! Here's the receiving blanket Mother made you—Patsy has the matching one—and, oh! A lock of your hair. Theresa was furious when she came for a visit and Mother had chopped it all off!"

She hands me an envelope that says "Baby's First Haircut" and the crocheted blanket, which looks like it used to be shades of pink. "And here's the stuffed elephant you would not go to sleep without. Mother fought you over that thing for years, but you never would part with it. Do you remember living here with them when you were just a bitty thing?"

I have a few memories of Grampa and Gramma Walker from when I was three or four—Gramma's bony hands holding a cigarette as she pushed me on the old metal swing set in the backyard, smoke swirling up the chains. The cool, fresh scent of Grampa's aftershave as he scooped me up on his shoulders. I shake my head.

"Not much. I remember Grampa waving at me from the porch when Mama and me drove away one time. When was that?"

"That was after Mother died. You were around five years old. She and Daddy looked after you for so long, I think they forgot you weren't theirs! Well, you all started out together here, of course, you and your mama. And Theresa must've left for Chicago when you were about a year. But then she swooped back in and took you away with her the day after Mother's funeral." Aunt Trish flips through a pile of cards and throws them in the "leave" trash bag so hard the bag falls over. "We all cried buckets of tears when you left, but Daddy most of all."

"Huh." A pang of sadness for Grampa—and Gramma—hits me. I hold the elephant up to my cheek, trying to squeeze some baby memory out of them, but its fuzzy trunk doesn't remind me of shit. I set it aside in my own "love" pile and open my box.

Three white mugs that say "Spirit of Peoria," and two orange sombreros go into the "let someone have" basket, and I stick my hand in for more. I pull out a dark case that looks like it holds a little guitar, or a violin. At the rate we're getting through stuff, Aunt Trish and Uncle Leo will be dead and gone before we get done clearing out this room.

"Oh, my heavens. Theresa's ukulele. Would you look at that." Aunt Trish unzips the case and pulls out a brown instrument with four strings on it. She gives it a strum, and we both jump back at the noise it makes. "Time was, Theresa wouldn't be more than five steps away from this thing. She played morning, noon, and would've played all night, but Mother made her keep it in the living room at bedtime. Give it a whirl."

I make the same noise as Aunt Trish when I pluck at the strings. "This is supposed to be music?"

"With some practice. Not that I would know—Theresa wouldn't let anyone near it if she could help it. She used to put on little shows and make all of us watch her sing and play. How many times did I hear 'Rainbow Connection'? Her playing wasn't too bad, but nothing like she made it out to be."

"So, 'let' or 'leave'?" I ask her.

Aunt Trish looks from me to the ukulele, then back again. "How about 'love'?" She holds it out to me, eyebrows raised and a little smile on her face.

"Will Mama be okay with that?"

Aunt Trish pats me on the shoulder and turns back to her box. "Honey, it's all yours. If it mattered to her, she would have taken it with her." She means it kindly, but something about the words settle funny in my stomach.

Six

I'm out on the back porch after way too many trips down Aunt Trish's memory lane. We sorted everything in the room, and we finished off by hauling the sleeper sofa into the space we, surprisingly, cleared in the back room.

I'm trying to get the hang of Mama's ukulele. Turns out there was a little book in the case that sorta explains how to do the chords and shit. I get the C chord and strum it a few times. I don't know shit about music, but I keep moving my fingers on the lines—frets—until it just feels . . . right to me. The next chord is so hard I'm tempted to walk down to the basement and toss the uke in the "leave" bin. Or smash it like a rock star would.

But I'm not gonna let some toy instrument win. I will get this if it kills me.

When I finally get the chord right, the sound I make is 100 percent worth the headache, full and sweet and like it's meant to be. It's hard to believe I can make something sound so beautiful.

Patsy plops down next to me on the back steps, jiggling my

arm and making me *sproing* a note. "Since when do you play guitar?"

I play the parts again, fixing the note Patsy fucked up. "Ukulele. It was Mama's."

"Aunt Theresa? You sure?"

"According to your mom."

Patsy winces when I mention her mom, then flips her hair like she's leaving yesterday behind her. Typical Patsy. Last night she was about ready to claw me to death, and today she's back to normal. She grins and grabs the ukulele out from under me.

"Give it back," I say. "It's mine now." I swipe at the uke, but Patsy hugs it closer to her, plunking and strumming all over the place. "Stop torturing it!"

"Uh, like you're any better?" Patsy tosses it to me and leans back on her elbows, laughing.

"Your phone charged?" I ask her. "I want to find a video so I can *get* better."

"Yeah, but I'm out of data again." She sighs and turns the phone over and over in her hands. "Stuck with this piece of shit forever, I guess." She leans up close to me. "Bliss, I have to get to beauty school or die trying. No matter what Mom says."

"Yeah, well, 'The beauty industry will take all your money . . .'"

"'And suck the life out of anyone who tries to earn an honest living.'" We say the last part at the same time, then crack up.

"Seriously, though, why do I get punished just because Mom was a terrible business owner?"

I shake my head. "You think you'd still want to do hair and shit if you'd grown up with it?"

"Maybe." Patsy looks at her nails, then sighs. "I just have cosmetology in my blood."

"Nothing you can do about that, I guess."

"If I can't use my birthday money, I'm going anyways. She can't stop me." She taps my arm. "And I have just the way. Did you see Aggie last night? From health class?"

I shake my head. "Was she at Granny's?"

"Well, River was being such a dick, she didn't exactly feel welcome. Her and her girlfriend left pretty quick."

Whatever. "So?"

"So I think she got us a job. Walking beans. A few weeks. Are you in?"

"What the hell is walking beans?"

"Working for a farmer."

I crack up. "Us. On a farm."

She doesn't laugh.

"You're serious."

She nods. "They need people bad, and the pay is real good. We start on Monday."

No matter how hard I tried, I couldn't find a job this summer. Without a car or experience, I was pretty much screwed. I'm not saving up for beauty school, but if I could save up for a car, it would change my life.

The smell of fresh-mowed grass cuts through the afternoon air as I try the chords again. "Sure. Whatever." I shift my feet.

"Still hurt?" Patsy asks. "Maybe don't try walking to town barefoot."

I give her the finger and we laugh, then I strum one more chord, and the string breaks right as a car horn blasts from out front.

"River," we say together.

"Now I need new strings. Great." I zip the ukulele case and hand it to Patsy. "Put this on my bed so I can go?"

"Some guys come to the door for their girlfriends."

"So?" I hold out the case.

"It'll cost you."

"How about I throw you a party on Saturday?"

River honks again.

"Fine," Patsy says. "Good thing he's not an asshole."

Just before full dark, we are sitting in the back of River's truck on an old blue sleeping bag, waiting for the drive-in movie to start. There's families everywhere, kids playing and even making s'mores on camping stoves by their cars. A little kid stumbles past the truck and drops a handful of Matchbox cars. He cries until his mom scoops him and his toys up.

"God, I loved those cars when I was a little shit," River says. He spits into his Mountain Dew can. "When I was really small, before they split up, Mom and Dad and me would all go to their jobs together. I'd play on the floor with my cars while Dad primed a house, or Lisa taped off some windows."

I snuggle in close, even though it's hot as shit, because I

have never heard River say even one-tenth this much about his family.

He looks at the previews on the drive-in screen like he's seeing his past. "One time, Dad made me a racetrack out of painter's tape and used one of the silver paint pans for a ramp, and I shot my cars all over the place for hours and hours."

He spits again and laughs a low laugh. "That ended with me getting my ass beat when Dad slipped on a car and fell over with the roller still in his hand, getting white paint all over the brown carpet. He whipped every single car at the fresh-painted wall. They have white paint on them to this day, and I have never been able to look at brown carpet since without my ass burning."

I look over at him, and even though his cheeks are covered with stubble, I see eight-year-old River in him so clear. My chest fills up with wanting to hug that little guy, protect him, force his parents to be better to him.

He squeezes me closer, then gets serious again. "But that all ended when Lisa ditched us. That's how Granny and me got so close. When Lisa was off finding herself, Granny was so pissed at her own daughter she let me live with her."

"Out there where we party?"

He takes his arm away from around me. "Why the fuck you think I have to be so careful? I have told you and told you, it's Granny's place right now, but she promised it to me some day. I just have to live with Dad for now till she hands it over, and I don't want no trash house."

And just like that, he's back to not talking about it. I lean into him, putting my head on his shoulder and my arms around him. River and me, we have to stick together. We're the only ones who understand. People shouldn't leave. *Moms* shouldn't leave.

I prop myself up on an elbow. "So you'll live at Granny's, but you'll drive the truck all over?"

River raises up his eyebrows at me. "*We'll* go all over. Cracker says I can pick my routes, so we can go anywhere they need shit hauled. Montana, Wyoming, Utah, all at eighty miles an hour with you in the cab next to me. We'll be the perfect team."

River and me *are* the perfect team.

I have a sudden memory of Mama next to me in the front seat of her ratty old Buick as we took off early one morning to go to the next modeling gig on the circuit. It was cold out, and I only had a blanket around me because Mama hadn't remembered to get me a winter coat yet. I musta been about seven years old, maybe eight.

"We're a team, Bliss," Mama had whispered, as she pulled onto the highway. "We are gonna make it so big, and then we'll have somebody else to do the driving for us. Anywhere we wanna go."

She did make it big, for a while, and I was a super good teammate. I sat very, very quiet in corners and watched the girls smile and pout for the camera, and held it when I had to go until Mama could hustle me into the ladies' room when nobody was watching. I snuck into the catering rooms to grab breakfast or lunch, since Mama was too busy to worry about stuff like that.

The catering rooms dried up when the good jobs did, and for some reason crappy photographers were more pissed about a kid hanging around—even a practically invisible kid—than the good photographers were.

Mama has a driver now, in Japan, and even though she said we were a team, Mama is there, and I am here. She thought they'd for sure let me come, too, but that has not happened yet in five years. Almost six. I stopped wishing for us to be a real team a long, long time ago.

Now River is my team.

The movie starts, and we watch it over the tailgate. The bad guys are all set to make their move against the superheroes when River makes his move, too. He scoops his dip out and turns to me on the sleeping bag, pulling me close. River kisses me long and deep, like he's kissing me into the future. He tastes like tobacco, and his lips are soft and convincing. The weight of him grounds me in the bed of the truck, and the lumpy sleeping bag scoots out from under us as we move around.

After, River lies back and lets me put my head on his chest so I can see the screen. A little breeze blows over us, making the heat of the day seem gentle and soft. The bad guys are winning, and the most important superhero won't join the crew, but I know he'll change his mind. My hair keeps drifting up to River's face, and the fourth time he picks a piece out of his mouth, he sits all the way up and scoots me off of him.

"Come on." River hops out of the truck bed. He opens the driver's side door and starts up the truck.

"It's not over yet," I tell him, but I climb out after him.

"Yeah, but we're leaving. Hop in," he says.

"Don't you want to see what happens?" I ask, after I pull the door shut.

"Nah," says River, putting the truck in reverse. "The good guys win. They always do."

River's mad when I tell him about the beans on the way back to town.

"The fuck you working with Patsy for? Let's you and me detassel corn. Deke says we can make a shit ton, and that way I can quit working for Lisa."

"I don't even know what detasseling is," I say, as he pulls up to Patsy's and parks just beyond the driveway. The darkness is thick and sweaty, and about a million bugs race around the streetlight like it's some kind of speedway. "Me and Patsy are for sure doing this job. Lisa will keep you on if you talk nice and promise to do what she says."

"Whatever." River shrugs and takes his dip out so we can kiss goodbye. He's kissing me up real good, and I'm starting to wonder if maybe he thinks we're gonna get it on again right here in the truck, when a car pulls up behind River and honks.

"What the fuck?" River asks. He barely moves, but I sit up to look behind the truck. The driver of the fancy silver car honks again. Its blinker is on, like it's going to turn in to the driveway.

River pulls forward just far enough for the other car to squeeze past. "Dickhead," he adds, then starts kissing me again.

The silver car parks diagonally, taking up the whole driveway. I look back again just in time to see a familiar form get out of the passenger side and shut the door.

Everything stops.

"Holy shit." I go hot and cold all over and close my eyes to keep the world from spinning away.

River stops kissing my neck. "What?"

I can't answer him. I can only stare as she totters down the driveway wearing stupid-ass red heels. She's got on a skirt that's all flouncy and a low-cut silky top that shows off like twenty-seven necklaces, and her hair is . . . my hair. It floats up beside her and billows out behind her as she wobbles down the drive. Every one of my muscles has frozen and I just watch her come closer.

"Mama," I breathe.

Seven

"*Your mama?*" *River* asks. "I thought she was in China or somewhere." He looks at me like I've lost my mind.

Which maybe I have.

She walks all the way up to the window of the truck, finger raised to give River a talking-to. I realize just in time that River still has his hand down my shirt, and I sit up at the last second and shake him off, my face burning as if she saw it.

"Listen, mister, when a vehicle has their turn signal on— oh, Lordy! Bliss? Baby? Is that you?" She opens her arms wide. "Mama's here! Mama's finally here!"

When I don't—or can't—move, she marches around and yanks my door open. "All the way from Japan, honey! Give your mama a hug!"

I slide out, and she tackles me in a tight hug. We are the same height now—maybe I'm a little taller; it's hard to tell with her high heels. Her bony shoulder blades are sharp under my hands, and she smells like she's eaten a whole tin of Altoids. But she's real and she's here, after all this time.

As suddenly as she grabbed me, she shoves me out to arm's length. "Let Mama get a look at you. Aren't you just perfect?" She circles her arm around my waist and drags me back to the truck. "And who is this?" She ducks her head to stare in at River, then jabs out a hand to smooth my hair out of my face.

"Mama, this is River," I try to say, but she talks over me.

"My baby! With a *boy*!" She claps a skinny hand to her cheek and looks from me to him, then sighs a loud sigh. "Where has the time gone?"

River just sits there, looking from Mama back to me, his mouth hanging open a little. I see in her a lot of the same things I see when I look in a mirror—same nose, same hair, mostly the same lips, but Mama's are thinner and smeared with orangey lipstick. Her eyes are lighter blue than mine, and ringed with so much makeup I wonder if Patsy got ahold of her.

Mama kisses her fingers and waves them at River. "Nice to meet you. I'm sure we will see you later," she says as she pulls me away from the truck and up the driveway. I look back at River as we go, and he gives a little half wave goodbye, looking as if he's just been run over by a truck.

"I can't believe I am so late. Clyde!" Mama thumps the truck of the silver car. "What's the holdup?" She links her arm through mine and walks us past the car. "As I told Clyde, there is no earthly reason there should be this much traffic in the middle of nowhere. Where is there to go?"

I look over her shoulder to see a tall bald guy get out of the driver's seat. He's wearing a white polo shirt and khaki pants, but he looks like he'd rather be in motorcycle leathers, or a T-shirt with rolled-up sleeves. He wrestles a glittery blue suitcase out of the trunk and follows us to the front door, where he stops to spit in the grass.

"Clyde, honey, this here's my angel, Bliss. My baby girl who's just about a grown-up woman!"

"I'll say," Clyde says. He looks me up and down, raising his eyebrows. "Like mother, like daughter, am I right?"

I shiver in the night air, and Mama slaps his shoulder. "Never you mind him. Bliss, baby! How are you so big, so grown-up? Old enough for boys? Now does *that* ever bring back memories."

She stabs the doorbell with a bright orange fingernail, then says, "Go on! Don't you live here? Open up!" I step into the house and all hell breaks loose.

"Don't ring the doorbell at this hour of the—" Aunt Trish's face freezes like a video when you pause it. "Theresa? Oh my god!"

There's all sorts of laughing and crying and hugging, and Patsy comes out of her room to see what all the fuss is about.

"Aunt Theresa?"

"This absolutely cannot be little Patsy. You're almost a grown-up woman, too! Do not call me 'Aunt,' or I will feel older than the hills." She wags her finger at Patsy, who stares at Mama like a magician just pulled her out of a hat.

"Theresa, I can't believe—you didn't tell us you were coming," Aunt Trish says, her face halfway between happy and horrified. "We would've prepared a room for you to—"

"I want you to meet Clyde, my personal savior," Mama says, all puffed up like she's showing a prize she won at the fair. "And driver."

"Nice to meet you." Clyde towers over Aunt Trish as Mama introduces them. His surprisingly small hands pat her on the back as he swallows her up in a hug. "Any sister of Theresa's is a friend of mine."

There's more hugging and crying and pretty quick we are all sitting down except Mama and Aunt Trish, who is in the kitchen tossing ice into glasses with such force, we can hear her all the way in the family room.

Mama flits around the room, lighting on objects the way a butterfly lands on branches in search of the best flowers, and I can't hardly take my eyes off her for one second. She about takes my breath away. She's scary skinny, wears way more makeup than even Patsy, and she's never still, not for more than a minute.

But she's *Mama*. Same hair, same way of swooping me up into whatever she's planning, same way of holding her head, like she's just about to get her picture taken.

Same as the day she left me.

"I just cannot believe it, that I'm back again in the town where it all started. And my baby! Bliss, you're so pretty I just want to cry," Mama says. I'm not sure where I'm supposed to go, if I'm supposed to follow her around or just watch, so I sit on the edge of the sofa near Patsy, ready to get up if Mama needs me. Patsy is looking at the two of us the same way River did, like she's not sure which of us is real and which one is the copy.

"Mmmm. Mother's old tea set. Remember when we were sick, she'd make special 'healing tea'? All milk and sugar? Only time she ever used it," she says, picking up objects and setting them back on the shelves as she talks about them.

"And you tried to fake being sick all those times," Aunt Trish says, "just to get the tea."

"But it never worked. Somehow she always knew." Mama and Aunt Trish share their first real smile since Mama walked in the door, then Mama turns back to looking through the shelves.

"I remember these silver candlesticks! And here's my crystal bowl." Mama smiles almost harder at the bowl than she did at Aunt Trish.

"Mother gave me that bowl for Christmas the year before she died," says Aunt Trish, passing out glasses to Mama and Clyde. Her face is pink and sweaty, and her eyes are maybe even more glued to Mama than mine.

"Of course she did. Gave away my bowl." Mama gives her head a little shake.

"Your bowl? She was very insistent that I have it," Aunt Trish says, her voice all trembly. "It's always meant so much to me."

"Well," Mama says, after a second, "you've taken good care of it for me." She trails a finger across the bowl, then turns to the next item on the shelf. "Remember when we made mud pies on these china plates? Ooh, were we ever in trouble for that!"

Mama laughs, and we ride her laughter, too, even Aunt Trish, who then says, "You mean, was *I* ever in trouble. Mother gave me the spanking, even though you're the one who brought them outside. Said I should know better, being older and all."

"We had some fun times, didn't we?" Mama smiles at Aunt Trish, who looks at her the way she looks at Patsy when Patsy finally does her chores without being nagged.

Mama turns to me. "Do you have any good snackies?" and it's like we are back in the Motel 7, and I'm bringing her cigarettes, special juice, and snackies while she rests up from a hard day's work, all the pillows behind her head and under her aching feet.

Patsy beats me to the kitchen and grabs a bag of flavored popcorn, just about knocking me over to get it back to Mama, who hugs her and hands the bag to Clyde. She grabs my arm while she talks about the most, the only, the best stuff she saw in Japan, and I'm right back in the front seat of the Buick, listening to her explain the next step in her career, telling her to take the next exit and go left as I read the map as best as I could with my eleven-year-old arm trapped up under her hand.

It's like we were just together yesterday, like five, almost six years are just erased, and things go right exactly back to the way they were before. All the memories I shoved away come piling back one on top of the other, and I remember all the little details I thought I'd forgotten. Like the electricity she brings to any room she's in, or the way people shine when she gives them her whole attention, or the way her hands move when she talks.

But mostly, I just did not really remember how goddamn pretty she is. Like, I can hardly look straight at her, my eyes don't believe that she's for real. Everything is just so perfect, it all goes together just right, her eyes and her nose and the way she tilts her chin—it's like looking at one of Gramma's roses and having your heart almost stop because there is not one single thing it could do to be any more beautiful.

"And Daddy's dictionary. You've kept everything, haven't you?" Mama finishes her circuit of the room and lands lightly on Clyde's lap in Uncle Leo's recliner. She leans back, covering her eyes with her forearm.

"Girls, girls, girls. They say you can never come home again, but here I am." She stands up. "Those bastards thought they could keep me away from my baby, and they were almost right. But didn't I have the last laugh?"

Clyde is just as glued to Mama as the rest of us, and he laughs a thick, wheezy laugh. "You tell 'em, babe." When he smiles, his whole face changes from scary to soft, almost cute.

"Theresa?" Uncle Leo comes in from his bedroom, rubbing his eyes. "Did we . . . know you were coming? This late?" He goes over to where Aunt Trish stands between the kitchen and living room, putting his arm around her so it looks like he's holding her up.

Mama laughs, and not one of us can keep from laughing with her. She's like fresh air, all sparkly and glittery. "Heavens, no, Leo. That would ruin the surprise!" Mama jumps up again and pulls me from the sofa. "Once I was dumped in New York, I realized I just had to get to my girl." She holds my hands and steps back to look me up and down again, smiling at me in a way that makes me wish she'd never left. "I just knew she was growing up without me, and it near about killed me. Clyde, here, got me all the way to my baby in twelve hours flat! What do you think about that?"

Clyde grins, lit up like a flower in the sunshine when Mama looks at him, then wilts when she looks away.

Mama says, "Come get acquainted, Leo. I just know you two will have a lot to talk about. Clyde drives a limo, and you do . . . car things."

Uncle Leo doesn't look like he wants to let go of Aunt Trish, who stares at Mama like she might disappear if Aunt Trish closes her eyes.

"Of course, you'll stay here," she says, in a wavery voice. "We just cleared out the basement, there's plenty of room down there, I just need to do a few things to set it up." Her eyes flick over to me, then get sucked back into Mama's.

"Now this, I have to see. Bring the bags downstairs, Clyde. I'll be right down. I just have to catch up with my little girl a minute or two."

They all disappear to set up housekeeping, and Mama and me are alone in the family room. Mama squeezes my hands. "Baby. I have so much to tell you. And I want to hear all about you: What do you love, what do you hate, what are your hopes and dreams, what's your plan for getting out of this ridiculously small town?"

"I—"

Mama pulls me to her in a fierce hug, squeezing all my breath out at once. "Oh! If this isn't just the most miraculous thing ever." She puts her forehead up against mine, closes her eyes, and is still for maybe the first time since she got out of the car.

I close my eyes, too, and there's nothing in the world besides me and Mama, our foreheads together like they've been a million times before, and I let myself slip into something that feels like home.

I lie in bed with a stupid smile on my face and hug the little elephant we found today. I am tingling from head to toe, like I stuck my finger in the electric socket, or got hit by lightning or drank a case of Diet Coke.

Mama came back for me. She truly did.

I am flooded with happiness. It's going to be just like I thought all these years. We are finally going to live together, like moms and daughters should, with movie nights and favorite delivery places and advice about boys and friends and the future. I am finally gonna have the mama I deserve, not an aunt who tries her best but has to like Patsy better. I am gonna be that person with a real mom at school conferences and an actual parent who signs the forms instead of a guardian. I am so excited about Mama finally, finally coming back for me, that I can't breathe, never mind fall asleep.

I make up my mind right then and there: I won't ask her for a single thing. So long as she stays.

Eight

In the morning, Mama is still, impossibly, here. Downstairs, in this very house. Aunt Trish makes her special baked breakfast, keeps it warm in the oven, then finally wraps it in tinfoil and shoves it in the fridge when it's nearly lunchtime and Mama still hasn't come upstairs. "Heat some of that up for them, Bliss. I can't wait any longer to make these deliveries."

Patsy's stretched out on the sofa watching TV, and I try to join her, but I can't stay sitting down. I'm as jumpy as Mama was last night. I tiptoe around the living room looking at each thing on the shelves with new eyes, wondering what Mama knows about it, if it's something she remembers from when she was little.

After a while, Patsy says, "You look alike."

"You think?"

"Almost like twins. You should model together."

"Nope." I run my fingers over the crystal bowl, the little diamonds carved all around it catching the late-morning light.

"Nope, you don't want to? Or nope, you don't look like twins?"

"Nope, I won't model with Mama."

Patsy divides her hair and starts French-braiding one side. "How long is she staying?"

"How should I know?"

"Why do you think she's here?"

"Um, because she misses me?"

"But why is she *really* here?" She pats the braid, then switches to the other side, finger-combing it smooth. "Like, why now? It's been a long-ass time. There's got to be a reason."

I don't answer her, just pick up the things Mama noticed on the shelves yesterday, then put them back.

"You really should ask to model with her. Just think what your life could be like!"

My stomach flips just thinking about it, and I slam my hand down so hard the bowl and the teacup shake. "No," I say real sharp. "And don't you talk about it, either."

"Jesus, calm down. Why not?"

I lower my voice and sit on the edge of the sofa. "It would piss her off."

"Aunt Theresa?"

"Quiet," I say, smacking Patsy with a pillow.

"How do you know what would piss her off? She's been gone so long. And she's only been here for like twelve hours," Patsy says in a fake whisper that's almost as loud as talking.

"*Not now*," I say real quiet. She raises her eyebrows at me, and I shake my head at her. She stares me down, and I decide to let it all out. "Mama always felt bad that I took such terrible pictures, so she never let anybody take my picture ever. Ever."

Patsy shakes her head, her black braids flipping back and forth. "What? But you're—! Why?"

"Anyways." I wait for her to look at me. "When Mama was in talks for the Japan job, there was this one photographer, Desmond, he took some candids of me and Mama, and he was hot to get us both on contract. I was like, twelve years old, and I never thought about modeling before, you know? All those years? That was for people like Mama, but this Desmond, he kept pushing for me, and I totally fell for it. I wanted to be like her, I wanted to be with her—hell, who wouldn't?" I've held this in for so long, it feels weird to hear it out loud.

Patsy sits up closer to me so she can hear. "Are you kidding me? What happened?"

I check the basement door, but it's still shut. "It almost messed up Mama's deal. She didn't want me modeling—"

Patsy slaps her hand on the couch cushion. "Oh, shit. She was jealous!"

"Nah." I wave that idea away. "It was supposed to be a perfect deal. But I almost blew it for her. And then I pissed her off more with all the begging."

I haven't thought about it in years. Mama's face when I kept saying, "Please, please, please." Her fingernails digging into my arm as she hissed, "Do not do one red thing to upset this man. I've got him right where I want him and you will not undo all the tap-dancing I've done to make this deal," into my ear as she pushed me into the waiting room where I sat alone until their meeting was over.

I swallow hard. "In the end, the deal Erika got for her said Mama only. She wasn't allowed to bring me with."

"Oh my god. She didn't want you there because you'd take her spotlight! And that's how you ended up here? You never told me *any* of this!"

"No." I finger-comb my hair, then twist it back into a ponytail-bun. I take a shaky breath, admitting it to someone for the first time. "She didn't want me to. I pushed her too hard, and the way she pushed back was to leave me behind."

"I think you're wrong." Patsy turns me around by the shoulders and starts braiding my hair into one big braid.

Patsy thinks I'm wrong a lot. Only this is the first time it's sounded like she's on my side when she says it.

"She left me behind. That's proof enough for me," I say. My phone buzzes.

River: Granny's tonight. Patsy's big bday is ON!

I text him back, and as I do, the door to the basement flies open.

"Hello, Lakeville!" says Mama. "I'm back!" And she is, even after I pushed her away by wanting her too much.

I hurry to the refrigerator to find the baked breakfast.

"Baked lunch, isn't it? I cannot believe we slept the day

74

away," says Mama. Both Patsy and me follow her every move like she's a fucking hologram that's going to blink out at any second.

River: Don't be late

Granny's seems like it's about a million miles away from here right now.

Mama follows me into the kitchen to watch me scrape plates and load the dishwasher. "Don't run that now—Clyde will have a fit if his shower is cold," she says.

My mouth is full of questions, but it stays glued shut while I fuss around the kitchen. Wiping crumbs, tidying the counter, scrubbing the sink are all normal things to do on a normal day, a day when memories of Mama from before get tangled up with real Mama here in front of me.

"I suppose you're wondering about Clyde," Mama says as she fiddles with the saltshaker.

I was not wondering about Clyde.

"Well, let me tell you, I've been focused on my career for so many years now, it's such a relief to finally be with a real, live *man*."

I rinse the coffeepot and shine it until it's crystal clear and watch the way Mama's face lights up with her story, the way her hands move to make a point, the way she swings her hair back over her shoulder when she pauses to take a breath. It's hard to take my eyes off her.

"Don't get me wrong: I wasn't really alone over there, but there were also rules. Rules about how and when to eat, how and when to talk—why, I almost got sidelined the first year for putting my arm around one of the sponsors when I'd had a little too much sake at dinner. I was just trying to cheer the guy up, put a smile on his face, but that very nearly did me in."

I'm seventeen-year-old me, cleaning up the lunch, but I'm also ten-year-old me, sitting on a hotel bed, listening as Mama tells me absolutely everything about her day. I can practically smell the musty carpet, the fresh-air deodorizer, and Mama's hand-and-face cream that she put on both of us every night.

"I absolutely had to lean on Daisuke, my manager, to make it through, and if that ended up with us being more than just business partners, well, take me to court, sir. A girl needs some breaks if she's going to survive, right, honey?"

We both laugh, and I remember that nothing in the world feels so good as being the one to make Mama happy.

My throat closes up a little because I don't even know this manager guy. Never even heard his name before. I swallow and push that thought away. It's too close to pestering Mama, and I'm never doing that again. She's here now. That's all that matters.

"But back to Clyde. After I ended up in New York City, that crazy Clyde showed up at exactly the right moment in time. Thank the stars above, I was Clyde's last fare, and when I was too sleepy—beyond exhausted!—to give him an address, Clyde took me home with him to his very own apartment, where he stuck me under a cold shower and let me sleep—alone—in his very own bed."

"Not for long, though, right, babe?" Clyde walks through the kitchen wearing just a towel, and I take one look at his hairy chest and quickly look out the window.

Mama puts her hand on Clyde's damp shoulder and smiles. "Well of course that touched my very heart, and that, I believe, is the minute my feelings for Clyde started to become real. What a gentleman!"

My hand gets warm, and I flash to Blake, with his big shiny truck, reaching out to shake it as he introduced himself: a different kind of gentleman than Clyde, for sure.

Clyde wraps his arms around Mama, not worried for a minute about whether Aunt Trish's blue-and-yellow-striped towel is up to the job of keeping him covered. I wish he would go downstairs and put on some clothes. Or at least a shirt. I open the fridge and move stuff around so the leftovers will fit.

"Of course, I told Clyde all about my burning desire to go see my baby back home, and he was so supportive. He was tired of the New York limo life and ready for something new, so he volunteered—without me even asking—to drive us back home in his very own car—"

"Limo," Clyde says.

"Car that is also a limo," Mama says. "And here we are!"

"Yeah," I say, afraid to turn around and see if the towel's still up.

"And here I go," Clyde says. He tromps down the stairs and

I close the refrigerator door now that it's safe to look.

"Oh dear," says Mama. "Here I've gone on and on about myself, and you haven't told me a word about you!"

"It's okay," I say.

"No, it is not. Here." Mama pulls me over to the table and sits me down across from her. "Oh," she cries, and suddenly tears are streaming down her face. "Bliss! Baby! How has it been so long?" Even crying, she's prettier than anyone I know. "I just cannot believe you went and grew up on me, baby girl."

Her voice is so sad, so lost, that I have a hard time finding any kind of answer at all. "I . . . did."

Mama jumps up, wiping her eyes on one of Aunt Trish's kitchen towels. She snuffles, then claps her hands together and says, "So, who are you? Who is Bliss? I've just missed you so much! If there's one thing I've learned in the past few years, you've got to listen, truly listen to a person's heart. And I want to hear what your heart is saying, baby doll."

"I guess, I mean, I don't—" I don't even know where to begin. I've saved up shit to tell her for so long that I stopped saving it up.

"I know! You can start by telling me about that yummy fellow you were cuddled up with last night. Boyfriend? First date?"

"River is . . ."

"Babe!" Clyde stomps up the stairs. "We gotta go. Right now. I did not pack deodorant, and you do not want to be around me when the day warms up."

Mama looks from me to Clyde, then back at me. "Well. It looks like I'm leaving."

I suck in a quick breath, then I remind myself she's not leaving for good. Just for the drugstore. Still, the room already feels emptier than it did a minute ago.

"Here's an idea, baby girl. Is Penguin Pizza still around?"

"Best pizza in town."

"Well let's have dinner tonight. Just the two of us. Clyde here can fend for himself. And you can tell me all about your main squeeze. Do kids still say that?"

"Did kids ever say that?"

"God, you're hilarious. See what I've missed, Clyde? My baby is hilarious. Don't forget, pizza as soon as we get back from our errands. Just us girls."

"I won't forget, Mama."

Me: Be there after dinner with Mama
River: Make it quick
River: We got shit to do

I shut off my phone.

River can be mad all he wants.

Nine

The afternoon crawls past, even when I help make dinner with Aunt Trish and clean my side of Patsy's room. I take down the picture of me in seventh grade before Mama can see how stupid I was back then. I will never tell her that I spent the whole first year she was gone reading books on how to talk in Japanese so I would be ready for when she came to take me back with her. I will also never tell her how hard I cried when she called Aunt Trish and asked if I could stay another year, how I threw away the Japanese book, even though it was a library book.

I wait, and I wait, and I wait, and Mama and Clyde don't come back. The afternoon slowly turns to evening, and my stomach rumbles in the family room while Patsy and them eat the meat loaf I made. Uncle Leo doesn't say anything, but he pats me on the shoulder as he walks by on his way out to his garage workshop. I don't even get mad when Patsy comes in and switches off my baking show and puts on *America's Next Top*

Model, season eight—again. Instead, I just go get some water from the kitchen.

Aunt Trish straightens up from the dishwasher, puts her hands on her hips, blows one stray piece of hair out of her eyes. "There's plenty of meat loaf left, if you want."

"I'm not hungry."

Aunt Trish sighs real big. "Your mama, she means well, honey. Time just has a different meaning for her. And commitments. She always did forget whatever was in her head if something else popped up. It's no reflection on you. You should eat."

Pressure builds in my stomach, and before I know it, it explodes out of me. "I don't need the damn meat loaf! I'm eating Penguin Pizza. With my actual mother," I say, like I would if it was Patsy I was talking to, not Aunt Trish.

She jerks her head back like I slapped her or something, and I know I should say sorry, but I can't make the words come out.

Aunt Trish's eyes look like a dog's when you lock it out of the house. I can't stay in here with the meat loaf and those eyes.

I check my phone—does Mama even know how to text?— and go back to Patsy's room and sit on the trundle.

I pull out the ukulele, but I forgot about the broken string. At dinner, I will ask Mama about her ukulele, and maybe she can teach me how to play it, and how to fix the string, and it will be like she never left.

If we ever get to dinner.

I pluck the not-broken strings, just random, and look

around Patsy's halfway-clean room, and out of nowhere, it hits me that I've lived here for almost six years. In this room. So why do we all call it "Patsy's room"? Even me. How long do you have to live at a place before it counts as yours?

I pick hard on the strings, almost hard enough to break the ones that are left. I thought music was supposed to calm people down and make them happy, but I'm getting more and more pissed with every note. Did Aunt Trish and Uncle Leo ever really want me here?

I wonder if Mama forgot about me already. My phone buzzes, but it's not Mama.

River: Get out here before everybody else shows up
Me: After we eat

My stomach growls.

The house shakes as the front door slams, and I jump off the bed.

Finally.

I go towards the family room, but the loud voices stop me in my tracks.

"Knock it off, *Theresa*!"

"Clyde, it was high school. *High school.*"

"It was *tonight*. Now. Right in front of me."

"Clyde, honey. Brendan Oliver always had a thing for me. It was pathetic. Isn't that right, Trish?"

"Don't pull her into this."

I peek into the family room, and there's Mama, hanging off of Clyde's arm with both hands. His whole bald head is all red, and anything that might have been cute about him is long gone. There's a bunch of giant wrinkles on his forehead where his eyebrows are pushed together.

"It was just a hug, Clyde."

They are blocking the TV, and Patsy stares at them like they're Tyra fucking Banks herself. Aunt Trish stands in the doorway to the kitchen with a dish towel and the clean meat loaf pan. Her face is all pink and blotchy, but she doesn't say anything.

"People hug when they haven't seen each other in a long time."

"Not like that, they don't." Clyde shakes her off his arm, and Mama chases him towards the basement door. Mama grabs his hand, and I step back so maybe they won't see me watching. I pull the ukulele close to me, protecting it.

"Clyde. Baby." Mama's voice goes all soft and high, and she pulls his hand up to her chest. "You're the only one I want to hug." She leans in towards him all melty and kisses his hand. "Not some hometown loser."

"Don't pull that shit with me, *Theresa*."

The whole house holds its breath, afraid of what might happen. A guy Clyde's size, he could trash the house and take us all out without even barely trying. Each of the three ukulele strings cuts into my fingertips, and I wish I was back on the trundle instead of out here.

Mama puts both her arms around Clyde as far as they can go and snuggles up to him. "Brendan is a terrible driver. Wouldn't last one quick minute in New York City."

We all watch Clyde to see what he will do.

"He won't last a minute here if he ever grabs you like that again," says Clyde, all mean, but they both laugh, and we all can breathe again. Clyde slaps Mama on the butt, then puts his arm around her and leads her down the stairs to the basement, saying something that I'm probably real glad I can't hear as he slams the door shut behind him.

I guess we're not having pizza.

I move to turn around, and Aunt Trish sees me. She opens her mouth like she's going to bring up the meat loaf, but I duck away before she can force it on me.

"Come on, Patsy. River's waiting."

There's tons of leftover beers from the other night, but Long Tom brought even more, since he wants to celebrate Patsy in a big way. So that means River has to get his drunk on quick, because he'll be busting people's balls the rest of the night making sure nobody hurts the house.

He takes it real serious, too. One time he jumped up while we were getting it on and threw on his pants to run out to the end of the lane to get rid of some out-of-town assholes who wanted to trash the place. Like he just knew what was up without even being out there. He's always watching, keeping Granny's place safe.

Like when Nathan and them show up again.

"Aw, let 'em in, River," Long Tom says when they come up onto the porch. "It's Patsy's birthday." Long Tom always has this sweet, innocent smile on his face that only partway comes from the weed. He really does just want to party with every soul he's ever met.

"Tom, Tom, Tom . . . ," River says, hooking his arm around Tom's thick neck and bending him down close to talk into his ear. "Happy birthday to Patsy and shit, but these assholes can't stay."

"They promise to be good," Long Tom says.

Nathan hears him and looks at me first, then Patsy, and smiles up at River, all innocent. "I'll be *real* good."

Patsy smiles and bounces on her toes when River nods once to let them in.

I turn right around and go to the kitchen for another drink, as River says hi to Shanna and Lyle and a bunch of others who come in right behind Nathan and them.

"He came back," says Patsy, following me and grabbing on to the back of my shirt while I fill my cup from the keg. She's practically jumping up and down.

"I guess my *asshole boyfriend* didn't ruin everything after all," I say, wiping foam off my lip. I look around the empty kitchen with its wilty-flowered wallpaper that Granny musta picked out special a long time ago. I bet there were never beer bottles all over the counters or stacked-up empty pizza boxes in the corner when this was Granny's home. River said he didn't want a trash house, but he must not mean actual garbage.

"Ladies." I sidestep almost into the stack of pizza boxes when I hear Nathan's voice behind me. Chills go up my back.

"Nate!" Patsy's eyes are bright, and she just about drops her full beer cup. "Hi!"

Nathan smiles his slow smile, and his eyes land on Patsy, then me for a long second, making shiver bumps rise on my arms. Then he throws an arm around Patsy, squeezing the back of her neck and bending down to say, "Happy birthday. You legal now?"

I don't stay to hear what she says back to him.

I should've had the meat loaf. Or some kind of dinner, even if I couldn't have Penguin Pizza.

I see this now. Now that I've had two beers and two shots of the stuff Deke and Neveah are mixing up in the living room. I stand up, wiping my mouth from the taste of whatever I just drank, and the room wobbles along with me. I grab a sip of beer from the cup I'm still holding and walk as straight as I can to the kitchen, where sure-to-god I better be able to get some water.

I walk in, and there's Patsy. Her smile is huge, and her shirt is buttoned all catawampus.

I look around. "Where's . . ." I make my mouth say it: "Nathan?" I half expect all my teeth to fall out along with his name.

Patsy's smile drops away like it was never there. "Why do you care?" Her hair is mussed, and her lipstick is long gone.

"So, are you two"—I point to her shirt that used to be buttoned right earlier tonight—"getting pretty friendly?"

"Is that so hard to believe? That Nathan picked me to talk to?"

"More than talk, looks like."

"Like you're the only one a guy could want."

"But Nathan, he's . . ." I don't know how to say it.

"What? Cute? Funny? Mature?" She giggles, twisting and retwisting her too-black hair on top of her head. "A good kisser?"

"I don't trust him."

"Yeah, well, *you* don't have to, since he's with *me*." She smiles at me and shrugs her shoulders.

I want to tell her so bad. Stop her from making a mistake she will 100 percent regret. And also wipe that shitty smile off her face.

But now, now she will never, ever believe me. Her eyes light up again as Nathan comes in the back door.

"*Je suis retournee*," says Nathan. "I'm switching my major to French, you know." His eyes poke holes in me and Patsy both, then land on Patsy, who giggles.

River comes in right behind Nathan, and he looks at Patsy like he's never seen her before.

Patsy bounces over to Nathan, and he shakes his dark brown curls out of his eyes and puts his arm around her. They go into the living room, acting like they've been together for months.

"What's she so happy about?" River pulls me into the dark

hallway and squishes me up against the wall. He grinds against me and kisses me up real good. "Patsy's never happy like that."

He moves down to my neck, and his hands dip under just about every piece of clothing I have on. I barely notice for thinking about Patsy.

"Nathan." I sorta want to hurl just whispering his name. Shiver bumps rise up as soon as I do.

River pulls away hard, practically taking skin with him. "You just call me *Nathan*?" His eyes go all snaky, cold and dark, and his hands freeze, one up my skirt and one down my top.

"Jesus. No! *Nathan's* why Patsy's happy."

There's a long minute while River's stare bruises my eyeballs. "Patsy, huh. He seemed like he knew you. Did you ever get it on with him? I bet you want to get it on with him."

My bones about freeze. If River knew the truth about what happened with Nathan all those years ago, he would lose his mind. And he will never let this go all night long. Not unless I can distract him some way.

So I lean into his hands, and pull him close, and hope that's enough to make him forget that he's pissed.

Which seems to work—River looks me up and down and finally goes back to kissing, and after a few minutes his hands chase away the cold that Nathan's name leaves on my bones and heat me up until I barely even remember who Patsy is. There's a loud cheer from the front room, and River pulls back, looking at me like he wants to eat me up. His eyes are half-closed, and his lips are all soft and shiny from the kissing, and for once, I wouldn't mind us sneaking off to Granny's room to forget everything but him and me right here.

Another cheer.

"Aww, man." One more really good kiss. "I gotta get back out there." He slaps me on the butt and starts to walk away.

But something makes me grab his hands and pull him towards the bedroom door, try to keep him with me. "C'mon." I wrap his arms around me and pull him close behind me, and I can feel how interested he is in what we've been up to. "Leave them to it, they're probably fine."

And just like that, River stiffens up and pulls away. "Jesus Christ, Bliss. What the hell are you doing?"

"I just thought—I mean, I thought you wanted—"

"The fuck you think this is? Some shithouse those assholes can destroy?" He pushes me away from him and stands there with his hands up in the air. "This is Granny's house. Where I plan to live someday. But not if those clowns tear it up."

I'm breathing super hard, part from River yelling at me and part from being all worked up from the kissing. I also, it turns out, have to blink away a few tears before I get my eyes under control.

"Okay, so you don't want to—" I reach out to him, but River backs away.

"Not in the middle of a party! Think, Bliss, what happens if I'm not there? Broken things. Broken things happen if I'm not around." He shakes his head. "'They're probably fine.' Sure, Bliss. I'm sure they're fine."

And with that, I'm alone in the hall, with only Granny's pink flowered wallpaper to keep me company.

Granny's house shrinks down on me, and I can't get a whole breath all at once.

I need to get out of here.

I stumble out the back door.

Ten

I go out back, but the air is heavy and full and there's people everywhere I look. Deke and Cracker laugh and whistle as I walk past the picnic table, smoke so thick it's like I'm inside a one-hitter, and I flip them off and keep walking.

Why didn't I bring a beer with me, is what I want to know. Gravel crunches under my feet, and I stumble past the shed, past the waist-high weeds, back into the night where the moon hangs skinny like it's laughing at me, too.

I stop when I get to the edge of the field, far enough away that I can't hear the party anymore, only the breeze and the night bugs singing away. Even though it's like 200 percent humidity out here, I can finally breathe a whole breath in, out, and in again.

My stomach growls, and I wish I had that meat loaf right now.

Mama didn't forget about our dinner. She just got distracted, is all. I can't push her too hard. If I push her too hard, she's gonna slip away again.

And I know better than to bug River like that in the middle of a party. He doesn't have time for fooling around. He cares. This house means something to him, and that means something to me.

And Patsy? Patsy's not some almost-thirteen-year-old kid who doesn't know any better. Maybe Nathan is different now. Older. Maybe he won't say, "Don't cha wanna be my girlfriend?" to her like he did to me.

The turned-earth and bean-plant smells are heavy in the air, and the lane jogs off to the left, so I follow it, only wobbling a little. If only I could walk far enough to get away from Patsy, Nathan, and River . . . and Mama. I squint over at the beans, and as far as I can tell, they don't need to be weeded. Or walked. Or whatever the hell me and Patsy are doing to them next week.

"Hey," says a guy's voice, down the lane a ways. I go real still, trembly all over, and just about shit my pants. I will be so pissed if I get murdered right out here behind Granny's. My leg muscles tense, ready to turn and run at any second.

"Sorry," he says again, and a phone's light pops on and blinds me.

Do murderers say sorry?

"Didn't mean to scare you. Here," he says, his voice sorta familiar, and lifts the phone higher like the Statue of Liberty's torch so we can both see. "You from the party?" His words are slurred, and he sways on his feet, so the light sways with him as I can finally see his face, and suddenly it all comes together.

"Blake?"

He squints at me, stumbles, and lowers the phone a little as he steps closer. His face breaks into a smile that is so sweet it almost makes up for Patsy and River and my grumbling stomach.

"Bliss from the road!"

I nod. His smile slips a little bit, and he lifts a finger to his lips, and it tugs at my middle how cute he is.

"Shhhh." He looks both ways, like he's checking for cops. "I cannot give you a ride right now because, it appears, I have been drinking."

He's not the only one who's been drinking. Those shots are for sure catching up with me, because he's soft around the edges, a little blurry. His dark brown eyes are shiny from the phone. Or the stars. I'm not sure which.

I nod again.

His eyebrows come together, and he bends over, taking the light with him, to motion at my feet. "You have shoes!" He laughs up at me again, and the way his eyes light up makes my day just a little bit better. "It's good to wear shoes."

"You were at Granny's?" I ask him, and he shines the light in my eyes again. I turn away, waiting for my eyes to adjust. "At the party?"

"I was. I sure was. With Shanna and Lyle, but Dad kept texting me, and those last two shots were maybe a mistake. So I took a walk."

"Me too."

He grins at me and I grin at him and we just stand there, me and Blake of all people, and about a million bugs singing their little hearts out. He's taller than I remember, and his chin has a little dimple, and he opens his mouth to say something when his phone beeps real loud.

He squishes his face all up as he reads the text, then sticks his phone in his pocket, flashlight still on, where it beeps two more times right in a row.

"Everything okay?"

He looks at me like I just showed up out of thin air, then shrugs. "Depends on who you ask." He's still slurring about every other word, and one of us is swaying back and forth, but I couldn't for sure say if it's me or him.

"Did you ever wonder . . . ," he says, then looks at me, his eyes soft with confusion, "how the people we love the most can make us the craziest?"

It's like he can read my mind. "Yes," I say, and we stand there staring at each other, just nodding our heads. Lightning bugs flash on and off around us, and I jump when he turns and walks away from me, shining the light further down the lane.

"I wonder sometimes if they weren't my family, would I even like these people?" He stops, waits for me to catch up, then weaves down the lane again. "But when they say things like . . ." He taps his phone, and I watch over his shoulder as he tries to open his texts. "It was just here. . . . Shit."

The phone flies out of his hand and bounces on the road,

the light wavering all crazy towards the corn. I bend down to pick it up.

"Is it broken?" he asks.

"No, but—" The light shines on a big slab of dark pink marble. Or granite? Maybe it's granite. There's a bunch of plastic flowers on top of it.

"But what?"

I wave him closer and shine the light on the stone. "What is that?" I rub my eyes. I really need my beer.

We walk up closer. There's a picture of an elephant and a circus tent on the granite. I shake my head and work real hard to read the words on the tent, which keep sliding around on me. "'Kay. October 21, 1994,'" I say. "Is this a cemetery?"

"It's an elephant grave! There's a circus elephant buried here!" he says. Blake looks up at me, smiling like a little kid.

He grabs the phone and shines the light closer. "'In appreciation for over fifty years of devotion and for the joy you brought to millions of children of all ages. Greeley and Miller Brothers Circus,'" he reads, only slurring a few of the words. The total joy in his voice lifts me up from where I've been most of the day.

"Huh." I put my hand on the stone, and it's still warm from the day, smooth and dusty on the top. I touch the drawing of the elephant that's next to the words, and Blake touches it at the same time, and for a second, our hands are touching Kay and each other. We leave them there, on the picture of the elephant.

He looks at me, and there's that string again, pulling us

together. He finally looks away. "Do you think she's really here?" He waves his arm out around the stone.

"Nah. They can't do that. Can they? Just bury an elephant wherever they want?"

"You think we're standing on top of her?" He looks so worried when he says it.

"God, I hope not."

"Me too." His voice is soft, and the light just barely reaches his face as he stares off into the distance. "Elephants are my favorite animal."

He rounds on me, rakes his hand through, like, ten pounds of black hair. "Have you ever seen a real one?"

"I rode on one." I haven't thought about that in a long, long time.

"On an elephant?"

The memory busts out of where I've been keeping it, and it's so strong. Mama's hands pushing me along in front of her as we stumbled on the grass on the way to the elephant tent, me so excited I could hardly stand it, partly because of the elephant, and partly because Mama had picked me to go with her, when she could have taken anybody.

"Mama was the celebrity guest from the modeling agency, and she took me along. She made them let me ride up on the elephant with her."

I can almost hear Mama saying, "Bliss, we are at the top of our game! Celebrity guest!" as we sat up high on the elephant's back, just the two of us way above the circus. She had grabbed on to me, saying, "I hope we don't fall," but I felt safe with her behind me, her skinny arms wrapped tight around me.

Blake runs his fingers over the etching of the elephant. "I saw them once up close at a zoo. They looked so sad. And huge. I would have been terrified."

I look over at him. "They are really big. But I wasn't scared."

"Wow." He turns and looks at me for a long time with his lips curved up in that little smile, like I'm brave or something.

He leans close, and I lean closer, and maybe it's the beer, but a wave of wanting starts out small in my middle and grows until it's big enough to drown a goddamn surfer. All the wanting—Mama, Patsy, River—everything I've stopped myself from wanting for so very long, all of it crashes into me, leaving me drowning in needing Blake to believe I'm brave. Wanting to feel close to him.

Wanting to kiss him.

It seems like the rightest thing in the world for me to reach up and pull him close to me. He leans in, too, and I kiss him like I've never kissed anybody before.

We kiss for what feels like the rest of our lives there, leaning just a little bit on Kay's grave, the plastic flowers brushing my elbow. Blake's arms go around me, taking the phone light with him, and we share soft kisses in the almost dark until I pull away and look up at the stars. They sparkle in their places in the sky, thousands of little pieces of glitter, and I take a shaky breath.

What am I even doing? I don't kiss guys. They kiss me.

But here we are.

"That was . . . ," he begins, and goddamn if I don't reach up and kiss him again. My fingers find the soft hair at the base of his neck, and my head spins from the beer and the kisses. His lips are warmer, softer than any I've ever felt, and I wonder what it would feel like to have them somewhere else on my skin. Just thinking about it makes me kiss him deeper, leaning closer to press against him. His chest is solid, his arms, too—not buff like he works out, but like he uses them for something.

All of a sudden, he's gone; we're not kissing anymore. I open my eyes, and he reaches out and grabs my upper arms—not hard, just businesslike as hell—so we are standing apart on either side of the elephant grave, the light from his phone wobbling as he sways.

"You don't even know me," he says.

My stomach drops and I take a step towards him. "What?"

He puts one hand up like a stop sign. "You're drunk. I'm sorry—"

"Sorry?" My voice comes out sharp as broken glass.

"I should never have done that, out of the blue, I—" Blake turns, and I have to chase after him as he almost runs back down the road. The light from his phone bounces off the corn and beans and gravel road as we hustle back the way we came. What I wouldn't give to get away from here, away from this rejection, away from impossible things like circus elephants practically in Granny's backyard. But there's also a part of me that wants to rip the headstone out of the ground and put it in my pocket so I can have it with me every day to remember that things like this can even exist at all.

I am so fucked up.

"I am really sorry. You must think I'm—I didn't mean to—" Blake stops and looks at me, and I can hear the music and laughing from the party, and the lights from Granny's house and the shadow of the garage loom just down the road. "You seem like a good person—and maybe . . ."

I'm not sure what he's trying to say. All I know for sure is I should not have kissed him. Not because I have a boyfriend. Not because I'm drunk. Not because we hardly know each other. River showed me earlier, and Blake reminded me just now. I shouldn't have kissed him because I forgot that wanting something, the way I wanted to kiss Blake, always ends up hurting me.

"No problem," I tell him, and wave over my shoulder as I walk, way more sober now, back towards Granny's. "See you someday."

And I promise myself I've been cured of wanting. Forever.

Eleven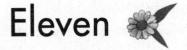

Patsy is over the moon about Nathan, and she drives us home singing along to some swoony country song on repeat. River never even noticed I was gone, so all I had to do when I got back was lean my drunk, tired ass up against the living room wall and wait till it was time to go home.

I have a complete brainstorm when I walk in and see the uke on my bed. I'm going to surprise Mama by playing an actual song on her ukulele. After I get the string fixed.

In the morning, me and Uncle Leo make homemade waffles and listen to this fishing podcast he likes. It's a perfect way to work off a hangover and turn loose of whatever it was that made me think kissing Blake was the answer to anything—Mama forgetting about dinner, Patsy getting together with Nathan, or River being pissed off at me.

"Not so much batter," and "Is there orange juice?" are the only things Uncle Leo says to me while we cook, and the steaming stack of blueberry waffles grows so fast the podcast isn't even over when everyone, even Clyde and Mama, show up, lured in by the warm blueberry smell.

Our waffles aren't perfect like they are when Aunt Trish makes them, but Uncle Leo and me smile and cheers our orange juice glasses together because they are damn tasty. Clyde eats four full waffles, but once Mama finds out there isn't any flax or whole grain in them, she turns up her nose and says she's going to make a smoothie. I want to ask her about last night and the pizza, but Clyde is glued to her side the whole time we eat, and I won't do it in front of him.

Finally, after me and Aunt Trish finish the dishes, Mama takes over the kitchen and we're finally alone. I watch her prep the smoothie for a few seconds before I say anything. She is bent over the chopping board, hair falling in her face just like mine does, as she hacks away at some green shit or other that doesn't want to be chopped. The stems are darker where the knife touched them, and they ooze grass juice, but they stick together like their life depends on it.

I should be mad at her for ditching on our dinner—but I can't quite cross that finish line.

"The other knife is better for chopping," I finally tell her, pointing to Aunt Trish's As Seen On TV knife set. "The ad was right. They are 'incredibly sharp and smooth.'"

She tosses the shitty one in the sink, and it clatters against the sides. "It's a sad state of affairs when I am the only one around who can make a decent smoothie. I'm near to starvation here." The TV knife slides right through the stems, splitting them cleanly, and Mama grabs another handful to chop.

"Have you tried Aunt Trish's? They are really good."

Mama slams down the knife and looks at me, her face all snarled up and red. "Of course they are. Of course. Anything Trish touches is perfect. So why wouldn't she make a perfect smoothie?" Her voice is as sharp as the As Seen On TV knife.

"I didn't mean—"

"Sure you didn't. Trish didn't. Didn't mean to make curfew every single night. Didn't mean to get grades so good they wanted to send her to college, for god's sake. Didn't mean to steal my baby right out from under me."

She stuffs unchopped grass into the blender by the handful, slams the lid on, and punches the button with a finger.

Steal me? My mind whizzes around with the smoothie until she pokes the Off button.

"Nobody stole me, Mama."

Mama snatches the pitcher off the blender base and sloshes some green stemmy shit into her cup, which she then chugs like she's teaching it a lesson. She takes a deep breath, then goes so limp, she almost misses the countertop when she sets the cup down. "Oh, baby girl. Look at me, taking out my frustrations on you. Not a reason in the world to do that."

She gathers me up in a tight hug, then lets me go so fast I almost fall.

"It's this house that does it to me. Especially my role model sister. I'll give you a role model. Tyra Banks, she's a role model!

But here at home, it was Trish, Trish, Trish. 'Trish made her bed this morning.' 'We never had to meet with *Trish's* teachers the entire time she was in school.' 'Why can't you dress more like Trish?'"

Mama paces around the kitchen, holding her smoothie but not drinking from it, waving it around while she talks to the point where I'm sure she's going to spill it all over the vinyl floor.

"I'm telling you, I was nearly ready to steal a car just to get away from here. But I'm a strong female, so I did the best I could while I counted up the days until I turned eighteen and could hightail it out. I made my own way. And I think it made me a better person."

I start to ask a question, but she keeps pacing and talking. She reaches out and pats my cheeks.

"Of course, it hasn't been easy, has it? Oh, how I've missed you! Every day was an absolute horror without you there. And thinking that I left you here in this backwards town—it's a good thing I have this smoothie to calm my nerves. Oh, Bliss, oh my baby!"

She throws her arms and her whole weight around me, and I gotta step quick so we don't both fall.

"You poor, innocent baby!"

River honks outside, but no way am I gonna leave Mama in this state. I walk her to the sofa and sit her down right up next to me. Her shoulders are way more bony than mine, and her skirt rides up while her top slides down, showing her twenty-seven necklaces all the way off.

I move to scoot away, but her hand clamps around my arm tight as a handcuff, so I stay right where I am. She dabs at her eyes with her free hand, then turns to stare deep into my eyes. Hers are reddish around the edges, but she's still so pretty I want to cry.

"I am so sorry, baby. So very sorry."

My heart sucks up this apology like a sponge, and I feel a little bit of softening around its edges. I lean into her the tiniest bit, more ready than I knew for the rebirth of our relationship, no matter how much I kicked down those old dreams, no matter how bad I felt about her forgetting our dinner.

"I am so sorry she did this to you."

"It's okay, Mama, you didn't— She? She who?" I go still everywhere but my stomach, where it's busier than the blender was a minute ago, trying to understand her apology.

She lets go of my arm to pat my hair. "Trish." She moves pieces of hair this way and that, stroking my head as she talks. "I should have known better. She tried to turn you against me, tried to make you perfect like her—I bet you make your bed and come home at curfew every night, don't you? Set the table and all that shit? I see how she has you cooking and doing the dishes, too."

I don't answer her as I look towards Patsy's bedroom with my made bed in it, and the kitchen, where I've made so many meals with Aunt Trish and Uncle Leo, and my ears get hot when I remember how proud I was when I learned how to cook, and how hard I've worked to be so good that Uncle Leo and Aunt Trish won't care that they got stuck with me.

I jump when Mama hugs me again.

"You precious, precious girl. How were you to know? Mama is so sorry Trish got her claws into you—must've been like a second chance to fix everything that was ever wrong with me—but you were too strong, weren't you?"

She pulls my head to her shoulder as River honks again. "Well, Mama is here now, and everything is going to be all right. I'm going to fix it so you won't ever have to make your bed again. Just you wait and see."

We sit that way until Clyde calls up the stairs for her, and Mama sets me free to leave with River.

Twelve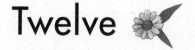

River's not too hot about bringing me to the music store before we go out to the lake, but he's in a good mood because detasseling's gonna start this week, so he doesn't fuss too much as long as I don't make him come in.

I know as soon as I walk in that this was a stupid idea. The music store is way bigger than it looks from outside. It's dark and not really air-conditioned, and it smells like wood and oil and old carpet. I'm surrounded by all kinds of instruments that probably have weird names, and everything costs an arm and a leg, and all I want is to turn around and get back in River's truck and the hell with a string for a stupid ukulele.

But this is Mama's ukulele. Aunt Trish said it was hers, and when I play that song, her favorite song, I want Mama to see that I can strum it like she did. And maybe make it sound like actual music. And she will be so happy that it'll be like I'm giving her something, something that just the two of us can share.

Whoever works here will know about the strings and shit,

since I can't for the life of me find what I need. But the store is like a maze, and I'm about ready to give up when I hear voices.

"Just the strings, son?" says someone with a low, dusty voice. Sounds like he's just past this shelf. I take a step, then stop cold.

"Just the strings. I'd love to take the guitar, too, but it's not meant to be, today."

Holy shit. It's Blake. From last night. My ears go hot at the sound of his voice.

I freeze in front of a bunch of violins, trying to remember if a bell rang when I walked in the door, if I can get back there before anyone sees me. Why are there so many different kinds of violins? They hang on the wall in row after row, bigger ones, smaller ones, light brown, some as dark as Blake's eyes as he pulled away from me last night after our kiss.

Kisses.

"Thanks for coming in," the worker says.

"I'll be back once I build up my bank account."

It's him for sure, and he's leaving the store, headed towards me. My skin prickles, and if there was a place to hide, I would sure as hell hide, maybe climb inside that big drum, or duck behind the rack of recorders.

"Oh," Blake says, and it's really him, standing by the violins, and my head swims like it did when we stood by the elephant grave. "Hello." He ducks his head and gives me a little smile, and for a second, all I can think about is how cute he is.

Then I remember how much trouble that kind of thinking got me in, and I hug the ukulele closer to me, put it between us.

He takes up the whole aisle, all brown arms and legs looking like he belongs here.

"Hey," I say, my mind going like a thousand miles an hour. I don't look at his hands or his mouth, so I don't think about how close we were, or how far apart he pushed us.

"I was not in the best shape the last time we met. I owe you an apology—"

"We're good," I say, before he can tell me again how sorry he is. It was just a few kisses. Nothing important.

He nods, smiles, and says, "Then we're good."

He looks at me seriously. "What are you looking for?" he asks, and it's like he's asking about life and the world and a million years of the future. Pictures of Mama, airplanes, roads, and elephants flash through my head before I shut that shit down and focus on getting out of here as fast as I can.

"Strings."

"For that?" He nods towards the ukulele. "Can I take a look?"

I hand him the black case, and something inside of me opens up as he pulls the zipper around and takes out the ukulele. I don't pay much attention to his fingers as they slide across the wood, and I don't notice that it's almost exactly the same color as his skin. And just as smooth.

"Beautiful," he says, and I know he's just talking about the instrument, not about anything else, even though he looks right at me and grins. He swipes across the strings and the twang makes both of us wince.

"It's broken," I tell him.

"Easy enough to fix," he says. "Let's get rid of these old strings first." He bends his head over the pegs. His hair is blacker than last night's sky, and I scrub my fingers on my skirt to wipe away the softness that I remember from touching it.

He brings the ukulele up and tucks it under his chin. It looks so small in his hands, but he holds it like he's been doing it all his life. "Let me just—" He turns a peg, and I grit my teeth, waiting for the pop of a string breaking, but nothing happens. Blake grins over at me like he's worked a magic trick. He slides his fingers down the neck of the ukulele, then threads the broken strings in and out of the complicated knots that hold them on. One string slips away from him, but he bends his head closer and tries it again. Pretty soon, both the strings are off, curled up in Blake's hand.

"Need some help?" The dusty voice belongs to a middle-aged guy who pokes his head around the display case, seeing what we're up to. "Come on back. We'll get you set up with some new strings."

Blake hands me the ukulele, and we follow the guy to the counter at the back of the store.

Blake stands right next to me, so close I can feel the heat from his arm as I lay the instrument on the counter. He's as close as he was last night when we stood at Kay's gravestone, and I don't know if it's his real arm or the memory of it that I feel against mine. He hands me the broken strings. "These are yours."

"Fuckin' right they are," says River, who is all of a sudden behind me—I didn't hear the door jingle when he came in. "The fuck's taking so long? Deke and them'll be gone by the time we get there." He looks from Blake to me and back again, measuring the space between us.

"He's getting the strings," I say, pointing to the back where the guy disappeared. I slide the uke over on the counter as I move away from Blake real slow so River doesn't notice how close we were standing.

"He is?" River steps closer and hangs his arm around my neck, pulling me away from Blake. "And who's your little helper here?" He jerks his chin at Blake and mashes me into his side. River's on high alert, like a hunting dog sniffing the air for the scent of prey.

Blake's eyebrows are raised so high they make a wrinkle in his forehead. He does the handshake thing he did with me that first day, only now he's not laughing. "Blake Wu. We met at your place last night?"

River looks at the hand, then looks Blake right in the eye, like he knows Blake did more than just meet me at the party. His arm tightens around me, and I can tell he wants to ignore the handshake. Then he leans in and folds me up as he shakes Blake's hand with the arm he's got around me.

"Wu?" he asks, not letting go of Blake's hand. "Where you from?"

"Chicago," says Blake.

River shakes his head. "No. Where are you *from*?"

Blake looks right at him and says, a little slower and louder, "*Originally, Chicago.* And now, here."

When River doesn't say anything, Blake says, "You're River, right? We met last night."

River nods. "Right. You was with Shanna and Lyle and them?"

"We met at U of I orientation," Blake says, his voice way calmer and steadier than it should be. "Discovered we're neighbors." River still has hold of Blake's hand, and he leans forward, so I'm stuck between the two of them.

I look up at Blake, almost as close as he was last night, catch my breath, and it hits me hard. Kissing Blake was 100 percent cheating on River. I knew it at the time, but standing here crowded in with all the guitars and trumpets and shit, it seems very big and very real. I cheated. On River.

I forget how to breathe for a minute, and I remember last week out at the lake when a squirrel fell off a branch into the water. It swam around in circles, moving faster and faster, just barely keeping its head out of the water, until Deke scooped it up with his net and dumped it, all wet and mad, on the dock where it shook itself and ran off.

There's no net here in this music store.

"You work here, then?" River asks, finally letting go of Blake and waving a hand at the music shop, his voice a dead giveaway that he's steaming mad. He pulls at the hair tie on his wrist over and over, and it makes little thwacking sounds as he stares at Blake, waiting for him to answer.

Blake doesn't even have the good sense to back up from where he stands. His face is so open and trusting, like he has no clue that River can tell there's something between us and wants to fucking kill him right now.

Blake laughs. "No, I don't. I stopped in here for some guitar strings and when I saw Bliss here—"

"When you saw my *girlfriend* here—" River lets go of me, and I lose my balance as he steps towards Blake.

"When I walked in the store and saw your *girl*friend"— Blake says the word in two parts, very clearly, and my ears burn that this is news to him—"and her stuck strings"—he looks at River, whose face is now like two inches away from his and bright red—"I thought I could help."

I never have seen River hurt anybody since we've been together, but he looks mad enough to start now. "I can get the strings later," I tell him. I pull on his arm, trying to get him away from Blake before he loses it. River doesn't answer me, and he doesn't budge.

Either Blake is an idiot, or he doesn't scare easy, because he just stands there while River breathes into his face. River is scrawny and scruffy compared to Blake, but his pissed-off makes him seem bigger than he is. His shoulder blades stick out, and his hands make fists at his sides.

Blake, on the other hand, looks like he's just waiting to hear the fuckin' weather report or something. He looks down like two inches into River's eyes and just waits, and the whole room feels like a balloon that's about to pop.

"Got 'em!" says the music store guy, who looks super surprised to see River and Blake nose to nose when he steps out from the back. "Uh, let me string it for you."

River claps Blake on the shoulder, way harder than is friendly. "See? Let *him* help," he says, and the tension goes right out of him. He juts his chin at the music store guy, then he turns away from Blake. He grabs my shoulders and plants a kiss on me with plenty of tongue, putting his hand on the back of my head and pulling me close. I don't even have time to respond before it's over. He pulls away and looks at Blake over his shoulder. "You need something else?"

Blake looks at me, not laughing at all. "No," he says, and scrubs his hand through his hair. He raises a hand and gives a sharp wave.

"Good to see you again," he says, and walks out of the shop, leaving it empty no matter how many instruments line the walls.

"Wu. Thinks he's hot shit or something," says River, after the music shop guy hands me back the fixed ukulele and I pay him.

"'We met at U of I,'" he mimics. "College boy. But I guess I showed him, didn't I?" He puffs out his chest and slaps me on the butt as we walk out of the store.

A little breath of wanting flows through me: wanting River to leave Blake alone, wanting back that moment before he came in the shop, when me and Blake were alone; but I shut it all the way down before it grows any bigger. Wanting doesn't make good things happen. Sometimes it makes everything worse.

Thirteen

The edges of the sky glimmer pink and gold as Patsy drives us to the meeting point for walking the beans. Patsy is pissed because I grabbed the last can of Diet Coke.

"Maybe if you hadn't been getting ready for prom with all that eyeliner," I say, but as usual, when Patsy doesn't get what she wants, it's because I stole something that should've been hers.

"It's not all about *you*, Bliss."

We are meeting up at a church on the south side of town, and they will take us out to the farm from there. Patsy parks by the church doors.

"Aaannd we're the only ones here. I could have slept longer." I try to fix my hair into some sort of braid, but it's not going real well.

"Oh my god. Just let me do it." Patsy's so quick with her fingers, my hair flows into two braids in less than a minute.

"Thanks."

"You have to learn. You are so pathetic." She rubs her eyes.

"Why is it so goddamn early?" Patsy puts her head down on the steering wheel and closes her eyes, the two knots on top of her head looking like bear ears.

A brown station wagon that I don't recognize pulls in next to Patsy's Malibu. Next comes a blue pickup. "Is that them?"

"The fuck am I supposed to know?" Patsy says, without even looking.

"You're the one who—"

She looks up, squints at the truck, and puts her head back down. "Nope. That's Aggie and Beth."

I look behind us and see a big pickup pull into the lot. That must be the boss, because the others slam their doors all at once, ready to go.

Patsy hauls herself out of the car while I get the cooler out of the back.

Two younger boys I don't recognize shuffle their feet and look down at the ground, and Aggie yawns and says hi. Her girlfriend, Beth, wears a painfully pink bandana and has a red metal lip ring. The boys are Jimmy and Clark Woodson. Brothers. Interchangeable. From out in the boondocks—not our school.

I'm fussing with the cooler, trying to make the water bottle fit inside. The others introduce themselves to the boss, and I shut the cooler and stand up. "I'm—"

"Bliss Walker," says a warm voice. The sunrise lights him up as he steps forward.

Blake.

Blake Wu is our new boss.

Of course.

"You know him?" Patsy hisses in my ear. We are smashed in the back seat of Blake's pickup with Jimmy and Clark. The same pickup I was in just the other day. I frown and shrug at Patsy, then close my eyes and lean my head on the window, wondering if I should get out now and walk back to town, before I have to explain River to Blake, and Blake to Patsy.

Patsy clamps her hand around my wrist. That's gonna bruise.

"How?"

I can feel her eyes stabbing into me.

"Long story," I whisper back, not opening my eyes.

She grabs tighter. "We have time."

"Later."

I look in the side mirror the same time as Blake does, and his eyes are full of questions. I look away, wishing I had better answers for him. And why should he care about River and me anyway? After all, he's the one who pushed me away the other night, and he seemed fine at the music shop yesterday.

The county fair is not for another two weeks but I feel like I just got off the Octopus ride. Down is a little bit up, my stomach can't decide where in my body it belongs, and I need to grab on to something to be sure that I'm standing on solid ground.

It's not too late to turn around. Detassel corn with River. Shop with Mama.

Nope. We're here. The farm. Shit just got real, and this is my punishment for cheating. I will walk these stupid beans and try and remember that me and River are a team—the only team that counts.

All the air in my body drains out in one big whoosh. River didn't want me here in the first place. What if he finds out I'm working with Blake? And I can't breathe. I swallow and swallow, trying to catch my breath, and then I look into the side mirror again, and there he is.

Blake doesn't grin, exactly, but the softness in his dark eyes lets me take a breath—a couple breaths—and I'm not on a ride at the fair anymore but solidly in the back of Blake's truck, off to start my career on a farm.

The rows stretch out before us for what looks like miles, and a tall sticker bush stands over the dark, squatty beans in the first row. Blake points. "Beans." Then points again. "Weed." He pulls the weed to one side with his gloved hand, and then holds up a stick with a thin, curved blade on the end of it. "Bean hook." He puts the blade behind the stem of the weed near the ground. "Here you go. Just—" He tugs the hook towards himself in a quick motion, then lets go of the plant. It falls to the ground, leaving a meaty stem a few inches tall that cuts off sharply where the bean hook went right through it.

He looks up at each one of us in turn, saving me for last. "Remember, that could be your skin. BE CAREFUL."

"I'm starting with ten toes and that's how many I'm gonna

end up with," Beth says. Patsy glares at her. It's too early to be funny. Plus, Patsy loses her mind when she sees blood, even just from a hangnail. Aggie shakes her head and pats Beth's back.

"You are responsible for any weeds in your row." Blake sounds like an infomercial or a teacher. Like any old boss. "If your rows aren't clean, you have to walk them again while the rest of us move on. Got it?"

The boys are swiping at air with their hooks already, and Blake sends them in first. Then Aggie and Beth. Patsy looks from me to Blake, who watches the others in their rows.

"Later," she tells me, with a look. These rows are plenty long. Maybe she'll forget to ask me by the end?

Yeah. Maybe. Maybe it'll start snowing in the middle of July, too. I put my gloves on and start walking.

The sun peels back the darkness, leaving a soft golden light that will surely turn into blistering heat before noon. The beans are wet with morning dew and the leaves slap against my bare legs with every step. Soon everything from my cutoffs down is soaked.

I walk maybe twenty feet before I find my first weed. I hook it like Blake showed us. The blade slides through the stem with a smooth motion that makes me want to slice up every plant I see, way sharper than the As Seen On TV knife. I drop the weed, and then jump as a shadow falls over me.

"Good technique." Blake stands in the next row over, judging my cut. He motions at my feet. "Smart move, wearing shoes," he says, making the same joke as the other night.

Does he even remember the other night?

"I thought I'd give it a try." I clamp my mouth shut so I don't ask him about guitars or ukes or things that happen near elephant graves.

His eyebrows come together for a second, and then he shrugs his shoulders. "Get your strings fixed?"

"Yep." Fresh start and all that. Any old boss.

We walk side by side in our rows, the leaves swishing against our legs with each step. Blake pauses to slice down a tall, bushy weed.

"Nice work," I say before I can stop myself. "You're hired."

Blake's laughter floats off in the pale blue sky and the green fields that surround us. A space opens up between my shoulder blades and I breathe a little easier.

"Clark! Hold up!" Blake hollers. He squints off at the first rows where even I can see at least two tall weeds Clark and Jimmy missed.

Blake looks back at me and shrugs his shoulders. "Quality control," he says, and steps carefully over to their rows.

It's not uncomfortably hot yet, but it's gonna be. I look ahead, don't see any obvious weeds, and walk a few feet with my eyes nearly closed, enjoying the sun on my face. It's almost peaceful out here.

"'Bliss Walker,'" Patsy mimics Blake. She's stopped in her row, waiting for me. "How do you know him?"

"He gave me a ride the other day. When River's truck got stuck."

I see her face change when she puts it together. "Of *course* he did." She stares off towards Blake, and her face pinches up like it did when Aunt Trish liked my red velvet cake, or when Uncle Leo asks me to help him in the garage.

"Why do you care?" I finally ask.

Patsy gives me a long look. She takes a step forward and violently hooks a small tree. She holds the severed weed in her hand with her pink garden glove, and I wiggle my fingers in my old ratty gloves.

"*Why* do I care?" She throws the plant down. "Because you can't have everything, Bliss. You just can't." Patsy reaches out and hooks a white flowering weed, dropping it to the ground, and stalks off down her row.

I go back to the rhythm of the beans. Walk a few steps, pause and slice, walk some more, pause, slice. I give up worrying about Patsy pretty quick and try not to think about wet shoes, hot sun, or the water break that won't come for a long-ass time. Patsy's always been like that: if I get one piece of pie, it must mean there's none for her. I bum rides from her and share clothes, but if Patsy wants something, even if it was meant to be mine, she gets it.

If she really knew what happened with Blake, I would never hear the end of it.

"Congratulations!" Blake calls out from ahead of me. "One down, lots to go."

Blake sends Clark and Jimmy back down their rows again to catch the weeds they missed, and Patsy glares at me as we all loop around to walk back the other direction. It's not like I meant to invade her life. I would've rather been in Japan with Mama than move into her room. But I did like I was told and tried to stay out of the way, and worked my ass off meanwhile so Aunt Trish and Uncle Leo knew I was grateful.

Nathan was the only thing that I ever "had" that Patsy wanted for herself.

Just because Nathan was Patsy's crush from way back when, she will never forgive me. And since I was crushing on him, too, I would've done just about anything for him. On the day he gave us a ride to his house when it was raining, and Nathan picked me over Patsy to stay and play pool, she thinks I stole him from her.

It sucked that me and Patsy still had to share a room after that, but I never could tell her what happened. Especially since Nathan went off to college the next week without even saying goodbye. I was going to tell her, but what would I say, that Nathan said, "Don't cha wanna be my girlfriend?" and then did boyfriend things to me for the first time ever?

That I couldn't say no because he flat-out told me he'd go get Patsy if I didn't let him?

Even though it's about a million degrees out, I shiver just thinking about it.

After a while, Patsy and me went back to doing stuff together, but she was always on the lookout from then on, always keeping score.

Who am I kidding? Patsy's been keeping score since before we were born.

***

"Lunch," yells Blake. It's not even ten thirty, but it feels like we've been out here for fucking ever. I take my starving, thirsty ass over to where Patsy, Aggie, and Beth are collapsed on their coolers with their eyes closed. My shadow falls over them, and Patsy opens one eye, gives me a long look, and then closes it again, leaning over just barely enough for me to grab my food.

The melted ice water slips down my throat, and I close my eyes, lost in its relief. I take my soggy PB&J off to the side, eat my apple, and look around at the never-ending fields.

"That's some pink hair," Clark says to Beth, as she takes her bandana off.

She tugs at her lower lip ring, and then laughs. "Shit. I was going for red. Guess I failed that final."

Soon her and Patsy are comparing hair dye and face jewelry—Patsy wouldn't dare, even though she's old enough—and it turns out Beth is living Patsy's dream of going to beauty school.

"Thinking of dyeing yours?" Blake says, back from looking over our first few rows. He stands behind me in my shadow, lifts his water bottle to his lips.

I shake my head. "You?"

He chokes on his water but manages not to spit any out. He shakes his head, coughing, and puts one long palm up. "No, thanks." He coughs again, laughing.

"You okay?" I take a step closer to him.

He coughs again and nods. "Sorry."

He holds up one finger and takes another drink. His arms

122

are lean and ropy, and he looks strong enough, but he doesn't have the huge shoulders and neck I've seen on most of the farm kids at my school.

"There." He flashes his grin at me, takes off his hat, and runs his fingers through his hair, making it stand up all over. "I'll stick with my own color, thank you."

"It's perfect," I say, then wish I could take it back. Blake looks right at me for a second, and I wonder what he remembers from the other night. He was pretty drunk.

"Blake," Beth calls out, "where do you go to school?" Her eyes are closed, and she has a goofy grin on her face as Aggie gives her a shoulder massage.

Blake closes his water bottle and stuffs it back in the cooler, his motions smooth and calm. "I just graduated high school up in Chicago."

"Why the hell are you down here if you could be in Chicago?" Beth asks.

"Well, back in my vegetarian phase, my family got a little obsessed with organic food. They were ready for a change, so Mom found Dad a grant for minority farmers—he's Chinese—and next thing I knew . . . boom! We were the owners of Good Neighbor Organic Farm."

"So you've been a farmer for a whole month now?" Beth asks.

Clark and Jimmy are seeing who can throw a dirt clod farthest, which is kind of hard to judge when they all land in the dirt. Blake shakes his head at them, smiling a little bit. "Well, I was here last summer, but I went back with my grandparents for senior year to play soccer. I burned out midseason and wanted to transfer, but I was stuck up there."

Aggie looks at Beth. "Stuck in Chicago? One is never stuck in Chicago."

We all laugh, then Patsy stabs a look at me, asking Blake, "And how do you like it here so far this summer?"

Blake looks at her, then at me. He gives me a small smile, then turns an even bigger smile on Patsy. "So far, so good." He takes a swig of his water.

Patsy actually smiles at him. It's a bean-walking miracle.

Blake puts the cap back on and looks at his watch. "Break's over, guys. You and you"—he points at Clark and Jimmy—"I'm watching."

Clark pokes Jimmy in the ribs.

"The rest of you all did a great job. Can you take two rows each this time?"

"Two for the price of one, boss," Beth says. She ties her bandana back on, grabs Aggie's hand, and pulls her towards the rows.

Patsy is still sitting on her ass on top of the cooler. I take a few steps towards her so I can put my water bottle back. She looks up at Blake, who stands behind me a ways, then looks at me and raises her eyebrows, tilting her head at me. Her bear-ear buns wobble a little bit as she gives me a small, mean smile.

"Ready, Bliss?" She knows I can't go till she gets off the cooler. "Think you can handle two at once?" Patsy picks up her bean hook and saunters off.

Fourteen

The rest of the morning passes the same way: walk, pause, slice, turn, and check. I picture the ukulele's frets and practice fingering the chords to "Rainbow Connection" in my head. Before long, I am covered in a film of dirt, sweat dripping down my back. I wish I'd worn a bikini top like Aggie and Beth.

I had no idea there were so many kinds of weeds. I like volunteer corn the best. It's just corn from the next field over that's growing in the wrong place, and it's very satisfying to cut. Just when I think I might lose my mind, Blake tells us we are on our last down-and-back of the day. Me and the other girls have walked at least twice as many rows as Jimmy and Clark, and ours are way cleaner.

"Nice work," Blake says to me.

"You're welcome to take over," I say, pointing to a bushy plant.

"Oh, no. I'd never take a weed that wasn't meant for me." He looks at me a long minute, and I feel like I should just stay there, explain everything, keep talking about the weeds and the beans, let the sun go down while we stand in the middle of this field that stretches all the way from here to the edge of the earth in every direction.

I bend down and slice the last weed. He picks it up and studies it, so close I could bump elbows with him. The tiniest breeze dances by, and I lift my braids to catch it on the back of my neck.

Blake looks up like he just realized where he is. "Oh, hey," he says. "It really is a grave." He looks like a little boy, earnestly explaining some LEGO airplane or something.

I look around, confused. "Here in the beans?"

"No, no. I looked up that elephant, Kay? It's her grave. She's really there." He says it like a peace offering, like I already explained about River, and Mama, and Patsy, and like, yeah, maybe we kissed that one time, but that's in the past and he's okay with leaving it there.

"She's buried there," I say, like I agree with him and we are just two friends talking about the random elephant grave we saw, or like a boss and his worker just shooting the shit.

"Right there."

"Huh." I smile at him.

He smiles back and says, "It's a cool story. Thousands and thousands of kids gave their pennies until they raised enough money to bring her to America from India where she was captured."

"Wow," I say, slicing a smaller weed. I think of the elephant

Mama and me rode, its big dark eye with the long lashes, and how the elephant seemed to take up the whole sky. "She must have been so scared, being captured like that, taken away from her family."

"Yeah. She never had a chance to live the life she was supposed to live," Blake says, looking off to where the last clouds are finally leaving. "They decided it all for her." He stands for a minute, then cuts two weeds real fast before walking on.

If Kay's mama had been with her, would she have been scared to leave the only home she'd ever known? Maybe having her mama would've made up for everything else she left behind.

Jimmy and Clark are using their bean hooks like swords, jumping rows while they battle.

Blake whips his head around. "Hey, knock it off!" He jumps across the rows to stop them, as close to running as he can get while carrying the bean hook.

Idiots.

Alone again, I get back to work. My shoes are still damp from the morning, but the leaves brush my dry legs now, all the dew burned off by the sun. Aggie and Beth are singing up ahead, and Patsy joins in.

How old was I when we rode that elephant? It was in the good years of Mama's job, so maybe I was eight or nine. I don't remember anything about the first little apartment in Chicago, but Mama sure did.

"I swore after we got out of that shithole that we were gonna live like queens, and that's what we're doing. I put in too many nights of hell to turn down free room service just because your chicken nuggets are spicy. Your crib was in the bathroom, Bliss. The bathroom. Stretch out on that queen-size bed over there and eat your goddamn room-service nuggets."

I was about seven when Mama's jobs got hotter. Her agent would call, and we'd head out wherever she told us to go, sometimes leaving in the middle of the night to make it on time. A few times, she hooked us up with a charter bus that had its own bathroom for her and the other girls, and Mama loved that.

It was almost more than she could stand when she got picked to be the celebrity guest at the circus. At the last minute, she decided I could come, too—"Mother-daughter celebrities! Won't they just love that?"—and it took me all day to believe I was really there. I remember the thrill of being plunked down in front of Mama like a hundred feet off the ground on top of the elephant. Mama's arms were around me, holding me tight up there, protecting me, making me feel brave. The thick gray skin of the elephant was soft, except for the little fuzzy hairs on the top of its head, and the giant ears brushed my knees like a leathery blanket. The smell of elephant poop mixed with Mama's perfume as she pulled me close to her, squeezing me tight.

Riding on the elephant, feeling Mama's arms around me, was the first moment that felt real that whole day at the circus. Maybe the first time in years.

I remember that I felt real, too.

* * *

"Everything hurts," Patsy says as we drive home, the first words she has said to me since lunch. "And my shoulders are burned. But it'll be worth it when I save enough for beauty school."

"You know she'll never let you go," I say, real low.

"Watch me."

I can barely hold my head up enough to nod. If she asks me about Blake right now, I won't be able to tell her anything—truth, lies, or anywhere in between. She plugs in her dead phone and it beeps when it has a charge again, then buzzes with like forty texts, and I go to read them to her, like always when she's driving.

"Leave it"—she pulls the phone away from me—"it's nothing." She stuffs it on her lap, but not before I see that the texts are all from Nathan.

I raise my eyebrows up at her. "Nothing?"

Her face gets red. "I call first shower."

River's busy with poker night out at Granny's, so I grab the ukulele from Patsy's room and take it out back to practice some, but just as I finally get a chord right, everybody in the whole house decides to come sit on the patio. Someone's mowing their lawn nearby, and a far-off dog barks and barks. Patsy drags the sprinkler to the back of the lawn, then twists the faucet until a plume of water bursts out of it. Mama and Aunt Trish come out of the house bickering about the crystal bowl like they have every day since Mama came.

"I'm telling you, that's *my* bowl," Mama says. She struggles to pull apart two stacked chairs, shrugging Clyde off, and almost tips herself over when they fly apart. She recovers quickly and sets the chairs up for her and Clyde.

"Maybe it was yours once, but Mother gave it to me." Aunt Trish offers Mama and Clyde beers from the flamingo-decorated plastic tray. She sets matching flamingo glasses of lemonade in front of me and Patsy, then sags into her own plastic chair. "She really, really wanted me to have it."

"But it's not yours." The *tink-tink* of Mama's fingernails as she drums them on her beer bottle competes with the sprinkler as the water drops move across the lawn, and her voice cuts through them both.

I'm only half listening to their same argument as I fiddle with the uke, going between two chords and getting the second one wrong every single time. I try once more, then I lay the uke aside and roll my neck to shake off the frustration.

"Where did it come from, if you know so much?" Mama asks, and I perk up at her new line of questioning. "Where did Mother *get* the bowl?" Mama crosses her arms in front of her chest like she scored a point, her many bracelets jangling together.

Aunt Trish shrugs. "Doesn't matter. She gave it to *me*."

Mama goes to take a drink of her beer, then stops with it halfway to her mouth. She closes her eyes for a long moment, then sets down the beer, like she's caving in to a demand.

Her blue eyes go hazy, like she's stepped out of time for a minute, and she starts talking in a dreamy voice. "I was dying here, you understand? With Mother's rules and her lectures. 'Don't feed that to the baby,' and 'You're going to spoil her,' every time I tried to help dress her or put her to bed. No matter how I tried, I couldn't get it right. So I had to go. Mother wouldn't let me take Bliss, but she was mad that I left her behind. I couldn't win."

Clyde pats her knee, and Mama gives him a gentle smile. "Mother used to call every Sunday night. 'To update you on the baby,' she'd say, but mostly she freshened up the guilt trip and complained about money. One week, right after I hung up, I passed that bowl in the window of a jewelry shop, and it came to me like a miracle—I needed to give it to Mother, to thank her for taking care of Bliss, to show her I cared. I walked right in and asked to buy it. But it was over a hundred dollars."

"A hundred dollars?" Patsy whistles. "For a bowl?"

Mama smiles at her. "Saving up for that bowl was the first time I'd ever really managed money, even though I'd been on my own for a long time. I was so excited when I had enough to make them wrap it up for me, I could have flown back to Lake-ville that instant!"

Mama's eyes light up, and she looks around at all of us, and I know I'm not the only one who is picturing her handing the bowl to Gramma with her face all shining and proud.

"I don't remember—" Aunt Trish starts, but Mama holds up her pointer finger, her face shifting, darkening.

"Oh, you wouldn't. Three months I saved up for that bowl. Mother took one look, shut the box, and told me I was wasteful, selfish, irresponsible, and a bad mother. Then she stuck it in a corner, set a basket of dirty laundry on top, and went to change the baby's diaper."

Even Uncle Leo is shaking his head, and Clyde sucks a breath in through his teeth. Mama looks carved out of glass, like she might shatter into a million pieces if the wind blows the wrong direction. The only sound is the patter of the sprinkler as it works its way across the grass.

I wish we were the kind of family that hugged people when they were sad, but all I know how to do for Mama is see the tears in her eyes through my own watery view. "Mama—" I start, but Aunt Trish talks over me.

"Well," Aunt Trish says all businesslike, "maybe that's what she said to *you*." She stands up and begins gathering empty cups and bottles back onto her tray. "All's I know is years later, when she was in that hospital bed weak as a kitten, she grabbed my arm and wouldn't turn loose of it until I told her I'd look out for that bowl. She made me promise twice."

Mama puts her hand on Aunt Trish's arm. "Really?"

"Really." Aunt Trish pauses. "Now can someone help me get these things inside?" All of us except Mama jump up to help Aunt Trish load everything back to the kitchen. I'm about to open the screen door to go back out, but the sound of the ukulele freezes me in my tracks. Through the shadow of the screen door, I see Mama with her head bent over the ukulele, and she's doing way more than learning a chord.

The first notes drift in like little drops of sunlight, bright and happy, but searching for something, too. She plucks through the intro, then slides right into the chords, and she whisper-sings along: "Why are there so many songs about rainbows?"

I can't hardly breathe, it's so perfect. Mama is bathed in the setting sun, all bright and warm, and I want to watch her like this forever. The mesh of the screen door fades in my view as Mama makes her way through verse, chorus, verse, her fingers sliding from one fret to another like she's been doing it every day of her life.

Aunt Trish crowds up behind me, but she hears Mama, too, and instead of pushing me forward, she puts her hands on my shoulders and leans up close for a better view. I have to wonder, as I stand here, if Mama ever played this song for me when I was a baby learning to walk, or what other songs she would have played if she'd taken the uke instead of leaving it in the basement when she went to Chicago.

Mama's voice, usually so confident and sure, is light and airy, and as she sings I want to put my arms around her and answer all her wishes. The light turns her skin bronze, and I have to pinch myself because this isn't a mama from my dreams, this is my real mama, here on the patio, close enough to tell me about her dreams and maybe let me have some of my own.

The last notes hang on the golden light, next to the long shadow of Mama curled up in the molded plastic chair. Aunt Trish and me stand there in the doorway, and the screen comes back into focus, a black grid overlaying the impossibility of Mama and her song.

Then, "Theresa!" Clyde yells from the kitchen behind us. "You coming in?" and I push against the screen door, still caught in Mama's spell.

"That was beautiful," Aunt Trish breathes, and Mama looks up at her all guilty, like she was caught with her hand in someone's purse.

Questions spill out of me before I can stop them. "Do you know any other songs? Can you teach me? You're so good at it."

"Oh, honey, you don't want to learn *music*," Mama says as she sets the uke on the table and skitters away from it like it's about to bite her. "You want to learn something, watch me show up on time for a shoot, or smile like I'm told. That's the stuff that matters."

I stand there still as a statue while Clyde pulls her back in the house, and soon I'm the only one left outside. The faucet for the hose squeaks and groans as I turn it off, and I hold the ukulele close as I look out over the darkening lawn and wonder about having to choose between all the things you love.

Before bed, Mama puts her arm around me and walks me through the living room. We stop by the shelf with the bowl, and Mama looks down at it, then smiles at both of us in the mirror that's hanging there. "Look at this mother-daughter team. Don't ever cut your hair, baby girl. I got a hack job my first year in Japan, and it was hell and a ton of extensions until it grew back. Trust me on this one." She smiles and for a second, I'm not sure if it's her or me I'm looking at in the mirror.

***

Getting up and to the church is so much harder the second day. Before she starts the car, Patsy pulls out her phone. When she sees me looking, she hunches over it like it's showing which lottery numbers are going to win.

Of course it's Nathan. I don't ask, and Patsy doesn't talk about him, which is fine with me. Just because he has history with me, doesn't mean he can't be good to Patsy. But the way he looked at me over her shoulder the other night makes me scared he won't be.

I shake my head to send Nathan back deep into my memories where he belongs and close my eyes as we cross the railroad tracks and bump down the road.

When we get there, Aggie's truck is already parked in the lot. I lay my head back and close my eyes and hear a faint sound coming from her truck. I push through the fog in my head to remember where I know that sound from.

I drag my head off the headrest and look over. Damned if Aggie isn't sitting there, going to town on a ukulele. I never even heard of the thing before last week, and here's someone else playing one right before my eyes. I can't stop staring at the way Aggie just slides her fingers from one chord to another, like it's easy or some shit.

"That noise has got to go," Patsy groans from the driver's seat.

I step out of the car before I know what I'm doing, ready to talk to Aggie, but before I get there, Blake pulls to a stop right behind the Malibu and he steps out, all clean lines and steady walk.

"Hello," he says. His grin pulls my own mouth into a smile. "Back for more?"

For a second all I can think about is us kissing by the elephant grave, and I breathe, "Yeah," then shut my mouth real hard.

Because that's not what he means, of course. He thumps the truck and says, "Good. The beans await," and opens the door for us. I drag my mind away from the elephant grave and fix it right here in the truck. With the beans.

The sun is coming up hard, and the early rays shine off the road, trying to blind me with the reflection. I close my eyes and listen to them all talk.

"Why didn't we see you last summer?" Beth asks Blake.

"Well, we worked pretty hard starting up the farm. Plus, I was driving back and forth to Decatur for classes three nights a week, so I didn't really meet any people."

"Ugh. Why?" Patsy says.

"Well, at the time, I was hell-bent on being an engineer, and I wanted to be ahead when I started college."

"Was?" Beth says, pouncing on the word. "Not anymore?"

Blake sighs and fiddles with his hat. "Not technically."

"Not technically anymore? Or not technically an engineer?" Beth laughs.

"Both?"

The truck bounces as we turn down the gravel road towards the fields. They are spread out for miles, like a green Astroturf blanket.

"It's a little complicated. I got myself admitted to the engineering school . . ."

"And you changed your mind?" Patsy asks, as Blake stops the truck.

"I realized I wanted something else," he says, and we hop out for another day of walking beans.

The beans are wet like yesterday, only it's hotter earlier, so I'm sweaty and soggy at the same time. I let my feet follow the path and my hands do the work, and the rest of me just soaks up the sun and the dirt smell and the birds chattering to each other. It's honest work.

"Hey." Blake stops in his row and pulls out his phone. "Look what I found." He leans over the beans to show me a picture of an old-time newspaper article of a baby elephant riding on a trailer in a parade.

I squint to see the words. "'Kay the Elephant Arrives!'"

"They had a huge parade and built a special elephant house and everything. Just for her. She was like a superstar at the zoo. She was their claim to fame."

"Wait. Zoo? I thought she was a circus elephant?"

"She started out at the zoo. But then, she—"

"Ho!" a voice hollers from off by the cars.

Blake looks around. There's somebody way off at the edge of the field, standing by a white pickup and waving his hands at us.

"Dad." He sounds like Patsy does when Aunt Trish shows up with a list of chores we should have finished already. "Hey," Blake yells to his dad. "Be right out."

Then to me, quieter. "Uh-oh, the boss caught us slacking off. I'll never hear the end of it." He doubles his pace down the row and I automatically hustle to keep up.

"Take your time," Blake says. "It's only me he's judging here."

"Is he a hard-ass?"

Blake zaps two tall weeds right in a row and hurries off. "You mean, is he a perfectionist who expects me to also be a perfectionist and gets frustrated when I'm not perfect?" He looks over at me and laughs as we speed down the row. It's probably just the way he laughs around anybody, but it feels like it's special, just for me. "No. He's not a hard-ass."

We both laugh then, but I see the worry in his eyes.

Blake's dad meets him at the end of his row and stops, blocking me from getting around him to my next row.

"Do you know how much acreage we have to clear, Blake?"

They look an awful lot alike. Except for the frown on Mr. Wu's face.

"I do."

"There isn't time for you to play on your phone."

"I know, Dad."

"I can find a new crew boss if this is too difficult for you."

"It's not—"

"We agreed on the conditions, son. Harold is still holding that spot for you over at his lab."

I want to get past them or go around them, but I'm afraid if I move, they will realize I've been listening in, so I stay put.

"Isn't a hands-on education better than some lab? Come on. Look how clean these rows are, Dad." Blake waves his hands at the rows we just came from. "I'm learning farming from the ground up."

Mr. Wu sighs a loud sigh and slaps his hands together, like he's cleaning them off. "Keep your crew on task. Not a single mistake." He looks over at where I'm standing and jerks his head in a nod. "Continue."

As I count the rows over to the next one I'm supposed to go down, I try to put Blake's dad's words into Mama's mouth, and I almost cry it makes me laugh so hard. I feel sorry for Blake that his dad's such a hard-ass. Nobody's ever pushed me that hard in my whole life.

Mr. Wu watches until we stop for lunch, then he gets in the white pickup and heads out. I want to say something to Blake, tell him we'll be good workers for him, but the rest of the day he just watches us work, pointing out missed weeds and praising clean rows. Like any old boss.

River has to finish the lawn at Granny's, then him and me are gonna go get some ice cream. I watched him push the mower back and forth around the front yard for a while, and now he's working on the back. I don't know how he can stand it—I'm hot and sticky just sitting here on the old picnic table. He still has half the yard left, and the mower's drone is making me wish he had a hammock out here so I could close my eyes and drift off.

He's really fighting through the lawn: the grass is so tall it's flopping over every which way. I lie back on the table and watch one perfectly white, fluffy cloud float across the sky, and then the drone of the mower chokes, coughs, and shuts off.

"Shit." Ears ringing with the interruption of silence, I sit up and watch River pull the cord once, twice, three times before he unscrews the gas cap. I jump down and join him, looking into the dry tank of the mower.

"Out of gas?"

He lifts his cap and runs his fingers through his hair, then jams the cap back down. "I almost made it." He gestures to the half of the yard that's still tangled green, then heads off to the shed and comes out with the red plastic gas can. He shakes it at me, the gas sloshing around inside, slapping the sides hard enough that I know there's not much in there.

"Aw, man." He wrestles with the yellow ring around the black spout until he wrenches it off. He shoves the can in my direction, and the sharp gas smell pinches at my nose. "Look at that. No gas. If Lisa won't pay me, I can't buy any goddamn gas, and if I don't have any gas"—he opens his hand and lets the can drop, his voice getting louder and louder with every word—"I can't finish the fucking yard." He chucks the spout away from him and it flies end-over-end across the yard, landing under some trees back by the shed.

River sighs, and he deflates like a birthday jump-house at the end of the party, his arms sagging to his sides as he turns to look at me.

"Can you . . . ask her again tomorrow?" I say in a small voice that I hope can sneak past his anger.

River walks away like he didn't even hear me, and I pick up the gas can and scurry after him out to where he's searching the grass for the spout. He finds it, picks it up, and stands there, slapping it against his palm like a policeman's club.

I try again. "Maybe if you explain about the gas?"

River turns to me then, and it's like he's back after being gone for a while. He breathes out a laugh, slings his arm around my neck, and kisses the top of my head. "That's the thing, Bliss. You don't explain things to Lisa. You either do it her way, or"— he reaches up into the tree we're standing under and twists a green fruit off of it—"or you just don't *do* it." He wings it at the side of the shed, just missing a square patch of paint before it bounces into the overgrown grass. River throws two more, missing the square each time, before he hands one to me.

"Apples?" The fruit is hard as a baseball, dark green and dusty.

He points to the brown stem and four leaves at the top. "Persimmons. Ever had one?"

I shake my head, and he turns his over in his hands,

studying it. "The very first day Granny brought me here to live with her, it was just before Thanksgiving and it was freezing out. Granny gave me her old hoodie as a coat—it came down to my knees, and she rolled the sleeves up to fit. We came out here to this tree—no leaves, it looked dead, except it had these orange things hanging all over it."

"I thought harvesttime was early fall."

"Not for these." He tosses the persimmon straight up and catches it. "Granny said you know they're almost ready when they fall off the tree, but you have to be sure you've got a ripe one."

I throw my unripe persimmon at the shed, hitting smack-dab in the square, and we grin at each other. River high-fives me.

"God, Bliss, I wish you could try one. Granny made me choose one I thought was ripe, and I picked the shiniest orange one off the ground. She let me take a big old bite out of it." He pulls me close and twists a piece of my hair in his fingers, and he shakes his head. His blue eyes are soft now, only memories in them and none of the mad. "I thought I had swallowed a bag of cotton balls. It was dry and sour all at once, and I couldn't spit it out fast enough."

I laugh, picturing it. "Granny got you, didn't she?"

"She couldn't hardly catch her breath, she was laughing so hard. Then she told me, 'The only cure for an almost-ripe persimmon is a ripe persimmon,' and she held another one out to me. There was no way I was going to let her trick me again, especially when it was so soft I thought it was rotting. Then

Granny said, 'Lisa always hated persimmons. Says they're the worst fruit in the world.'"

"You're smarter than Lisa," I say, and River kisses me.

"So I grabbed it away from Granny and chomped down on it and—damn—that persimmon tasted like maple syrup and brown sugar all rolled up together. Granny said it's the sweetest fruit there is, and I believe she's right."

He twists the stem, picks at the leaves. "Granny taught me how to predict the winter by looking inside the persimmon seeds—if it's shaped like a spoon, that means snow to shovel, if it looks like a knife, there's gonna be cutting winds, and a fork means a mild winter. They were right every single time we looked, but Lisa just laughed at us, called us old-timers and asked about the *Farmers' Almanac*."

His phone buzzes. "It's like she knows I'm talking about her." And his face clouds over as he reads his text. "Shit."

"What?"

He throws the persimmon and hits the target. "Shit, shit, shit. I've still got Lisa's keys. We have to get them to her before she loses her mind." River takes a few steps towards the truck, then turns to grab the gas can and the nozzle. "I told her I wouldn't forget to give them back. And then I forgot. Shit."

River is quiet as we race into town to meet Lisa. I shrink into the bench seat as we bounce down the brick-paved streets, barely slowing to turn corners until we reach the house they've been painting. It's a two-story house with a wraparound front porch with big white pillars and a railing, the kind of house a rich family lives in. There's a ladder up against the far side of the house and blotchy tarps on the ground. The house either used to be tan and they're painting it white, or the other way around. Lisa's midway through the job.

I grab River's hand as we go past the porch and around the side, and there's Lisa, up the ladder, scraping fat curls of paint off the siding next to one of the second-story windows. The scraps float past her cargo shorts and drift down to the pile on the drop cloth. Lisa looks like a girl version of River—same blue eyes, same hair, only hers is in a ponytail under a red baseball cap. She's been nice enough to me the few times I've met her, but mostly she just ignores me.

"Lisa," River calls, but she doesn't answer. He calls again louder, and finally he yells, "Mom!" and she turns away from the house.

She jerks her earbuds out and squints down at us, then scrapes an extra-long curl off the house and watches it drop. Her sharp voice stabs into us both. "River." She picks paint off the scraper, then nods towards me. "And Bliss."

My name sounds like a piece of garbage the way she says it, and River about squeezes my hand off, but I answer her as if she'd been nice.

"Hello, Lisa."

She points at River. "So. Are you proud of yourself?"

My fingers are about to go numb in River's. He looks at Lisa but doesn't answer.

She makes her voice all high like a little kid's, mocking River. "'Let me run the power washer. I'll leave it cleaner than you've ever seen.'" She waves at the speckled house. "Bullshit. It's back to scraping for you." As I look closer, there's a clear line where half of the house has been worked on, and half hasn't.

River juts his chin at the less-clean side. "I had to leave early. I'll do it over."

"You bet your ass you will. If any other worker left one of my sites in this shape, he'd be looking for another job." Lisa turns around again and scritches faster at the wood with her scraper. River walks over to the pressure washer, which is like a lawn mower with a hose attached to it, like we use at the car wash.

"Not *now*." Lisa's voice makes me want to curl up in a little ball around River to protect him. "I been trying to leave for an hour already, but *someone* took my keys." She scrapes even faster.

River fumbles around in his pocket and tosses the keys up to Lisa, mumbling, "Sorry."

She snags them out of the air, then says, "You done with Granny's yard?"

River stuffs his hands in his pockets. "I ran out of gas."

"I gave you gas money last week."

"It's a big yard."

"I gave you more than enough. When are you gonna learn,

River? Seriously?" Her voice goes up and up, higher and louder with every question. She puts her hands on her hips. "If I was this irresponsible, no one would ever hire me. Is that what you want? To be a deadbeat like your dad?"

River stands like a statue as Lisa goes back to scraping. She's working so much faster it's like someone turned the "speed" dial all the way up. She stops abruptly, and points the scraper in our direction. Her voice goes deadly quiet. "It's time to choose, River. Get your shit together or throw your life away. It's up to you."

She looks him in the eye as she stuffs her earbuds in, then makes a big point of turning her back on us.

We stumble out to the truck, both of our ears ringing from Lisa's lecture. I wonder what I would do if Mama yelled at me that way. When I've been in trouble, Uncle Leo is always good for a story about when he was young and how he got smarter as he got older. Aunt Trish sure knows how she likes things done, but Lisa is a whole other thing. Even worse than Blake's dad.

The first time I tried to make a pie, the crust was so tough we had to leave most of it in the pie plate when the knife wouldn't hardly go through it. Aunt Trish didn't yell, or make me feel stupid, she just told me pie crust is fussy every single time. She showed me what to do, gave me tricks to use, and the next one was better, and the ones after that weren't perfect, but they weren't far off. I think if she had yelled at me like Lisa, that would have been the last time I ever stepped foot in the kitchen.

"I'd like to give her a persimmon or two," I say to River, and he almost laughs. "Don't let her get to you. Go back tomorrow and prove her wrong." I shove my hands in my pockets as we reach the truck. There's something in one of them, and when I pull it out, it's the five-dollar bill I grabbed to pay for ice cream. I grab the gas can from the bed of the truck and hold it and the money up like I'm standing on the gold-medal steps of the Olympics. "Gas money!"

River grabs me up in a big old bear hug and then we head back into town to buy some gas.

Fifteen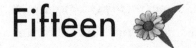

Getting up early does not get easier the more we do it. I'm so tired, I go through the bean rows automatically, and when it's time to quit for lunch, I have no memory of how I got to this side of the field.

I come out of my rows just as Patsy tells Aggie and Beth, "Nate is just so different from the other boys around here. You know. He's *special.*"

She smirks up at me. "Oh, hi, Bliss."

I take my sandwich and move away from them.

Clark and Jimmy are jumping back and forth over the ditch, cracking up when they fall on their asses, calling each other names.

"Sorry about yesterday." Blake's shadow falls over me and I squint up at him.

"Yesterday?" I was going to let it go, but if he wants to talk about it, that's up to him.

"I'm sorry that you had to hear all that," Blake says in a

low voice, crumpling his sandwich wrapper. His shoulders are hunched over and he's definitely not smiling.

"It wasn't so bad," I say.

He shakes his head. "I had to wear my dad down for weeks before he let me head this crew. I'm surprised he hasn't sent a drone out to follow our progress or something."

I look over at Clark and Jimmy, wrestling at the side of the ditch, just as they almost crash into all the coolers. "I don't know what he's worried about. You seem to have everything under control."

"Yeah, totally." Blake laughs and looks at his watch. "Back to work," he calls out. He scrambles up and offers me his hand, which I grab before I really think things through. He pulls me up to standing, and I look up, up, up, past his hand holding mine, past the cords of his neck as they rise from the V of his shirt, all the way to his dark eyes shining down at me. His hand is touching my hand, every finger wrapped around my fingers, and if I'd known I wouldn't be able to pull away, I wouldn't've ever put my hand in his.

Patsy's laugh rings out, and I don't have to even look to know that she's watching me and Blake, but I drop his hand like it's the sharp end of the bean hook and walk past her. She can think what she wants: we weren't doing nothing wrong.

The sun is seriously up now, burning off all the moisture from the leaves and sucking it into the air. Patsy, Aggie, and Beth stand together as I wade into my row. Right as I pass them, Patsy says loudly, "And, Aggie, you remember *River*, Bliss's *boyfriend*? He was in your English class last spring. *Most* people can't forget *River*."

I slice the first weed I see. I probably pull a bit harder than I have to.

Patsy and them file in the next few rows, and their laughter and joking should rub off on me, but the happier they are, the more my throat tightens up.

I trip on a big dirt clod, catch myself, and keep walking.

Later, I end up next to Blake. Before I know it, I'm asking him, "So Kay was a zoo elephant *and* a circus elephant?"

His face is all hopeful and serious, a little wrinkle between his eyebrows. "You want to hear the story?"

"Not if it's on your phone," I say. "I don't want to get you fired."

"Got it all memorized," he tells me, patting the phone stored safely in his pocket.

"Okay, go."

"So, Kay was the star attraction at the zoo for years and years, and everybody adored her, especially her trainer, Bob. He didn't let anyone else care for her."

"That's sweet."

"Yeah, well, one day something spooked Kay, and she crushed Bob against the wall."

"Oh no! Was he okay?"

Blake looks at me all concerned, and he leans towards me across the rows. "He died the next day."

"Oh no." Shivers race over my whole body in the hot sun, and I have to stop for a minute. The elephant I rode on with Mama was so slow, so gentle, I never thought it could be a killer. I feel almost sick.

Blake takes off his cap and runs his hands through his hair. "I know. But Bob knew she didn't mean to kill him. He wasn't mad at her."

"No?" I sound like a little kid. But for some reason I really, really need to know that Kay, who I didn't even know existed, like, a week ago, never meant to hurt anyone.

"No. The paper said he died 'unresentful.'" Blake makes quote marks in the air.

Blake's face is so sad. I want to make him feel better. "So they gave her to the circus?"

"Yeah." He smiles but gets serious again real quick. "This rinky-dink circus bought her and toured her around for another fifty years. She was saved, but it still wasn't a great life. Most circuses could only afford one elephant, and they are meant to live in groups, like families."

"She was all alone?"

"Off and on. Except for—"

Blake's phone rings and he squints down at it.

"Sorry, I have to take this." He stops and turns away in his row, and he says, "Dad?"

It's a lot to think about, Kay being a killer. Even if it was an accident. I leave Blake way behind and walk almost the whole row, picturing it. I'm so caught up in cutting weeds and thinking about Kay that I don't notice Patsy stopped in her row until I'm practically on top of her.

"Hey," she says, "Beth is gonna show me some beauty school stuff at her place tonight." She looks off to where Blake stands, talking on his phone. "So if you need a ride anywhere, you'll have to get your boyfriend, *River*, to take you. You remember him. Right?"

I wish there were some weeds to slice, but this row is clean so far. How mad would Blake be if I started tearing up his beans? "So fucking funny, Patsy. I thought River was an asshole?"

"Oh, don't get me wrong; Blake is a way better guy, but even assholes don't deserve to get cheated on. You have to tell River about your new boyfriend. I mean, boss."

"Look at you with all your relationship know-how."

"At least me and Nate know what a relationship is," she says, and the lid blows on the words I've been keeping boxed up for years now.

"Here's one thing Nate knows. I was almost thirteen," I say, tripping through the dirt. I'm not loud, but I can tell Patsy hears me from the way she keeps her face forward, not moving her head even an inch towards me as we walk.

"You and me both were, that day we got a ride home in the rain from him. You left with his friend Matt. He—Nathan—" I make myself say his name, "told me I could be his girlfriend. And then he . . ."

Four or five tiny gray birds flash and dart past us, chittering happily. I take a deep breath.

"I didn't say no, if that's what you're wondering. I never said yes, either. And I . . . I was afraid—he said he would pick you instead, if I wouldn't. He said I could be his girlfriend, and then he had sex with me for my first time ever. I was almost thirteen and he said I could be his girlfriend, and it wasn't nice. And he never called me or talked to me ever again."

My heart has escaped my chest and is beating all through my body, especially my stomach, where it's making me feel like I'm gonna be sick. I swallow and wipe my hands on my shorts before I swipe the next weed.

Patsy doesn't say a thing, just walks down her rows, and I wonder for a second if maybe she really heard me, if maybe I was wrong about her not believing me.

But then, she turns and shakes her head at me real slow. Finally, she says, "Nate? Would never do that. I know you can't believe he likes me, but you don't have to make up stories about him." She stomps off down the row, slashing weeds every which way she goes.

I stand stock-still in my row, staring at her, with my mouth hanging open. *Make up stories*?

Eventually, I move forward again, wondering if maybe Kay the elephant just reached her limit with Bob, if she was just so tired of him poking and pushing at her and she never meant to kill him, only to make him stop.

Sixteen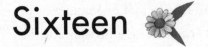

I practically sleepwalk through the rest of the beans, and almost before I know it, we are loading up in Blake's truck to go home. Patsy and Aggie and Beth are like new best friends, and there is no way Clark and Jimmy can have this much energy after a full day in the hot sun.

I peel myself out of the truck, and Patsy stalks off, leaving me to get the cooler. Blake hands it down from the back of the truck, saying, "See you tomorrow? I'll need you more than ever."

I get a little lurch in my stomach. "You will?"

"There may not be as many workers," he says, nodding over at Clark and Jimmy.

Oh. "Really?"

"Really." He draws his finger across his throat. "My dad is not just a hard-ass about me."

"Well. Nothing can keep me away," I say. "Walking beans is my life now."

He grins, and I grin, and I can't seem to make myself say anything back to him, but I also can't seem to leave the truck and get in Patsy's car. Finally, she calls over, "Any time now," and we smile one last time before I head off.

The silence in the car is as big as a bean field. Patsy's not looking at me, and I'm sure as hell not looking back at her any time soon. I plug my phone in and it buzzes and buzzes with about a million texts.

River: I'm here at the church, where are you?
River: Aren't you done yet
River: Where you at?
River: Jesus Christ, Bliss
River: Fuck it. Text me when you're home

River came to the church? He's supposed to be at work. The ride to Patsy's takes practically forever, but I text River to come get me after I shower. I know he's pissed because all he texts in return is "K," but it's better than nothing.

My hair isn't nearly dry, but River's coming soon, so I grab a Diet Coke while I wait for him.

Mama comes upstairs, looking like she's ready to go out dancing, or to a nightclub if we had any of those around here. She checks her makeup in a hand mirror, and then she smiles real big and nods over at the dining room table where Clyde props up a computer tablet.

"What's going on?"

"Thanks to the use of technology, I am talking to SMOOCH corporate in New York from right here in the middle of nowhere," Mama says.

A hole opens up in my center. She just got here. She can't leave again so soon.

Then she calls, "No, no—not like that, Clyde, honey! You'll give me double chins and bingo wings with that angle!" Mama squeezes at her upper arms, which have less than zero loose skin hanging down. "And these overhead lights—ugh!—look at the dark circles they give me." She pats at the bags under her eyes, or where some would be if she had any.

"What . . . what are you talking to corporate about?" I make myself ask, crossing my fingers that it's not as bad as it sounds.

In answer, she comes right up close to me, and just when I think she's going to tell me, she shows me her teeth. "No tooth crap?"

"They look good. But why—"

"Well, you can never be too careful. We women have to be strong and clear and not take no for an answer," she tells me. "Keep their focus where you want it, and you'll have them eating out of your hand."

"What is your focus?"

She doesn't answer, so I say, "Can I listen in till I have to go?"

"Clyde!" Mama hollers, like she's cut herself and needs a doctor. "Clyde!" He comes storming in holding an armful of books and Aunt Trish's white bedside table lamp, cord dragging behind him.

"What? Are you okay?"

"Oh, Clyde," Mama tells him. "My baby girl wants to learn from me—if this isn't a dream come true, I don't know what is." She dabs at her eyes, then pulls me close and touches her forehead to mine, then walks me over to the couch. "You sit right here, and you can see the whole thing."

Mama goes to position herself before the camera. Clyde holds the lamp over his head to shine the light on her as she leans her chin forward, arranging her blouse so it falls just a little bit open, like it happened accidentally.

She smiles at herself and says to Clyde, "I've thought of everything. What could possibly go wrong?"

Little chimes sound from the tablet. Mama pushes her shoulders back even more, and says, "Thomas, it's been far too long. How is your family?"

A voice like a car salesman says, "Doing great, doing great. But the question is, how are you?"

Mama smiles, and I can't tell if she's smiling at Thomas, or the little picture of herself in the corner. "Oh, Thomas, I'm sure you know, time spent with family is time you'll never regret." She claps her hands together. "But enough about me. Erika told me my name has been coming up a lot recently, so I thought I would save you the trouble of trying to track me down."

"She said that? Well, we have been planning a revamped—"

"Thomas." Mama leans in close to the screen. "I was the

face of SMOOCH for so many years."

"You were. But that was—"

River honks from out front, stopping Thomas from whatever he was saying. He tries to speak again and is interrupted by several more honks.

"River's early," I tell Mama, wishing I could make him stop while staying in here to find out what this call is about.

"One moment, please." Mama smiles at the camera while she hisses, "Make it stop!" to me through her smile.

I want to stay so bad, but Mama waves me towards the door behind her, and Clyde jerks his head at me to get out of the house. As I fiddle with the door, I can see Thomas, big as life on the screen. He's about half-bald and a little chubby, definitely not one of the models. River honks again long and hard, and I can tell he's getting pissed.

"As I was saying— What in the world?" Thomas stops dead in the middle of his sentence.

I open the door, then turn to whisper, "Sorry," and give Mama my best smile before I leave.

"Who in the *hell* is that, Theresa?" Thomas says, his voice rough enough to stop me where I stand. "Is that your sister?"

Mama's back goes stiff, and she turns to me slowly. "Bliss," she says, in a voice that sounds like we've never met before in our lives. She snaps her fingers. "Come say hello."

I'm chained to the floor, unable to move. In my head I can hear eleven-year-old me saying, *Please, please, please,* and see back-then Mama's face as she plunked me down hard in the waiting area, her face all red and mad at me for wanting to model like she did.

I'm not fucking this up again. I just can't. River honks once more, and I'm pulled between the two of them, but Mama's force ends up being way stronger than River's. I go over to her like I'm being sucked into a whirlpool.

"Stop lollygagging," Mama says. "Thomas here would like to meet you." Her voice is iron as she looks over her shoulder at me, and I can't read on her face if she really wants me here or not. My stomach is flipping and flopping, and I wish whatever technology makes this video conference possible would stop working right this minute.

"Thomas, meet my daughter, Bliss. Bliss, say hello to Thomas." I practically whisper hello, and Thomas leans way forward on the screen.

"Bliss was just leaving." She doesn't want me here.

I try to pull away from her, but Mama has her arm around me like one of those snakes that squeezes their food until it's dead.

"Good god, Theresa, it's like looking at you, twenty years ago. She could be your clone. Sweetie, have you ever thought about getting into the business?"

"I've kept her out, Thomas. Let her have a normal child-hood. It's so important these days that children have a stable upbringing."

"How old are you, honey?" Thomas asks.

"Almost eighteen," I say, at the same time Mama says,

"Sixteen." I look at her all confused—she knows how old I am, doesn't she?

Mama laughs a brittle laugh and hugs me way too hard. "To me, she'll always be my baby."

"Well, Theresa . . ." Thomas looks at me like a coyote that just saw a rabbit cross its path.

River honks again, and the sound helps me pull away from hungry Thomas.

"I have to go." I squirm out from under Mama, throw a smile their way, and try not to run towards the door, even though I still don't know what the conference is about.

As I open the door, Mama tells Thomas, "These teenagers. Hormones all over the place, right? Now about the new campaign . . ."

I hurry out to tell River what took so long.

Patsy pulls in as we are leaving, and she leans out her window as she drives past us. "Make sure you tell River all about your new boss." She honks twice and pulls into the driveway.

"I thought you said you were done early," River says as he takes my kiss on his cheek. He's still in his work clothes, and there's white paint in his hair and on one forearm.

"This *is* early. It's short days because it's so hot."

River takes off his hat, turns it around, and puts it back on, then takes it off again, and he can't seem to look at any one thing for more than a few seconds at a time as we drive off.

"The fuck was Patsy talking about?" River asks as I wrap both arms around his skinny upper arm and lay my head on his shoulder. His muscles twitch under my fingers as if he's about to fly off.

I take a deep breath and say, like it's not a big deal, "So Patsy got us this job, you know, and the boss turns out to be the same guy from the music shop the other day. Crazy, right?"

River looks at me so long I'm afraid he'll crash the truck.

"Fucking college boy? From Lyle and them?"

"His name's not—" I stop myself and nod, not trusting my voice any further than necessary.

He looks at the road again. "Don't fuck with me, Bliss. This is the last thing I need today." Which Patsy probably knew, which is why she said something.

"It's not a big deal."

River drives for a few minutes in jumpy silence. "Screw beans. Come detassel with me. We might start early."

"What about Lisa?"

River used to quit working for her once a week, tops, before me and him got together. Somehow, I've managed to talk him into not quitting and not killing her this entire summer.

River looks away from me, settles a dip in his lip. "Lisa was all over my ass by nine a.m., bitching about 'quality over speed' and some other shit, so I bugged out early."

"Aw, River, I thought we talked about this."

"I don't need her shit. How exactly does knowing how to

paint a goddamn house help me drive a big rig? Besides, she's too picky. It's a fucking house! Nobody gives a shit if I paint side to side or up and down."

I fiddle with the hair tie on his wrist, sliding it first one way, then the other. "How long did you make it?"

"Ten o'clock. Two hours of that bullshit. She doesn't rag on any of the other guys like she does on me. Her own fucking son. You'd think she'd feel guilty for ditching me all those years and go a little easy on me, but nope, not Lisa."

My arms and legs ache, and I think I have a sunburn. I wonder if I would hurt this much after painting houses. Or detasseling corn. Probably. I should be more upset with River, but him and his mom will make up soon. They always do. I'll talk him out of it later, when I'm not so tired.

"And then, Lisa hits me with it, right when I was ditching. 'I thought you'd want to know. Granny's gonna need a care provider.'" He mimics her voice. "'It's going to be expensive. We have to sell her place.'"

The words linger in the cab of the truck. Sell Granny's? River always, always thought the place would be his.

"See if I ever work for that bitch again."

"She's your mom, River."

"Nah. She's just some lady who had me, ditched me, and keeps fucking up my life in as many ways as she can think of." River reaches in front of me and turns up the scream metal as loud as it will go, and we drive around and around until I'm pretty sure we're gonna run out of gas, before he turns down the lane to Granny's. He has not said one more word about Lisa selling the place, and I am sure as fuck not asking.

We park in the drive and River finally puts his arm around me. He tangles his fingers in my hair, then pulls me close. Granny's white house glitters as the early-evening sun angles out from behind it, and the completely mowed lawn glints in the sun's rays. River plays with my hair, twisting and tangling it all the hell up until I'm worried how I'll get a comb through it later.

River jerks his hand away, taking a few pieces of hair with him, and shuts off the truck. Then he sits there with his hands on the steering wheel, staring at Granny's house. I sit next to him, waiting.

And waiting. We sit there for so long I can't sit still much longer, but I can't be the one to move or say something first.

A far-off dog barks, and a horsefly lands on the windshield. I follow its progress as it tiptoes up to the top of the windshield, then turns towards my side and makes its way across. Its shiny black body seems way too heavy to be carried by the clear, veiny wings. Just as it crosses in front of me, it takes off.

"Allison fucking Hanson is coming by tomorrow to look it over."

"The Realtor?"

"You know any other Allison Hanson?" River moves for the first time in a long time, turning to stab me with burning dark blue eyes, taking his hat off and running his hands through his shaggy hair till it stands up all over. "I been out here cleaning for hours before I went and got you."

"That sucks."

He stares out the windshield again. He squeezes the steering wheel.

"What sucks is that I lived more of my life out here than anywhere else. What sucks is that even though we talked about it for years and years, Granny lost her fucking marbles and forgot—forgot!—that she ever had a grandson, that he ever lived out here with her, that she promised him that this place could be his." He takes a shaky breath. "It's mine."

My heart turns inside out for him as he starts the truck back up and puts it in gear.

"And Mom—Lisa—doesn't believe a fucking word I say about it." He cuts the wheel and floors it, turning a doughnut on the gravel drive. I brace myself on the dashboard just in time.

He slams to a stop, and we both cough on the gravel dust that floats up into the evening sky. River looks over at me again, looks at me like I'm the one who's selling Granny's place, like I'm the one who forgot about him, like this is all my fault.

"Oh, River," I whisper, and reach over to pat his leg. He's told me some of that before, but I never knew Granny forgot all about him.

I duck up under his arm. "I'm sorry." I'm not sure what I'm sorry for, everything and nothing, and I can't do a thing to make Granny remember him, but I wish, oh I wish I could.

He turns off the truck. "So yeah, I guess you could say it sucks."

He sounds so lonely and sad; I just want to put my arms around him and give him anything he needs to feel better. I go to kiss him, but he won't have none of it.

I know what's worked before when he's been upset, and I kiss my way down to his lap. It isn't until he helps me unzip his jean shorts that I know he's going to go along with me making him feel better.

After, I go to kiss him, but he pulls back, eyes hard again, and opens the door.

"Come on," he says, and jerks his head at me to follow him into Granny's.

It's getting darker, that summertime darkness that gets dimmer and dimmer and makes you think there's something wrong with your eyes, that if you could just blink a few times, everything would be bright and clear again. My whole body is limp, and I wish I could go home and go to bed. My neck has a kink in it, and I wish I'd put some fuckin' gum in my purse like I meant to the other day.

But we work until it's full dark, loading the truck up with all the trash, leaving Granny's so clean nobody would even guess all the shit that's gone down there all summer. Not even Allison Hanson.

The night air blows in the truck windows as we drive to Patsy's. I lean on River and try to keep my eyes open. I cannot wait to climb into bed and pass out.

My hair keeps blowing in River's face, and he finally elbows me to sit up away from him so it will stop. I grab his hand, but he doesn't squeeze back.

I wish I could help him somehow. Maybe I should quit working for Blake.

No.

My stomach tenses up at just the thought. It's hot and tiring and hard work, but I picture the wide-open sky and rows of beans rolling off into the distance and I know I'm going back tomorrow.

It's not like I'm picking bean walking over River, or anything. I'm not.

River pulls up in front of the house. "Thanks, Bliss," he says, real sweet, "for helping." And I make my way up the driveway, where the house is dark except for the porch light. I didn't think it was so late.

Aunt Trish is wide awake on the sofa, watching the clock instead of her show. "Did you forget something?" Her voice is sharp and cold.

My stomach sinks as I realize it's way past curfew. I told her I was missing dinner, but that was hours and hours ago. I open my mouth to explain, and Mama comes out of the bathroom trailing a cloud of steam. She has a green facial masque on, and Aunt Trish's ratty old pink robe hangs off her even though she's wrapped the belt around a bunch of times.

"Finally!" Mama says. "I had to start without you. There's still plenty of goop to do your face, too." She pulls my elbow towards the bathroom, and I follow, confused. Did I know about this? Mama grabs my chin and slathers cool green mud on my cheeks, dripping on my shirt and the bathroom floor.

Aunt Trish appears at the doorway. "Bliss has some explaining to do. Thirty-seven minutes' worth of explaining, as a matter of fact."

"I didn't think . . ." I can't spit out my reasons. Or my apology.

"Keep still," says Mama, who quick ties back my hair and slaps mud on my forehead and chin.

"No, you don't think, do you? I've been worried out of my mind, sending texts that don't get answered, picturing you dead by the side of the road—or worse—Bliss, you need to think of someone besides yourself. Have a little courtesy."

I instantly feel terrible. Patsy's usually the one making us miss curfew, or she comes up with a story so we can sleep out at Granny's.

"I haven't been late in—" I say, trying not to move my mouth.

"Lay off, Trish." Mama's voice is as cold and heavy as the face masque.

"Curfew is important, Theresa."

"Not to me it's not. She's clearly fine. Or she will be once we unclog her pores."

Aunt Trish folds her pudgy arms. "So that's all it takes, is it? Clear skin? A pretty smile?" She shakes her head slowly. "Not everyone can waltz through life trading on their good looks."

Mama steps back like she's been punched in the gut, and I

reach out my hands to protect her, but then she tugs on the belt of the bathrobe and leans towards Aunt Trish. "Oh, but following all the rules? That's going to get her out of this secondhand house in this backwards town?"

"It was good enough to leave your daughter in all these years."

Mama gasps, and I do, too. My hands are in fists by my sides, and I swear I could punch Aunt Trish right in the stomach.

Mama puts her hands up to her cheeks, getting fresh green goop on them. She opens and closes her mouth, cracking the masque.

Then she bursts out in tinkling laughter. "My daughter, Trish. *My* daughter." She puts her arm around my waist and squeezes. "Go to bed, Trish. My daughter and me are going to have some bonding time."

The masque dries and tightens on my face, beginning to itch, but as long as Mama's got her arm around me, I'm not moving a single inch. No matter what.

Seventeen

My ass is dragging but my pores are clear as I climb into the Malibu with Patsy way before sunrise. She was asleep when I got in the room last night, so I don't think she heard us in the bathroom.

Patsy chugs her Diet Coke—the only one there was—and says, "Tired?"

Like she can't tell from the way I'm leaning against the door with my eyes closed.

After a while, Patsy clears her throat, then asks, "So what is it like? Having your mama here?"

Maybe she did hear us last night.

I touch my masque-smoothed cheek, remembering Mama's fingers on my skin. "It's nice. She's always got something going on."

"She sure does," Patsy says. She drives for a minute, then shakes her head. "My mom would never do face masques at midnight. Especially not if I had to be at work super early."

It's too bad that Aunt Trish doesn't want to bond with Patsy the way Mama wants to bond with me. But I don't want to rub it in, so I just say, "Mama has her own ideas about things, I guess."

Patsy laughs and says, "Hard to believe they're sisters, isn't it? One's a hard-core mom, and one's all about having fun." She goes to finish off her Diet Coke, but instead she holds the can out to me. "Here. So you don't fall asleep in the beans."

I smile at her, then close my eyes as I finish off her drink.

The truck is less crowded without Jimmy and Clark, but Blake manages to fill the space just fine. I don't know what River was so worried about. It's not like I'm going to break up with him. Especially now that he's losing Granny's.

I've never really broke up with any of my boyfriends; we always just reached a time when I got tired of getting it on anywhere they could find a place, and we just stopped being together.

River's different. I mean, he loves me more than any of my other boyfriends did—plus River needs me. He can do so much in his life, if only somebody'll believe in him.

But for some reason today, Blake is everywhere I look. A crow yells from behind me, and when I turn to see it, Blake is back there with Aggie, laughing as they walk and cut weeds. A tiny car moves across the horizon, making its way down the far-off highway, and he is standing there watching it pass. I bend down to tie my shoe, and when I stand, his movement catches my eye.

It doesn't matter. Whatever it is about Blake and me, it is

not happening, plain and simple. I fucked up that night at the party, but that's all. If he would just stop looking at me and quit asking me stupid questions and acting like he cares about what my answers are . . .

I make sure to keep some distance between us at all times, and if I accidentally smile back when he catches my eye and smiles at me, I quick put my head down and walk the beans hard to make up for Clark and Jimmy being gone.

As I get close to where everyone is eating lunch, I hear Patsy talking to Aggie and Beth where they sit in the shade of Blake's truck.

"Oh, you'll love this story. My mom and dad got married *first*, like you are *supposed to*, and then they got busy and ended up with me. They picked out this baby shirt that said, 'Grandma's Little Angel,' and they gave it to my gramma for Valentine's Day. She of course lost her shit and started crying all over Mom and Dad."

"Cute," says Aggie.

But I know what's coming. And it isn't cute. I should be getting my sandwich, but I've kind of lost my appetite, knowing where this story goes.

Patsy keeps blabbing. "Which should be like the first positive memory of my life, but just wait. Bliss's mom was there at the dinner, and after everybody had calmed themselves the fuck down, all happy and shit, she just randomly says, 'Oh, hey. That's around when *my* baby is due,' and not one person at that dinner even remembered the little Patsy bun in Mom's oven.

They only remembered the Bliss bun in Aunt Theresa's oven, which completely should not have been there because she was barely eighteen and just started modeling up in Chicago, and she's not even sure who the dad is."

Jesus.

Is Patsy *this* upset about the Nathan stuff? I barely breathe as I move farther away from the truck, hoping they don't see me.

"Sad," says Beth. "But how fun that Bliss lives with you. My big brother ditched me all the time, so I never had anyone to play with."

"You'd think. But I have to share my room, and they made me get rid of my chandelier because it gave her headaches. And now she's making up stories about Nate when we were younger." Patsy stands up and looks right in my eyes. "If she won't get out of my room, she can at least get out of my business."

I make myself pick up the cooler and go sit away from everyone—Blake, Patsy, all of them—while I choke down my sandwich.

Maybe she's right. Maybe I was trying to turn her against Nate, telling her what happened. But he deserves it.

A shadow falls over me. "Are you all right?" Blake says.

I shrug.

"That was . . . pretty harsh."

"It's just Patsy. I'm used to it."

He raises his eyebrows like he doesn't even begin to believe me, then shakes his head. "Family, right? So complicated." He sits down across from me.

"Yours seems fine."

"If by fine you mean always stressed-out and constantly disappointed."

"Really?"

"Let's see. Promising older brother refuses to run the family farm. Disappointing younger brother chooses five different career paths in four months, quits every sport, club, and job he's ever been in . . . father hasn't smiled in months, maybe years. No, in fact, I was wrong. We're fine."

We laugh together, but I say, "You sure had me fooled. All this time, I thought you were perfect. Patient, funny, and a good teacher, too."

"Huh." He pauses. "Same here. You seemed smart, observant. Clearly I was misinformed."

He's so far on the other side of wrong. But something warms in my stomach just the same.

Blake looks at his watch and stands up. "But I do have the cure for family drama."

"You do? Would it have anything to do with beans? Or weeds?"

"I was right the first time. You *are* smart and observant."

Blake is not wrong. Once I get back into the rhythm, I can sort of leave Patsy behind and zone out while I slog through the thick air chopping weeds. I tie my shirt around my waist so I can cool off in my bikini top. Before I know it, we are loading up the truck to head back to the church, another day behind us.

Patsy and them head to Aggie's car, and Blake and me laugh for a second while he hands down the coolers. Right as I turn towards Patsy's car, River steps out of the shade where his truck is parked. How did I not see him there?

He ambles over to us. "Blake Wu."

Blake stands head and shoulders above us all in the bed of his truck. His open face has a half smile, like nothing ever bothers him, and he squints down at us.

"River."

River looks Blake over. Patsy watches the whole thing, her narrowed eyes going back and forth between River and Blake.

"What are you doing here?" I ask River, a little too loud.

"We're going for a swim, babe," he says. "Hop in." He jerks his head at his truck. With Blake watching, River's voice seems bossy and mean. Almost like he thinks I'm stupid or something. For a second, I wish I could climb in next to Patsy and leave River standing here in the parking lot.

But then I remember about Granny's, and I shake the feeling off, walk the cooler over to Patsy, and hold it out for her to take.

"It's nice the way River talks so sweet to you," Patsy says, and her eyebrows go way up.

"Bye, Patsy." I half jog to catch up with River, who is already in the driver's seat before I even reach the truck.

"What are you, trying to get a suntan?" River eyes my bikini top.

The truck is running, but he hasn't pulled out yet.

"Maybe," I say. "Why are you here?"

"I told you. Cracker and them are at the lake. You do the beans like that?" He cuts his eyes over to where Patsy's leaned against Aggie's car with Beth. "Don't see Patsy and her lovers letting it all hang out."

"You know Patsy's with . . ." I can't even say Nathan's name, and if I could, River would know something was up in about two seconds. I hope to hell telling Patsy wasn't as big a mistake as it feels like right now. "Patsy doesn't like girls. Besides, Aggie and Beth are crazy about each other."

"Like you're crazy about your boss?"

I go cold all over. What does he know? My hands clench up tight together in my lap. "That what you want, huh? You and that college boy, rich fucker? I seen how you are together."

I let my hands relax, lay them flat on my legs. There's nothing to worry about. He doesn't know about that night at the elephant grave.

Even without Blake watching, the straight meanness in River's voice hurts my ears. Before I can say anything, though, River says, "Once I lose Granny's that's what happens. You going after him and every other rich boy. Guaranteed."

Wait. "Granny's? So soon?"

"Motherfucking sign went up today," he says, and now I know where all the mean is coming from. This can't be easy for him. I push myself up under River's arm as he turns off towards the lake. His shirt sticks to his side from all the humidity, but I squeeze in tight and put my hand on his leg.

River pushes me off him. "Jesus, Bliss. You've got beans and shit all over you. Wait till after we go swimming, would you?"

I go to argue with him, tell him it's just dirt, but I give in, let him say what he wants, like always. It's so much easier than being mad. Especially when he needs me like this.

Eighteen

"*Don't be mad* we left before everyone," I tell River as he pulls up in front of Patsy's later. "It's just, Aunt Trish will be pissed if I miss dinner."

Well, she's probably still pissed from last night, but it was worth it to spend time with Mama.

"I'm not mad," he says, but he won't look at me, and he keeps his hands on the steering wheel. My throat tightens up, and my back gets all stiff.

"I'd rather be with you," I tell him, sliding my hand up under his black T-shirt, wet from his dripping hair. I snuggle close so he can feel me against him. I look up at him, but he's staring out the window like there's a movie playing out there.

His chin is sharp, and his jaw muscles twitch, so I know he doesn't believe me.

"You know I would."

His chest is damp where the shirt stuck to it, and I lean over to kiss his neck, which smells like sunscreen and lake water. I can't leave him like this, mad and all crazy about Granny's.

I work my way up until I reach his lips, which are hard and don't budge when I kiss them. I try to slide my tongue between them, but he won't let me in.

I have to try harder.

"Too bad it's broad daylight," I say in a sexy voice. "I could climb on top of you right here." I lean into him and kiss him again, and he almost kisses me back.

"I should just do it anyways," I say, and his lips, under mine, slide into a smile.

"Yeah, right."

"I will."

"Won't." His arms slide around me. "Not in a million years," he says, finally kissing me back.

The tightness in my throat eases, and I don't think about Aunt Trish's face last night as Mama and me slammed the door on her. I just kiss, and kiss, and lean over a little bit as River slides his hands into my top to get at my boobs.

"Halloooo!" I hear, and I look up to see Mama's face right up against River's window. "Playtime's over, kids. Mama's home."

Clyde appears next to her, and my face turns seven shades of red.

I jump away from River, straighten myself up, and grab my bag. "Text me," I say, and jump out of the truck.

Mama and Clyde hoot with laughter as I run into the house.

Aunt Trish's lips are in a straight line, but she says hello, so maybe she's not too upset about last night. It's not her fault she didn't understand that Mama and me needed girl time. I feel bad that her and Patsy don't have as much fun together as we do. If only she could let Patsy go to beauty school, maybe they'd get along better. But none of that's my fault.

Still, I hustle through a shower so I can help her out with dinner.

"I'll do the salad," Aunt Trish says, sounding more tired than her usual self. "Can you collect dishes from the garage? Leo's stolen all my mugs again."

Uncle Leo is working on his boat. Like always. The combined smells of motor oil and burnt coffee and faint cigarette smoke left over from before he quit smoking wrap me up and let me step out of time.

A cheer comes from the little TV on the workbench as someone hits a high fly to center field, and I could be any age from twelve on up, listening to the game while I sit and watch Uncle Leo work. The exact same stuff is spread out over the counters—engine parts and half-empty oil cans, an orange extension cord and a zillion tools whose outlines wait for them on the pegboard wall. Uncle Leo only puts them back once or twice a year, digging around on the bench instead to find the 5/16 wrench when he needs it.

I go right to my usual seat without thinking—the stool is dusty, but Uncle Leo has left it right where it used to be. Just like

I never left, like I never stopped coming here once me and Patsy started high school. Uncle Leo gives a little half smile and points to the bench in front of me. "Rag?"

I pass him the cleanest rag I can find, and he wipes the grease off the engine part after he nods his thanks. He's not as skinny as he was when I used to hang out here—he blames it on quitting smoking—but otherwise, he's just the same as when I was little. Him and Patsy both have those wide shoulders and big hands, and if he didn't have his summer cut, his dark wavy hair would curl around his ears just like Patsy's does.

I never missed having a dad—Mama said she didn't know what happened to him anyway—but sometimes I wonder if he would have let me watch baseball with him, or make waffles on Saturdays like me and Uncle Leo do.

"I've almost got her ready," he says, and jerks his head back at the silver fishing boat, which takes up all the space a car would use if this was a real garage and not Uncle Leo's workshop. "Might be able to get her out next week some time."

I don't remember the last time the boat was out of this garage, and I sure as hell don't remember the last time I was even out here.

Somebody steals second base, and the crowd cheers on the little TV. "She wants the mugs," I tell him.

Uncle Leo winces, his round cheeks bobbing up and down, then scrubs his hands through his buzz cut. "All of them?"

We look at the workbench together as the pitcher walks the batter, searching for multicolored coffee cups hiding in all his

180

other shit. There are one, two, three—

"All six of them."

He moves aside a notepad and holds up a yellow mug. "Seven. At least."

"I can't carry all of them," I say, laughing.

"You gotta help me out, kid. I show up with this many dirty mugs and Trish'll have my head." He dumps bolts and nails out of a storage bin. "Put 'em in here."

The door bangs open, and Mama stands there, lit from behind like somebody plugged her in. When I think of all the times I wished for her here, imagined her showing up just like this, pictured her scooping me up and taking me away with her, I get a pain in my stomach.

"Oh, thank god. You're here." It's impossible to tell if she means me or Uncle Leo, so we both just stand there like parking meters, waiting for her to put a quarter in.

The smile on her face is bigger than I've ever seen it. "Hurry, baby. I snagged a reservation for six o'clock: you need to know how to talk to these people. Go get ready!"

"For what? I don't remember—"

"Dinner. Did you not hear me say I got the reservation? We have to leave in five minutes to make it on time." Her grin could not be any bigger. "And you do not want to miss this meal. Trust me."

"River and me have a—"

"He's small-town, Bliss. When you see what the world has to offer us, you'll look back and wonder how you wasted your time on a backwards, dead-end, hometown boy. No matter how sexy he is. Now come on!"

She whirls around and the door bangs shut behind her, just missing her hair.

The garage feels darker, like after someone shines a flashlight right in your eyes, then turns it off, leaving you with the memory of the light and unable to see in the deeper darkness.

Uncle Leo clears his throat. "Well. I guess you'd better get these mugs inside. Sounds like you're going out." He leans over to dump a green mug into the sink before balancing it on top of the rest. He hands me the bin and looks at me all serious before he lets go. "Theresa. She always did have big plans. You should know that."

I can't hardly look at him, his eyes are so kind. It makes me all squirmy inside.

"Trish and her, they don't have it easy. Never have. But bottom line, Trish would do anything for her baby sister."

I pull the bin, but he doesn't let go.

"Anything. Unless she was hurting somebody Trish cared about." He smiles. Then says, "This backwards, hometown boy's here if anybody needs him."

I nod, and the mugs rattle as Uncle Leo turns loose of the bin.

"Thanks." I smile so he knows I mean for more than the mugs.

Nineteen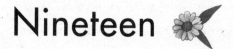

Clyde holds the door for us, and Mama and me both climb in the back of his car. Limo. Whatever it is. Even though it was over an hour ago, they are still cracking up over catching me and River going at it in his truck.

"God, Clyde, if I had a nickel for every time I had to have car sex! That was the best part about finally growing up, having a proper bed."

"Damn straight," he says, and reaches back to squeeze her knee, then turns to spit sunflower shells out the window. "But how about limo sex?" He laughs his big laugh, and I squeeze my eyes shut to get that image out of my mind.

"Bliss, honey, don't you worry. Soon you'll be dating men with apartments. Actual homes! This is all just a phase," Mama says.

The fields rush by as we go down the highway—corn, beans, some fields clean, some not—and I remember how pissed Aunt Trish was a few years ago when she came home early and caught me and my boyfriend Denny laying on the sofa together. We hadn't had time for anything but kissing, but she didn't know that, and she kicked him out right then and sat me down at the kitchen table for a lecture that lasted about an hour before she ran out of warnings and stories and promises of how terrible my life would be if I got pregnant or worse.

I didn't tell her that Denny was not my first real boyfriend, and she never caught on that I'd already had sex like a million times, so I just nodded my head like this was the first I had heard of any of this information. She wouldn't let me see Denny for like a week, and she watched all my boyfriends like a guard dog every time they came near the house for a while. We never talked about it again, but I knew she was watching.

"Quick stop, then off to dinner," Mama says as we pull in to the mini-mart. "Need any condoms?" She and Clyde crack up as they get out of the car, leaving me in the back seat all alone.

When we take off again, Mama is wound so tight she might just fly apart. She laces her fingers through mine and squeezes. "You mark my words; we will remember this night for the rest of our lives. And having our own personal driver is just the beginning. Oh, baby girl, I'm so excited for us!"

Clyde gives a little salute from the front seat. "Just cause it's not a stretch limo doesn't mean you can't have star treatment, a driver of your own."

Mama's jitters run all the way down to her hand, which

twitches against mine. She pulls my hand close, flips it over, and inspects my fingernails. "Good Lord, baby. We have got to fix these nails. All that farm work has ruined them."

"I'll have time when I'm done walking the beans."

"Time! Time is one thing we do not have," Mama says, and she clamps her free hand over her mouth. "Clyde, didn't I tell you I'd spill the beans?" Then she turns to me. "Not your kind of beans, sweetie. But I have big, big news!"

Clyde shakes his head slowly, eyes on the road. "Keep it together, Theresa."

A pit opens up in my stomach. No time? "Are you . . . leaving?" I ask, and the seconds spin out while I wait for an answer I don't think I want.

"She thinks we're leaving, Clyde," Mama says, and screeches a few laughs.

"She does," Clyde laughs back.

"Oh, Bliss. You are a hoot." Mama pats my arm. "Baby doll, just relax and enjoy your dinner. I promise you will not be disappointed."

The restaurant is inside of a mall, so we window-shop while we wait for our beeper to go off. Mama and me like the same kind of plates in the window of the department store, and she takes my side against Clyde when he says they're ugly.

We pop into the store and pretend to pick out glasses and mugs and placemats and towels, and then Mama drags me over to the baking section.

"Cookies!" She runs her fingers over the cookie cutters on display. "I can teach you to bake."

I start to tell her I already know how to bake, I'm a good baker, but she puts her arm through mine and keeps talking. "Can't you just see us? We'd make the best cookies. And then we could sit and eat them on those blue placemats with . . . those blue napkins. No . . . white ones. We might even let Clyde eat some, if the plates aren't too ugly for him. Oh, we are going to have so much fun, the three of us."

That doesn't sound like leaving talk. That sounds like . . . she's staying?

I don't even care that my stomach is growling and folding in on itself, I'm so happy to hear Mama's plans for our kitchen and our living room, in our very own place. By the time we are done looking, I'm pretty sure I've figured out the big news Mama wants to spring on me: she's staying here in Lakeville. *We're* staying here together. I'll still act like I'm surprised when she tells me, though.

I haven't let myself think about Mama staying even once since she came back, but since she started it, now I'm picturing us in a place of our own, with placemats and curtains and all that shit. There's some little houses over by school that would be nice for us. Or maybe Mama found an apartment we can rent. I don't even really care that Clyde will have to live with us, too, just so long as I get my own room. In a house—a home—with Mama.

The beeper shivers in my pocket, and I hand it to Clyde and

follow them into the restaurant. Once we get seated and order our food, Mama bounces on her chair and wiggles, and it's like me and Clyde are the mom and dad, because he says, "Settle down, Theresa," and I make her take a drink of her water to calm down.

But the more excited she gets, the more excited I get, and I wish she would just come out and say it already so we can celebrate.

Clyde's and Mama's meals come out a whole five minutes before mine. If they asked, I woulda said to go ahead and eat, but they don't, and they are both practically finished with their food when mine finally shows up.

"Well, that is just wrong," says Mama. "You should do something."

I don't know what to say to that.

"I am serious, baby girl. Just smile real pretty and tell him to just give it to you. If I had to count the number of freebies I've gotten for a smile . . . anyway, it's their fault it's late."

"You got that same smile as your mom, kid. If you turned it on me, I might even dump your mama."

I decide then and there that I'm never smiling at Clyde for as long as I live.

"Clyde, you would not!" Mama slaps his arm, but she's laughing. Like it doesn't even bother her that he would hit on me. "But honest to Pete, baby, use what you've got. Life is so much better."

I decide to focus on my food, but I barely get two bites in my mouth before Mama sets down her fork and stares at me until I set down my fork, too.

"So." Mama smiles ear to ear at me.

"So," I say back, trying not to smile as big as her and failing big-time.

"I think I got it all figured out." She grabs my hand across the table.

"Yeah?" I lean forward, thinking of all sorts of promises of how I'll make this good for us. I won't care where we live; I won't get all fussy about what color we paint my room; I will be easy to live with, even if it kills me.

Anything so we can be a family in our own house.

Mama laughs again and bounces once more, then gives a little squeal. "I cannot believe I have kept this under wraps for the entire dinner."

"Me neither," says Clyde.

"Hush, you." Mama smiles at him, then turns back to me. "Bliss, honey. I did it. I worked it out. Take a good look at my face, because you are looking at half of the hottest mother-daughter modeling team to hit Eastern Europe." Mama's voice goes higher and higher as she talks. "Europe, baby. You and me. We're going to Europe!"

Mama hops up from the table and pulls me out of my seat. She hugs me tight and jumps up and down, and somehow, I jump, too, even though I can't feel my arms and legs.

"It's our dream, baby. Our dream come true!"

Our dream come true.

I don't even have to act surprised—I was all set to hear that Mama was staying, that we'd have a home together here, with placemats and cookie cutters—I never ever thought she'd really take me with her overseas. Not after last time.

"But you said I couldn't come. That it was—"

"Times change, baby girl! SMOOCH wants *us* to model, and this mother-and-daughter team is not going to let them down!"

Mama's mouth moves and says more stuff about the job and the travel and probably some other things, but the sounds don't really go all the way into my brain, they just swirl around my head as I try to make sense of what she said.

Europe. Together.

Holy Shit.

"Christ, is that the time? Theresa, we have to hit it," says Clyde, poking at his huge phone with his tiny fingers. "You've got that call."

The waiter comes to check on our food.

"Bring the check," Mama says. She shoves my bowl at the waiter, who dumps Mama's plate into it and stacks them up.

"I wasn't finished," I say, and the waiter turns ten colors of red and freezes with his hands on the dishes.

"Sorry. So sorry. I can bring you another," he says. He looks like he might cry.

"No, no. She's fine. We're in a hurry."

The waiter looks at me, still frozen.

I'm frozen, too—my brain tries to move forward, make words and shit, but every way my thoughts try to turn, the word

Europe rises up and sends them zooming back on themselves.

I take a deep breath and wave the waiter away.

"You sure?" The bowls teeter in his hands.

"She's fine. Leave the check." Mama's upset they charged us for my dinner, and I try to follow the discussion. "He simply stood right there staring at my baby girl instead of clearing the table. Ten percent is much more than he deserves. Why, in Japan—"

"We're not in Japan, Theresa."

Mama hugs me around the neck, puts her forehead against mine, and goes all singsong on me. "We're also not in Europe, but we're gonna be!"

I hug her back and try to stop my head from spinning.

Modeling.

Overseas.

With Mama.

On the way back, Mama sits with me again for star treatment, but she spends the whole ride home telling Clyde the story of how hard it was for her to wait to tell me, and he cracks sunflower seeds and praises her for keeping the secret all through dinner.

I look out the window, my stomach just as empty as on the way there, but my head a billion times fuller.

Mama just about dances in the door, dragging me behind her. "Trish! Pa-tricia!" Mama grabs the remote and turns off the baking show Aunt Trish and me always watch when we fold laundry. She pulls me over to the sofa and sits me down next to her, right on top of a pile of clean bedsheets. "Trish, you will never in a hundred years guess what Bliss and me have planned!"

Aunt Trish straightens a stack of towels that Mama bumped and raises her eyebrows. "You're running off to join the circus?"

Mama laughs and leans over and grabs Aunt Trish's face, kissing her smack on the middle of her forehead. "No, silly! Better! Way better!" Mama is like a balloon that's gonna pop any second if she can't let out her news.

Aunt Trish's eyes wobble back and forth from me to Mama, then she sighs and says, "What do you and Bliss have planned, Theresa?"

"Eastern Europe!" Mama pulls me right up close to her so our two heads are touching side by side. "You're looking at the most amazing mother-daughter modeling team to hit the scene in the whole century!" She jumps up, knocking the towels to the floor, and pulls me up with her. "Strike a pose, baby. Our first mother-daughter catwalk!"

Before I know what I'm doing, we are strutting up and down in front of the coffee table, stopping in front of Aunt Trish with our shoulders back and our elbows out. Mama laughs and dances, and she's here and real, and so goddamn happy that my spirits rise to match hers. I grab Uncle Leo's work shirt from the top of his pile and sling it over my shoulder like I've seen on *America's Next Top Model*. I wonder what they do on *Europe's Next Top Model*?

"Trish! Isn't this the most incredible idea? We can't lose with this angle."

Aunt Trish looks at me, and her eyes are tired, like somebody just told her she's got twenty more loads of laundry to go before she can sit and watch the end of her show. "Bliss, honey, is this what you want?"

"Of course it's what she wants! What she's always wanted! It's what any teenage girl in her right mind wants," Mama says, and reaches up to put her arm around my shoulders. "It's win-win, Trish. We'll get a killer contract, and I'll get to rescue my baby from a boring, small-town life. She'll travel the world and make a name for herself as one of the Walker Girls—no, Walker Women—and she can learn a new language and so much more!"

Heat is coming off of Mama like she's my own personal sun. Her eyes are bright and shiny, and they light a tiny spark in my middle, a small flame of hope and possibility. I feel warm for the first time in a real long time as I put my arm around Mama's skinny waist.

Aunt Trish moves very slowly as she picks up the towels and dumps them back in the laundry basket. She takes a blue one out and carefully matches the corners, then the edges, shaking it so it lines up before she folds it again and again and starts a new pile. Mama is quiet, waiting to hear what Aunt Trish says, but she practically buzzes under my arm.

"So you've learned a lot of Japanese in your time there, have you, Theresa?" Aunt Trish's voice is as flat as the yellow towel she sets on top of the blue one. "Made a name for yourself?" She snaps a blue hand towel out to straighten it. "Bliss has one more year of school. What do you intend to do about that?"

Mama sags a little bit underneath my arm, and I want her to stay happy, to stay excited and full of her plans that include me for the first time in almost six years, so I decide right then and there: I'm all in on the Europe plan. We can see castles and eat strange-sounding pastries and speak a new language.

"I can get a tutor. Or take that test that lets you pass high school—the GLE?" I blurt out.

Aunt Trish's eyes widen, and her head snaps back, like I cracked a whip in her face or something. "You want to get your GED?"

"Yeah, that. I can study real hard and take it before we leave."

"And when will you be leaving?" Aunt Trish is not having any of this.

I've seen Aunt Trish shut down Patsy a million times when she gets her back up, and all I can hope is me and Mama together are strong enough to go against her.

"Oh, Thomas said somewhere near the end of the month." Mama smiles.

"Theresa, that's barely enough time to—"

"THERESA!" Clyde roars from the top of the stairs. "You about done up there? We got us some celebrating to do." He holds up a full bottle of whiskey and acts out drinking right from the bottle. His gut wobbles in his white T-shirt, and I try and remember if anybody said whether Clyde was coming to Europe or not.

Mama takes her arm away from me and walks towards him. With Mama gone, the little flame of hope flickers in my middle, and if Aunt Trish does anything to stomp it out I might never forgive her. I don't even look at Aunt Trish as I follow Mama to the stairs for our celebration.

Clyde slaps Mama on the butt and hooks the arm with the whiskey around her neck. Then he sees me behind her. "Oh no you don't. This here is a private celebration." He wiggles his caterpillar eyebrows at Mama, and she turns to look at me.

"Grown-up fun, baby. You understand. Go call all your little friends and tell them the big news." She wiggles her fingers at me, then closes the door to the basement so fast I have to jump out of the way or get my toes caught.

"Mmm-hmm," says Aunt Trish from behind me.

I turn away from her and walk down the hall to Patsy's room, moving slowly and carefully to keep the spark from going out. Mama's taking me with her. Nothing will stop us this time. Nothing.

Twenty

"*Bliss. What the* fuck?"

Patsy is standing over me, and every light in her room is on. I fell dead asleep wearing all my clothes as soon as I came in here last night, but it feels like just seconds ago. I close my eyes again.

"Come on. We have to bust our asses to meet up with Blake."

"In a minute."

"Move." Patsy rips the sheets off me and throws my clothes at me. "Your. Ass. Aggie has an audition, so they might not come, and I am not walking beans all by myself."

I'm finally awake, and I shake off my heavy dreams while I throw on my clothes. There's not time to braid my hair, so I yank it into a pony, and it's so tangled it hurts to even finger-comb it. Patsy's hair is done up in some twisty braid, and she looks like she's ready for the junior prom. "Nice do," I tell her, maybe a little mean.

But she doesn't even notice. "Thanks. Beth is really talented."

The only good part is there's two Diet Cokes in the fridge on top of the cooler. I give one to Patsy and I wade through a half-awake fog, following her out to the porch. Where I stop dead on the top step.

"Oh no." I squeeze the cooler and my bag and Diet Coke and shake my head. "No." There are puddles all over the drive-way, and the sky is full of heavy gray clouds.

"It's only rain. It's not supposed to storm until like tomorrow. Or even later."

"You don't know that."

Patsy looks at her watch, walks back up the steps, pulls the cooler and my bag out of my locked arms. She tosses them in the back seat of the Malibu.

"Move it." She comes back to the steps, gets behind me, and pushes me to the car.

"We can't work if it's raining."

"Blake texted all of us last night. Which you would know if you ever kept a fucking charge. We don't work if it's lightning or thunder. We do if it's just rain."

She shoves me a little to make me get in the car. "And this is just rain. I knew you would bust a tit if it was gonna storm, so Mom and Dad and me watched the weather for you, even after you skipped out on dinner." She slams the door. "So you're welcome."

Patsy joins me in the car, then backs out and tears off to the church.

I ignore her comments and poke her in the arm. "There's no storm?"

"Jesus Christ. Just rain."

My eyes are burning and scratchy, and I almost fall asleep as we make our way to the church. All of a sudden, I remember clear as day: Mama is taking me to Europe.

Soon.

"Stop," I say, smacking Patsy on the arm.

Patsy slaps my hand away.

"Take me back."

"Nope."

"I'm not going."

"Wrong."

"Patsy." I grab her arm. "Mama and me are going to Europe. By the end of the month. I'm going to be a model. I don't have to walk the beans."

"Oh yeah?" Patsy raises up her eyebrows at me. "Where in Europe?"

"Eastern Europe," I tell her.

She takes a drink of her Diet Coke, then slams it into the drink holder. "First, it's not a thunderstorm. Second, the end of the month is not today. Third, fuck you if you think I'm missing my chance to save up for beauty school just because of some bullshit story your mom is telling you."

"Bullshit story? We have a deal for a mother-daughter modeling job."

Patsy pulls into the church parking lot and slams the car

into park. "I told you she was here for a reason."

"And I'm the reason," I tell her. "She wants me with her."

Patsy shakes her head. "I don't buy it. You're not dumb, Bliss, so don't be stupid. When has your mom done anything for you, like . . . ever? There is a reason, and if it's not all about her, let's just say I'll believe it when I see it. We all will." She takes the keys out of the ignition and jams them in her pocket. "But feel free to sit here until after lunch when we're done. Or walk your ass home. Don't suppose your phone is charged?"

I sit in the Malibu alone as Patsy climbs in Beth's car to wait. Aunt Trish is never gonna come through and let Patsy go to beauty school, and she can't hardly stand it that Mama has plans with me. She's jealous, like always. There's nothing she loves more than poking holes in my happiness.

I can hear Patsy's muffled laughter and singing and Aggie's uke strumming from Beth's car. Right then and there, I decide the rainbow song is going to be my thank-you to Mama for taking me to Europe with her. If I walk the beans, maybe Aggie will help me learn it.

So when Blake pulls up, I get into his truck. Patsy smiles like she knew I'd go along with them, but I just shrug at her and climb in the back.

Patsy climbs in and shuts the door. "Aggie's audition is later, so they're going separate," she announces, then pats her hair and looks out at the rain as we drive.

* * *

Patsy was partly right earlier. It's not storming. But it is raining. And raining. The raindrops aren't very big, but they just fall, and fall, and fall. The far-off trees are blurry dark lumps, and everything else is the same color gray all the way to the horizon.

Our hair, of course, is soaked, and mine weighs about ten pounds. The rain makes the dirt between rows into a foot-sucking mud pie. There's a squelching sound every time I pull my foot up to take a step. I think we cover one down-and-back in the time we made it through two or even three yesterday.

The crazy thing is, everybody's freakishly happy. Like, so fucking happy. Like squishing through the mud with a wicked-sharp stick and slicing up weeds is the most fun thing ever. Patsy and Aggie and Beth crack themselves up singing every Disney song ever invented, and Blake and me follow along, smiling.

The whole time they are singing, I'm trying to think of how to ask Aggie about the uke without sounding like a dumbass or a stalker. I'm turning it over in my mind when Blake catches up with me.

"You're not a singer?"

"I don't know the songs."

"A girl who doesn't know every word to every Disney song?" And I'm so funny again. I look over at him through the rain, and he's got that grin on his face.

"I didn't see the movies when I was little. Mostly only after I was older."

"Is that even allowed?" He looks at me, then cuts a small tree.

"I do keep waiting for the Disney police to show up."

We squish forward, cutting weeds every few steps, getting rained on. Just me and my boss, not talking, not smiling, just squishing through the mud and cutting weeds here and there.

Finally, I say, "I still can't believe Kay was a killer."

"Not on purpose. But, listen: one time, Kay made a break for it."

"She escaped?"

"She ran away, and she was free for almost a whole day before they caught her."

"What? How?"

"It was up in Chicago—close to my old house, actually. The article said Kay and another elephant, Barbara, were traveling with the circus. An airplane buzzed past the circus right when they were moving the elephants from the train to their tents, and Kay and Barbara both freaked out and took off running in different directions."

"Go, Kay!"

"Right? Imagine sitting on your swing set in your backyard and all of a sudden, *bam!* The fence slams down and an elephant comes walking in. An elephant!" Blake's smile is huge and bright.

I walk along, thinking about that kid on the swing. "I bet she blew their minds."

"Completely! Just think, all her life, she's been locked up, and then one day she's able to go anywhere she wants. I bet *that* blew *her* mind."

I go a few feet, slice a sticker bush and dodge it as it comes down. "I think she musta been scared."

"Scared? Kay?" Blake looks at me, his big eyebrows raised way up.

"Well, yeah. All her life she knew what was expected, what she was supposed to do. And then she was all alone, lost, in a big city. I wonder, did she even know where she was trying to go? Or did she just run away as fast as she could? I bet nothing looked familiar and everything smelled weird."

We walk in silence for a few minutes, and then Blake shakes his head. "See, I picture her happily busting fences and stomping flowers, so excited to try something new. Whatever she wants."

He laughs his warm laugh, and the rain lets up to just a drizzle then. Or maybe I just don't notice it so much.

Twenty-one

Even though the rain stops, everything is soaked and dripping and squishing for the rest of the morning. I'm pretty sure I have a rash where my wet shorts rub against my legs, and I can only guess how pruney my feet are inside my soggy shoes.

Steam rises up from the beans, the mud, and the five of us. I thought if only it would stop raining, the walking would be easier, but that is not the case. The fucking sun comes out and pushes down on us with its heat, making a sandwich of hell as we walk. Only it's more like torturously slow marching because we have to pull each foot out of the sucking mud with every step.

Right before lunch break, I end up walking even with Aggie. We had health class together, and she's been out to Granny's, but we haven't really been friends before now.

I want to ask her about the uke, but the words are stuck in my throat, and my lips are sealed shut. I'm going to count to three, and then I will say something, anything about her playing. One, two—

"Aggie," Blake says, making both of us jump as he catches up with us in his row. "What time do you leave for your audition?"

"Noon? I thought I'd go home and clean up to make a good first impression."

Blake flashes a smallish smile at her. "You're pretty good on your ukulele. How long have you been playing?"

"I really only started about two years ago. I never played an instrument before, but the minute I got that uke in my hands, it was like I was home, like I'd always been able to do it."

"But those chords are fucking impossible," I blurt out.

Aggie swings her head over to me, a big smile on her face. "You play?"

My ears get hot and I swipe at a cornstalk that doesn't really need it. "If you call knowing just a G chord and a C chord playing."

"Those first chords! I thought I was dying, trying to make my fingers twist all around to get it right."

Blake laughs, too, saying, "Guitar isn't any easier. My friend Joel kept saying, 'Dude. They're *your* fingers. Own the frets.'"

They talk about songs and chords for the rest of the row, comparing guitar to ukulele, and instead of feeling like an outsider, I feel like I almost belong in the conversation, like I'm nearly speaking their language.

We come out for lunch break, and Aggie hangs back by the end of the row, asking about my ukulele and how long I've had it and what I'm doing to learn how to play. I tell her the whole story of Mama and how I want to learn the one song, and she tells me we should get together so she can teach it to me.

We drift over to the coolers, and I am so relieved I didn't have to think up a way to ask Aggie, and I'm super jazzed to get taught by practically a pro, and I can't believe I almost didn't come today.

I catch Blake's eye and I smile at him, glad he asked Aggie about her playing. He smiles back.

Patsy, however . . .

"We've been out for fucking ever. What took you so long?" She stands in front of the cooler with her arms crossed.

"Walking the beans, Patsy. Same as you." I take a step to the left.

Patsy steps to the left, too. Her fishbone braid or whatever it was didn't last long in the rain. She's got her hair up in a wilty bun, and there's dried mud on her cheek. She stands like a soccer goalie, daring me to get past her to the cooler. Her eyes are the exact color of the sky, except they are one thousand times colder.

"Can I get my lunch?"

"I don't know. Can you?"

I can feel Blake watching us. "Not with you blocking the cooler, I can't."

"This is how normal people get things. They work for them. Sometimes, they don't get them at all."

"I need to eat, Patsy."

I get up real close and look down into her pissed-off, sky-blue eyes. I swear there's murder in there. Or at least a couple of good hair pulls. Who knows what set her off this time?

"I just want my—"

"Oh. My. Fucking. God." She jumps up and rips the top off the cooler. She reaches in, grabs my shit, and shoves it at me.

When I grab hold of it, she pulls the sandwich bag to bring me close. She narrows her eyes at me and mutters, "Someday, Bliss. Someday you'll want something enough to get it yourself, without having it handed to you on a silver fucking platter."

Blake's voice cuts between us. "Let's eat fast, everybody. Beth and Aggie have a tight schedule." Not exactly talking to Patsy, but not *not* talking to Patsy.

"Whatever." She spins around and stomps off.

Beth raises her eyebrows at me, and I just shake my head and pull out my sandwich. Beth and Aggie start talking loudly about their plans to get to the audition, and I shove food in my mouth. It tastes like the mud I'm standing in.

"Everybody ready?" Blake asks, and we pick up our bean hooks again. He points out the next field, which is across the ditch and across the road from where we are eating. "I think we have time for one more down-and-back before Aggie has to go."

He leads Aggie and Beth along the edge of the ditch to where the dirt road is built up across it. The rows start about even with where we ate lunch, but the ditch is completely blocking the way. We have to go around.

"Bliss! You coming?" hollers Aggie.

Patsy and me look at each other, then at the cooler between

us. Finally, I shrug and walk it over to Blake's truck, parked just off the dirt road.

"Better hurry. Your new best friend and boyfriend might get started without you," Patsy says in a low voice. "We all saw you two earlier when it was raining. And you can be sure River will hear about it."

"About what? Nothing—"

"Happened. Nothing ever happens, does it, Bliss? And you never mean for anything to happen, do you? You don't notice me making friends with Beth and Aggie and you don't mean to steal them away from me."

"Patsy, I—"

"I can't believe I tried to help you by getting you this job. That after everything, I felt sorry for you. And you return the favor by stabbing me in the fucking back. Again." She starts towards the others, then swings back towards me. "But why even bother if your precious mama is taking you away from here? Nate was right. You really are trying to ruin anything that's mine."

Patsy grips her bean hook and backs up a few steps, looking across the ditch to where everyone's waiting. "It's probably bullshit, but seriously, I hope to hell it's not. I hope that you go to Europe and leave me to my house, my parents, my boyfriend, and my friends." Patsy is madder than I've ever seen her, and I'm pretty sure everyone can hear her.

"Uh, guys?" Blake calls. "These beans won't walk themselves. Time is money, you know."

"Patsy—"

"Just because your mom ditched you with my family doesn't mean you get to steal my life from me. And I'm not gonna be late because of you."

Patsy turns away from me and jumps the ditch. She almost makes it, too.

If only the grass wasn't so wet from the rain.

If only she wasn't holding her bean hook in her hand.

If only she didn't try to catch herself on the other side of the ditch and forget she had a sharp, curved blade on the end of the pole in her hand.

The hand that swings back at the end of the jump, trying to propel her forward onto the far edge of the ditch. And slices the bean hook through the front of her thigh like it's just another stalk of volunteer corn.

"Oh," she says.

I shouldn't be able to hear such a small sound from so far away. But it's like Patsy is breathing right in my ear. The air has gotten so thick, and everything is moving so slowly.

Patsy crouches on the edge of the ditch, just barely keeping her balance. I look at her leg, and she looks at her leg, and the cut yawns open like a mouth, but instead of teeth, it has red bubbles of blood that burst and pour down her leg, and Patsy and me both just stare at it, like if we look long enough we can keep her from being cut.

Patsy drops the bean hook, and it tumbles back into the ditch. She turns and looks at me, blue eyes wide.

"Oh."

Twenty-two

"Ohmygod, Patsy, you're cut." Blake pounds across the road and sweeps Patsy up in his arms before I really understand what's happened.

Patsy can't be cut. She just jumped the ditch, is all. Maybe scratched herself.

"Bliss. Get the door." He's running towards the truck, carrying Patsy like she's made of air. She stares straight at me with a blank look.

"Beth. Call my dad. His number's on the cooler," Blake hollers over his shoulder as he runs.

I wade through molasses and reach the truck just seconds before he does. Blake shoves Patsy in the cab, then steers me in after her by my elbow. I can't seem to move in this slowed-down world.

Blake hikes his shirt over his head.

"Hold this over her leg. Push down." I'm frozen in place.

He puts his shirt in my hands, then grabs my shoulders. He locks eyes with me.

"Help her. Patsy needs you." He slams the door behind me.

And suddenly it hits me. Patsy cut her leg. Patsy's hurt. The bottom drops out of the universe, there is no up or down, and I reach out to steady myself. I look down and realize I'm holding Blake's T-shirt pressed against Patsy's leg. The world snaps into sharp focus again.

Blake is behind the wheel lightning fast, and we tear off down the road. I push a little harder and I look up at Patsy.

She's still just staring at me.

"I missed the edge," she breathes. "Wasn't my best jump." Her eyes are palest blue now, the color of the slushies we used to get back when we were twins and rode bikes in the summer.

"You'll do better next time," I say. My voice is all trembly. I smooth it out so Patsy doesn't get scared. I can't let her think about the cut or she'll lose her mind. "Or take the road like normal people."

She and Blake both laugh then, her laugh a little confused and his a little too loud.

"Who's walking the beans?" she asks.

Blake looks at Patsy, then down at her leg before he answers her. It's not really bleeding much, but I push on it anyways.

"Don't worry. We've got it covered."

"Bliss?" The skin around Patsy's eyes is all white and pinched and she reaches for my shoulder. I swear to god this is the longest drive to town I have ever taken in my life. Every telephone pole crawls past. Street signs hang off in the distance, then slowly grow larger until we come even with them, then they take their time fading past us. I can almost count the blades of grass along the road.

I lean into Patsy so she can hold my shoulder and I can hold her leg. To distract her with something, I say, "So Beth showed you some stuff from beauty school?"

Patsy's eyebrows come together like she's thinking real hard. Then she brightens. She still hasn't looked anywhere other than smack-dab at me since we got in the truck.

"She showed me a bunch. A Dutch braid, triple-cross, mermaid braid, and a couple others. Your hair would be perfect to practice on, but we used Aggie's and mine and it was fine. Beth is learning so much at school. I wish—"

She winces as we make the turn into town. I'm afraid to look at her leg, afraid she will look down at it, too, and lose her shit. Better to keep her talking.

"Which one did you like the best?"

"Which braid? Dutch is sorta classy—your hair is perfect for a Dutch braid, maybe a little too curly, but if we brushed it out real good it'd be fine. Mermaid is . . . ," she jabbers on, and I nod and smile like I'm paying attention so she will keep talking.

We are back to town now. The hospital isn't too far from here. At a stop sign, Blake looks over at me and nods, so I go on asking Patsy more questions. Maybe she will keep talking and forget why we are in the truck. And that she was super pissed at me when she jumped.

Tried to jump.

"What braid did Beth do on you?"

"If it didn't get ruined, you could see it was an upside-down French braid into a twisty bun. I don't know why it didn't last in the rain . . ." She runs down like a balloon that's losing its helium.

"Um, so, Beth is in school to learn how to do hair?" Just a couple more blocks. Why can't we turn left on red? We could go *right* on red. There's nobody coming the other way.

"I told you, she got a full ride. It's expensive otherwise. If only Mom would let me use my birthday money." Her voice gets wistful, and I almost ask her more about beauty school, but we are finally at the hospital.

I've only been here once to see some great-aunt about a million years ago. Where do we go? The sign says "Emergency," but it doesn't look like we can park by the doors.

Why is this so fucking complicated?

"I'll grab someone or a wheelchair. Sit tight." Blake pops out of the truck, and me and Patsy are left alone.

I risk a quick look at her leg. I thought it would be bleeding all over the truck and Blake's shirt, but there's just a thin red line across her thigh.

"Bliss?" Patsy's voice is tiny. She sounds like she used to back when I first stayed with her, when we thought we were just together for one school year. Before all the Nathan stuff.

We would stay up late watching scary movies, then Patsy would only go to sleep if I was right next to her.

She leans closer. "Stay with me?"

"Always." What is taking Blake so long? I thought an emergency meant lots of running around and hurrying and shit like that, but Patsy's emergency seems to involve lots of slow, agonized waiting.

"Bliss." Blake is outside the truck with a guy in cartoon-covered scrubs who pushes a hospital bed. "We're gonna slide you both out till the doctor can take over."

The doctor comes around on the other side of Patsy, and we inch, push, wiggle, lift, and slide her until she's lying down on the hospital bed. He asks her all kinds of questions in a calm voice, and she answers most of them.

I'm not sure how we do it, but we get her out safe, then take off into the emergency room. I run to keep up.

Blake has mine and Patsy's bags, and I dig for my phone as we run. "Call her parents." I shove my phone at him. "They should be here." We turn a corner of the longest hallway I've ever seen.

Blake frowns at my phone. "It's dead."

"Use hers, then. Trish and Leo. She needs me to—"

"Bliss?" Patsy sounds like when we were little, and the lights were out, and she was afraid to go to sleep.

"I'm right here."

* * *

It turns out that the doctor is really a nurse named Isaac. We tell him what happened, and he nods, like nothing could surprise him. He leans over her arm, and in a quick second, she's hooked up to some tubes and shit. He pushes buttons on a nearby machine, then says, "A little something for the pain."

He squirts yellow stuff on Patsy's leg, trades Blake's shirt for gauze and tape, then steps to the computer and types for a few minutes. The littlest hand on the big round clock on the wall creeps from one number to the next, slower than even school-time.

"What's taking the doctor so long?" I fuss.

"I'm not dying, so there's not as big of a hurry," Patsy says. Those pain meds must be kicking in.

"Good clean cut," says Isaac. "Plus the pressure? Kept it from bleeding as much." He goes back to typing. "You're lucky you had your friends to help you."

Patsy leans her head back and closes her eyes.

Blake steps in. He hands me Patsy's phone and whispers, "They're on their way." He looks almost more shaken than Patsy, but he smiles at her and says, a little too loud, "I thought we agreed the hooks were only for weeds."

Patsy smiles a tiny smile at him and closes her eyes. "Sorry."

Blake crowds next to me by Patsy's bed, and the room feels safer with all of us here together.

Isaac peeks under the gauze, then looks at Blake and says, "And you're the one who brought her in?"

Blake ducks his head.

"Quick thinking, man. You might've saved her life. Another inch, she would've cut the femoral artery. Probably have bled out by now if that had been the case. At any rate, good job."

Bled out.

My heart has suddenly realized what happened, and it pounds like I was the one who carried Patsy to the truck at a dead run. The air conditioning of the room hits my still-damp clothes and hair, and I get goose bumps on top of goose bumps. I keep seeing Patsy balanced at the top of the ditch, keep seeing the bean hook fall to the ground after cutting her, keep imagining it slicing an inch in either direction and making Patsy "bleed out." The strong smell of the disinfectant surrounds me and the room swims in my vision.

I must make some sound, because Blake leans against me, not looking at me or saying a word, just standing there, his elbow against mine, his solid shoulder leaning in, and my heart slows down and the room goes back into focus.

Patsy's okay.

She's gonna be okay.

I'm okay.

Until I realize Blake is standing there without a shirt on, that he gave his shirt to me to put on Patsy way back at the field. That he's leaning up against me with all his warm brown skin that shades into a darker brown farmer's tan on his arms and neck.

Then I'm way too hot, and I feel stupid for not noticing

him before, then stupid for noticing him at all, then stupid for worrying that Patsy can tell I'm noticing, then pissed that I am thinking of anything but Patsy.

I pull away from her a tiny bit, and she holds on to me for dear life. "Don't leave me."

I squeeze her hand. "Not until you're good and ready." And when she is, I'm gonna go see if somebody has an extra shirt that Blake can put on. Patsy shouldn't have to think about him giving up his shirt. She's got enough to worry about.

Aunt Trish arrives, rushing in like Patsy cut off the leg instead of sliced it open. Uncle Leo is next, and we all crowd in the room together. Blake and me leave when the doctor sends us out.

She is telling Patsy, "You're going to need quite a few stitches," as we go out to the waiting room.

"It's still light out?" I say, amazed.

"Right?" Blake says. "It feels like it should be the middle of the night."

I just want to curl up on a chair and go to sleep for a thousand days. Or at least have a Diet Coke. I set down Patsy's and my bags and Blake goes out to move the truck, and when he comes back in, he's wearing a gray T-shirt with the orange U of I logo on it.

"Don't get too close," he says when he sees me look at it. "It's been in the back of my truck for a very long time."

He also has two ice-cold, dripping bottles. One of water, one of Diet Coke.

"Pick your poison. Not much in the vending machine."

"This," I tell him, and grab the Diet Coke. He twists the cap off the water, and I watch him tilt his head back to drink it. His smooth throat moves as he swallows the water, one gulp at a time.

I shake my head to clear it and crack my bottle open. The cold, fizzy drink coats my scratchy throat and soothes my dry mouth. It's gone almost instantly, and I feel a whole lot more human, but I keep seeing Patsy jump, over and over and over.

"She tried to jump the ditch," I say.

"One minute she was standing there, and the next, she was cut," Blake says. He looks off in the distance, and I wonder if he's seeing it, too.

"She could have bled out," I say.

"She's so lucky."

"I just stood there staring at her. You were there so fast." If I keep telling it, maybe I will understand it.

"My reflexes just took over."

I take a deep breath. "If only she hadn't been so mad at me, maybe she wouldn't have jumped the ditch."

Blake shakes his head. "If only I hadn't tried to rush her back to work."

"It's not your fault."

"It's not *your* fault." He stands up, pacing back and forth next to me. "I'm the boss. Was the boss. Dad knew I'd mess it up. 'One mistake, son.' This is a big mistake."

I stand up next to him. "You saved her life."

He looks at me, and his face is haunted, like he's the one who sliced her with the hook. "He said I wasn't ready, and he was right. 'Time is money,' I told her."

"This wasn't about you. We were fighting when we should've been working."

Blake pulls out his phone and looks at it, sends a text. He collapses onto the chair and puts his head in his hands. Good thing he's just my boss, or I might want to pat his back, or touch his knee, or even hug him until the tension went out of his body.

Instead, I sit next to him, still as I can make myself. The silence stretches between us, and I finally say, "You okay?"

Blake laughs once, shakes his head, and laughs again, holds out his phone to show me the text from his dad. "'We'll talk about this when you get home.' That's what he said."

Blake puts his hand out, like for a handshake, and even though it's a terrible idea, I take his hand. He looks at me like he did when he pushed me away after we kissed, like he's just broken some law or spilled the last drop of water in a desert.

He says, "It's been nice working with you. If you want to stay on, I know whoever my dad hires will be happy to have you."

The warmth of his handshake distracts me from what he's saying, but then it sinks in. "He's going to fire you?"

"Not if I can quit first."

"You can't quit!"

"Sure, I can. I'm real good at it."

"But why?"

"Why?" Blake looks down at our hands, still clasped

together between us. "Patsy's stitches are why. Clark and Jimmy are why." His sad brown eyes bore into mine. "I should've listened to Dad and gone to work at that lab. He was totally right."

"But if you quit, aren't you proving him right?"

"I can't stay. It's a huge mess. The fields will never get cleared. No Clark and Jimmy, no Patsy, I wonder if Aggie and Beth will come back. . . ."

"I'm in," I hear myself say. "As long as you need me." And the minute I say it, I know it's true. Nothing can stop me from walking the beans with Blake. "Don't quit."

He gives me a twisty little smile. "I bet you've never quit anything in your life."

I shrug. "You don't know that."

He shakes his head. "Nope. I can tell. The way Patsy talks to you, and you just let it roll off, like she can't hurt you. And then you hold her hand when she needs you, even though she's been nothing but mean to you. As far as I can see, that is. Maybe she's nice to you in secret, when no one's watching."

"She's not," I say, even though sometimes she is, and we smile, but then he gets serious again.

"Really, though. You keep going, even when everything around you is on fire."

"You can do that, too, you know."

He pulls his hand away from me and grabs his head, like it might bust open at any second. He leans towards me. "Don't you ever just want to run away from it all?"

"You mean, more than every day?" I say, and we laugh a little. I watch an ambulance pull away, lights off. "Patsy'll come around. She always does. We're cousins. Running away wouldn't fix anything. Right?" I shiver, and for the first time in hours, I remember about Eastern Europe. I'll be running away from it all soon enough, I guess.

Blake looks down and murmurs, "Sometimes you have to leave to save yourself."

I touch Blake's arm. It's warm and solid under my hand, and his muscles flex when he clenches his fist. "Prove your dad wrong, Blake."

He looks at me like what I say might actually mean something, like he might listen to me of all people, and I have to look away before I do something real stupid. I think about modeling with Mama halfway around the world, and I remind myself that if I go with her—*when* I go with her—I'll be running towards something, not away from anything.

Twenty-three

Uncle Leo wants me to bring Patsy's car home from the church, so Blake and me haul ourselves back out to the truck. I'm so wrecked, my eyeballs throb every time my heart beats.

"You okay?" Blake's voice comes from far away.

"Probably." I lean against the window.

"Here's a pillow." Blake tosses a dark blue sweatshirt to me. It has the big orange U of I logo embroidered on it, a match to Blake's T-shirt.

I bunch it up under my head and lean against the door-frame. It smells like sun shining on warm earth, like Blake smiling at me, and I want to wrap my whole self up in it forever, safe from the world and from everything that's happened the last few days.

A familiar honk jerks me back to reality. We are at the four-way stop, and there's River right across from us, going the opposite way. We cross the intersection, and as we pass him, River puts his hands out, palms up, and mouths, "What the fuck?" His face is all snarled up and mad.

He guns it and peels out through the intersection.

So much for my nap.

"You want me to turn around? Catch up with him?" Blake looks back over his shoulder, and he slows the truck.

"If he wanted me, he'd have stopped." The rest of my head is thumping along with my eyeballs now. Each hair feels like it's squeezing into my scalp, pushing aside every other hair to hold its place.

River is never going to believe me. Even though Patsy's at the hospital with eleventy-million stitches, he'll still think I wanted to be with Blake. Like I planned it or something.

I need to think about something else. I smooth the sweatshirt out on my lap. "So, you're going to U of I?"

"End of August."

"You excited?"

"Mostly."

"Why only mostly?"

"Well, I got admitted to the school of engineering, and now I think I want to switch to agriculture, so I have to work that out with my dad and the school, but all in all, it's where I've always wanted to go."

"Always?"

"Since I was seven or eight years old. Mom took me to a homecoming football game, and I felt it right away. *This is my place.*"

"This is my place."

221

"Where is your place?" he asks, in that way he has of asking questions that make them seem bigger than the words.

"Huh?" My mind churns through all the possible places I'd like to be.

"Where is your place? Do you have a dream college?"

"College? I'll be lucky to make it out of high school. I'm maybe gonna take that test to graduate early, the GED, before . . ." I open my mouth to tell him about Europe, but I can't make the words come out. Maybe Patsy was right. Maybe it's all bullshit. Or maybe if I say it out loud, the whole thing will disappear like smoke into thin air. Maybe I'll wake up and find out it was all a dream.

Instead, I tell him, "I almost dropped out last year, but Aunt Trish wouldn't let me stay at her house if I wasn't in school."

"Dropped out?"

"I'm not really . . . a school person. I never really learned how to do school."

"You're certainly smart enough."

I shrug. "Mama dragged me around with her from town to town from the time I was four and a half years old. I never went to real school until I was in sixth grade, when I moved in with Patsy."

"You were homeschooled?"

"More like motel-schooled. I've done every workbook you could find at a drugstore, from *What Your First Grader Should Know* up to *Preparing for Fifth Grade*." I lay out the sweatshirt and fold the arms together in the back, then tuck the hood in so all I can see is the big orange logo.

"Your mom didn't teach you?"

"Nah. She was too busy modeling. It's a good thing Gramma taught me how to read when I was four, because Mama was not the person for that job."

"You taught . . . yourself. You really are smart."

"Not hardly. Every few weeks, Mama would remember my homework and demand to see how good I was doing. She thought I was a genius because I got all the answers right. She never knew I copied 'em from the back."

"Ha! See? I would never have thought of that."

I trace the bumpy stitches of the embroidered letters. "Yeah, well, I felt bad about it, but I walked around for years letting her think I was some egghead."

"And?" We pull into the church parking lot, and Blake parks next to Patsy's car. He turns to me and runs his fingers through his hair, looking at me all serious.

"And what?"

"And you're gonna go to college, right?"

I hand him the sweatshirt. "I told you, school and me, we don't get along too good. I could do those books, but I never learned how to take notes in class, and I missed every science there ever was, and the first time I had to turn in a book report, even the teacher laughed at me."

"Then what do you plan to do?"

"For what?"

"You know: next year. After high school. With your *life*."

"I dunno." I take a deep breath. "I guess I can decide after Europe."

"Europe?"

My stomach goes all wobbly, and I want to take it back, but now that I've started, it's like the dam is broken and it all comes spilling out. "Mama and me are doing mother-daughter modeling in Eastern Europe, at the end of the month."

His eyes go all wide. "*This* month?"

Oh, shit. "Don't worry, I can finish the beans before we go."

Blake raises his eyebrows up. "Good to know." He looks at me then, really looks at me, and his eyes go all soft, like he's ready to hear anything I want to say. "So, a model? That's what you want?"

His eyes are so kind it almost hurts. I shrug. "Yeah." I take a shaky breath. "I did. I really, really did."

"Do you still?" He tilts his head and looks at me, and his eyes remind me of the elephant I rode, deep and dark and a little sad, surrounded by giant lashes. For a second, I fall into them, and I let myself remember how much I wanted to go with Mama when I was little—to Japan or anywhere—and how wrecked I was when she left me behind. I've worked so hard to let go of that wanting, to fit myself into life with Aunt Trish and Uncle Leo and Patsy and keep myself from wanting things that can't ever happen.

I pull myself away from Blake's eyes, focus on what really matters. "Mama is over the moon about it," I tell him, and I smile as I pull on the strings of the sweatshirt. "So happy."

"And how about you? What makes *you* happy?"

What makes *me* happy? Why would he ask me something stupid like that? I laugh, and push my hair out of my face, and I tell him, "Patsy's gonna be okay. That's what makes me happy."

And he smiles and nods, but his eyes tell me he'll take that answer for now, but he knows there's a better one.

Blake lets the truck idle next to Patsy's car another few minutes. He doesn't say anything, and neither do I, and I'd like to tell him that what would make me happy right now is to sit here like this for about another ten hours, all peace and quiet.

Finally, though, I say, "I'd better go." I grab my shit and Patsy's purse and hand him the sweatshirt. Well, I try to hand it to him.

"Keep it. For luck, finding your place."

I climb out and say goodbye. Blake pulls away as I unlock Patsy's car, then he makes a slow U-turn and pulls up beside me, his face appearing as the window slides down. He holds out the cooler. "Did you want this? For tomorrow?"

"Tomorrow?" I squint up at him. The sun is finally out, and it's burning up the world to make up for not being around this morning. "What's tomorrow?"

He pauses, then says, "Beans?" He ducks his head and looks so hopeful, like a puppy waiting for a biscuit, that I want to pat him on the head and say, "Good boy," just to see him smile.

I take the cooler. "Is that so . . . boss? I should still call you boss, right?"

Blake cracks a small smile. "That's up to my dad. But I think

I will follow the advice of a very wise woman and stay. If he'll let me."

A little thrill runs through me. Wise. Yeah, right. I'm smiling at him, and he's smiling at me, and our hands are just touching on the handle of the cooler. We both jump as River pulls in the parking lot and screeches to a stop crossways in front of Blake's truck. I pull the cooler away from Blake and turn to River.

"I waited here for over an hour," River calls out the window.

Blake says, "We had a little—"

"Talking to my girlfriend, here, college boy. Unless there's something you two have to tell me?" He looks from me to Blake and back again, then takes a drink from a can in a koozie that is probably beer, judging from the lazy way his words are coming outta his mouth. Maybe not his first one today.

"I'm Blake," Blake corrects him, and his voice is even and flat, like he's talking to a wild animal that might bite him if he shows any anger or fear. He looks at his phone. "I guess we are a little later than usual." His smile is open, but in a way that shows that he's being super careful how he talks to River.

"Patsy's hurt," I start to say in the baby voice, but a new feeling busts up out of me, hot as the sun and burning just as bright, and I let it shine right out. "And stop with the 'college boy,'" I say, strong and clear.

River shrugs, and I keep going, my gut switching from wanting to protect River from stuff that might make him mad, to wanting to protect Blake from River. "I never said you should come get me today. Besides, we were at the hospital with Patsy and all her stitches. She almost *died*, you know." Sweat rolls off my forehead, and I grab the sweatshirt and the cooler closer, even though they make me hotter.

Blake says, just low enough for me to hear, "And sometimes you have to leave to save yourself," and I'm not sure if he means him, or me.

"Well, I'm here now," River says. "So see ya. *Blake.*" He waves, a short, sharp flip of his hand.

Blake looks at me. He says real quiet, "Do you need me to stay?"

I look at River, scraggly and small in his old white truck, and I sigh. "He's okay."

"Okay, then." He pauses. "Good seeing you again, River," Blake says, with a smile so fake it's like somebody drew it on with a crayon. Blake puts the truck in reverse, then he says, "Tell Patsy I'll check in with her later," and leaves the parking lot.

River reaches out his window and slaps the door of his truck a couple times. "Hop in," he says, like either he doesn't notice how mad I am, or he doesn't care.

"I have to take Patsy's car home."

River takes another drink, then flashes his movie-star smile at me. "Lead the way, baby."

River not noticing that I'm mad makes me want to kick his truck, or dump whatever's in the koozie over his head. I settle for driving Patsy's car a little too fast back to the house, and by the time we get there, the mad has passed, or turned into so much exhaustion I'm afraid I might pass out.

River follows me up the empty driveway to the door. "Busy day, huh?" How many beers has he already had? More than two, seems like.

"Patsy jumped the ditch with the bean hook, and . . ." River's dark blue eyes say he's not interested. He puts a foot on the bottom step and takes a swig from the can, tipping his head back so far I'm afraid he'll lose his hat. I can almost hear the sun blasting its heat on us.

"And you and your boyfriend were the only ones who could help?" He laughs a slow, easy laugh.

"He's *not* my boyfriend."

"Sure as fuck not," River says. He goes to put his arms around me, then pulls back. "What, did you roll in the beans? There's dirt all over you."

"It rained. A lot."

River takes another swig of the beer and follows me into the house. The cold air from the window unit reminds me just how wet my hair and clothes still are.

"Hello?" I call out, "Mama?" I open the door to the basement, but it's quiet down there. I need a shower bad and a Diet Coke worse, so I shut the door and head into the kitchen. River follows me and grabs my butt, then leans his chin on my shoulder from behind.

"Nobody here." His arms creep around me.

"They're probably out celebrating." I bend over to search the fridge for a Diet Coke, but all I find is River's hands all over me.

"Celebrating what?" he asks.

Celebrating what.

He doesn't know. He doesn't know about Europe.

I can't hardly breathe, so I look behind the margarine and the eggs, then move some leftovers and run my hand over the shelf, reading all the labels real hard.

He kisses the back of my neck. "What's the celebration?"

Real milk, one percent milk fat. Homogenized, I read, over and over, while I think of all the ways I could tell him.

Later. I'll tell him later.

"They'll be back any minute. Patsy was almost out when we left the hospital."

River takes another swig of his beer, then sets it on the table. "We. You and . . . *Blake*?"

His voice has a sharp edge to it, but his hands are soft on my hair. He tangles his fingers in it and uses it to pull me around to face him. Even though I smell like dirt and sweat and soggy everything, River pulls me to him and buries his face in my neck.

"Ahh, man. Even covered in fuckin' mud you are smokin' hot. How could I ever live without you?" He hugs me tight and kisses my neck. That dirt cannot taste good.

"They're gonna be back."

He tilts his head and gives me a classic River look, the one that made all the girls fight over him last year. His eyes are darkest blue, like the sky in the last few minutes of daylight, and

229

his hands haven't stopped wandering around on my shirt and shorts.

"We'll hear the car. C'mon." He kisses me then, and I tense up, waiting for more, but all he does is kiss, kiss, kiss. Little, quiet, beer-flavored kisses with just a taste of tobacco. His cheek is rough against mine.

Maybe River *can* take my mind off everything but him. Nothing else in the world but what's here in front of me. I sink into him, into the kisses, then I'm jerked back to reality. How *will* he live without me?

I have to tell him.

"River, I—"

"Shhh," he says, his beery breath soft on my cheek. He pushes my hair behind my ears, then twirls it around his fingers. He kisses me again, but all I can think about is how I'm planning to leave him to go to Europe, right when Granny's is taken away from him, too.

I break off the kiss. "River. I'm going—"

"Bliss?" Aunt Trish throws open the door and River jumps and yanks his hands out of my hair.

Twenty-four

Aunt Trish glares at me and blows out an irritated breath. "Patsy needs her phone." She flat-out ignores River.

"It's out in the car," I say, and step towards the door.

"Not now! Daddy's helping her in." Aunt Trish taps her fingers together in front of her mouth as she scans the room. "Pillows, ice, afghan," she mutters. "Help me out, Bliss."

Pretty soon, Patsy appears in the doorway. She has a huge bandage on her thigh, and crutches, and she winces every time she moves. Uncle Leo is so close behind her he's practically walking for her, and he pats her back with every step. Patsy's face is white again, and she shrugs off each one of Uncle Leo's touches.

"Clear the way," Aunt Trish says to River, in about the meanest voice I've ever heard her use. "Can't you see she's hurt?"

River steps aside, looking like he'd like to clear all the way out of here.

Patsy shoves away the stack of pillows I made on the sofa.

Uncle Leo holds her hands to lower her to the sofa, and he practically flies to clear the coffee table so she can put her foot up. Aunt Trish flutters around, tucking in the ice pack, moving the remote control so Patsy can reach it, paying no attention to Patsy's jerking away from her every touch.

I go stand over by River and try and blend in with the walls.

"Ohmygod. Stop," Patsy says. "I'm not a baby."

Aunt Trish and Uncle Leo stand there, shoulders slumped, with identical sad faces. "But, honey . . ." Uncle Leo puts out his hands, palms up. "We want to help you, sweetie."

"Where is my phone? Nate will be worried sick. And my Diet Coke?" Patsy pushes at Aunt Trish's hands, which can't stop themselves from smoothing Patsy's hair.

The pain meds have definitely worn off.

"Seriously?" She turns to me. "Bliss. Get my phone."

I spin around and pull River out the door, remembering just in time to grab his beer from the table, hoping nobody noticed it.

River stands by Patsy's car, holding his empty koozie while I dig Patsy's phone out. When I finally shut the door, he pulls me close.

"Jesus Christ, was that intense. Let's get out of here. The lake is waiting." He gives me a long, slow kiss that heats up near the end, then puts his forehead against mine and sighs. "Aww, Bliss. I could just eat you up."

We could drive to the lake, park under the trees, leave our

clothes behind, and slip into the murky water, skin on skin covered in water, no thoughts or worries in the way.

But not today. Today is for Patsy, who has a million stitches because of me.

"I don't think I better leave just now."

"Come on. Let's ditch. Patsy on a good day is bad enough. Hurt Patsy? Get me the fuck outta there. Besides, I need you to come plan out the goodbye party I'm fixing to have at Granny's place this weekend." He runs his hands up and down my sides.

"Goodbye?"

"Do you not listen? Fucking Lisa is bound and determined to sell the place. She can make me sell it, but it sure as hell won't be pretty."

He kisses me again, pushing me against the hot car like that'll keep Granny's from being sold. Patsy's phone gets smashed in between us, and I can feel the seconds ticking away since she asked for it.

"River—" I finally pull away.

He turns his head towards the street as a truck pulls up.

A shiny red pickup truck.

"Well, well. Your boyfriend couldn't stay away."

Blake holds a big old bunch of yellow flowers in his hand as him and Mr. Wu walk up the driveway. Blake squints into the sun, lifting his chin in a nod to River and me, and trails his dad up the driveway. River stays right where he is, pinning me under him against the car, making it so I can't even move or wave hello or anything.

"Bliss." Mr. Wu greets me with a small wave and nods at River. "Blake is here to make our apologies to your cousin." He nudges Blake with his shoulder. "What a terrible accident." He doesn't say anything about whether Blake is fired or not, or about River practically humping me up against the car in the middle of the driveway.

I struggle against River to get out from under him and follow them. "She's inside. Let me take you in." I give River a mean stare, but he acts like I could've stood up any time I wanted, like he wasn't keeping me trapped against the car. "River was just leaving," I say.

"Oh, I think we all better check on Patsy," River says, and hangs an arm around my neck, practically dragging me up the steps. "Such a terrible accident."

I give him an even meaner stare, and he shrugs his shoulders and opens the door.

I stick my head inside. "Mr. Wu is here."

Blake holds the flowers like he does it every day. He shows them to Patsy, and Aunt Trish and Uncle Leo shake hands with Mr. Wu, and I can feel River watching, taking it all in.

"My son would like to apologize."

Blake looks small and sad as he says, "I'm sorry, Patsy." His voice is low, and I try to tell from his face if his dad made him quit working.

"Sorry? But you saved my life." Patsy looks up at Mr. Wu. "Blake carried me to the truck. He saved me." Patsy's attitude from before has gone clean away, scared off by the flowers and the attention. She describes every gory detail of bone, muscle, skin, and whatever the hell else the plastic surgeon stitched up with fifty-seven stitches, then she starts over again telling how Blake carried her to the truck.

Blake stands just behind his dad, ducking his head every time Patsy mentions him. If this was a drinking game where somebody takes a shot every time the word *Blake* gets said, that somebody'd be real drunk about now.

"I just did what any boss would do," Blake says, and before I can catch myself, I look over at him standing there, still holding the stupid daisies or whatever, and he gives me a tiny little smile that I almost give back before I stop myself.

"Any shitty boss," River says into my ear. We are wedged into a corner out of the way, and every time Blake looks our way, River squeezes me up tighter in his arms.

"Blake tells me that you have committed to finishing the job," Mr. Wu says, turning to me. "We'll work straight through the weekends."

"If it's with Blake." My mouth opens all by itself and lets the words out. All eyes turn to me, and River stiffens behind me as I look from Patsy to Aunt Trish and Uncle Leo, and then finally to Mr. Wu, whose eyebrows could not possibly go any higher on his forehead.

I swallow. "I mean . . . ," I say, and I'm about to come up with a good way of asking if Blake is fired without making River think I like him or anything, when the front door bangs open and Mama comes through.

"What is this, a used-car lot?" Mama says. "There's so many vehicles out front, I ought to charge a fee. Why, we had to park halfway down the block!" Even if she wasn't so pretty, nobody would be able to take their eyes off her, she's so full of life.

Her and Clyde scan the room. "Guess we missed the invite," Clyde says from behind an armful of grocery sacks. Blake and Mr. Wu both look confused, and Blake looks from Mama to me and back to Mama again.

Aunt Trish goes into full-on mother-bear mode, chugging her arms as she stomps across the room to where Mama stands. "It's hardly a party when a child is injured, Theresa. Did you even get my text?"

Mama's face falls, and the entire room slows down, a music box running out of steam. But then she brightens, and it's like the sun comes out from behind a cloud, like we forgot what warmth and light felt like in those few seconds it was gone.

"Did I get your text?" Mama says to Aunt Trish, then she waves Clyde forward with the sacks he's carrying. "Did I get your text? How's that for getting your text?" She shoves Clyde towards Aunt Trish.

Clyde thunks the plastic sacks down on the coffee table so close to Patsy's leg that we all flinch, and Uncle Leo steps forward before he realizes she's okay. "Diet Coke and more Diet Coke," Clyde says, and he peels the white bag away from the cardboard case like he's unwrapping a million dollars cash. "And all the pain meds you'd ever want—I didn't take none of them, I swear. They're all legal." He shakes the second bag and four different kinds of pills rattle onto the coffee table, barely missing Patsy's foot. He grins like he just invented aspirin or something.

Mama fishes in her purse, and we all stare at her, like she's the reason we are all here, not Patsy. Even River relaxes a little bit while we all wait to see what Mama will do next. Finally, she says, "And the best medicine: chocolate and trashy reads. Heal you right up." She goes to give it all to Patsy, but everything slips out of her hands and lands on the floor. Blake jumps to help her, kneels and scoops the whole pile up, then hands it all to Mama, even the flowers he'd been holding.

"For me?" Mama swallows Blake up in her smile as he slowly gets up. "I just adore flowers."

Blake reaches out a hand to take back the flowers, then pulls it away and glances down at Patsy, like he's not sure how to get her flowers back from Mama, or if Mama even knows they're for Patsy, not her.

"Blake's my boss," Patsy says. "He brought me flowers. Aren't they pretty?"

Mama pauses a second, then laughs and squeezes herself onto the sofa between Patsy and the end. "Well of course they are." She looks at Patsy's bandaged leg, then quickly looks away. She dumps the magazine, chocolates, and flowers into Patsy's lap, then grabs Patsy's arm and stares deep into her eyes. "How are you, really? Be honest."

Patsy shrugs. "It's not that—"

"Don't you let anyone tell you it doesn't hurt. We women

have to stick together and show the world how strong we are."

"I mean, there's a lot of stitches. I guess I could use some more—"

"We can take gallons more pain than any man—why, if men had to give birth, the world would be a different place, don't you think?"

Patsy nods but doesn't answer, and Mama looks around the room for agreement, her eyes finally landing on me.

"Bliss," she says, and jumps up from the sofa, tipping Patsy a little sideways. "I nearly forgot." She turns to Aunt Trish. "Now, Trish. I need you to take good care of Patsy, here. She's been through so much today; you need to look after her well-being while we're out."

Aunt Trish sputters and her face turns pink and bunches up, but Mama grabs Clyde's arm and turns towards me before Aunt Trish says anything. "We have to hurry, before we lose the light."

"Light?" I say, a little croaky.

"Everyone knows late-afternoon light is the best for portraits," Mama says, and she pulls me away from River as easy as pulling a grape from its bunch. "We have to hurry if Clyde's going to get good head shots of this mother-daughter team. Thomas wants them tonight, if we want to leave town anytime soon."

"I haven't showered . . . ," I begin.

Mama stops and looks me up and down. "We can make do."

"Look at her, Theresa. She's still soaking wet," Aunt Trish says. "It doesn't have to be right this moment. She's had a hard enough day."

Any tiredness I had disappears in a flash. "I'm fine," I say right at Aunt Trish. "We can make do."

Mama looks from me to Aunt Trish, who looks mad as a wet cat. Mama claps her hands together. "Time's a-wasting. Come on, baby girl. We have to get ready for Europe!"

Mama grabs my elbow and hustles me to the door, but not so fast that I don't hear River say, "Europe?"

Twenty-five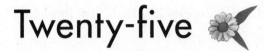

Patsy stops me, putting her open hand out towards me. "My phone? Nate must be worried sick."

I freeze by the door, afraid to turn around and see River. Mama tugs on my elbow.

Patsy snaps her fingers. "Bliss?"

"What's *Europe*?" River says, slow and low.

I hand the phone to Patsy without looking at River. Or anybody. I move real careful and still, like I'm walking on ice or carrying a pail of water on my head. My whole face is burning hot, I can't find a single word to say, and the room is way, way, way too quiet.

"What's she talking about?" River says, louder.

"You didn't tell him?" Patsy looks up at me, her black hair spilling out of its ponytail. She grabs the phone and frowns at it, then meets my eyes with her clear blue ones. "You didn't tell your *boyfriend* you're going to Europe?"

I turn around and look at the maddest, meanest River face I

have ever seen. "I was going to—" I say, at the same time Mama calls out.

"Bliss, honey, the light! We're wasting this precious light," she says, like she didn't hear me or River. She nods at me. "Shake a leg, baby."

River's face goes seven shades of red, and he turns and shoves past Mama, knocking her sideways. Blake is there to catch her and pull her aside as River slams the door behind him.

"Manners, young man," Aunt Trish huffs. "Honestly."

"Are you all right?" Mr. Wu asks Mama.

I take a step towards the door, then stop and look around at all the faces. My ears burn from all the things that nobody is saying out loud, and I want to stay and explain why I didn't tell him, why he's so upset, why he ran out so fast. I also want to run after River and tell him that I'm not leaving, not yet, and I would've told him, I really would, if today hadn't been such a shit show. I can't look at Blake, because he's already in my head, asking over and over, *What do you want, Bliss?*

"Well, what are you waiting for? Go after your boyfriend." Patsy leans forward, then makes a too-loud-to-be-real moan and grabs her leg.

I swallow and head out the door after River.

He's behind the wheel, counting the money in his wallet. He's got one elbow out the window of the truck, and his shoulders are all slumped down.

I put my hand on his arm, and he yanks it back in and starts to counting again.

"River—"

Nothing.

"River, I—"

"Goddammit, Bliss. Just—fuck. How the fuck do I only have four dollars?" He lines the money all up so it's going the same way and smooths it out flat. "I can't even get a fucking six-pack for four dollars."

"I can explain—"

He whips his head around to face me. His eyes are mean blue, and his face is as red as Blake's truck.

"Oh, I. Bet. You. Can." Little spaces of hate between the words. River folds the money and pushes it in the wallet, then tosses the whole thing on the seat next to him.

I lean my head in the window. "Mama—"

River puts a hand up between us and starts the truck.

"I was gonna tell you," I say.

"Mmmm-hmmm. Before or after you left?" He smiles, a thin smile with his lips pushed together tight. "What's your boyfriend going to say when you tell him that you aren't so committed to walking his fucking beans."

"I told him . . ."

River goes still, and his eyes freeze all the way up to ice blue. "You told *him*?"

My guts drop to my toes. "She just . . . it's only been—"

The truck roars as River guns the engine two, three, four times. He stares out the windshield, then finally turns to me. "How long have you known?" All the light that was ever in his eyes is gone, and all that's left is this empty blue stare. "I waited almost a year for you. And this is what you do to me?" He turns his hat around, so the brim is at the front, grips it hard with both his hands. "I can't even decide what's worse: you and the fucking professor, who you tell everything to, or you planning some trip to Asia or someplace without saying a word to me." He sighs, and says real low, "Out of everyone, I thought at least I could count on you. I guess I was wrong." He jams his hat back on his head.

"I—" I reach out to River's arm, and he flinches away from me.

We both look up as Blake and Mr. Wu come out of the house. The early-evening sun makes everything look golden, dreamy, like it's a memory of something that already happened.

River puts the car in gear. "Goodbye, Bliss," he says, real loud. "Or however you say it in Europe. Have a nice life." He roars off down the street, just missing Blake's truck.

Blake's dad shakes his head as they reach the end of the driveway. "So dangerous. Cars and teenagers: not a good combination." He looks at Blake like he was talking about him, and Blake shrugs his shoulders. Mr. Wu points at me. "We have it all arranged. Blake will come get you in the morning, and you two will continue to clear the fields. No distractions." Just like before, it sounds like he's talking to Blake, even though he's looking at me.

Blake stands stiffly, but when I look at him, his eyes are open, and clear, and calm. Like he doesn't have plans for me or questions for me, like he doesn't want anything from me at all. My shoulders loosen and my hands let go of the fists I've been holding them in for probably the last ten minutes, and a little breeze lifts my hair and cools my hot cheeks.

"There you are!" calls Mama. "Hurry, hurry," she says, thumping the limo as she opens the door for me. Right. I about forgot her and the light and the head shots.

"See you in the morning," Blake says as I drag myself up the drive.

Mama directs Clyde to this one spot in this one park, and by the time he gets the angle right on his phone, Mama is crabby as hell. She pushes and pulls my hair, jabbing bobby pins all over, muttering about Thomas, the light, the background, and the "goddamn beans."

"Stand like this," she says, and I try to stand like her.

"No. Turn your head. Lift your chin," and I do like she asks.

"Jesus, do I have to do everything? Here," Mama says, and she moves my arms like I'm one of the Barbie dolls her boyfriends used to give me back when we went from motel to motel following the modeling circuit.

I go to brush my hair out of my face, and Mama slaps my hand away. "Leave it." She steps back and shakes her head and turns my shoulders a few inches. "*Tonight*, he says. Thomas, you are so lucky it's not raining," she mutters.

Clyde takes a few pictures, but Mama stops him over and over to fix me, or my hair, or the angle of the picture. Finally, she wrinkles her nose and throws up her hands. "I cannot work with this. Next time, you clean yourself up before a shoot."

"You said we can make do."

"We made do!" Mama snarls, then presses her fingertips to her temples. "Sit down." She snaps her fingers and points to a nearby bench. "Clyde, honey. Just grab a few of me before the light goes entirely, so we haven't wasted our whole day."

I take my sweaty self over to a bench and don't say a word about the shower I wanted to take hours and hours ago. I collapse on the seat, too tired to even be pissed. If I didn't still have mud caked on my legs, I would believe that Patsy getting hurt was months and months ago, or some sort of nightmare I imagined.

I watch Mama walk and pose in the fading golden light, spinning around for the camera, sometimes smiling and sometimes not, and I want to reach out and touch her, grab her, make sure she's not some dream I'm having. A dream where I leave everything behind: pissed-off River, hurt Patsy . . . Blake, too, and it's only Mama that matters, and who I am when I'm with her.

Twenty-six

After the light fades down to nothing and Mama and Clyde bring me back, I charge my phone all the way up and text and call River about a hundred times, but he's not answering. River was just mad when he left; he wasn't breaking up with me, I'm pretty sure. I would've told him right away—but there was bean walking, and Patsy, and I wanted to tell him in person.

I shut the door to Patsy's empty room, and I stand there in the middle of all that silence. Nobody to get hurt, or mad, or tell me how I've ruined everybody's lives or some shit like that. Just me in the whole room, all to myself.

I pull out the ukulele and hunch up on the bed so I can do tiny strums that hopefully won't wake Patsy up where she's sleeping on the sofa. So what if River is breaking up with me? When I go to Europe, it won't matter anyways.

My mind starts to go round and round again, so I work on the three chords more, then pick out the opening notes to "Rainbow Connection," and every time I play it right, those nine little notes wrap themselves around my heart and after a while I'm finally calm enough to go to sleep.

Walking the beans without Patsy turns out to be almost fun.

We tell the hospital parts of Patsy's story to Aggie and Beth like four times before they are done talking about it, but then we just go up and down the rows like usual. I leave my phone with my lunch, so I don't wear out the battery checking it—the longest River has ever been mad is like a half a day, so I'll for sure hear from him by lunchtime.

Blake acts the same as normal, except for around the bean hooks, where he watches us real close. He jumps every time one of us swings a hook for the first little while, then he gets used to being around them again. It takes me a little longer to get comfortable with mine—I see Patsy's cut leg every time I slice a weed.

Blake walks in the next row over all morning, and when I don't talk, he doesn't talk either. He smiles at me a few times, but he mostly just lets me be. It's extra sticky out today, and the air is so hazy the trees way off at the edges of the fields are fuzzy and wavery. But it feels good to be out here. *I* feel good. The beans don't care if I know how to stand like a model. The sun doesn't shine hotter or colder because I couldn't tell River that I'm leaving, and the wind doesn't blow any harder because Patsy is at home with a million stitches. I just walk, and cut weeds, and soon this field is more clean than not.

Before I know it, it's break time, and then lunch break.

Aggie is jittery with waiting to hear if she made callbacks, but she tells me a couple ways to make the uke easier and offers to help me in person later on. Beth does something to my hair that pulls it back and keeps it out of my face for the whole rest of the day, even without a hair tie. She says she'll show Patsy how to do it, too.

Blake keeps getting up to check the hooks where we've left them, and the time, and counting how many rows we have until we can go to the next field. When he finally does sit down, he doesn't really talk. I check my phone about a million times to see if River is done being mad, or if we are even still together.

Finally, after I'm done eating, I tell Blake, "Thanks for coming to see Patsy."

"No problem." He takes a drink of his water. "You sure look like your mom."

I nod.

"I guess people tell you that all the time."

I shrug.

"I want to see!" Beth says. "Will she be there later when me and Aggie come by so we can meet her?" She pokes a dirt clod until it breaks apart.

"She's kind of hard to pin down," I say.

"I got that impression," says Blake. "How long till you leave for Europe?"

"The end of the month?"

He shakes his head. "Oh, man. When we visited my dad's parents in Shanghai my mom was crazy for three solid months beforehand, trying to get everything ready. Passports, rental cars . . . I think she had to-do lists of to-do lists. All she wanted to do was impress my grandparents—I can't imagine what it takes to move somewhere for work."

"Yeah?"

Beth smashes the last of the dirt clod, and it raises a puff of dust. "Just to go to Mexico for my aunt's wedding was a huge pain in the ass," she says, then pokes Aggie. "Remember trying to find your birth certificate?"

Aggie rolls her eyes and laughs.

Blake looks at his watch.

"I know, I know. Break's over," Aggie says, and she pulls Beth to standing.

My stomach flips around as I follow them, but it's probably just something I ate.

The rows are longer after lunch. It's hard not to notice things about Blake when he's right there two rows away from me. The way the sun makes him squint just a little bit, or the way his arms bunch up when he's cutting a tough weed. I try to hook the weeds as smooth as he does, but my arms don't move all graceful like his do.

Sometimes I can forget Blake and me ever kissed, and he's just my boss.

Other times, it's hard to look at him and *not* think about it. Or about what I would do if me and River really are broke up. Like when Blake and me get to the end of our rows and we both turn to go in the same row at the same time. His arm bumps up against mine, and for a whole down-and-back all I can think of is dark skies and lightning bugs, and Blake tasting like beer and starlight.

I shake my head to knock those thoughts clean away. "Was your dad mad?" I ask him. "He didn't fire you, I guess."

Blake scrunches up his eyebrows and looks off to where Aggie and Beth are working. "He was . . . disappointed."

"That's not too bad."

"Sometimes, it's worse."

"How?"

Blake studies a weed before he cuts it with a sharp jerk. "It's like you're proving them right, like they should have never believed in you in the first place. Like you can't do anything without messing it up. Again."

"But he let you come back."

"Eventually."

"What changed his mind?"

He gives a little laugh. "He decided he was proud of me for my perseverance. And the 'maturity' I showed by wanting to come back." He makes air quotes.

"So that's good. Right?"

"It's good." We walk till we are about halfway down the row, then Blake stops and turns to me, looking all serious. "Thank you," Blake says. "If it were up to me, I would have given up."

I shrug. "But you didn't," I say, and turn to keep walking.

"You don't."

I stop.

He keeps talking. "Your cousin, your mom, all those people. No matter how they act, you don't give up." His eyes are steady on me, and even though we're two rows apart, it feels like we are standing as close as we did at the elephant grave. The rough spots in the bean hook handle stand out under my fingers as I grab it tighter, but I can't answer him. I can't tell him that it's so much easier to go along with things than to make a fuss, to want things, to make people mad.

Blake clears his throat. "So," he says, and turns down the row again. "How did the photo shoot go? Did you catch the light in time?"

I tell him about the park and Mama. "She just forgets that I don't know everything she does."

"I think . . . parents have trouble remembering that their kids are separate people from them."

"Your dad will come around," I tell him. "Mama's just getting used to me again."

"How long has she been back?"

We walk and cut, and I tell him the whole story of how Mama left, and how she came back, and how we're leaving soon. "I remember it, how it used to be. With Mama." I stop and look at the dark green rows of beans, lined up for miles like a giant combed them neatly into place. Blake stops, too, waiting for me to finish. "Sometimes it's like she's a tornado that rearranges everything the way she wants it, then disappears without looking to see what she's left behind."

251

Blake and the hazy blue sky don't say a word, and my mouth keeps going. "Or maybe she doesn't even care." A single bird coasts over us, high in the sky, riding the air currents like it has all the time in the world. "But it feels so good when she wants you around, when you can do something, anything, to make her happy. A person would follow her to the ends of the earth, even."

We both stand still and watch the bird until it's out of sight, then Blake laughs and says, "Or at least to Europe."

We laugh, and we walk again and cut weeds like we're in a race to get to the end of the row.

Aggie and Beth go home to shower before coming to see Patsy. I check my phone, then I toss it on the seat of Blake's truck. "It's dead."

"Waiting for a call?"

"Anything, really." I don't say from River, and Blake doesn't ask. But a hole opens up between us in the silence.

When we get to a red light, Blake finally looks over at me and says, "You don't have to do it, you know."

"Do what?"

"Whatever people want you to do."

"You mean River?"

"I mean anybody. You can do whatever you want. Go to college or, I don't know, study music like Aggie, or hair like Beth." Blake looks at me like he 200 percent believes that I could go off to college with him, like it's a thing that makes sense and nobody would ask what I was doing there.

"You don't know that." My voice sounds like when Patsy talks to Aunt Trish. Or me, sometimes. Sharp and deadly.

"I didn't mean—"

Now I'm the tornado, or maybe there's a fire inside of me. Either way, it's hot and loud and fast. "You don't know what I can do."

Blake jerks back from me as my voice gets louder, and I don't even care.

"You don't know anything. College is fine, for honor rollers and Chicago people. But when there's not a whole ton of choices, you have to pick what you can. I might be good at modeling. I might."

Blake looks over at me while he drives, eyes all big and mouth open a little. I keep going.

"Sure, I could go to community college. Take night classes, even. Or go off and live in a dorm somewhere. But I'm not made out to be a nurse, or a teacher, or some sort of, I don't know, auto mechanic. You have to know what you want before you start that shit, or there's just no point at all, and a huge waste of time and money, and it's not worth it."

I finish up, real loud, right as we pull up to Patsy's house. The silence that's left in the truck is so loud my ears ring from it.

He nods. "You're right." His eyes are serious, and the shine that's usually in them is gone. "I don't know what you want."

"No." I grab my shit and jump out of the truck. "You don't."

Twenty-seven

I walk into the house hoping maybe it's calmer in there, but that sure as hell is not the case.

"Nate!" says Patsy, before I'm even in the door, but when I walk through, she gives me a dirty look and says, "Oh, it's you."

Patsy's on the sofa wearing clean clothes and a ton of makeup, and her leg is propped up with about six pillows. There's enough empty cups and plates and wrappers on the coffee table by her foot to fill a grocery sack.

"So what?" I ask her.

Patsy looks at her phone, and says, "He's coming to see me at—never mind." She slaps the phone onto the sofa beside her. "Help me up? I've had to pee for an hour."

"Where is everybody?"

Patsy gives me a mean smile. "Where is everybody? Well, let's see. Mom and Dad had to go to work, so your mama and her idiot boyfriend are supposed to babysit me."

I look around. "Where are they?"

"Well, now, that's the question, isn't it? We ran out of those damn sunflower seeds, so they went to the store to get some. Over an hour ago." She reaches up so I can help her stand. "Not like— Don't touch my— Jesus!" She pushes me away and grabs the crutches.

I don't say a word, just help Patsy to the bathroom. And back to the sofa. And get her pain meds, which she was late for, while she bitches the whole time. My skin itches with dust from the beans, but I clean up her mess and sit with her until Beth and Aggie come, and then I am finally free to take a cool, quiet shower.

The minute I step out of the bathroom, I can hear Patsy crying.

"Nate said! He said, 'That sucks.' And then when I told him I needed him to come over, he said, 'Tomorrow for sure.' Well, it's tomorrow, and where is he?"

I walk real quiet into the bedroom, where I get dressed and check to see if River texted and wait for Patsy to stop crying about Nathan, which takes a good long time.

After a while, Uncle Leo comes home with pizzas, and when Aunt Trish gets here, we all eat in the living room with Patsy and hang out.

Aggie shows me some uke stuff that I suck at, and Beth teaches Patsy how to do that thing with my hair. My phone is charged up, but River's still not talking to me, and the not knowing is busting my head in two.

"Can I use your car?" I finally blurt out to Patsy. "It won't take long."

She looks at my phone and raises her eyebrows.

"Oh, Bliss, no," says Aunt Trish. "It's late."

"Yeah," says Patsy. "Maybe too late."

I just look at her, and she says, "Text Aunt Theresa. Maybe she can pick something up for you. If she's coming back at all."

I stand up with my uke. "Forget it. See you all tomorrow."

When I get to the bedroom, I text Long Tom.

Me: Tell River to call me.

Patsy's got to be wrong. It's not too late, even though River's never been mad this long before.

I get out the uke book while I'm waiting for him, and finally I get an answer.

Long Tom: That's not a good idea.

I text River one last time anyway.

Me: I miss you

I sit on the bed with the ukulele and the book and try to learn some chords. My fingers keep slipping as I remember the look on River's face right before he drove away. *Out of everyone, I thought at least I could count on you*, he said.

I thought he could, too, but it's beginning to sink in that I'm really leaving. I look around Patsy's room, at the matching yellow comforters and the hole in the ceiling that used to hold Patsy's chandelier. An emptiness settles right in my gut, and I try and fill it up with the music, but tears drip down onto the chord book. This time next month, I'll be playing the ukulele in my new bedroom, somewhere in Eastern Europe with Mama.

I want—I *need*—to go so bad. Is this what she felt, before she left me here last time? An ache so big that it wanted to swallow her up?

Five minutes—or five hours, I can't tell which—later, I wake up, my brain thick with sleep. I'm lying with my head on the ukulele book, the uke is still in my hands, and all the lights are on.

I'm partly in the grip of a dream. River is planted in a row with the beans, and he keeps trying to play a G chord on a beer bottle, and the sound won't come out right. Finally, he picks up the dirt like it's a carpet and shakes it like we used to shake the parachute in gym class, so it makes a huge rumbling sound.

Thunder.

The clock doesn't make sense to me, and I'm still half in the dream. Five seventeen. Is it time for dinner?

Then another low rumble of thunder rolls through the room, and I click into alertness. It's morning. And it's storming.

I lie there, paralyzed, listening to the rain pound on the roof. My backbone is twangy, and my arms and legs are tight as I lie very still, waiting for the sirens that will send all of us into the basement.

Aunt Trish tried to calm me down about storms when I was

younger. "God and the angels are having a little bowling game, sweetie. Soon the angels are gonna lose, and they'll cry so much we'll see it here on earth."

But I knew better. I knew that a sound that huge must belong to something that could reach right into my house and snatch me away if it wanted to.

The thunder shakes the house again with a sound that comes from everywhere—inside me, outside, even underneath me. I can't even move to cover myself up or put the uke away. I stay super still with my head pillowed on the chord book as the rain slows down some.

The next thunder is farther away, and I wait a good long time to hear another rumble faintly in the distance. I look at the clock: 5:37. Blake will be here to get me in just a few minutes. He wouldn't make me go out in a storm, would he? Patsy said he has radar and shit, so he would know if it's safe or not. I hope.

I wait until 5:40, and when there's not another thunder I put away the ukulele and shimmy into my bean clothes. I jam a baseball cap on my head and check my phone, but there's nothing, from River or Blake. I tiptoe past Patsy and open the fridge to grab my lunch.

And—thanks to Clyde, I guess—a Diet Coke. I slide out the front door and sit on the steps to wait for Blake. The limo is parked at an angle down at the bottom of the driveway, so I know Mama and Clyde made it home last night, at least. The air is heavy, and the driveway is shiny, but the rain has stopped, and the thunder has finally gone away completely.

Blake is two minutes late and can't stop apologizing.

"Checking the weather one last time," he tells me. "It's clearing off, with more storms later."

My backbone scritches up again. "How much later?"

"Late afternoon. We can just beat it."

We head out of town, me watching the clouds off in the distance, and Blake watching the road, not saying anything. There's no sun, but the edges of things start graying up as morning comes on.

Blake drums his fingers on the steering wheel. "You—" He takes a deep breath and lets it out. "You were right. Yesterday. I'm sorry."

It takes me a minute to stop thinking of the storm and remember how mad I was at Blake yesterday. I try to be mad again, but I can't find the anger under the worry about the weather. "Okay."

Blake goes on. "It's none of my business, really. But you're so— You have so much— You shouldn't—" He clears his throat. "I'm sorry."

"It's not a big deal," I say.

Blake stares off at the road through the windshield. "Everyone has choices." He looks at me, then forward again as we pull up to the field. Blake parks the truck but leaves it running, waiting for Aggie and Beth.

He grips the steering wheel and his whole arm flexes, all the way up to where his blue work shirt ends. "It's just—here. Here's an example." He points out the window at the beans on every side. "Take this farm."

"Huh?" I say.

"Our entire farm is a choice. Good Neighbor is an organic farm."

"So?"

"So, it's that, or Questron." He raises his dark, straight eyebrows at me like I should know what he's talking about.

"That's who River wants me to detassel corn for."

"Really." He pauses, then keeps going. "We can either farm the Questron way, with pesticides and genetically modified seed, or the organic way, with none of that."

"That doesn't seem like a hard choice."

"But it is. My parents had to choose to farm like everyone else—cheaper and faster, no weeds or bugs—or go full-on organic, which is more expensive and a lot more work. They picked organic."

"Good for you. And your family. You picked a way to farm." The anger I was looking for flares up in my middle and grows with every word. "What does that even have to do with me?" I say, louder.

Aggie's car pulls up beside us, and I scrabble around for the handle of the door, so I can get out of here.

"Bliss." Blake's voice is low, quiet, but insistent. I turn and look at him, and all I see is his soft eyes and his hand reaching out to me.

The words sit there between us, and the fire inside of me grows smaller. "Yes?"

He sighs. "I'm not trying to tell you what to do. What I mean is—" He runs his hand through his hair. "Do whatever *you* want, not what everyone else wants."

I open the door and climb out, then stick my head back in. "How do you know that I'm not?"

Twenty-eight

Beth and Aggie both have their phones out by the time we get out of the truck. "Is it gone?" I ask them.

"Only nice green rain off to the west," Aggie says, and holds her phone up next to her smiling face. "Nothing severe till later." Her and Beth sing and laugh and practically dance around as we get to work. I make sure to let Beth and Aggie go between me and Blake in the rows, in case he wants to lecture me some more about how I should listen to him and not other people.

"So you're in a good mood," Blake says to Aggie.

Aggie smiles so big we don't need the sun to come out. "I made callbacks," she practically sings. But then her face gets serious. "Except . . . you're gonna kill me."

"I am?" Blake says.

"It's today. We need to leave early. Like, lunchtime."

Blake tugs at a sticky weed, then we all walk for a minute without saying anything. Finally, Blake says, "You're right. I am going to kill you."

262

I look across the six rows between us as he flashes Aggie a big smile.

"I'm serious," she says. "You're already behind, with Patsy, and firing the boys. Won't your dad be—"

"You know what," Blake says. "Don't worry about it." He leans down to pick up a chopped-off volunteer corn. "We can make it up later." He peels the leaves off the corn, dropping each one to the ground as he talks. "This is your dream, right? This audition?"

Aggie nods.

"It could change her whole future," Beth says.

Blake tosses down the last piece of the corn and starts walking again, so we all do, too. "For a future-changing opportunity? I'll figure it out."

"We'll be okay," I tell Aggie. "Me and Blake will make it work."

"If you're sure," she says, and her grin comes right back on her face. She walks down the rows so fast it's almost hard to keep up with her.

"We're leaving in an hour," Aggie says as we stumble back to work after break.

"Sounds good. What is this audition?" Blake asks her.

"Well, it's a straight shot from here to Nashville—full ride—they teach you here, then send you there when you're ready, which I will be."

"Wow. My dad would be over the moon if I could commit to something like that," Blake says. "What do your parents think?"

Aggie pulls off her hat and wipes her forehead, then looks at him. Her ponytail bounces as she shakes her head. "Since they kicked me out, they don't get a say in my life, so I have no idea."

Blake's eyes get big, then he nods, and we all go back to the beans.

The whole time, I try to imagine wanting something as much as Aggie wants this gig. Not like Europe, but some new idea that I had all on my own. Even thinking about it makes me dizzy, like the bean rows are shifting and tilting.

I stomp my feet a few times in the sticky, reassuring dirt. Europe is the best choice there is, and Mama will be so happy. Maybe I'll even turn out to be good at modeling. That's enough choices for me, I want to tell Blake, as I hurry to catch up with the others.

I thought it would be super weird, just me and Blake and rows and rows of beans and the whole big sky and nobody else for miles around.

But it's not. It's just, like, normal. We sit on our coolers to eat, and we don't say too much. No talking, no lectures, just lunch. For now, my brain is empty of everything except beans and sky.

After, we chop down weeds like we've been doing for the last trillion miles of beans. I wonder if we've gone as far as one of those marathon races. I'm trying to remember how long those are when Blake checks his phone and looks at the darkening sky; there's a line of clouds there that weren't before lunch.

"They're fine. Still pretty far," he says.

"Okay."

The light is fading as we walk our rows. The dark gray clouds weigh down the sky, and I force myself to look at the ground for weeds.

"Look," Blake says in his lecture voice. "For all I know, you've always wanted to be one of those Gap models, or *America's*—or *Europe's*—*Next Top Model*. The point is, I *don't* know."

And he goes on, but I'm not really listening to him—I'm listening to the stillness in the air and watching the pencil-gray clouds swirled with white that now cover more than half the sky.

Blake looks up at the churning clouds, then back at his phone. "It looks nearer than it is. What I'm trying to tell you is, if you're doing what you want, chasing your dream like Aggie, that's awesome."

I keep watching the sky, now almost completely covered in heavy, angry clouds. I hustle down the row to where the truck waits without cutting any weeds. "Terrific," I say. "But I can't be here anymore."

Blake looks at me, nods, and says, "All right." He catches up to me, and we pop out of the row into the open space by the road. We turn and kinda trot back to the truck, keeping our hooks safely away from our bodies so we don't end up like Patsy.

I can't look at the clouds full-on, because if I do, I will lose my shit for sure. The wind picks up even more, blowing my cap off, sending it behind me a few rows over.

"Leave it," Blake huffs as we grab our coolers and head to the truck. Every hair on my arms is standing straight up now, and the muscles in my legs twitch, wanting me to get the fuck out of here.

We get to the truck, and Blake opens my door for me, then tosses our bean hooks under a tarp in the back.

He starts up the truck, then pulls out onto the road.

His phone buzzes, then beeps one long beep. "So, no big deal, but my dad says we should go up to the house. We've got a good storm cellar there. He and my mom are both over in Decatur."

"Sure," I manage to get out. There is nowhere I can look. The clouds I refuse to focus on are greener and nastier, and the wind has come up and is pushing at the truck. I squeeze the armrest like I can keep us safe from the storm by holding on. Raindrops spit, first just at Blake's window, then all over the truck. Soon, they are big, fat drops that bounce on the hood after they hit.

We turn down a drive that has a big sign arched over it: "GOOD NEIGHBOR ORGANIC FARM." It sways back and forth in the wind. Right after we go under the arch, the rain comes down all angry, like it's trying to smash everything to smithereens.

Blake parks in front of the old-fashioned farmhouse, turns off the truck and looks at his phone. "Well . . ." He scoots closer to me so we can both see the radar on the screen. There are angry red boxes all around the map, and the radar shows clouds with red and orange centers and dark green edges covering the town. The red bar at the top has "TORNADO WARNING. SEEK SHELTER IMMEDIATELY," and other scary words scrolling across it.

I point at the red boxes. "Warnings," I say, my voice all trembly. "Not just a Watch."

"Bad news, right?" Blake points at the house. "The shelter is around that side. You ready to run for it?"

"I—" I catch my breath.

"On three. One, two . . ."

I can't even say "three!" with him. I shove out the door and follow him.

We are sopping wet within milliseconds. Blake herds me towards the storm cellar, and I'm glad he's staying close, because I can barely see with all the rain. As we round the corner, I feel little bites on my arms and head.

"Here comes the hail," Blake shouts near me.

There are two slanted gray doors that lead down to the cellar, kept shut with a giant padlock. "I have to unlock it," he says, shakes his keys all around until he finds the right one, then pops the lock and pulls it out of the metal hook thingy on the door. He pulls the handle, fighting the wind, and finally swings the door outward to open it.

Cement steps lead down under the house.

"Go ahead." Blake holds the door up so I can duck in, then

he follows me and pulls the door shut behind him.

Just as he gets in, the tornado siren blares from our phones and off in the distance, all at the same time.

Tears prick at the corners of my eyes.

I will not cry.

I will not cry.

I will not cry.

Twenty-nine

The wind whips around outside, trying to pull open the storm doors. Blake fights it to keep them closed, standing on the bottom step.

"I just have to close the latch," he says over his shoulder.

I'm standing just behind him in the gloom, waiting for his say-so before I go any deeper into the cellar.

"Aha! Gotcha!" He pounds on the doors overhead once, then lowers his arms and turns around.

"That should hold it, but we should get away from the door," he says. The siren's whine gets under my skin, softer now with the doors shut, but fighting it out with the wind to see which is louder. He pats his thighs and looks around. "Let's take inventory of what we've got here."

"Yeah. Isn't it a . . . little dark?" I try to keep my voice light. I am wound so tight; I could run from here to home in about two seconds right now. I am ready to put a blanket over my head and not come out till the sun is shining. Patsy used to stuff popcorn through the holes of the afghan until the watch or warning was over and we could go back upstairs. It's never once been an actual tornado.

Blake looks at me, his cheeks still wet from the rain. He's lit up in the slice of light from between the two doors. His eyes glow like stars have fallen into them.

He reaches over to my left, and I jump out of his way, then let out something that is half laugh, half sigh.

"Sorry." He holds up a camping lantern. "This should help." He punches a button, and light jumps from the tiny lighthouse window.

The doors rattle in a big gust from outside. "Is it close?" I squeak.

"Hey." Blake looks at me—really looks at me then. He stretches up and hangs the lantern on a hook I didn't see and could never get to. "Are you okay?"

"I'm . . . not a fan of storms. That's all. I—"

Blake puts a hand out towards me and I freeze where I stand. He stops himself before it touches me, then pulls it back. "You've got some hailstones in your hair. Do you want to get them out, or leave them to melt?"

I touch my head, finding little chunks of ice here and there. I rake my fingers through my hair and come out with a few of them in my hand. The wind is getting louder and the sirens are still going.

"You missed a couple." He laughs, and I paw through again.

"Hopeless," I admit.

"Want help?"

"Thanks." He steps towards me and reaches out to my hair. He softly works a hailstone free. His touch is gentle, and he frowns in concentration. I focus on his blue work shirt in front of me, buttoned all but the top two buttons. The edge of his suntan shows as he turns just a little, a solid line of lighter brown edging the darker brown V left from his shirt collar, and his chest moves up and down as he breathes.

I look up farther, to where his hair has run into one glossy black sheet, not a single hailstone in it. He smells like rain and earth, and I can feel the steam coming off his damp clothing.

"Come on, you," he murmurs. He smooths another hailstone out of the snarls, and I barely feel it, his touch is so light.

"Any more?"

He catches the edge of his bottom lip with his front two teeth and closes his eyes, as if he's feeling my head for a message hidden there.

The wind and the sirens are still out there, but my arms and legs grow heavy, and I could stay here like this forever. My heart beats in strong, slow thumps rather than the jackrabbit rhythm it was keeping before. Blake slides his fingers to the ends of the strands and opens his eyes. "There. All clean."

I stand stupidly right next to him, and then I make the mistake of looking up at him. As soon as those soft dark eyes smile down at me, I know I am in deep trouble.

I pull my eyes away, only to have them land on his lips. A boy shouldn't have lips that soft, that full. It's—

Whoa. I need to back away, step away. Keep my distance, but I cannot fucking move. Why am I not moving?

His smile deepens, and we stand there, frozen, his hands hovering over the ends of my hair, my hands itching to reach forward, to feel his shoulder muscles move under the damp shirt, to see if the hair on the back of his neck is as soft as I remember. My breath is coming faster now, and I can't seem to remember exactly why keeping my distance is so important. . . .

Thunder crashes so loud it rattles my teeth, making me jump.

"Umm . . . Let's go farther inside." He brushes past me.

I cannot fucking talk now, either. What the hell?

"Come on back," Blake says, putting out a hand to show me where to go.

I shake my head to clear it and follow Blake deeper into the storm cellar. The wind makes a kind of hollow *whoo* sound and the doors jump and buck to get open. My twitchiness returns even stronger, and I wonder if there's an afghan down here.

"Sorry it's just a dirt floor and cement-block walls. I know some people put TVs and bars in theirs, but this is just an old-time storm cellar."

The doors thump again, and I close my eyes, but I still picture a tornado whipping them open and pulling us out, one at a time, up into the spinning cloud, never to be seen again. I take a deep breath and let it out real slow.

"Will it keep out a tornado?"

"Has so far."

"Then I guess it's all I need." He leads me back about ten more feet and turns a corner. The light makes the shadows bounce around to where nothing looks real. Another gust of wind rattles the doors, and the siren keeps wailing, but quieter now that we are inside.

Blake motions to a gray wooden bench in a little cubby. "That's under the main beam. If the house gets ripped off its foundation, we should still be safe here."

"Ripped . . . off its foundation?" My mouth goes dry. "It's gonna get ripped off its foundation?"

"No. But if it did, this is structurally the safest place in the house, according to my dad. Have a seat." He motions at the bench, and I go sit at the far end.

Distance. Distance.

He stops at a shelf just outside the cubby. "I thought we had . . . ," he says.

I strain to hear what he's saying. I've got my arms crossed around myself. What I wouldn't give for my warm, dry afghan and Aunt Trish's basement right now.

"Got it!" Blake pops into view, carrying a plastic box the size of a carry-on suitcase. He's grinning like he just won the lottery. He sits down right next to me and puts it on his lap.

He opens it and pulls out an old patchwork quilt. He raises his eyebrows and holds it out to me.

It's no afghan, but it will do. I nod.

Blake drapes it across my shoulders, then checks his phone. "No signal down here." He taps it a few more times, shakes his head, and looks up at me for a long minute, then says, "We'll just stay here until the wind stops."

My breath is coming fast and shallow. I can only look at him. This is not happening. This is not happening.

Blake leans closer, and his shoulder is firm against mine. He keeps up a steady stream of chatter. "So, basically, we are in the safest place we can be."

"I can think of a lot of safer places. Like Hawaii. Or Japan. Even Europe." My lungs can only fill halfway up at a time.

"Okay, how about this? This house has stood for more than a hundred years. I think it's good for one more day." The lantern casts strange shadows, and it feels like it's the middle of the night, it's so dark in here.

My ears pop, and the doors rattle again. How can a tornado really be coming?

"What do we do?"

A tornado is coming.

"Well . . ." Blake digs in the box.

It's getting louder.

He holds an object in his hand.

It wants to destroy us, pull us apart, send us flying.

Pick us up and drop us miles away.

"Do you like fruit cocktail?"

"I . . . what?"

"Mom packed some snacks. This stuff keeps for years. Which is a little frightening when you think about it. But do you like fruit cocktail? Fruit cups? Says here there are peaches, pears, grapes, and cherries."

"We could die in the next few minutes and I'm supposed to . . . eat a fruit cup?"

Blake digs in the box some more. "Unless you prefer butter-scotch pudding?"

Thirty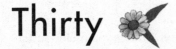

So we eat fruit cups. I search out the cherries first, then go after the other fruit.

Blake checks his phone again and shakes his head, and we listen to the wind howl and the doors rattle. Like the storm is mad that we won't let it in. I fight to keep my distance while Blake sits right next to me on the bench.

And the tornado is still coming.

"Will we hear it from down here?"

"They don't exactly sneak up on you," he says with a little smile.

"Not. Funny. What if it's headed straight for Aunt Trish and Uncle Leo's house? Or where your mom and dad are?"

"Hey." He looks me in the eye and says real low, "I'm scared, too. Only an idiot wouldn't be scared. But we'll be okay. Here." He digs out the one lonely cherry in his cup and holds it out to me on his spoon. "For you. Do you want it?"

I look at it, but don't see it. I shake my head, and thunder crashes and then the air pressure drops, pushing down on my sinuses and making my ears pop again. We look at each other, wide-eyed, and I lose my shit for real. The shaking starts in my back, moves up to my shoulders, then down my arms. I'm not cold, but I'm shivering like it's twenty below zero and I'm not wearing a coat.

"Bliss?" Blake puts a hand on my arm. It's heavy, and I can feel his heat through the quilt, but I can't stop shaking. "Are you okay?"

My laugh sounds a little crazy even to my ears. "It's just . . . all those times I was afraid of storms. All those times I freaked out. I had nothing to be afraid of. But now it's really real, and I—"

Blake takes my cup and spoon and sets them down on the floor with his, then gently takes hold of both my upper arms and turns me to face him.

"Stay with me. Some old farmer built this cellar. He knew what he was doing, and it's not going to blow away." He rubs up and down my arms briskly, like he's drying me off.

His fingers catch in the quilt, and it slips off my arm, causing him to rub my bare arm all the way down to my hand. The feel of his hand on my skin makes me shiver again, but this time it's not from being cold.

He pulls his hand away as if he's touched something hot, and his other hand freezes on my arm on top of the blanket.

"Sorry," he breathes, then he grabs me with his eyes again. "Just stay with me."

I should stop myself. Think of River, even if we are broken

277

up. But once I give in to it, it blocks out everything else, and I don't want to think. I lean in and put my lips on his, drop the quilt so I can put my arms around his neck, and I'm completely not surprised to find his lips are just as soft as I remember. I don't want to think about what's right and what's wrong, or even what's happening outside. All I can think about is how very much I want this right now. And how very much I hope Blake doesn't push me away.

But his arms wrap around me and he kisses me again, a real kiss, and I forget how to breathe, and I never want to leave this exact spot for the rest of my life.

The wind howls, and the siren wails, and I vaguely hear hailstones bouncing off the cellar doors like popcorn popping.

Vaguely.

He kisses me so gently, like he's telling me a story with each touch of his lips, and it's like the first kiss of my life, like the storm is in my head, like I want to climb inside his skin.

We kiss and kiss, and then we are somehow halfway undressed. We pull the quilt under us as we lie on the hard-packed dirt floor, and we are more and more undressed. I don't remember ever feeling like this, not ever.

I slide my hand up his arm, and it makes me want to cry, his skin feels so good under my fingers, and I pull him closer, learning the shape of his sharp, perfect teeth, tasting the faint syrupy flavor left from the fruit cups, breathing his breath into my lungs.

He shifts me slightly and touches my stomach with his flat

hand. I stop the kiss to force myself to breathe again.

"Okay?" Blake whispers. His eyes are burning and are so deep they have no end.

I smile. "Better than okay." I kiss him again, and every hair on my body stands up.

There are too many clothes in the way. I yank off my bikini top and Blake pulls me close so our bare chests have full contact. He kisses me, and asks, "You sure?"

"I want this," I tell him. "You're the one who said I should know what I want."

He laughs, but I'm not laughing because that's all the world is, is those eyes and those hands and the feelings between us.

Every part of my body wants Blake closer and closer. Patsy is always saying I drag guys into bed with me, but it's always been 100 percent their idea. Right now, this is all me.

Blake pauses to slide up and kiss me, and I reach down to move more clothes out of the way. I brush the front of Blake's shorts as I try to undo the button, but it's good and stuck.

"Help me," I tell Blake.

Blake quickly unbuttons and unzips his shorts and slips out of them. I bend to touch him, and I get a wave of memories of this moment with different boyfriends. I freeze for a second, my hands on Blake's hips.

He leans up on his elbow and puts his other hand on my hand. He looks at me. "We can stop if you want." He leans forward a little bit.

Relief washes over me. I lean to meet Blake's kiss. He puts

his arms around me, and I just enjoy the kisses. How can they be so soft and so full of everything at the same time?

The cellar doors thump again, and I go back to touching him all over. My head is busting with the idea that *this* is what I could've had all these years. Was it my fault? Or did all my boyfriends just do it wrong?

Blake is doing it so right. No way are we stopping any time soon. I open my eyes, and Blake is staring at me intensely. His dark eyes look right at me from where he has one hand planted on my belly, and he is smiling at me as he kisses down my stomach. And farther.

Right away there's a roaring in my ears, and I am hot from my head to my toes. An elephant stampede could run through the cellar—ten tornadoes could peel off the roof—and I don't think I would care.

When I can move my own arms and legs again, I reach for Blake. The second I touch him, he says, "Oh no."

I pull my hand away. "What's wrong?"

"No, no, no." He frowns. "I don't have . . ."

My heart sinks. "You don't have a condom?"

"I do not have a condom."

We look at each other, and all of a sudden, we both crack up laughing.

"When I left the house this morning, I wasn't planning—" Blake breathes a sharp breath in when I first put my mouth on him, then he touches me on the shoulder.

He clears his throat. "It's okay. We can just . . . stop."

In answer, I just keep on going, returning the favor. And he doesn't stop me until he's done, and then right after, Blake leans over and kisses me.

Something melts at the core of me, something blooms, some wall breaks down as we lie there, listening to the thunder as it fades away. After a while, Blake hands me my clothes. He waits while I put each thing on. Then he puts his own clothes back on. We keep stopping for little kisses, and our hands can't seem to be more than a few inches away from each other. I can feel every movement as he stands, feel the space between us when he shifts away, feel the heat where he's close enough to touch.

"Are you . . . are you okay?" He smiles my favorite smile.

I nod. "Are you? I mean, just because it was someone else's idea, you didn't have to do it."

He laughs. "So you were listening to me."

"A lecture like that? I took notes."

His face turns serious. "I meant every word, even when I was saying it like an ass. You really do deserve to have what you want. You are strong, and loyal, and if modeling is what you want to do—"

Then it hits me. "I'm going to Europe." Thunder rumbles off in the distance.

"If that's what you want."

"But, we just— What about—" I sit down hard on the bench. "Blake," I start. I just want to say his name like a million times in a row, to feel the way my mouth moves saying it and hear it float past my ears. I've never felt this way before, like by leaning in to kiss him, I woke up some part of me that's been hidden deep inside. I reach up for his hand. "I'm going to Eastern Europe. Like, soon."

"Forever?" He sits next to me, our knees touching, like we have to be in contact all the time now.

I just stare at him, then all of a sudden, I'm laughing so hard I can hardly catch my breath. Blake smiles at me until I calm the hell down, and I can finally say, "I never even thought to ask that."

Blake raises up his eyebrows at me.

"I have no idea how long we'll be there. All that mattered was that we were going." I look at him, and now I want to know exactly how long we will be gone, the exact date we will be coming back. How many hours, days, months? "I guess I should find out."

He nods. "I'd like to know, too." He stands up, pulling me with him. "It sounds quiet out there. We should probably go see if the storm passed, check my phone."

I sigh. "Yeah, we should." We stash the stuff where it came from and head over to the doors. How long ago did we come in here? I feel like nine million years have gone by. "Back to the real world."

Blake catches me by the hand in front of the doors. He kisses me again, soft and short. "Are you okay? After . . . this? Working together and everything?"

"I'll have to see if that's what I want," I say.

We laugh.

"Ready?" I ask.

Blake nods and unlatches the doors and looks back at me before pushing them out. His phone beeps as soon as we step out of the cellar. I lean up against him on the steps as he thumbs through his phone.

"Is it coming?"

He looks at the screen. "Nope."

"Nope?"

"It already did. About a mile south of us."

"You're joking. A real tornado?"

He puts his arm around me. "A real tornado. No major damage. Now past us and all the warnings are over and—we've got to get you home. There's a lot of messages from your family."

We climb the steps out into a goddamn mess. Leaves are everywhere and branches, large and small, lie in puddles and on the wet grass. Some lawn chairs are tipped where they were blown against the shed, and a bike with its wheel bent sideways is in the exact middle of the yard.

It snaps on in my head like a switch: it passed right by us.

My back twangs again, and there is a roaring in my ears. This is the real world. There's probably houses—my house?—with their roofs peeled off like cans of soup. Walls blown down. Cars thrown around like that bike. It's worse than I ever imagined.

"I have to call them. They have to be okay," I say. I go faster to get to the truck, fighting my way through air that is somehow not any less humid after the storm.

"Careful," Blake says, and reaches back to grab my hand to

steer me around a big tree limb just outside the cellar. His hand feels good in mine, but strange, like our hands aren't the same ones that were all over each other just a little while ago, like we are different people already. "We'll need more than a bean hook to chop these branches up," he says, and I try to laugh, but the sound can't get past the worry that's swelling up my throat. Blake squeezes my hand as we clear the branches.

"They're all right, I'm sure of it," he says, and I want to believe him.

"What the fuck, Bliss?"

I look up into River's eyes as he comes around the corner of the house.

Thirty-one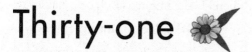

Blake and me drop hands at the same instant, and my face gets hot.

"Fucking Patsy."

"Is she okay?" I ask him, but he talks right over me.

"What a goddamn setup! She's all calling, and texting, they're all flipping a tit that you're out in a tornado, and . . . fuck, Bliss!"

River looks from me to Blake and back at me. River looks different, like he's not the person I spent the whole summer with, like he's changed in the two days since I've seen him. His eyes blaze as blue as they always have, but they look at me like a stranger might, with not even a tiny bit of warmth. My stomach folds in on itself, that cold mixing with the hot relief that Patsy and everyone are safe, and I struggle to take in River, here, next to Blake in the aftermath of the storm.

"A tornado touched down half a mile from here, man," says

Blake. "We're lucky to be safe. We holed up in the storm cellar." His voice is calm and even, like that's really all we did. I'm standing close enough to reach out and touch him if I wanted to, but now that River's here, Blake might as well be miles away.

River squints his eyes at Blake, looks him up and down, then looks at me. "I know about the tornado, professor. Everybody knows about the goddamn tornado."

Blake's jaw twitches, and he says, "It's Blake." His smile is like lightning, sharp and quick. "Remember?"

"Whatever." River hitches up his shorts, then juts out his chin. "Blake." He stares me down with his dark blue eyes. "Not everybody spent the storm 'holed up'"—he makes air quotes—"but what did I expect? Fucking Patsy."

"She was worried—" I start to say.

"I come out here ready to *save* you. Forgive and forget, fresh start and all that shit, and this is what I get? Holed up, my ass." He whirls around and stalks away, slowed down by all the fallen branches.

The distance between me and River grows, but I can't make myself take one step away from Blake. I feel like a piece of saltwater taffy, stretched into ribbons between them.

I was surprised as hell when me and River started going out. All the girls were crazy about him, and I never knew I had a chance until that night out at Granny's. It felt so good to be wanted by him, I never thought much about whether I wanted him.

But if wanting is what I felt about Blake in the storm cellar,

I never even came close to wanting River. So why can't I just let him go?

Blake glances at me, then runs his hand through his hair. His moving unfreezes me.

"I have to explain to him," I say to Blake.

He tilts his head and frowns, like I'm speaking another language, but he doesn't say anything.

"River, wait," I squeak. I trot off after him, splashing in the puddles and dodging fallen branches.

River is almost to his truck when I catch up with him. I reach for his arm, and he yanks it away. He won't look at me, just opens the door and jumps in.

"River—" I start, then I zip around and climb in before he can leave. "I haven't heard from you in two days. For all I know, we are broken up."

He turns his dark blue eyes on me, and I have never seen him look so sad. His shoulders are slumped, and he doesn't even reach for the keys to turn on the truck. He shakes his head slowly back and forth and squeezes the steering wheel in time with the head shaking.

I want to tell him it's not what he thinks.

But it *is* what he thinks.

"Well, *are* we?" I can't stop myself from looking out at Blake, where he stands by his truck, waiting, looking from us to his phone and back again.

River runs a finger over the blue hair tie, and I can almost feel the dent it's made from him wearing it every day for over a year. His voice cracks as he says, "Perfect," then drums his fingertips on the steering wheel.

"What?"

He turns in his lazy way and lets out a big sigh. "I said, your timing is fucking perfect. Losing Granny's and the only girl I've ever loved, all on the same day."

"They sold it?"

He slams the steering wheel. "Here's what I don't get. You don't tell me you're going to—to fucking Europe—and then you turn around and dump me for some rich fucker who works in a music store—"

"He doesn't work in a—"

"Fucking fuck, Bliss, I don't care where he works. What I care about is that you lied to me and cheated on me and now you're dumping me."

"I'm not—" I take a breath. "You didn't answer my calls, or my texts," I say, wondering why I can't just say goodbye and hop out of this truck like I should. "For two days, I didn't know if you were alive or dead."

Blake has started dragging branches into a pile, looking over at us after each one.

"You lied to me, Bliss!" River grabs his hat and pulls it off his head, then jams it back on. "Who decides to leave the goddamn country and doesn't even tell their boyfriend about it—but everyone else in town knows. Who does that?" He looks like a little kid, one who doesn't have a friend in the world.

"I was going to tell you," I say in a small voice.

"I knew you'd let me down. This is what I get, all that time waiting, knowing you were the one I had to have," he says. "You said we were a team. And Granny's will be gone by tomorrow when I get back from detasseling, or Tuesday at the latest, and after that, I'll have nothing." He slumps in his seat. "Nothing."

I picture River, sitting in his truck, watching me leave for Europe with Mama, and it near about kills me to think of being the one to leave him all alone.

But I'm going with Mama.

But I want Blake.

Do I want him enough to destroy River?

Blake and me wouldn't have much time, anyways, not enough time to really start something.

Maybe I just imagined all the stuff that happened in the storm cellar. All the things I felt.

Maybe it doesn't matter.

We both jump when Blake knocks on my window. I open the door.

"I need to go meet my parents, but I can drop you off on the way," he says.

His eyes are so warm, but I can see they are full of questions. I need to get out of this truck. Leave River behind and go with Blake.

"I got her," River says.

Blake looks at me, and I don't say a damn thing. My head spins, and I can hear his lectures about choosing, and loyalty, and I remember again that every single time I've ever wanted something, it's gone to hell in one way or another, and I decide right then and there that I'm going to freeze the storm cellar in time, so nothing can ever ruin it or change it, so I can take it with me to Europe and everywhere. It will stay a time when I wanted something with all my heart, and I got it, and it didn't ever have a chance to turn out bad.

"Well. Okay, then. Here's your stuff." Blake hands me up my bag and cooler, his eyes full of confusion. His hand doesn't touch mine as I grab the stuff. "We'll pick up where we left off tomorrow," he says.

I think about leaving, and being left, and choosing, and I make a decision.

"Um, Blake?" I try to get his name out of my mouth quickly, without tasting it. "I, uh. I won't be here tomorrow. I'm going to detassel corn with River."

Blake's eyebrows come together, and he takes a step backwards like I hit him or something.

I look over at River, and he has almost the exact same look on his face.

"Yeah," I say. "Sorry. I, um, meant to tell you before. See ya."

River moves into action, starts the truck, and heads back out the circle drive. I am leaving all my insides behind, and I'm not 100 percent sure why.

I refuse to turn my head to look back, but I can't keep from looking in the side mirror. Blake stands right where we left him, and fuck if there isn't a rainbow in the sky behind him.

I force my eyes to face the front, blink away the hot tears that threaten to spill out, and River and me head down the driveway.

I study all the houses we pass for tornado damage, but they all look pretty normal. We come to the first stoplight in town, and River strokes my hair a few times, then combs through the hair at the back of my neck. For a second, I imagine him pulling on those tender hairs, pulling my head back, back, back, until I break down and tell him everything that happened with Blake, everything we did and said and all the new things I discovered in the middle of the tornado.

But he only slides his hand down to the bare skin of my shoulder under my shirt and squeezes.

"You really up for detasseling? It's not pussy work like walking beans."

"I said I was."

He nods, then makes the turn to Patsy's. There aren't as many branches down here in town, but there's tons of green leaves stuck all over the sidewalk, like stickers in a sticker book, and even though River said they were okay, I still go a little limp when I see Patsy's house all in one piece in front of me.

River parks behind Clyde's limo and we sit quiet for a minute. I check my phone but shut it down when I see there's like a hundred texts.

Aunt Trish: Where are you?

Uncle Leo: Are you okay?

Patsy: Don't freak out but there's a real tornado coming

And so on.

River pulls me close.

My head hurts so bad I can barely look him in the eye. "Thanks for driving me home." I slide over and almost fall out of the truck, I'm so tired. I wince at the sound the door makes when it slams.

"See you later," River says, and then he pulls away.

"Bliss. Thank the Lord," Aunt Trish says as she grabs me up in a hug so tight I almost drop the cooler. "You didn't answer our texts, and we thought—"

Her chest shakes as she sobs. "You must have been so frightened," she says into my hair.

"I'm okay," I say, but my head is throbbing, and I might have a couple of tears in my eyes, too. "Are you?"

"Super fun getting to the basement on crutches," says Patsy, "but the tornado missed us. We watched it on TV, though— thanks for letting us know you were safe and all."

Maybe I imagine it, but there's a tiny waver in her voice when she says it, and I give her a little smile, which she gives back.

I tell them about getting to the storm cellar just in time, and River bringing me home. I look around the living room, even though it hurts just to turn my head. "Is Mama okay?"

Aunt Trish hollers down the stairs. "Theresa. Bliss is here."

Uncle Leo comes in the front door as Mama rushes into the living room and throws her arms around me. "Oh, baby!" She sniffles loudly and dabs at her eyes, which are red and puffy.

I pat her back. "I'm okay, Mama, I—"

"I was so scared. Absolutely terrified. The storm was so close! The thunder nearly shook the house down. Terrible, just terrible."

"I'm safe, Mama. We're all safe." I look over Mama's shoulder at Aunt Trish, who has her eyes narrowed, like Mama sassed her, or didn't take out the trash when she said she would.

Uncle Leo pats my arm. "You had us all pretty worried. When we hadn't heard from you, well"—he squeezes my arm and swallows—"I'm just so glad you're all right."

I pat his shoulder and say, "Me too."

"Bliss?" says Aunt Trish, her face asking a million questions, like she can see everything that's happened between now and the last time she saw me. I lean into her for a second, let her hold me up, then all of a sudden it's too much, her arm weighs like a thousand pounds. I bust out of her hug and stand between her and Mama.

"Just a headache," I tell her.

She goes to feel my forehead, and I duck away before she can touch me.

"I'm fine."

"You too?" Mama says. "We really are two peas in a pod. All that stress—I can't even see straight."

"I'll bring you something for your head," Aunt Trish says, and Mama says, "Oh, thank god."

Aunt Trish stops and turns back to Mama. "Something for *Bliss*," she says, and her voice is sharp, like it's a knife she'd like to stick in Mama. "For the *child* who was out in the *storm*. Probably scared out of her mind. Help yourself to anything in the medicine chest, though, Theresa," she says, and turns towards the bathroom.

Mama looks so small, so fucking shocked, like a fish that's been thrown onto land. I want to put my arms around her and sit with her until her head feels better, and I want to scream my pounding head off at Aunt Trish for being so mean.

"What is *wrong* with you?" I snap. I stomp past Aunt Trish to the bathroom and bring back the bottle of Tylenol. I shake out a handful and pop two of them in my mouth, dry-swallowing them, then I dump the rest back in the bottle.

"Here, Mama," I say. I look over at Clyde's stupid face, where he stands there not doing nothing.

"Let's get you downstairs," I tell her, and I put my arm around her, and I don't take it away until I've tucked her into bed on the pullout with a cold rag over her eyes, just like Aunt Trish used to do for me.

In my dreams, whenever Mama came back, she and Aunt Trish would spend their days laughing around the kitchen table, sharing memories of when they were girls as they asked about our friends and boyfriends, offering advice on eating healthy and telling us to be home by curfew.

Instead, at dinner Patsy is so grumpy she snaps at everyone, and Aunt Trish looks like she'd rather be anywhere but here. Mama is up and down throughout the meal, and I swear she doesn't even taste the food. She ignores Aunt Trish, feeds bites of her food to Clyde like he's some kind of pet, and finally announces that she's going to bed early.

"It's so exhausting preparing to go overseas," she says. "On top of a tornado! But you'll be so excited when you see what I'm planning," she tells me as she heads downstairs, pulling Clyde behind her.

Aunt Trish offers Patsy a bowl of apple crisp and ice cream for dessert, and Patsy snarls at her. "How fat do you want me to get? It's bad enough I have to sit around this place all day."

She stomps off to the living room with her crutches. Uncle Leo raises his eyebrows, and Aunt Trish says, "She's upset about Nathan. It's been almost three days, and she hasn't heard from him."

Before bed, River texts.

River: 6 a.m. sharp

It's not until I'm turning out the lights that I realize I never told anybody that I'm detasseling with River instead of walking beans with Blake tomorrow.

That's the thing about choices. Blake is right that everyone has them, but sometimes you have to choose what's best for others, even if it leaves you wishing you could choose something else.

Something that would have been for you.

Thirty-two

I barely sleep, and I'm up almost before my alarm even goes off. First thing I do is check the weather to make sure it's not going to storm, then I wait for River on the front steps. When the lights of his truck show from down the block, my stomach gives a little lurch, and I realize I'm picturing a red truck pulling up in front of the house, not River's rusted-out old white one.

Before I can get all caught up in thinking about the storm cellar and the wide-open bean fields and Blake in general, I hop in and squeeze up close to River in the truck for the ride to the meeting spot for detasseling. He is even a worse morning person than Patsy, so it's a real quiet ride.

At the meeting place, we get on a school bus that will take us and a bunch of other kids out to the cornfields. River squeezes into the very back seat with me. He puts his arms around me and falls directly asleep with his head on my shoulder, trapping me so I can't even turn my head or I'll pull my hair out.

When he wakes up, he starts in to making a list of how he's going to spend his detasseling money. "First things first, this will be a party to remember. We'll buy out the fucking liquor store. Then, maybe some leftover fireworks," he adds. He's got a bunch more, but the bus pulls up to the cornfields and we have to get out.

The sun is horribly bright, but everyone else is wearing jeans and long sleeves, and some even have sweatshirts on, even though it feels like it's already about ninety degrees out. Maybe the shorts and bikini top I wore for the beans aren't right for working in the corn.

The crew leader, Verniece, gathers us all up and explains what we are doing. She's a big, tough-looking lady with a short haircut and little eyes.

"All right, first-years. This here is Questron's hybrid field. You got your eight rows planted: six female one variety, two male another variety. Them tall one's the male rows: you can see the tassels stickin' up high, over most of your heads." She scans the crowd, checking heights. "Machine's been through, cut off the six female rows, so most tassels are gone. Your job is to clear out any left behind. Gimme that."

She waves her hand at one of the guys, who hands her an entire cornstalk that was lying on the ground. "Tassel's the male part of the plant." She points to the very top of the plant. "Corn's bisexual—no laughing—and we gotta be sure this corn stays only female. Your job is to find them tassels, grab them"—she pulls hard on the top of the stalk, and the first three or four leaves squeak as they come away from the plant—"yank 'em out, and toss 'em on the ground. Any of them left on the corn, they'll pollinate the other females. Your job is a one hundred percent clean field. And don't touch the two male rows."

Verniece squints her eyes and looks around at all of us. "It's not hard work, just hard to keep working. We'll break for lunch in a couple hours. Take your water and sunscreen. Questions?"

Nobody says anything.

"Keep up with your crew. No dragging behind, no fooling around. Ya do a crap job, you're out of a job. Got it?"

We all nod, and she points us to our rows.

This should be a lot like walking beans, minus the sharp sticks. River and me walk over with the first group. He goes in the first row, and I'm right next to him. It turns out that even though they cut the female rows down short, every corn is trying like hell to make a new tassel. I stop and check each stalk and tug to see if the top is a baby tassel that will squeak out, or if it's just a female's leaf that will stay attached. It's a lot of reaching up and pulling down, and the corn leaves are scratchy and sharp.

River pokes his head through the corn. "Jesus, Bliss. You don't have to check every single one. The machine did most of the work. Didn't you hear? We're just cleanup."

"All the ones I checked had tassels."

"You're slowing us down."

The corn gives a little shade, but it takes away any breeze that might come up. I'm already exhausted, and I'm getting beat up by the corn plants.

River waits for me to catch up to him. "Can't you go any faster?"

"Leave me behind, then."

So, he does. At least the ground isn't muddy like it was in the beans; yesterday's sun dried everything up after the storm. The two jobs are a lot alike—find something in the field that doesn't belong and cut or pull it out. Easy enough. The rhythm is even kinda the same: walk, reach, pull, toss. Walk, reach, pull, toss. What I want to know is, why in the hell is this so much shittier than walking the beans?

I guess I should be glad I have to concentrate to get the job done. My mind doesn't wander like it did in the beans. As soon as I start to drift off, I have to pull extra hard, or I'm surprised by a nontassel stalk that I thought I could pull out, but I can't, or I trip on a dirt clod. The corn is not quite spaced right for my steps—it takes like a step and a half to get from one corn to the next, so I never get into a smooth rhythm.

Instead of my mind wandering, I see flashes of memories, like a slideshow. I see Mama, rubbing her temples at dinner last night as she pushed the coleslaw around on her plate while talking about some Japanese salad that's healthy and filling and so much better for you than American food.

And Patsy, glued to her phone and glaring at me as she sat

alone on the sofa waiting for Nathan to show up, even though he never did.

River, and the hurt and angry look on his face when me and Blake were holding hands after the storm cellar yesterday.

And Blake.

I blink my eyes hard until I don't see him no more. Don't smell his fresh, sunshine smell, don't feel his skin under my fingertips. I squeeze my eyes shut every time I hear the memory of his voice, retaste our kisses, remember his eyes meeting mine and smiling so sweet.

I keep picking up my feet and taking the next step forward because I decided on this, I chose to work with River instead of Blake. This is where I need to be, and this is where I'm supposed to be. Until we leave, Mama and me, I belong *here*.

I reach up, bend another cornstalk down, and pull the male part of the corn out of the stalk, tossing it on the ground behind me.

"Hey, baby." River stands at the end of my row. I'm so far behind the others, it's not even funny. He catches me around the waist and plants a kiss on my dry, thirsty lips. I taste blood in the kiss, but River doesn't seem to mind. He's got a dip in anyways, and he spits off to the side while he stands there with his hands on my waist.

"Fuckin' sucks, don't it? All that's keeping me from losing my fucking mind is the thought of those six-packs stacking up with every tassel I pop out."

"Back in, you two. And keep your hands to yourselves." Verniece glares at me, even though River's hands are on me, not the other way around.

"Awww, Verniece. Soon as Bliss is done with me, you are next in line, girl," River tells her all flirty.

Verniece gives River a dimpled smile, then glares back at me again. "You heard me. Get back in there."

The day crawls past. At lunch, I find tiny white scratches all over my arms from the sharp edges of the corn. This guy Derek has red welts instead of scratches.

"I guess I'm allergic to corn," he says, and I hope mine don't get that bad.

I start to wonder if I wasn't better off walking beans, until River sits down next to me and smiles. "I wasn't sure you were gonna do it, but it was good you came out here with me. We are racking up the big bucks." His face falls a little bit. "If I can't have Granny's, at least we can make the last party count. And when you come back from your little trip, we can start over in our own place, a new place, with no memories but the ones we make. Just you and me."

River whacks me on the arm with the back of his hand. "Hold on. That's it. That's fucking it! We'll make this a going-away party for Granny's . . . *and* for you," he says, and he stands up, pacing back and forth in front of me as he pulls out his phone. "Jesus Christ, this will be legendary."

* * *

On one of the last few times through, Verniece is at the end of the rows, standing in front of a pile of tassels almost up to her knees. She has two crew bosses whose whole job is to follow each person to see how they are doing with getting the field 100 percent clean.

"I'm going to have to put another crew through this field tomorrow. This here's all the tassels you all missed. It better not happen again, people." She looks right at me when she says it, but I know my rows are clean.

On the bus ride back, River gets all emotional about Granny's place. "Can't believe it, to be honest. God, I remember running around outside when I was just a little shit, bugging Granny while she worked in the garden."

"There's a garden?"

He laughs, but not in a happy way. "Not for a while—Lisa and me was supposed to keep it going, but she's always busy, and I know fuck-all about when to plant and what to weed, even after watching Granny all them years." He looks out at the passing fields like he's seeing the ruined garden.

Then he brightens up and grabs my hand, puts it in his lap. "Take my mind off it, babe." He raises his eyebrows at me as he moves my hand around.

"On the bus . . . with everyone?" I shake my head and try to pull away, but he's holding on tight.

River leans back from me, his dark blue eyes wide, then

he laughs and leans in and talks low in my ear. "Aww, Bliss. Nobody's gonna see," he says, and looks up and down the aisles. "All of them is passed out."

I look around, and he's right, the only one not sleeping is Derek with the corn allergy, and he can't see from where he sits, I don't think. But the thought of touching River here on the bus makes my hand curl up and pull away from him.

"No," I say, more sharp than I meant to. But I'm hot, and my arms are tired, and I know what it feels like, now, to want to do something, and I cannot make myself do this. Even if it could make River happy.

"Jesus, Bliss." He smacks the seat in front of us, then turns his back on me and pulls his cap low on his forehead. "I'm taking a nap."

I shrug, make a little pillow out of my hands, and lean against the window of the bus. I did a lot for River today already. Don't my sore feet and itchy arms count for anything? Field after field of corn goes by as my hair blows in the breeze from the open window.

When we get to his truck, River has forgotten all about being mad. He downs a hot Mountain Dew he had on the dash, and he jabbers on and on about the party. Two kegs, body shots, and a garbage can full of electric lemonade, which has a secret ingredient he doesn't want to name.

My eyes just barely stay open, and partway through his planning, I drift off, waking up when we get to the house, where River hardly slows down the truck for me to get out before he races off to buy shit for the party with money we didn't even get yet.

As I stand in front of the mirror yanking out each one of the thousand and two tangles in my hair, Mama knocks on the bathroom door and swings it open.

"Bliss, honey," she says. She holds out a glittery purple suitcase like it's a prize she just won. "We have to get this show on the road. Europe's waiting, baby girl."

"What . . . today?" I say, confused. I follow her into Patsy's room, where she throws the suitcase on the bed while I stand there watching, wrapped in just a towel.

"No, no, no. But I found just the best bargain. Matching suitcases! Aren't they perfect? We need to start packing. Before we know it, we'll have to hit the road." Mama opens and closes drawers in my dresser, flinging things onto the bed.

She pauses and looks at me with tear-filled eyes. "When I left here, I only had the clothes on my back. I had to leave everything behind. Even my precious baby girl. But I came back for you, didn't I? And now we never have to be apart again."

"When, Mama? When are we leaving?" I ask, my voice a tiny bit wobbly. The room spins a little—as much as I want to go right away, I'm not sure what I would do if it were today. Or even tomorrow.

"Soon enough," Mama says. "Soon enough. Now the trick to packing is to narrow it down to your favorites, and only bring those. Start there."

I quick put on shorts and grab a T-shirt, wincing as I pull

it over all the corn scratches on my arms, then start handing Mama my favorite skirts, tops, and shorts. Just about everything I pick makes Mama wrinkle her nose and shake her head.

"Clearly, you need some new things before we go. I know! We can do mani-pedis, then hit the mall. Then we can—what on earth have you done to yourself?"

Mama jerks back from my scratched arms. My wet hair has soaked the back of my T-shirt, and I look around for my towel. "It's from the corn."

"Oh! My precious girl! I am so, so sorry you had to work all those terrible jobs." She holds my hands in hers and inspects my arms, front and back. I look up, and she has tears in her eyes again. "They won't scar, surely? I cannot believe Trish let you girls out in the fields. Well, I thank the stars that I can steal you away to somewhere civilized before you wreck your skin permanently."

"Mama, I don't mind the work. The money is good, and I—"

Mama squeezes me close again, clinging on to me, then pushes me out at arm's length. "And that is why I love you. Such a good girl."

"But I—"

"Don't you worry. Now go get a towel. You got me all wet."

After we finish, I hear a familiar sound in the backyard. Out Patsy's window, I can see her and Beth and Aggie sitting in lawn chairs. Aggie has her ukulele, and she's making awesome sounds come out of it. I grab a Diet Coke and go join them.

"Bliss." Patsy smiles a knowing smile at me, and Aggie stops playing. "You back from work? How are the beans?"

"Wouldn't know. I was with River. Detasseling corn." I look at Aggie and Beth, trying to see if Blake told them anything.

Patsy smirks over at Beth. "Tell her."

Beth looks over at me and raises her palm up. "You missed a real fun day."

"Fun how?"

Aggie somehow makes the uke sound like it's sad, then angry. "Let's just say, we got to see a whole new side of Blake."

"The crabby side," Beth says.

"Maybe *the tornado* was too much for him," says Patsy, and she looks at me, all round-eyed innocence. The way she says it makes it sound like she knows about me and Blake. But there's no way she could.

"I still can't believe it. A real tornado! Most exciting thing to ever happen in this town, and we were in Decatur instead of here," Beth says. "Were you outside when it came, or in the truck? Blake didn't say more than two words today."

"We made it to Blake's storm cellar."

"I would have shit my pants," says Aggie. She lightly picks a little tune on the ukulele, plucking the notes faster than I can think.

"Oh. Wait. How were callbacks?"

Aggie doesn't even stop playing to answer. "I think good. They thought—I don't know. I won't hear for a few days."

"Good luck. God, Aggie. Look at you. I have to concentrate

completely when I'm trying to play, and you can hold a whole conversation."

"Keep practicing. That's all it takes—millions and millions of hours of practice." She grins at me and hands over the uke. "Here, show me your progress."

Aggie doesn't laugh when I show her the two whole chords I can do every time without screwing up. She shows me how to hold my fingers better on one and helps me pick out a few new tunes while Beth keeps Patsy laughing.

I try a little harder to be the boss of my fingers on the frets. On the bus earlier, my fingers curled up away from River. Now they are reaching for the notes, stretching and stacking up to make chords and chord changes. The music gets into my soul somehow and smooths out some of the shit from the last few days.

Aggie takes a turn with the uke, playing some complicated fingering that sounds like drops of water bouncing on a pond in springtime, making it seem cool out here in the heavy summer heat. Maybe, someday, I can do even a part of what Aggie does. For now, I will settle for learning the song for Mama.

Aggie hands the uke back to me while Beth helps Patsy with her crutches so she can go into the bathroom. I am picking out the notes to "Rainbow Connection" when Aggie leans over and puts her head close to mine.

"Take a look." She holds out her phone.

I stop playing and whip my head up. Her clear green eyes

are kind and understanding. I look at the screen, and the texts between Aggie and Blake almost kill me, especially the last one.

Blake: Ask Bliss if she's okay?

I look up at her, and Aggie puts one hand up, palm out. "I don't want to know anything you don't want me to, but you weren't there, and he's worried you aren't all right."

I stare at the phone.

"Are you okay?" Aggie asks in a low voice.

I can't talk. My throat is tight. I look down at my fingers, make sure they are just right for the new chord position. G string, C string . . .

"Bliss. Are you? You can tell me if you're not."

One tear drips down on my arm as I strum. I nod. "I'm okay. I'm leaving for Europe, and then it won't matter." I knock on the uke and hand it to her. "Now teach me how to do this song."

Aggie and me pass the ukulele back and forth, and I get every single chord of the song right by copying her.

I can't wait to play the song for Mama. I think I'll play it for her, and for everyone, on our last night here. She will be so surprised.

Thirty-three

Day two of detasseling is an almost exact repeat of day one. I go through the rows even slower than yesterday, but if I miss a tassel, it's only because it grew after I passed that cornstalk. At least I remembered to wear a long-sleeved shirt today, but I have to force myself to keep the sleeves buttoned as it gets hotter and hotter.

River's work picks up some, after Verniece gave him the stink eye when we got off the bus. "She thinks she's got me figured out. Guess I'll show her who's boss," River told me as he headed down his row.

I get corn scratches on top of my corn scratches, and blisters on one hand and both my feet. All in all, it's a great day.

When I get home, Mama is waiting by the front door. "Let's go! Won't be another week and we'll be up in the air. We simply must shop!"

"Really?" My cooler slips out of my hand, but I catch it before it hits the ground. "Next week?"

"At the very latest," says Mama.

"You got your passports, right?" Patsy says, handing me her pillow as she juggles crutches, blanket, and water bottle. "Work visas and everything?" She is finally done living on the sofa and ready to sleep in the bedroom now that she can use her crutches without falling over.

"Do we, Mama? Aggie and Beth said all that stuff is a real pain," I say.

Mama waves her fingers at us. "Don't you worry. Corporate has a plan." She links her arm in mine. "And it starts with replacing your godforsaken wardrobe, sweetie."

Clyde charges through the living room, whipping past Patsy so fast she wobbles on her crutches. He grabs her shoulders to steady her, then clumps over and puts his arms around me and Mama, and the dirt and sweat on my shoulders surely rubs off on him. "We ready?" he booms out.

"We are," Mama says. "To the mall!" She pulls on my arm, and I find myself pulling back. Shaking my head.

"Bliss?"

I swallow. "I'm not going nowhere until I shower."

"What? You're fine," says Mama. "You're beautiful. I just throw a little lipstick on and I'm ready for anything." She takes a step towards the door, but I can't make myself budge.

I learned my lesson: there's no way I can "make do" ever

again. I know how that ends. "Ten minutes, Mama. All that heat and humidity, I can't try on clothes like this." I hang there, halfway between doing what Mama wants and sticking to what I want. What I need. My heart bangs around in my chest so hard I'm afraid it will bust through.

Mama stares at me like I just told her that kale actually makes you fat, her mouth open a little and her eyes blinking at me. Then she shakes her shoulders, pats her hair, and turns towards the kitchen. "Suit yourself," she says over her shoulder to me. "Clyde, honey, come check the pantry and we'll make a shopping list."

Patsy raises her eyebrows at me, her light-brown part showing in the too-black hair, and I walk away real slow but inside, I'm running. I take the fastest shower I ever took, and I'm dry and dressed in record time so Mama won't be mad.

"Ready," I say, busting into the kitchen where Mama and Clyde are bent over the table, writing on the back of an envelope.

Mama doesn't even look up, just puts up one finger to let me know she'll get to me in a minute and keeps writing. "Clyde, baby, I cannot believe how fast you go through those seeds of yours . . ."

It's more like fifteen minutes before Mama gets up, stretches, and folds the envelope into her purse. She slowly turns and looks me up and down. "Now, don't you look fresh as a daisy?" My shoulders loosen, and I smile at her. Why did I think she would be mad?

I follow them out to the limo, and Clyde gets behind the

wheel. I wait for Mama to get in back like last time, but she climbs in front and shuts the door. I stand there, confused, and Mama's window goes down.

"Climb in," she says, waving her hand towards the back door.

"Don't you want to sit in back? With me?"

Mama's smile stretches her bright red lipstick but doesn't quite reach her eyes. "Oh, I wouldn't dream of sitting so close. You might get too sweaty to go shopping. Now get a move on. Time's a-wasting."

I climb in slowly, and off we go, no star treatment this time. My damp hair lies heavy on my back and neck, reminding me how dirty and sticky I'd been before my shower. If I had just thrown on a little lipstick like Mama said, she would have been sitting back here with me telling me all about her shopping plans, instead of all quiet up front with Clyde. I wish for a second I could go back and do what Mama wanted, but the leather seat squeaks under my clean legs, and I'm real glad I'm not covered in dust and sweat and pollen. I'll do everything else Mama says today from here on out.

We shop harder and faster than I ever have before. Mama warms up to me when I say yes to a pair of four-inch heels that she just loves, and she finally smiles at me as I try on the tightest, shortest, flounciest skirts she can find, so I don't even dream of telling her no when she follows me into the dressing room with her arms full of silky tops with strange ties around the neck and the waist, and sheer lacy sections in weird places.

"Sweetie, once we update your makeup a little bit, you will

look so good in this wardrobe. It's perfect for you." I look over, and Mama has shucked out of her clothes and is struggling to get a tiny top off the hanger and onto herself.

She grins. "Let's do it. Give Clyde a preview of the Walker Women, mother-daughter models. Just think, Bliss. Next week! Two weeks at the most. A chance to travel, and model, and get out of this crummy little town." She hugs me, then wiggles into a short skirt. "You are so lucky!"

We walk—"Show us your strut, baby!"—out to where Clyde sits, buried in shopping bags. He grins so big when we step up to the giant three-way mirrors, the two of us reflected thousands of times: same hair, same face, even the same way of standing when we come to a stop, even though I'm the only one who pulls at the skirt and the neck of the lowcut top.

Mama sighs and grabs my hand, her lighter eyes meeting my darker ones in the mirror. "Just let 'em try to stop us. No way SMOOCH can say no when we're together! We're gonna make all your dreams come true, baby girl."

A lump rises up in my throat as I look at her smile, the smile I have missed for so long, the smile I would do anything for. I look at my own, matching smile, which is not quite as big as Mama's. Maybe she knows better than me what my dreams should be and how to make them come true.

"Oh, Lordy," Mama says, and drops my hand, making a face. "Your cuticles are simply awful. We can't forget manicures! But first: the makeup counter. We need to get you some concealer, honey."

After the third makeup lady asks if we are twins, I stop correcting them and let Mama have her fun. I swear there's, like, five pounds of product on my face when I'm done—even Patsy has never done me up this much. Too bad she's not here to share in all the fun.

I only make one mistake, when Mama picks out a lipstick color I would never wear. I hand her a way lighter one, and she looks at me like I smell bad or something.

"Have you lost your mind? That color is terrible with our skin."

I try and tell her I can't walk out of here with bright red lips, but she stiffens up and pulls back from me, her eyes cold and brittle.

"I think I know what I'm talking about, Bliss. If it looks good on me, it will look stunning on you. Go ahead," she tells the makeup lady.

After that, I do my best to agree with whatever Mama says, and after a while, she smiles and bounces as she whizzes around the makeup station bringing over about a million different kinds and colors of makeup.

We are standing at the checkout counter near the front of the store while Clyde pays for the six bags full of supplies that Mama swears I should never be without. I bend down to pick up a bag, and when I stand up, I am face-to-face with Nathan. Patsy's Nathan. He looks at my bright red lips, my shaded cheeks, my eyes that have an entire rainbow of shadow behind the mascara.

"Bliss?" A slow smile spreads across his face, and shiver bumps raise up all along my arms. "Whoa." His dark ringlets are the same as they've always been, and I can practically smell the chlorine from the park pool all those years ago, hear the people splashing, feel my stomach tighten up from him noticing me, a kid from across the street.

I shake off the past and land hard in the present, bringing all my pissed-off with me. "Where you been?" I say, my voice raspy. "Patsy texted you days ago to come see her." It's hard to talk with all the lipstick on, but white fire burns in my middle, and I want to let it loose on Nathan.

He smiles again, and his eyes are on me like hands, like bad air that sticks to my skin everywhere he looks. "She didn't say you'd be there." He lifts a hand, like he is gonna touch my hair.

I duck away from him, looking for Mama and Clyde, but they walk away, not even noticing I'm not behind them. I turn to follow them, pulling myself away from Nathan's reach. "Text her back, Nathan," I say over my shoulder through gritted teeth, choking on his name as I hurry away.

The nail salon is the exact same one we went to when Mama told me she was leaving me. Same shiny green-and-gold wallpaper, same fake tree in the corner, even the same cracks in the chairs.

I can't tell if Mama knows it's the same place, but I almost expect to see a little blond girl next to me trying—and failing—not to cry while her hands and feet are under the drying lamps.

Clyde is getting a manicure, too, and they laugh about that

for a while. "Did you ever in your life think you'd be getting a *man*-icure?" Mama says.

I have to pick a color, and I stare at rack after rack, looking at them for so long that I start to drift off, imagining the nail polish bottles are cornstalks and I have to pull the tassels out of them.

The nail lady puts lotion on my hands and arms, and it stings when she rubs it into the thousand tiny corn scratches. But then she massages my hands, and I forget all about any other feeling than the relief of having my sore, tired hands rubbed and squeezed, the tension slipping away until I feel like a wet noodle. I almost fall asleep while she paints the dark blue polish on one finger at a time.

Mama and Clyde don't exactly forget I'm there, but they mostly ignore me as they giggle together at the drying table, and I finally let myself relax into the same chair I sat in all those years ago. For a second, I'm twelve years old again and the pain of being left behind rips through me like a knife. I start to breathe fast, but then Mama looks over at me and smiles, and I remember that we are here together and we are staying together.

Before I know it, we have gotten through the manicure without anything bad happening, and we are at the counter while Clyde pays. I look over at Mama, and I feel a rush of love for her that's so strong it almost knocks me over. We are safe now, headed off for an amazing future, just her and me and probably Clyde.

There's a little elephant statue on the counter, and I run my finger over it, my shiny polish almost an exact match for the blue of the statue. My sleepy mind wanders, from the elephant, to Kay buried under the ground near Granny's, to Blake, to the stuffed elephant Aunt Trish found, back to Blake, and then to the elephant ride with Mama.

"We rode on an elephant once, didn't we, Mama?" I say, as we walk out into the heavy evening sunshine.

Mama's eyebrows come together, and she gives her head a little shake.

"At that circus? You were the local celebrity? Remember?" There the memory is—I can feel her arms around me keeping me safe on top of the elephant, and I'm filled up all over again with knowing that she picked me out of everybody to come with her that day. Just like she's picked me to go to Eastern Europe with her.

Mama snaps her fingers. "Oh, my stars and heavens, yes. I do remember that."

I can't help but smile. The humid air seems less hot, and I shake off the sadness of the salon and the bad taste in my mouth from seeing Nathan.

Mama claps her hands together and her bright red polish glitters in the sunshine. "We rode the goddamn elephant! How on earth could I have forgotten?" She turns to Clyde. "You would never believe it. Worst goddamn day of my life. First I'm forced to be the 'local celebrity' for some Podunk town in the middle of nowhere with some ratty, smelly old circus, and then I find out the only reason *yours truly* has to do it is because I have a kid, and 'Kids equal circus, Theresa, and that sells tickets, which have our name on them. Free advertising,' so I couldn't not say yes."

Clyde whoops his gross big laugh and hugs all up on Mama. "I bet you showed them," he says, and slaps her on the ass.

Mama laughs and says, "We did, didn't we, baby? Of course, I was terrified. I was holding on to you for dear life up there. Wasn't it horrible?"

But I can't answer her. A wave of darkness starts up at my head and rolls off of me, spreading in every damn direction. As it floats off further, I get more and more alone in the middle of this busy parking lot, surrounded by a thick black cloud of nothing.

"Bliss?"

But all I can do is stare at her.

Worst goddamn day of her life.

I follow them to the limo, and it's not until we are halfway home that I look at the clock and realize we shopped straight through dinner. It doesn't matter. I guess I'm not hungry after all.

Thirty-four

I go right to Patsy's room and lie down on the trundle.

I pull the ukulele out from under the bed, and I'm unzipping the case when Patsy slams open the door and thumps across the floor, banging the crutches into furniture and walls, her face as red as Mama's new nail polish.

"What. The actual fuck. Were you thinking?" she snarls at me. She hangs on the crutches, her hurt leg off to the side, and she looks at me like, if she wasn't using the crutches to hold herself up, she'd be using them to beat the shit out of me.

"Hey, Patsy. How you doing?" I say. I'm way too tired to get caught up in her bullshit. Especially after the day I've had.

Patsy holds out her phone, but I can't see the texts she's showing me, so she helpfully snaps them at me. "'Bliss told me to text you,'" she reads, "'*Bliss* said I need to come see you. WILL BLISS BE THERE IF I COME BY LATER?'" Patsy is so loud she's almost screaming now, and I don't blame her because of course Nathan did that, of *course* he put it that way to Patsy.

"That asshole. I told you he was a dick."

"*Nate* is a dick? *Nate* is an asshole?" Patsy looks at me, really looks at me for the first time, and sees all the makeup and the manicure and shit. "Jesus Christ. Did he see you looking like that? You act like you don't know, but I see through you. First River, then Blake, now Nate? What number of guys will be enough?"

"I—"

"Oh, wait. It's always been Nate, hasn't it? And you've loved watching me twist and cry and wait for him to come over, haven't you? And all you have to do is bat your fake eyelashes— which are on crooked, by the way—and say 'Nathan!' with that horrible red lipstick and he'll come running. Well, it's not gonna work this time." Patsy's hair hangs around her face in greasy strings where it escaped from her ponytail. She turns to leave the room, but her crutches make her slow.

I want to feel bad for Patsy, but there's nothing left inside of me. I'm as empty as the wide sky over the bean fields. I can't even find the anger I had just a minute ago towards Nathan. "Okay," I mumble.

"Okay?" she says. "O-fucking-kay?" She turns and her crutch catches on my sparkly purple suitcase, and she wavers and almost falls. She whacks it with the crutch.

I grab the suitcase out from under her, the purple glitter flaking off in my hands. "Well, don't worry. Soon Mama and me will be in Europe and you won't have to think about me anymore." I look around her room. "You'll have this place to yourself in like a week, and you can have all the boyfriends in the world, then."

Patsy stares at me, her mouth open, then she starts to laugh. "Wait. You really—" She catches her breath. "You really believe all that shit?"

"All what shit?"

"Europe. It takes weeks and weeks to get a passport. Longer than that for a work visa. Where *did* you go to take your passport photo? How *was* your trip to *Chicago*—the only place you can get a visa? Did you see the Bean while you were there? Eat some pizza?" She flops back on the bed, her leg hanging off stiffly. "Which country are you even going to? You do know there's more than one in Europe, don't you? As much as I would love to kiss your ass goodbye, you are fooling yourself if you think for one minute that you will ever visit Europe—or wherever the hell you think—with your mama. I'd be shocked if you even made it as far as Iowa."

"You're wrong," I say. "It's being taken care of."

Patsy lifts her hands in a *whatever* motion.

"You are wrong."

She has to be wrong.

I need to get out of here. I grab the uke and, seeing Patsy's keys on her dresser, grab them and shake them in her face as I walk past. "Taking your car. Maybe your precious Nathan will finally come while I'm gone."

I charge past Aunt Trish, bumping her on the elbow while she dusts the stupid shelf holding Mama's bowl with an old rag.

322

"Careful," she says. She pauses. "Is Patsy all right?"

I can barely see her through all the anger rising up inside me like a shook-up Diet Coke. "Patsy's not just all right. She's always right. And I'm always wrong."

Aunt Trish stares at me, her mouth open. And before I can say anything more, I turn around and walk out.

I take the Malibu, and I drive around and around town, trying to get away from Patsy and her stupid questions and Aunt Trish and that dumb, hurt look on her face. I drive past the junior high, and I remember the first day of school, how Patsy walked right next to me all the way in, how big the school was, and how everybody looked at me like I was some weird animal on display at the zoo because of being a new kid.

I go past the park, and the square, and all the places Patsy and me used to go, first on our bikes, and then in the Malibu. Everything looks strange, new, like I just came to town, not like I'm leaving soon.

I try to go back to the house, but the third time I go past the turn I have to admit I can't do it. I can't see Patsy laugh at me or sit there with Mama while my head is full of the questions Patsy put there, alongside the fact that my memories don't mean anything I thought they did.

The worst goddamn day of Mama's life.

She can't really mean it. I remember she picked me, she wanted me there, she held on to me and kept me safe.

She was keeping herself safe.

Without paying too much attention, I find myself on the road to Granny's. Hot night air blows in through the windows, and the Malibu almost drives itself out there from habit.

I pass the mailbox where Blake found me that day, back when Mama was just a wish I had and Europe wasn't even a dream. I can see his eyes smiling at me as he went to shake my hand, and I go red all over again remembering the way I hugged him.

I go real slow down the lane to Granny's. Sure enough, the word *SOLD* is swinging from the "FOR SALE" sign at the top of the drive. But there are no cars, and I park and get out and walk around.

I can't even get sad about Granny's as I walk past the front porch where we sat shooting the shit so many times, or the picnic tables where Patsy and me beat River and Long Tom at beer pong that one time. Will I miss this when I'm gone? Will I miss River?

The hot breeze that comes past could pick me up and blow me all the way to Europe, passport or not, and I wouldn't hardly even notice.

I need to see that grave.

I need to touch that headstone, look at that picture of Kay, feel the letters cut into the pink granite, something solid and strange and true.

I grab the uke and walk past the shed and up onto the road that leads to Kay's grave. Lightning bugs wink on and off in the fields on either side of me. Uncle Leo told me those are the males, saying, "Here I am, here I am," to the females.

I almost miss the turn, but I find the pink granite marker, looking just like it did the night me and Blake found it. My gut clenches up, and I have to sit down in front of the headstone because my legs won't hold me up anymore. I open the case and play around with a few chords, then let my fingers wander.

Poor Kay. What did she want more than anything? Probably not to die in the middle of nowhere, working too long for a circus she never asked to join. She probably wanted to run in the fields as fast as she could with her elephant friends, going left when she wanted to go left, and stopping for a drink and a snack whenever she wanted one.

Instead, she had to wear a hat and stand on a ball and give people rides around and around the ring.

My stomach growls as I watch the lightning bugs, and I let a few wishes slip through the cracks where I've locked them away. What if Mama had decided to stay, instead of going to Japan? Or, before that, what if she hadn't dragged me around from job to job? I could have finished school, maybe even paid attention enough to do something after graduation. Maybe I could have taken some extra classes, found out what I'm good at, found a thing I cared about as much as Aggie cares about her music, or Beth loves beauty school, or Blake—

Another wish, but one I have to shove back before it takes over my whole mind. I can't for one second think about the storm cellar, or I will break apart into a million pieces.

I fumble the chords three times in a row, and I set the uke in my lap, leaning my head back on Kay's etching. I am too old for this circus shit. I am past thinking of elephants as some sort of magic animal, some sort of good-luck charm. I am going to walk away from here and never think about Kay again, never think about her gravestone or who I found it with. I need to be strong and stick with the choices I've made. The chords I know.

I stand up, my hand on the gravestone, which still holds the warmth of the day's sun, and hear tires crunch on the gravel road and headlights flash across the lane. I stand there, pinned in place by the lights, and like always, my phone is back at Granny's in the car, so I can't even call for help.

The car—it's a truck—doesn't move, and I don't move, and all I can do is stare at the dust as it swirls in the headlights, making little whirlwinds.

Finally, the truck shuts off, the headlights disappear, and the door slams as someone gets out.

I grip the headstone in one hand, the uke in the other, wondering . . . hoping . . .

"You're here," he says, and of course it's Blake. He steps closer, and even in the dark he looks clearer, sharper, better than I've worked so hard to forget. My whole body leans towards him, like all the cells inside of me move to be closer to him.

"I'm here," I say, then I can't find my voice to say any more.

My head fills up with words, and my throat chokes on every single one of them.

He looks at me, then looks away quickly. He puts his hands flat on top of Kay's grave, like he's soaking up the leftover sunshine, and stares down at them. "I, uh, I've been coming here to think," he says. "Sometimes."

He's just inches away from me, and I grip the headstone hard to keep from reaching out for him. The etching of the elephant is rough under my fingers, and I force myself to look away from Blake and down at the picture. I rub my thumb over the curve of the big top.

My voice is hoarse when I finally find it. "I wish she had died free, instead of tied up in the circus." If I look at him, I won't be able to block out the last time we were here, or the tornado shelter.

"Did you know why they only use a rope around an elephant's leg to hold it? Weighs more than a car, and they tie it up with a single rope. Do you know why that works?"

I shake my head at Blake, keeping my eyes on the trees at the edge of the field.

"So, when they first get an elephant, when it's a baby, they put a strong rope around its leg. When it tries to run off, it can't. Because there's a strong rope holding it back. Right?" His voice is soft and relaxing, and I could listen to it for hours.

"Yeah. So?" I shake my head to clear it.

"So, the elephant has the rope put on every day. And every day it's too heavy, and the elephant can't get away. But after a while, it grows up. Grows up to the size of a car, or bigger, and when it's all grown up, it's held down with . . . the same size rope."

"The same size rope?" I blink at him, surprised, and then look away, because he is saying something I don't quite understand.

"Exactly the same. And, the thing is, the elephant doesn't even try to break the rope, doesn't even try to get away. Even though it could just pull the rope and snap it. Because when the elephant was a baby, it learned that it could pull all it wanted, and the rope would hold it tight, right? The rope was stronger than the baby elephant. And when the elephant grows up, it *still believes* that the rope is strong enough."

Blake turns towards me, and every single muscle in my body wants to turn towards him, but I hold myself completely still. "Hmph. I thought elephants were smart."

"They are." He leans towards me.

We stand there looking at each other, just a few inches of thick summer air keeping us apart.

"I'm not going to ask why," he says, looking off into the night. "But I sure wish you'd change your mind."

"I—"

He shakes his head. "You don't need to say anything."

We stand there all quiet, and my head is full of answers I could give him, but none of them seems good enough.

Finally, I ask, "How are the beans?" at the same time as he says, "How's detasseling?"

We look at each other and laugh, then we both look away.

"You first," he says.

"All right. Detasseling is okay. The corn is taller, but there's no sharp hooks."

He might have smiled, but I'm only looking out of the corner of my eye, so I'm not for sure.

I risk saying, "The boss isn't near as good," and then I wish I could take it back.

"Well, I was a terrible boss today, so . . ."

My hand moves before I can stop it, reaching out to touch his arm. "I said I would help—"

Blake stiffens up and looks down at my hand, then up at me. His eyes are so deep, and dark, and shouldn't be full of so much pain.

I take my hand away, but my fingers tingle with the feel of his arm under them. I block out the memories that want to come rushing back. "I'm sorry. For—"

"Don't worry about it." Blake says, like he actually means it. He looks off at the lightning bugs, closes his eyes, then looks at me, pulling me in like always with his soft smile. "You're doing what's best for you, what makes you happiest. I truly wish you the best. You're going to be an amazing model. As for me"—he shuffles his feet—"I used my dad's new respect for my 'excellent crisis management' skills—his words, not mine—to actually talk to him about the engineering thing."

"You did? That's great," I say, and I have to link my fingers together to keep from throwing my arms around him in another stupid hug.

"When the beans are all cleared next week, I have a meeting with an admissions counselor to talk about switching to the agriculture school or at least getting a minor in ag if I'm stuck with engineering." He smiles at me, but then it fades. "When do you leave?"

"Too soon, and not soon enough."

He laughs. "I know what you mean—there's so much to do. I remember! And then the travel itself: our flight to Shanghai could've been only thirteen hours but my mom's a bargain hound, so we had three stops, and it took over a day to get there. But it was cheap! Where are you flying out of? Chicago?"

I have no idea.

Patsy's wrong. It's not bullshit.

"It's taken care of," I say, louder than I meant to. "Thomas from corporate is taking care of it."

We're both quiet for a minute then, looking up at the sky. The stars wrap around us in a dome from horizon to horizon, and the night bugs whistle and sing and whirr, and we stand there, together but not together, in a little pocket of almost peacefulness.

Blake's phone buzzes, and we both jump. He looks at it, a giant lightning bug flashing on and then off when he's done reading. Only he's not saying, "Here I am." Instead, he says, "I have to go."

"Yeah. Me too," I tell him.

He won't let me walk back to the car alone, so once again I ride in the big red truck, and Blake lets me off just like the first day we met. But I'm not so stupid as to hug him this time. I know better than that.

He waits until I get in the car, then he follows me down the lane. At the turn, he goes right, and I go left, and I'll probably never see him again.

Thirty-five

The next day, River is all over the place, skipping tassels, having to do some rows twice, all while telling me every detail about the plans for his party. Which is, I guess, my party, too. My going-away party. Long Tom has found a band that's gonna play, and River is revved up talking about how he's gonna get extra tables for beer pong and borrow somebody's cornhole game.

His words go around and around and never quite land. I'm caught up someplace between seeing Blake at Kay's grave and the worst day of Mama's life. I try to sort everything out, but it keeps twisting up on me. The only thing that's real and true is the corn, and I come back to myself as I trip down the soggy rows and brush up against the sharp leaves as I pull tassel after tassel.

The sun pounds down on us, but it's almost good to feel the pain of its heat. Like it understands that sometimes you have to live with your choices, even if things aren't exactly what you thought they were.

River isn't doing so good here in the corn. Verniece is getting fed up with his lazy work, and the only reason his ass isn't fired is he has big blue eyes and a sexy stare that he uses on her all morning long, in between telling me all about my goodbye party.

After a while, I stop thinking about last night and decide to focus on good things, like going to Europe with Mama. I try to imagine the after part—after all the goodbyes—but pretty soon I've worked up a real panic about the whole trip. Patsy's and everyone's words swirl around my head: *tickets, visa, passport, arrival, travel*—on and on until I'm about to bust. What country are we even going to? For the first time, I want—need—to know. When we break for lunch, I can't hardly eat, my stomach is so upset.

River is so focused on the party that he hardly eats, either. Over and over, he says, "Nobody's going to forget Granny's goodbye party for a long-ass time. Guaranteed."

I nod and smile.

After lunch, I stumble through the dirt rows surrounded by tall green stalks. One of my stalks is already making an ear of corn and I stop to look at it more closely. The light-yellow silk peeks out of the fragile green ear and I reach out and touch it with a fingertip. It is soft and warmed by the sun, and I close my eyes for a moment. It reminds me of Mama, of sitting in front of her on that elephant with her hair hanging down around my face. I remember thinking I would do anything to get her to hold me like that, laugh with me like that, every day. Anything.

So much for that memory. I close my fingers around the silk and rip it out of the ear as hard as I can, then throw it to the ground. The thin strands float through the air to land on the clods of dirt like streamers after a parade.

I walk off, pulling tassel after tassel. Going to Europe, it's not about some memory from when I was little, the way Mama and me remember it completely differently. It's about new memories, about laughing with Mama every single day from here on out. Like Blake said, I'm doing what makes me happiest.

I come to a dead stop in the row. All this time, I've been waiting on SMOOCH to do everything and Mama to tell me when it's done. I plant my feet in the lumpy dirt and look up through the green corn fronds to the sky, grab a tassel, and yank it from the cornstalk. I'm tired of waiting around, tired of everybody else making plans for me. I've never in my life took over planning for something, but when I get home, I'm making Mama tell me when our tickets are for and what still needs doing about passports and shit, and I'm doing it.

I throw the tassel down the row, and it flops to the ground. No more sitting around waiting. I'm taking charge of our trip.

I march down the rows, full of plans and purpose.

River is all kinds of cuddly on the bus back to town, but the questions I have for Mama are so loud in my head, I can barely pay any attention to him.

He hugs me up close and kisses my sweaty forehead. "I am going to miss you so much while you're on your trip. And

I want you to know"—he pulls back so he can look me in the eye—"that you're the best thing that's ever happened to me. You belong with me, Bliss. I knew it ever since last summer, and I will never, ever let you slip through my hands. Not even if you go halfway around the world."

He leans over and kisses me, one of the sweet, slow kisses that used to melt my insides, and I kiss him back, but my mind is churning through tickets, and visas, and which day we are leaving and how I can get Mama to let me help her.

"We have to mix it up in trash cans first, then add the ice," River is saying, as we bump home in his truck, dusty, sore and sun-burned from the day's work.

"Mix what up?"

River drifts past the neighbor houses until we stop in front of Patsy's. He looks over at me, on his way to steaming mad. "I'm starting to think you forgot about me already. You half-ass kiss me, you won't even tell me when you're leaving, and you sure as hell haven't helped me with your party."

"I thought it was for Granny's."

"Of course it's for Granny's." River pounds the steering wheel with a fist. "It's for all the goddamn things. You, Granny's. Fuck, I won't be surprised if Long Tom moves away tomorrow."

My heart does a flip that reminds me I'm really truly going and leaving everyone behind, sooner than I think, probably. I reach out to give River a hug, tell him I'm here now, that he isn't all alone.

"Whatever happens, Bliss, you will not forget this night any time soon," he tells me. He grabs my wrist before I get out of the truck. "And wear that blue skirt tonight. It makes your ass looks hot."

Once I get inside, I know I should go straight down and ask Mama, but I get nervous about it. I pull out the ukulele and practice the chords I'm good at, letting the music drift into my pores, where it gets inside me and fills up the cracks in my soul. After a while, I play the rainbow song, and once I realize I've got it all the way down, I have an idea.

I'm going to play the song for Mama right this minute and remind both of us that even though the elephant memory isn't what I thought it was, we are still connected. We belong together; we're a team. Then, when she understands our connection, I will do what I said to myself earlier and take control over our trip, making her tell me what's happening and when, and what we need to do before we go.

I'm so excited by my idea that I jump up and practically run downstairs to where Mama and Clyde are probably still sleeping, but I slow the fuck down when I see who Patsy is tangled up with on the sofa.

Nathan raises up his eyebrows, then a slow smile goes from ear to ear as he burns up my pink tank top with his hot eyes. "Hell-o, Bliss. Come to join the party?" I step around Patsy's crutches and walk as slow as I can make myself go past them.

Patsy gives me a look that should split me wide open, even

335

though it's Nathan who's the problem. I can't help looking at the way his hand rests on Patsy's good knee. My own knee twitches, but I ignore Nathan and ask Patsy, "Need anything?"

She shakes her head, and her eyes shoot fire at me. "We're good."

I nod and turn towards the basement door. Nathan's hand snakes out and catches hold of the uke, and I jump like he's grabbed me instead. "Make up your mind, would you?" he says, in that syrupy voice. "'Come see Patsy,' you say, and now that I'm here, you're all mad." He looks over at her and jerks his chin at me, whispering loudly, "I think someone is jealous."

"Think what you want," I say, and the uke twangs as I twist it away from him.

"Bye," Patsy says in a singsong voice as I take a shaky breath and go downstairs.

The basement looks like the tornado made a direct hit here instead of missing us by a few miles. There's clothes everywhere, half out of suitcases and draped on shelves and boxes, and empty fast-food cups and bags are piled around like holiday decorations. Bags and bags from our shopping trips are stacked up in the corner, with at least one of the shirts Mama bought me puddled up on the floor next to them. Half the bowls from Aunt Trish's kitchen are stacked on the floor and every other flat surface, some empty, some with molding food, and lots with sunflower shells piled up in them.

Clyde is on his back snoring on the foldout, but Mama is awake next to him. She puts her finger over her lips and slips out from under the rainbow afghan, grabbing a robe to wrap around her naked body. I turn away and look at just about anything else.

"Gracious, baby. What could you possibly want? Clyde needs his sleep," Mama says as she leads me over to the steps, where she sits and looks up at me, eyebrows raised. Afternoon sun slants in through the window and lands on Mama, making her hair glow like the light around a candle. Even though she just woke up, she's so pretty it's almost painful to look at her.

My hands shake as I bring out the ukulele from behind my back. I put my arms around it like a baby, ready to play.

"Sweetie, whatever you need, could you just ask Trish or something?" Mama yawns. "You know about these headaches. Simply debilitating."

I take a deep breath and decide to go for it, now or never. I'll play, Mama will love it, and then when she's good and happy, I will tell her I can't just sit back and watch her plan our future. Not anymore.

The first nine notes come out a little slow, but I do them better the second time around. I play the first chord and sing real soft, "Why are there so many songs about rainbows?"

I can't watch Mama because I still have to look at what my hands are doing, but even though I screw up a few chords, it's the best I have ever done on the song, even when Aggie was helping me. I lose myself in the sweet notes and the chord changes, and I'm feeling good about it, especially when I nail the three chord changes right in a row, when Mama reaches out and puts her hand on my strumming hand.

"I'm going to stop you right there," she says, her nose wrinkled up at me, "and let you take that upstairs to practice, or whatever you're doing." She puts her fingertips to her forehead. "Every twang is simply grating on my head."

"But it's yours!" I say.

Mama shakes her head. "What?"

"This ukulele." I hold it out to her. "Don't you recognize it? Aunt Trish said you used to play it all the time."

Mama looks at it blankly.

"You took it everywhere and practiced all the time. No one could stop you. You played it just last week!" Even though I try not to, I sound like a puppy whining to be let out of its crate. "She let me have it, and I'm learning, too. To play just like you." I'm practically panting; I'm trying so hard to remind her.

Mama sighs, then lets out a tinkly laugh. "Do not listen to Trish if you want the truth about our past. If you asked her, she'd say everything in this house was hers, and that I was the one who barfed at the fair, when we all know it was her." She stands up, pulling her robe close, and squints at the uke. "Keep it if you want—I'm not the musical type, but once you practice some, you might be."

Mama slips past me and heads back to her and Clyde's room. She blows a kiss over her shoulder. "Sweetie. I cannot wait to model with you, but I need my beauty rest if we want people to think we are twins."

I stare after her, then I remember the other reason I came

down here. I was supposed to make Mama so happy she wouldn't care if I asked her about our trip.

"Passports," I bark out. "I'll get us passports." I chase after her, reaching for her arm. "I want to see the tickets. Did Thomas get our tickets? How long does it take us to fly there, Mama?" I'm fucking it up, I can tell, and I grab the sleeve of Mama's robe, the thin fabric bunching up in my sweaty hand. "Tell me what's happening. Should I take the GED? You can't leave me out. Let me help."

Mama jerks away from me, pulling her robe loose. She closes it and reties it, then tilts her head and puts her chin in her hand and says real slow, "You want to help."

I nod, blinking through the stupid tears that come out of nowhere.

"With travel plans. To Europe."

"Yes, I—"

Mama puts out a hand, and I go cold all over and wish I could go back, start over, leave the uke upstairs and never come down here, because I've fucked up, I can feel it.

"What . . ." She closes her eyes like it hurts her to even say the words. "What on earth do you know about travel?" She opens her eyes and then narrows them at me. "Why, baby girl, if I didn't have such a big heart, or wasn't so open-minded, I might think for a minute that you don't trust me. Your very own mama!" She gives a laugh that has cracks running through it and throws open her arms to pull me in for a hug. She kisses me on the forehead, a wet kiss that feels like a warning. Or a brand.

"But don't you worry. Mama has everything under control, and there is no way I'm going to bother you with tiny details. Just you rest easy and let SMOOCH handle things, and before you know it, we'll be over there eating—I don't know. Bonbons?—together."

The ukulele twangs as Mama squeezes me tighter. "But first, girlie, Mama needs an aspirin. Take that thing far, far away from me before it splits my head in two. Mwah!" Mama air-kisses me and pushes the uke away from her before she disappears into the spare room, shutting the door practically right in my face.

I can hardly breathe. I grab for that feeling, the new feeling, that told me I could take up as much space as I want, take control, but it's like a flag on the wind that whips out of my fingers every time I think I've got it.

I climb the stairs, dragging one foot at a time onto the next step. I catch a string under my finger and it pips out a note, laughing at me. I did a real great job of taking control just now. I totally connected with Mama—we have so much in common—and I'm sure she's going to tell me every little thing about our trip, starting now.

Fuck.

I shake my head and pull myself up another step.

When I'm almost at the top of the stairs, I hear Nathan talking to Patsy.

And he's saying it to her, just like he said it to me before: "Don't cha wanna be my girlfriend?"

Thirty-six

My bones go all watery, and I put my hand out to hold myself up on the railing. I shut my eyes, but I can still see Nathan's face right up close to mine, his rich brown curls bouncing on my cheek as he went at it way back then. At first, I was so pissed at Patsy and so fucking happy that Nathan picked me over her. And then I was just stuck, trapped, pinned down by the no I hadn't given him and the weight of his body on top of mine.

Because he knew what he meant by "be my girlfriend." But I sure as hell didn't.

"You didn't come see me," Patsy says, her voiced muffled by the basement door. "I wasn't sure I *was* your girlfriend."

The door looms dark in front of me, a thin piece of wood between me and Nathan's smooth answer to Patsy. I rub my arms to erase the memory of his hands all over me and to stop myself from shaking, and I look back down at the beanbag, limp in a dark corner of the basement near the closed door to where

341

Mama is sleeping. I take a step down, wanting to hide under an afghan, but like Blake said, I always have choices, and I think I'd rather face Nathan than Mama right now. I shift the ukulele to one hand, and the strings make a soft chord of their own when I let them go.

Patsy gets louder. "Stop it. I have so many stitches, Nate. I could have died, the doctor said so."

"Relax. You're too tense." Nate's voice is flat. Pissed. Low enough that I have to lean my ear against the door to hear him.

"Let's watch a movie. Tomorrow when I'm better, we can try again."

"*Tomorrow*," Nate sounds like he's explaining water to a fish, "Tomorrow I have to register for fall classes. *Today* I want to be with my girlfriend." He sounds whiny as shit. "Is that a crime?"

"Nate, I— Ow!"

If he hurts Patsy, I might just kill him. I put my hand on the doorknob and keep listening.

"I told you. We have to wait." Patsy's voice gets louder and higher with every word.

"Jesus Christ, Patsy. You're fine. Just let me . . ."

Silence, then Patsy says, "Stop," in a voice that means serious business.

I throw open the door, and I'm standing over the sofa almost before I know it, staring down at Nathan and Patsy. He has his hand in the waistband of her flannel pajama bottoms and he's trying to kiss her even though her face is turned away.

"Stop," I say, loud and mean and like I wish I'd said it all those years ago. "She said stop." I go to grab Nathan's arm, and my fingers recoil from the feel of his skin, so I try again, and this time I pull on a fistful of polo shirt. I haul backwards with all my might, and Nathan slides halfway off the sofa, landing with his full weight on Patsy's hurt leg, and the ukulele goes flying, twanging as it lands somewhere on the floor.

Patsy shrieks, "Ow-ow-ow-ow," and slaps at Nathan, and I pull at his shirt again to get him off her.

I'm yelling, and Nathan is yelling, and I pull so hard that Nathan comes crashing towards me, catching himself on my shoulder and my chest. I stagger to hold him up, and having the full weight of him right up on top of me, his dark chlorine-scented ringlets against my cheek, is like being shut into a coffin with no air to breathe.

I shove him off me with all my strength, but he teeters and grabs on harder, and we almost crash back into Patsy, but I grab the couch to steady myself.

"What on earth is going on?" Mama calls from the basement door, eyes wide.

Nathan ignores her and brings his nose right up against mine, his eyes open so wide the blue is a target in the middle of the whites. "Leave me alone, you crazy bitch!" he growls, and pushes me away hard, then takes off towards the door.

In slow motion I fall and fall and fall, smashing into Aunt Trish's bookshelves before I crash to the floor in a heap of broken plates, figurines, and, finally, the big glass bowl, which wobbles on the edge for one long moment before it shatters into a million pieces on the floor next to me.

"Oh my god," I say, staring at my arm, where there's a piece of the bowl stuck in it like a little tooth growing in the wrong spot. I can't move for staring at the sparkly piece of glass and the line of blood that's working its way down my arm from it.

"Oh my god," Mama shrieks. Like a superhero in a silk robe, she rushes past Patsy, who is half standing next to the couch, to where I lie on the ground like dirty laundry somebody left behind. The front door slams, shaking the house as Nathan leaves.

I hold out my hurt arm so she can make everything all right. "Mama," I say, and she looks at me, but her eyes are dull, like I'm maybe not even here in this room with her.

"Oh no," she says, and she sinks down in front of the ruined bowl, staring at its broken pieces. "I gave that bowl to Mother . . ." She bends over the wreckage, tears and yesterday's mascara running down her cheeks.

We're in the center of a tornado, the eye of the storm, just me and Mama, although I'm not sure she knows I'm here. Everything is still as death, and I don't remember how to breathe. My ears roar as Mama, not two feet away from me, shrugs her hair back from her face while she cups the biggest shards of the bowl in her hands. She holds the broken bowl like a baby, like she wants nothing more than to put it back together and make it whole.

But it will never be whole again. Never.

She looks at me then, and for a little tiny second, I think she will lean over and scoop me up, take care of me.

"Bliss," she says, her voice as broken as the bowl. "Help me." Mama holds the pieces out to me, a miserable child looking for a magic cure. "Help put it back." She grabs my hand like it's a life preserver and she's in the middle of the ocean. "You have to fix it. Please."

Blood drips from my arm, and the tornado roars in my ears: Sure, I can help her. But who's going to help me?

"Bliss." Patsy's voice comes from far away, and it's like she pushed Play on a paused video. I find myself flat on my ass in the living room surrounded by broken dishes and pottery. "Bliss." Patsy leans over me, reaching for me, supported by her crutches. "Oh my god. You're hurt?"

I can't make words with my mouth, so I just nod at Patsy.

"Here," Patsy says, and she pulls me to standing. I can't take my eyes off of Mama as she leans forward to pick up more pieces of the bowl. Patsy puts her arm around me as I feel around for the uke. "Are you hurt anywhere else? Can you walk to our room?"

I grab the ukulele and point to the crutches. "Can you?" I say, and together we limp back to the bedroom, leaving Mama and the broken bowl behind us.

Patsy wears some of her hair-dyeing gloves to grab the glass and pull it out, then squirts cream on the cut and bandages it up.

"Do I have to say it?" Patsy drops to her bed, letting the

345

crutches fall to the floor. "You're going to make me say it. Jesus Christ, fine. You were right. About Nate."

Her words go in my ears, but I can't hear them through the buzzing in my brain. I walk around the bedroom and pick up things—hairbrush, hair ties, Patsy's nail polish—hold them for a second and let them fall, not really seeing them.

"You saw it, right?" My voice is scratchy. "What she did out there?"

Patsy nods and reaches for my hand. "That was some fucked-up shit, I'm not gonna lie."

"I just—"

She squints up at me.

"I just wanted her to be a mom. For one second."

Patsy wipes her eyes and gives a little laugh. "Your mama couldn't take care of a stuffed animal, Bliss."

The memories flutter past, like fifty-two-card pickup. Waiting in the room for her to bring me dinner when I was six, only to have her forget because she had a stressful shoot. Bringing her ice packs at the motel when I was eight and she had a headache. Taking her side against Aunt Trish when she talked about us going to Europe just the other day.

I get the cold chills up and down my back. Like when you go into the movies on a sunny summer day, and the change from bright, sweaty sunlight to dark air conditioning makes you completely not able to see for a minute. And then when your eyes get used to it, you're like, *Yeah. Why couldn't I see these seats and this popcorn until now?*

It's not gone all the way, but the pissed-off feeling just pops and fizzles out. Because I knew, didn't I? I always knew. It was like some secret Mama and me shared but had taken a blood vow to never say out loud: what she needs from me is bigger than anything I could ever need from her.

"I thought she loved me. Wanted what was best for me."

"I think, in her mixed-up way"—Patsy pauses, reaching for her crutches—"she did." Patsy pushes herself up from the bed and teeters there, her blue eyes soft as she says, "I mean, she brought you here to us."

She did.

I nod, hugging Patsy so hard I almost knock her over. "I'm sorry about Nathan."

"I'm sorry about your mama."

"I wanted to be wrong about him."

"I wanted you to be wrong. Sorry. I was such a bitch."

"You're always a bitch, Patsy." She laughs, and I laugh, only a little hysterical, as we lean together, arms around each other. Once we both stop laughing, I look over and see the giant sparkly suitcase in the corner by the trundle. And it all adds up.

Mama forgets to feed me.

Mama dresses me like I'm her.

She went to the broken bowl.

She left me.

Mama left me.

"Oh, fuck."

I can't get any air in my body. I choke, because now that I

know . . . now that I see, clear as day, now that I know, there's no way in hell I can do it.

"I'm not going to Europe." I rub my arm near the bandage.

Patsy snorts a laugh. "You were never going to Europe."

"But I have to tell her." I look over at the bulletin board, where Mama's postcards used to hang. At the pile of clothes Mama bought for me. Or her idea of me. "I can't go with her. I won't."

Patsy nods. I pick at what's left of the manicure Mama got me, and I flash on Blake, lecturing me out under the open sky, and I finally get what he was talking about. I pick up the uke, strum one bad chord, and set it back down.

"It's not my dream." I sit down on Patsy's bed and hold out my fingers with the chipped polish.

Patsy pulls out her nail polish remover, and the sharp lemon smell fills the room. "Damn straight it's not," she says, and she wets the cotton ball and scrubs hard at the polish on my pointer finger, leaving my fingernail raw but clean.

Mama and Clyde don't come up for dinner, so me and Patsy get to tell Aunt Trish some story about how the bowl and stuff just fell right off the shelf, and how we cleaned it all up. Aunt Trish pinches her lips, and then her and Uncle Leo go out back to work in the yard. Patsy has somehow convinced Aunt Trish to let her leave the house for the first time tonight, and she uses every kind of makeup in her stash on us to celebrate.

I don't think about the party because I'm working up my

nerve to go downstairs and tell Mama that I can't go with her. I force myself to leave Patsy behind and go down the hall, and there is Mama, headed to the kitchen.

I watch from the hall as she gets a glass, fills it, takes a sip. She looks so small from here. So alone.

Mama comes through the living room, and I almost, almost let her pass. Let her go downstairs thinking we are heading off together, just like when I was little: Mama and me against the world.

But my throat closes up and every muscle in my body goes tense when I even think of it. I have to tell her. Like Blake says, I need to make my choice.

I shake my head to clear my thoughts, then I make myself call out to her.

"Mama?"

She jumps, and the water sloshes onto her hand. "Oh, dear Lord, you scared me to pieces. Hiding in the shadows like that." She's cleaned the mascara from her cheeks, and without it, we really could pass for twins. "What are you, a stalker?"

I've gotten used to hearing her voice in this house again. Is that all it takes? Nearly two weeks and you get used to something that's been gone for so long? For a tiny second, I imagine that this is Mama's and my house and we've always been together here, and this is just an ordinary night between two people who are so used to each other, they know what the other person is going to say next.

"Mama?" My voice is tiny, wobbly, like I'm using it for the

first time. "I . . . Come sit down." I sit on the sofa and pat the cushion next to me.

"Oh, baby, I would love to have me some girl time, but Clyde is waiting, and I have to get up early to call around to find someone who can replace that bowl," she says, glancing at the empty shelf. Her eyes bounce off it, and she takes a step closer to downstairs.

Just like always, I have to go to her instead of her coming to me.

"Mama." I take a deep breath and jump in feetfirst. "I can't do it."

"Oh, baby, you'll figure it out. Whatever it is. Now let Mama get to work. There's a lot to do before we go."

She moves to pass me, and I reach out and grab her arm. The water slops out of her glass and onto my foot. Her arm is skinnier than mine, scrawny even, and a rush of wishing pours over me when I touch it. Wishing she had strong, sure arms that could hold me when I'm scared and push me in the right direction when I need it. Wishing she could look at me and see a Bliss-shaped person, not a Mama-shaped reflection.

I can't help myself. I have a goddamn relapse. "Mama, do you think I should go to college?"

Mama blinks like I just asked her if I should join the football team. "College? What for?"

"I don't know. For finding out whatever I'm good at?"

Mama smiles a gentle, sad smile at me as she pats my hand, then peels it off her arm. She takes a drink of the water, and I wiggle my wet toes as I wait for her to answer.

"Oh, sweetie. With looks like yours, you won't ever need to be *good* at anything. Don't you see? You and me, we're not the college type—we don't need it, and it sure as hell doesn't need us."

"Even if I, I don't know, *wanted* to go?"

Mama's laugh busts out of her like a trumpet. "You don't want to go to college, baby girl. You're not the honor roll type."

A blast of fury rises up from my toenails to the top of my head, filling me with anger so hot it's a wonder every hair on my body isn't burning.

"Honor roll?" I say, and I'm shocked to hear my voice come out like normal, not like the roar of some dragon. "Honor roll? For all you know, I was on the honor roll every day of my life since you left me here. Seventh grade, eighth grade, ninth grade—maybe I'm a goddamn genius. But that's the hell of it, isn't it? You don't know. You weren't here."

Mama's eyes are huge, and she gasps and holds the glass to her chest, like it can protect her heart from what I'm saying.

"But even if you were here, Mama, I don't think you would know then, either. You look at me and mostly you only see your-self." The heat in my blood pops, and all the fire goes out of me at once, all the anger disappears, leaving a sadness so deep I feel it inside my bones. "And that's . . . okay. It's you, and you don't really know how to be any other way. But"—I take a deep breath—"I can't go to Europe with you."

It's dead quiet in the living room. Then Mama laughs, a light tinkling sound. "That's ridiculous."

I'm not mad at all—I'm practically made of sadness. I look at Mama, and I feel this big tenderness for her, like she's a bird with a broken wing, or an animal that's been held captive and treated bad for a long time. I want to smooth her feathers and let her free to fly off and live her life.

"I mean it, Mama. I can't go. Aunt Trish might never let me stay after how I treated her, but I can't go with you now. Not because I don't love you. I love you so much. So much." I take a deep breath. "You don't see me, Mama. But I see you—I finally see you—and because I do, I'm staying here. I'm going to finish high school and play my ukulele—*your* ukulele—and maybe try college, or tech school, or cooking school, to see what I'm good at. Because I know there is something I'm good at, Mama—and I am going to find it—I just know it."

The room is full of silence—I can just about see it, like the stuffing in a pillow, heaped to the ceiling, filling the corners and the doorways.

Mama shakes her head. She shakes it over and over and over. "No," she whispers. Her eyes are glassy, and she stares into her cup. She looks up at me. "You have to come. Mother-daughter, Bliss. That's the only way SMOOCH will take us. We're a team."

I swallow. "I can't. I'm sorry, Mama."

Mama whips her head around, her face all twisted up and red. "You're sorry?" She stomps over to the table and slams the glass down. "I hand you the fucking world on a platter, and this is what you do with it?"

"Mama—"

"Don't you 'Mama' me." Mama looks around, and her eyes land on the shelf where the bowl used to be. "This is all Trish's fault. YOU WIN, TRISH!" Mama screeches, her eyes spitting fire, and her hands reaching to the sky. "SHE'S ALL YOURS!"

Her words slice me open, and I just stand there staring at her, pieces of my heart pouring out of the cuts she's made.

"Theresa?" Aunt Trish and Uncle Leo come in from outside, breathing heavy like the house is on fire or something. Patsy comes out of her room, and Aunt Trish steps in front of her with her hands out like she's going to keep her safe from a grizzly bear.

Mama turns on them, her face like a nightmare. "You did it! You took the only thing I ever cared about! You turned my baby against me, fed her lies, told her not to go to Europe, SO TAKE HER. TAKE HER!"

My stomach feels like Mama took her fist and punched it in as far as she could, then pulled out every last thing I ever thought was true.

"Theresa?" Clyde sways on the top step, shirt unbuttoned and hairy belly hanging out. "What's taking so long? Get on down here."

"Mama?" I say, in a voice so small it could fit in a bottle cap.

Mama looks wildly from Clyde to Aunt Trish and back again, not even looking at me once.

"You heard him," says Uncle Leo, coming to stand beside

353

me. He places his hand on my shoulder. Without its weight, I might shatter into a million pieces. "I think you should go downstairs now, Theresa."

"Come on, Clyde." Mama finally looks at me, and her eyes are ice blue, empty, like she's already left me behind. "I can see we're not wanted here," Mama says, and she turns her back to me—to all of us—and, head high, glides down the stairs, not even slamming the door.

Thirty-seven

Everybody looks at me.

"Aggie and Beth are coming soon. I'm going to wait outside," I say, because I can't look at them, can't see if they feel sorry for me or want to say *I told you so* or—worst of all—want to give me a hug or some shit.

Patsy clomps outside on her crutches after a few minutes and plops down on the steps next to me. "God, I have to get out of there. Mom has a list a mile long of how I can stay safe and careful all night." She studies me. "Jesus, your hair is a wreck." She turns me around and quick smooths it out with her fingers, and I wish I could say thanks for not talking about what just happened.

Beth honks her horn as she pulls up, and I help Patsy down the driveway. I'm sticking so close to her I don't notice who is holding the back door open until we are almost to the car.

"Blake," Patsy says, smiling up at him.

I pass within inches of Blake as he holds open the door, and everything stops for a minute when I look into his eyes. They are every bit as soft as they've ever been, and as I look at him, it's like he knows—about the bowl, and Europe, and Mama, and his eyes get even softer, and he gives me a little smile.

"Today, Bliss." Patsy jabs me with a crutch, and I break away from Blake, and we duck into the car. Blake's leg and arm are smooshed against me as we ride out of town, no matter how much I lean against Patsy.

"Hard to believe. Last night ever at Granny's," Patsy says.

I practically forgot about the party with everything else going on. My heart is still beating fast, and I can't get Mama's face out of my head as she hollered "Take her!"

Some night for a party.

Patsy turns to me. "Stay with us. We can all go together later."

I sigh and shake my head. "River needs me there early. You're coming, right?" I ask them. Suddenly, I don't want to be alone.

"A little later," says Beth, "First, though, we have to"—she looks over at Aggie, then drums on the steering wheel, ending with a long blast to the horn—"celebrate! Aggie got in!"

We yell and scream, and Aggie tells us all about getting the call, her voice shaking and her face shining. Beth's grin is almost bigger than Aggie's, and I wish I could stay here and celebrate with them, be happy here with them. Blake holds out a bottle-shaped paper bag and says, "Champagne, anyone?" and we laugh all the way to Granny's, where they drop me off with promises to come back soon.

***

I tuck my white lace top into my good black shorts as I watch
Beth's car pull away, picking my way between all the cars
parked up and down the drive. I tried and tried to put on the
blue skirt like River wanted, but I couldn't make myself do it.
Aggie begged me to stay with them and help drink the champagne, but I promised River, and besides, I need to tell him I'm
not going away anymore.

Even before I step inside, I'm sorry I let them leave without
me, because if I had started drinking yesterday, I would still not
be drunk enough for River's party. All summer, Granny's has
been where people would drop by, have a few laughs, shit like
that. Relaxed, fun, mellow.

This party is on a whole other level.

For one, there's already about six times as many people here
as River's let in all summer. Second, I don't hardly know any of
them. I walk in the back door, through an already-huge crowd
playing beer pong. I know one, maybe two of the guys and none
of the girls out there. One keg is in the kitchen, and judging
from the half-full cups sitting on every counter and table, people have been hitting it pretty hard already.

A huge cheer comes from the front room, and I go in just in
time to see three guys holding some girl sideways while a fourth
guy does shots off her bare stomach. Tequila spills off her onto
the carpet, landing on the faded roses. Where the hell is River,
is what I want to know.

"Bliiisssss!" River throws his arms around me from behind

and grinds into me. He slides around me and kisses me with sour breath. I can practically see fumes coming off him, and shiver bumps raise up on my arms.

I push him off me. "What's going on?"

He slings one skinny arm around my neck and drags me into the hallway, kicking at empty cups and bumping into people with every other step. A guy finishes his beer and tries to toss the empty can out the window as we pass, but it hits the wall and slides down, leaving a beery trail. Two girls blow smoke rings at each other, and one of them crushes her cigarette out on the hardwood floor of the hallway.

I look at River, waiting for him to lose his shit, but he's staring at me with a goofy smile on his face, like he rubbed a magic lamp and out I came.

"You're here," he says, all wobbly.

"River. What the hell?" I wave my arm at the beer stain and the smoke rings. "Who let all these people in? You've been so careful all summer."

"Lotta good it did me." River slams a hand into the wall behind me, and I jump. "Fuck the summer. It's not my house anymore, so fuck this house."

There's a loud thump from the kitchen, something big falling, but River doesn't even turn his head. "River, what the hell happened?"

"What happened? Fucking Lisa happened, is what happened. Well, I say, fuck her." He pokes me in the shoulder with each word. Hard enough to bruise. Then he wraps his arms around me. "And you're leaving. Everyone's leaving." He slumps over, deadweight in my arms, then pops up suddenly. "Hey. Come on," he says, pulling me closer to Granny's room.

There's a loud crash of glass breaking in the house somewhere, and River turns his head, looks down the hall, and turns back to me.

I take a step towards the noise, but River pulls me away.

"The fuck cares?" He puts his arms around me and tries to kiss me. Just, like, a week ago, River almost lost his mind at me for even suggesting we get it on in the middle of a party.

Some guy—nobody I remember seeing around here before—comes running from the kitchen, breathing heavy. "There you are. The window, man. Booker's cut bad, bleeding all over."

"I'm busy, asshole," River says, and whoever he is, Booker's friend, shakes his head and goes back in the kitchen.

"River, you have to stop them. Someone's hurt. These people—who are all these people?—they're destroying Granny's house. If your mom finds out you had anything to do with this—"

River lurches away a few steps, then turns back to me. "Well, she's not gonna find out, is she?" He rattles the doorknob until it opens, and we fall through the door together. I keep him upright, just barely, and we stagger across Granny's bedroom, where he collapses on top of me on the bed.

"How you like your g'bye party?" River drags his hands across my chest and tangles them in my hair. His kisses are loose, sloppy, and insistent, and they do nothing to drown out the shouts and thumps coming from the rest of the house.

Maybe I can bring him back to reality somehow. I put my finger on his lips, and he bites at it, then laughs like he's the cutest thing he's ever seen.

"River." I wait for his eyes to mostly focus on mine. "I'm not going. I'm not going with Mama to Europe." The words feel fake, unreal, like a script I'm reading from, and I close my eyes to block out Mama's face as she screamed at me and the basement door as she shut it behind her.

River pulls back and stares at me, his mouth half-open, then pulls me into a rough hug. "This's great! Good! Good news. Don't go with her. Stay with me. We gotta celebrate." It's getting dark outside, and it's growing dim in the bedroom. River's face is red, and his eyes hang half-closed when he looks down at me. He pulls his fingers sharply from my hair, and I flash back to Blake pulling the hailstones out of my hair, each touch as soft as a kiss.

He shrugs his shoulders and reaches for me again. "You're staying." River gives me a loose smile. "Let's celebrate, baby." His eyes in the dim light are darkest blue, and the look that's in them is starting to scare me.

"River?" I try the baby voice. "River, what's going on here?"

"What's going on is you and me is gonna celebrate. God, you're so fucking hot." River's all up under my top, and he's struggling one-handed to get his shorts down. I start to let it happen like I usually do, but when he touches my skin something snaps inside me, like a rope breaking or a chain shattering. In one quick motion, I push away from him and wiggle to the farthest corner of the bed.

"No. I can't."

River looks at me like I'm talking in Japanese. He slides a hand out towards my leg, and I pull myself into a little ball in the corner of the mattress.

"Awww, baby. You know you want it." He crawls closer to me.

I wrap my arms around my legs. "No. I don't. This room, this party, it's not what I want."

River just stops there on his hands and knees, looking at me stupidly, his mouth hanging open, his red lips all shiny. Then he sits back and laughs. "But you do." He waggles his finger at me. "Don't tell me you're not leaving and then play hard to get." He crawls closer. "You're all mine, baby."

"River!" Someone's pounding on the door. Two guys open it up, and I take the chance to scoot all the way away from River when he turns towards them.

"Uh, man, bad shit is going down out here. Them guys from Alexandria showed up, and they fucking busted up the pong table when they lost, like I'm talking *in half,* then they started burning holes in people's shirts with their smokes."

The other kid says, "Booker's gone to get stitched up—man, can that guy bleed—and the second keg is gone missing. Maybe Booker took it when he left?"

River has noticed that I'm not on the bed anymore. I

straighten my top, and he looks from me to the guys in the doorway.

The first guy looks out in the hall, then back at River. "You gotta get out here, man. They won't listen to nobody else."

River stares at me instead of the guys at the door. His eyes are like dead shark eyes. No light, no feeling. He lies back on the bed and holds up both middle fingers.

"Fuck 'em. Fuck 'em all, is what I say."

Thirty-eight

One of the guys slams the door, and I hear people running up and down the hall. There's a loud thump on the wall that's shared with the living room, and I wouldn't be surprised if somebody busted through it.

I stay a few steps away from the bed. I'm not going to Europe with Mama, and I'm not getting it on with River even one more time.

But before I tell him that, I need to know what he's up to. "River, where is everybody? Where's Long Tom and them?"

He sits up and leans forward. "He wouldn't come. They wouldn't help me."

"Help you what, River?" I step closer to hear him better.

Even though I am watching his hands, River has them on my shoulders so quick, I can't even dodge him. He squeezes, hard, and gives me little shakes every few words.

"Jesus Christ, Bliss." His words are clearer than anything he's said all night. "This's a goodbye party. We're all here to say good-fucking-bye to Granny's house. Lisa's house, I guess. Sure as fuck isn't River's house."

"You've kept it from getting trashed all summer . . ." I don't even try to get loose from his hands.

"You. Don't. Listen," he says, little shakes with every word. "I am done with Lisa, and I'm done with this fucking place." He lets go and crosses his arms over his chest, suddenly grinning, proud of himself. "And when tonight is over, they'll get what they deserve. Not one fucking thing."

I picture the broken window, Booker's blood on the sill and the floor. "You're letting them destroy it?"

River's grin is all the answer I need. My whole body goes cold as River's plan comes to me, crystal clear.

"Now get back over here, baby."

I flinch as River pulls me closer. I have to get him out of here. "I, um. Where's the electric lemonade you told me about?"

He grins. "We finished off one batch already—I made myself puke so I could keep going. You gotta try some."

So that is how we end up in the backyard, after walking around piles of puke, broken glass, way more blood than I thought possible, and one passed-out kid that everybody is decorating with fast-food ketchup and mustard packets that used to be in the kitchen drawers.

People are dancing and talking, and there's a group of kids having chicken fights off by the garage. The weed and cigarette and beer smells mix together in a party perfume, and I cannot recognize one single person. The beer pong has been moved from the broken table—shattered, really—to the patio table, and everybody is cheering on some girl who looks about old enough for junior high but has perfect aim.

River doesn't even seem to notice. He's getting amped up again, and he puts his hands around my waist from behind and walks me over to the silver tin garbage can out by the basketball hoop. He slips his hands up under my top and runs his fingers under my bra, and I grit my teeth to keep from twisting away from him. He only stumbles once, and he grabs on to my boobs to hold himself upright.

I have to figure out a way to fix this.

The electric lemonade looks like piss, it smells like furniture polish, and there's little blobs of lemon pulp floating through it like drowned minnows. Maybe if I can get him a drink, then get him away from the party, I can text Long Tom to come talk some sense into him.

He dips me a cup, and I take a taste, and I almost spit it out it's so strong.

"Can't even taste it, right?" He hugs on me and drinks it like it's a Diet Coke.

A movement across the yard makes me look up over River's shoulder, and there, impossibly, is Blake.

He stands by the corner of the house alone, scanning the crowd. He's so still in the middle of all the drinking and dancing and breaking that is going on.

I feel it in my gut when he finds me, when he sees me, when his eyes lock on to mine. His look is as good as a touch; so soft, so calm, so sure. At first, he just stares, then he gives a little smile and he turns his head to talk to someone.

His eyes never leave mine, though. Even when Aggie and Beth and Patsy on her crutches come around the corner and they all walk towards us. He doesn't let me go; he holds me steady with his eyes.

"I—Bliss?" River wobbles as he turns around, and he squints at Patsy, who has limped to the front of the group. "Fucking Patsy. I should've known."

River sees Blake then. His body goes stiff, and I hear him squeeze his cup over and over. The only sound louder than the crackle of the cup is my heart, which pounds loud in my ears. I can't seem to get a breath.

"College boy." All at once, River crushes the cup and throws it on the ground at Patsy's feet. "Sorry. *Blake.*" He sneers. "I didn't invite you. Oh, wait. Actually, I told you to stay the fuck away from my girlfriend." His words are loose and slide into one another.

"Hello, River." Blake's voice is calm, quiet, and mild, like he's reminding River that today is Wednesday.

"Blake's with me," Patsy says. I can't believe how glad I am that they're finally here, in the middle of this hell party.

River grabs my cup outta my hand and drains it in one gulp. He throws it after the first one, and it lands a little closer to Blake than Patsy.

"You can all leave now. Bye-bye." River wiggles his fingers in a little wave.

I take a step towards them. Blake still hasn't looked away from me, not even when River was talking to him.

River grabs my wrist hard and stops me in my tracks.

"Let me talk to Patsy," I say, looking at River. "I'll get them to go." Maybe they can tell me how to get River to stop whatever's happening here.

River holds up one finger in warning, then lets go of me. I hurry over to Patsy, who hugs me as good as she can on her crutches.

"River's lost his goddamn mind," I whisper to her during the hug. "He's letting everyone trash the place. I don't know what to do."

Aggie and Beth circle up with us, and Blake is so close, so very close. He pulls at me, just by standing there, inches away from me.

"Are you okay?" he asks.

Am I okay? I don't ever want to be with River again, and Mama hates me. And River's flat-out lost his mind and wants to destroy Granny's house.

"Am I okay?" I repeat. I look at Blake—just a glance—then back at Patsy. "I'm so not okay right now."

"Can you puke on demand?" Aggie wants to know. "'Cause that's a real good reason to go home."

"What about the house?" I look at Granny's, bright white against the evening sky.

"You can't worry about it," says Beth. "It's not your problem." I look back, but River is leaning over the garbage can, getting another electric lemonade. How many can he drink and still stay upright?

"You have to take care of yourself," says Blake. I can feel his body shift from foot to foot, and my fingers are burning. They are just three inches from his but not able to close the gap.

"Let's get you out of here," says Beth.

"I can't just leave," I say.

A guy hollers from the porch, "The couch is on fire!" All the crazy people cheer, and a few of them go running inside to watch.

"Maybe I *can* leave," I tell them.

"Let's go," says Patsy.

River suddenly clamps his arm around my waist, freezing all of us. I look at Aggie, and her mouth is in a big O.

River slowly pulls me towards him. He looks over at Blake, who is still almost close enough to touch. "You're leaving?"

Blake clears his throat. "She's leaving. Now."

River looks from me to Blake, and back at me.

"Bliss?"

"It's not like that, River, I'm—"

"You're leaving me? For this fucker?" Superfast, River jabs out his fist and punches Blake in the side of the head.

Blake puts a hand to his ear and stares at River, who grabs my arms and spins me around.

"Let her go, man." Blake steps towards us. The side of his face is red, but it looks like River was so trashed that he couldn't get much power behind the punch.

He's not so drunk that it doesn't hurt where he's holding

my arms, though. He pulls me back with him, away from the others. He leans forward, right up in my face.

"You told me you're staying."

"Let her go," Patsy says, hopping forward on her crutches.

"Fuck you, Patsy." River kicks one leg towards the crutches, missing completely, but it's enough to stop Patsy from coming any closer.

"River—"

"Shut up, Bliss. You're supposed to be with me. We're a team." River pulls me close in a wobbly hug, running his hands up and down my back and my butt. He whispers into my hair, "I love you, baby. You're staying with me."

Mama didn't see me, and River doesn't, either. I picture Kay, tied up with a simple rope day after day after day, not knowing she could rip that sucker at any time and take off on her own. And I imagine her running through that town, busting down fences and tearing up gardens, feeling free, and alive, and on the run.

I'm not going to Europe with Mama. I'm staying here.

But not with River.

I stand up straight and grab River's hands from behind me. I put them at his sides, and I look up at his face, which is blurry, like all the drinks actually made him less solid.

I look at those blue-jean eyes that I've looked at all summer long, and I say, plain as day, "It's over, River."

His eyebrows drag down over his eyes. "What?"

"I'm done. I don't want this anymore."

369

"The fuck?"

"I'm sorry this won't be your house, and I'm sorry about Granny, and I'm sorry about a lot of things, but I've gotta go."

River reaches out and touches my face, strokes my hair, surprisingly gentle. "No, you don't. Stay."

I am shaking, even worse than I was in the storm cellar the other day.

"You can't go." River's voice is so small. "You and me, we got big plans." He stumbles a little and catches himself on my shoulder.

"They're not my plans," I say, spacing each word out, hoping he will understand. "They never were." I duck back from his hands, and turn to walk towards the car, away from River, away from who he wanted me to be.

I don't even look to see if Patsy's coming; I'm leaving now, and nothing's going to stop me. I pick up speed, my steps stronger than any I've walked for a very long time.

River calls out, but I keep going, looking across the lane to where the cars are parked. River comes after me, the crunch of gravel under his feet speeding up as he closes the distance between us, but he's in my past, and I'm hell-bent on going towards my future.

River almost catches up with me, but he's real drunk, and I'm determined to get away. When he's right behind me he makes a deep animal noise in the back of his throat that ends in him roaring "Blisssssssss," and he reaches out to grab me, but

I'm too far, too fast, and his hand brushes past my shoulder as I move forward, safely away from him.

Except I'm not. He misses my shoulder but catches my hair, pulling me backwards, back towards him, right off my feet and into the dirt at the edge of the lane.

For the second time today, I'm flat on my ass, but instead of Mama, it's River standing over me, sad, drunk River, holding what looks like corn silk in his hands, and he looks at it like he doesn't understand how it got there.

The whole back of my head feels like it's on fire, and I put my hand up to touch it. My fingers come away with blood on them. "You pulled out my hair?"

"You pulled out her goddamn hair?" Patsy says, hobbling across the lane with Aggie, Beth, and Blake. River holds the hunk of hair in his fist and doesn't say a word. He looks miserable, defeated, and I almost, *almost* feel sorry for him.

I scramble up, keeping my distance, and there's a loud crash from Granny's. A smoking couch cushion flies through the door and lands on the back porch. I don't know if River meant to pull the actual hair out of my head, but he sure as fuck meant to make me stop, and what I need to do right now is go.

But first, I tell Blake, "Give me your phone."

He hands it to me. I dial the number. It's only three taps, one ring, and then a lady's voice: "Nine-one-one, what's your emergency?"

I look right at River.

"Hello? I'd like to report trespassing and a loud party." I rattle off the address in a rush, then press End and give Blake his phone.

"You bitch," growls River.

"You don't want to do this, River. You love Granny's."

He looks at me, and his eyes are as sharp as broken glass. He stirs into motion. "Get. Out." His face is red, and he no longer looks small or defeated. He points at me, my own hair flapping in the breeze, then he paws at his wrist and rips off the blue hair tie, throwing it to the driveway. "Get. The fuck. Out."

I close my eyes and turn away from him. Blake is close behind me.

"Don't ever come back here again," River calls after me.

I keep walking.

Then I run.

I run past the garage and past the swing set and past the corn. I run until I trip on the loose gravel and scrape my knees all to hell, and only then do I realize that there's nobody behind me.

I look back at Granny's one last time, drained now of all the good feelings it used to carry. The house glows white against the dark blue summer sky, and from here, I can't see how they're tearing it up. No matter what, River kept Granny's safe all summer long, from parties I barely remember to that one time Long Tom made us all line-dance in the living room, and me and River's whole time together seems like it happened in that house.

And now it's all over. I will never stand next to River at the front door, watching him send away those clowns who he just knows will ruin the party. I will never stand in the kitchen when everyone else is on a beer run and pretend Granny's given me her house, me and no one else, and it's up to me to decide where the TV goes, and what color the couches should be. And if I want to have roses out back, or maybe fix the vegetable garden.

I never in my life thought that I would ever end up here, watching River burn this house he loves so much to the ground. I touch the bare spot on my head. I never in a million years thought he would hurt me.

I turn and walk farther down the lane, down to where Kay's grave is. It rises up out of the dirt like an old friend surrounded by millions of stars in the hot summer night. I sit down and lean up against the carved picture of Kay, and I wait, watching off into the distance as the red and blue flashing lights come closer and closer to Granny's. I hope Patsy and them are okay. If only I kept my phone charged like Patsy's always saying.

Lightning bugs signal "Here I am" all around the grave, and I think about what it must have been like for Kay to be brought to America without her mother, what she must have thought when the boat docked and the crate opened up to a whole new land.

After a while, the gravel crunches, and I look up to see Blake standing in the lane.

"How's your head?" he asks, like we didn't just run away

from a crazy person, like we are just hanging out on an ordinary Wednesday night in the middle of summer.

I touch it—no blood. There's definitely hair missing, though. And it's real tender. "Okay, I guess."

He comes and sits at the other end of the headstone, close enough that I could touch him if I wanted to. I reach for his hand, which is warm and solid just like always, and he doesn't pull away.

After a minute, I turn towards him, and his eyes catch the starlight, and they crinkle up like I'm hilarious.

I smile back at him and lean in.

He leans in farther, puts his arms around me, and looks down at me, all happy. I rest there, in his hug, quiet after this crazy day of Nathan, and Mama, and River. Blake doesn't make a sound, doesn't move, just holds me and holds me. After a while, though, I can't hardly stand it, and finally my hands meet behind his neck, where his hair is so soft it feels like butter. I pull him close to me, put my lips on his, and then Blake is kissing me like if he doesn't, he won't have any air left, and he will die of suffocation. Like my mouth is the only place he can find air. He tastes like sun and stars and summer, and I drink it all in.

Blake's phone buzzes, and he pulls it out to read the text, keeping one arm around me. "Patsy, Aggie, and Beth want to know where we are and if we're okay."

"Are we okay?"

"I'm okay," he says, smiling.

"Me too."

Blake texts Patsy one-handed, reading out loud. "'Here we are. At the elephant grave. We are okay.'" He deletes the last word, then retypes. "'We are more than okay.'"

Aggie and Beth and Patsy come get us after a while. "We had to go miles out of the way to get past all the cops," Aggie says.

"I wonder if they busted them?" Beth asks.

"I don't care," me and Patsy say at the same time.

Aunt Trish is passed out cold on the couch, and Uncle Leo is snoring in the recliner, but once they mostly wake up, they are both over the moon that we are home before curfew and all in one piece, especially Patsy. I wait until everyone is asleep, and then I get out of bed to go make peace with Mama.

I tiptoe down the stairs, past the beanbag and the afghans, and push open the door to the storage room. It's real quiet. Clyde isn't even snoring. I don't really want to wake him up. This is between me and Mama.

Before I even switch on the light, I feel it; they aren't there.

I squint at the bed, thinking maybe I just can't focus real good, but there's not even any blankets on the bed, and for sure no people in it.

No one is there. The room is empty.

The trash is all there, but the half-full whiskey bottles are gone, the clothes that were hanging all over are gone, even the sparkly suitcase is gone. Every single shopping bag, mine and Mama's, is gone. My guts all cave in like somebody punched me real hard, and I sink down on the bed. They must've snuck out while Aunt Trish and Uncle Leo were passed out in front of the TV.

Was Clyde's limo there when we came home? I turn to run upstairs and check the driveway, see if it's there, but I stop myself: I know it's gone.

She's gone. Again. Without so much as a goodbye. I should have known what would happen when I told her I wouldn't go to Europe. Of course she left me. All my emotions, every feeling I've ever had, rushes out of me in a giant whoosh, leaving me empty all the way down to my fingertips, my toes, the ends of my hair.

How will I make her understand if she's not here?

"I have to explain," I whisper, too late. "I love you, Mama. I just can't come with you. It never would have worked."

I didn't cry when Nathan attacked me. Or when Mama went for the bowl, or even when she screamed "Take her!" at Aunt Trish about me.

I didn't cry when I told her I wasn't going, or when I said goodbye to River, or even when he pulled out my hair.

But I sure as fuck do cry in this empty room, this room that once held boxes and boxes full of memories, and then Mama and Clyde and all their shit, and now, just me and nothing else. I cry and cry and cry until there can't hardly be any tears left in my whole body, and then I cry some more.

* * *

I wake up to a loud thump as something big falls near the door of the spare room. I sit up, hoping it's Mama, here to say "Surprise!" and we can hug and cry and shit.

Instead, Aunt Trish is chugging around in the spare room that is practically empty, no signs of Mama and Clyde, just cement floors, the bare foldout, and a few black trash bags by the door.

"You're awake," she says, her smile almost breaking her face apart. "I can't believe you slept through all my work. What do you think?" She waves her arm around at the now-clean room.

"She's gone," I tell her, and somehow my eyes find a way to make more tears.

"Of course, we'll need to get you an *actual* bed. A nice rug, and maybe a mirror, and you'll need a desk. Maybe over in that corner?"

"A desk? I—" I wipe my eyes with my hands and snuffle. I take a deep breath and stand up tall in the empty room facing Aunt Trish. "Mama's gone," I say, loud and clear. "She left me. Again."

This is it. This is when she sends me packing, forces me to go chase after Mama or to live at Beth's or somewhere. Where she finally pays me back for being such a shit to her the last couple weeks, and such a pain in the ass all these years, even though I tried so hard to fit in, to earn my place at their house. If she kicks me out, I won't put up a fight. I will figure something out. Take care of myself.

I look closer as Aunt Trish lifts her head up slow, like every year of her life weighs ten pounds, and they're all stacked on top of each other in her mind. Her makeup is all scrubbed off, her hair is flat on one side and fluffy on the other, and she has a giant sleep-crease across one cheek.

She reaches out a pudgy hand to me. "Bliss, honey . . ." She closes her eyes, then opens them, saying, "They must have snuck out while we were sleeping." Her mouth turns down at the corners. "I'm so sorry."

"I—" I can't get any words out.

Aunt Trish, moving faster than I've seen her move in years, comes over and puts both her arms around me, holding me up, helping me remember who I am.

"Bliss. Honey. It's just her way. When Theresa's hurt, she runs."

"Why does she always run away from me?" It's more of a wail than a whisper. And when Aunt Trish strokes my hair I lose my shit and start crying for real. Deep, heaving sobs so strong I might just shake apart. "She never wanted me."

Aunt Trish squeezes me and smooths my hair away from my soaked face while I just cry and cry. "Oh, Bliss. Theresa wanted you more than anything in the world. Still does. Oh, she wasn't ready for a baby, even she agreed with that. Her career was just starting off when you came along."

Aunt Trish's voice is like the yellow lines on a highway, pulling me forward, mile after mile, keeping me from veering off the road. "But the instant she saw you—I'd never seen anything like it. Theresa's smile always was beautiful, but when she looked at you, Bliss, the whole room lit up with it. With love for you."

"Really?" I squeak out, between sniffles.

"Did she tell you that you were supposed to be named Jane, after our mother?"

I shake my head.

"That was always her plan. But when she held you for the first time, when you opened your eyes and looked right at her, she instantly decided to call you Bliss, because you were more than plain old happiness."

"She must've changed her mind, then, to leave me behind so much."

Aunt Trish turns loose of me and hands me a gob of tissues. "Your mama always did have such big dreams. Mother and Daddy never knew quite what to do with her. Even after you came along. She tried so hard."

"But, what, then—"

"For months and months, your mama stayed here with you. But we saw how it was killing her. Then one day when she was mad at Mother, the agent called, and Theresa was out the door. She tried to take you with, but your gramma blocked the front door, not budging even an inch, telling Theresa she could leave if she wanted, but she couldn't take you till she had a place to live and a steady income, and not one second before. Your mama cried all the way to Chicago."

I throw away the used tissues. "You think she's crying now?"

"Oh, I'm sure she is." Aunt Trish grabs my shoulders and stares hard at me. "Theresa is crying her eyes out because she knows that it's her loss. That you're every bit as special as the day you were born, and she's the one who's missing out." She pulls me tight against her squishy body.

"You think so?" My mouth is muffled against her shoulder. Aunt Trish pats my hair. "Oh, my girl. I know so." Then her voice gets hard as rocks. "Your mama just made the worst mistake of her life, and she can run as far as she wants, but every day from here on out she's going to wake up and wonder why she let you get away."

She clears her throat. "So. What color do you want to paint? I mean, we could offer this to Patsy, and you could take her room, but I thought you'd . . . like a space of your own. . . ." Aunt Trish's face is all hopeful and worried, like she maybe brought me the wrong flavor of ice cream or something.

"I can stay? Here?" I say, real quiet.

Aunt Trish lets go to look me right in the eyes. "Of course, honey. As long as you want. I never tried to steal you, but you are as much mine as Patsy is. Your uncle and me, we just want what's best for you. We want you to be happy and find your way in life, and we figure here is about the best place for you to start. Anything you need, Bliss, just ask, and if it's in my power, I'll give it to you."

I wipe my eyes and look around at the room. My room. I take a few steps towards the door, then I turn around and grab Aunt Trish in a big hug, a good hug, a welcome-home hug.

My eyes burn while I hug her, and the emptiness from Mama leaving is a tiny bit smaller.

"Thanks," I say. "Maybe a deep blue." But that reminds me of something. Or someone. "You said you'd get me anything I need. What I need—what Patsy needs—is beauty school. It's the only real school for her. What I need is . . . you've got to let her use that birthday money."

Aunt Trish's mouth turns down at the corners, then she shakes her head and laughs. "She's not going to give it up, is she?"

"She knows what she wants," I say, and it hits me that maybe soon I'll find something I want that much. And then I remember something that I *do* want.

"I have to go," I tell her, and we hug once more.

I run upstairs and pull on shorts and a tank top, then shake Patsy awake. "Hey, Patsy."

She looks around all lost, then squints up at me. I hand her the crutches and her best scissors. "I need you to do something for me."

I set the ukulele on the passenger seat of Patsy's car and look back at the house as I pull away in the early-morning light. What did Mama think as she drove off last night? Was she mad? Sad? Relieved?

I'm all of those things and then some, and I wish more than anything that Mama and me could have worked it out. But the Mama that was here is the only mama I've got, and I have to learn to be okay with who she is and who she's not.

Either way, I'm okay.

The sky is getting lighter as I drive, and the morning air tells me this day is gonna be hot as hell. But I don't care. The sun is just peeking over the treetops as I pull up behind the red pickup and park next to the bean fields. I can see Blake off in the distance, bent over his row as he slices a weed.

I smile and run my hands through my hair, cut in what Patsy called a "spiky bob" so it covers up the chunk River pulled out. I reach into the back of the truck and pick up a bean hook, the long rows stretching out before me. The ground is solid under my feet, and the morning sun lights my way as I walk off into the field.

Acknowledgments

When I watch a movie, I stay until I see every key grip and gaffer, caterer and costumer named, and I am always blown away by how many parts are required to make a whole.

Creating a book also requires a tremendous community. My name is on the cover, but I am not the only person responsible. I can't thank my amazing agent, Suzie Townsend, enough for believing in me and Bliss. You answered every question I had, and I felt your support from miles away, as well as that of Dani Segelbaum, Miranda Stinson, Sophia Ramos, Kate Sullivan, and everyone at New Leaf.

I'm so grateful to editor extraordinaire Kristen Pettit, who has championed Bliss and helped me hone her story. The HarperTeen team: Clare Vaughn, production editors Caitlin Lonning and Alexandra Rakaczki—I feel as if I know you even though we've never met. Corina Lupp and Alison Klapthor, you made me want to write a book that lives up to your beautiful design. Thanks to production managers Meghan Pettit and

Allison Brown, marketing director Lisa Calcasola, and publicist Mitchell Thorpe, and thanks to my copy editor, Erica Ferguson, and proofreaders, Jaime Herbeck and Lana Barnes, for keeping me in line.

Cover artist Karmen Loh brilliantly brought Bliss to life in the most beautiful way. If I ever get a tattoo, it'll be of one of your flowers.

Of course, a book begins long before publication day. This book absolutely would not exist if not for my Hamline MFAC family, all my classmates, workshop participants, and faculty. Each of you added a special something. Mary Rockcastle, you've put together an amazing program.

Gary D. Schmidt, thank you for saying "Always follow that voice" and holding space for Bliss to blossom and grow from a whisper to a completed draft. Marsha Qualey, you helped me see Bliss through new eyes, and Mary Logue, I so appreciated your support as I tried my hand at revision. Special thanks to Jacqueline Briggs Martin and Phyllis Root for our biannual breakfasts, and thank you to everyone who read and responded to a draft, including Donna Koppelman and the ever-generous Debbie Kovacs.

Laura Ruby and Anne Ursu, I learned so much from you at Hamline, and even more at Highlights. Anne, your support along the way has nurtured and sustained me. Thank you also to Christine Heppermann for listening to my pitch at a moment when I was ready to give up and for renewing my faith.

Thanks to all my mom's night out friends, especially Laura Minnihan, Kat Paavola, Sheila Reschke, Dawn Rootness, Cathy Rude, and Leanne Steinbrunn. You all make me a better person. Patty Kelmar, thank you for being the spark and lifting me up. You make the world a better place.

Thanks to Jenny Palmer for all the coffees, Dori Weinstein, my inspiration, and Melanie Heuiser Hill for all the tea and scones and writer chats. Many thanks to Amanda Awend, whose spirit helped me arrive home each day with writing energy intact.

My amazing cohort, The Front Row, is bursting with terrific writers who are also great people. You have been there through all the incredible highs and crushing lows—sometimes on the same day—and because of you, I've been able to make it through with grace, humor, and only a few thrown chairs. I'm lucky to have friends like you and could write thousands of words about how special you each are. Sarah Ahiers, Josh Hammond, Jessica Mattson, Brita Sandstrom, and Zachary Wilson, along with Anna Palmquist, Kate St. Vincent Vogl, Gary Mansergh, Ronny Khouri, and Steph Wilson: my table is always open. Thanks to Anne Ahiers for all the great food.

To the real Kay the elephant, buried in my hometown in central Illinois, thank you for showing up just when I (and Bliss!) needed you. I hope you're running free somewhere.

Thanks to Becky Sun and Irena Wilson for critiquing the manuscript and being awesome family. Michael Wilson, you've brought me music and science and have been excellent company since I was two years old. Sarah Vaile, the best gift I ever received was getting you as a baby sister. I owe everything to my dad, Larry Wilson, who supports me and told the best bedtime stories, and my mom, Barbara Wilson, who modeled and nurtured my love of reading, and left us far too soon. Mama is most definitely not modeled after her.

To my lights, my life, Carly Coats and Cassidy Coats (and Cassidy's fiancé, Gannon Youakim): you are the reason for everything I do. I think you're wonderful.

And lastly, to Bliss, I am honored to tell your story. Thank you for whispering in my ear and starring in my show.